This book should be ret
Lancashire County Libra

By Suzanne Johnson and available from Headline

ROYAL STREET
RIVER ROAD
ELYSIAN FIELDS

SUZANNE JOHNSON

ELYSIAN FIELDS

headline

First published in 2013 by
HEADLINE PUBLISHING GROUP

First published in paperback in 2014 by
HEADLINE PUBLISHING GROUP

1

Cataloguing in Publication Data is available from the British Library

ISBN 978 0 7553 9771 6

Typeset in Fournier MT by Palimpsest Book Production Ltd, Falkirk, Stirlingshire

Printed and bound in Great Britain by Clays Ltd, St Ives plc

Headline's policy is to use papers that are natural, renewable and recyclable
products and made from wood grown in sustainable forests.
The logging and manufacturing processes are expected to conform
to the environmental regulations of the country of origin.

HEADLINE PUBLISHING GROUP
An Hachette UK Company
338 Euston Road
London NW1 3BH

www.headline.co.uk
www.hachette.co.uk

ELYSIAN FIELDS

I

The scariest sound in New Orleans' French Quarter is silence.

Even at four a.m. on a damp November Sunday morning, there should have been a few horns blaring, one or two belligerent drunks staggering around, a street hawker trying to solicit one more customer into a nightclub making its last call, the final trill of a trumpet.

All I heard as I followed Jake Warin along lower Dauphine Street were the falls of our footsteps on the concrete sidewalk. It was as if the thick mist that shrouded the gas streetlamps in golden balls of light had absorbed everything else and corralled the sounds from Bourbon Street into the confines of the street itself.

Just in case slipping into a gory police crime scene wasn't eerie enough.

We turned the corner at Ursulines and found our contact standing against the side of a generic sedan that had been parked across a gated driveway. He wore a New Orleans Saints cap, but his nylon windbreaker had NOPD stamped across the back in gold block letters that glittered in the misty light. It, plus the gun on his hip, offered a warning to anyone who might take a notion to rob him: don't.

"You owe me," he said, and he wasn't smiling.

Homicide detective Ken Hachette had agreed to let us into his crime scene as a favor to Jake, his former Marine buddy who'd recently trained to join a new FBI unit called the Division of Domestic Terror, or DDT.

Ken didn't know the DDT's brand of domestic terror would involve the preternaturals that had flooded into New Orleans after Hurricane Katrina tore down the metaphysical levees between the modern city and the Beyond. He thought it had to do with Homeland Security.

Ken also didn't know his friend had been turned into a rogue breed of werewolf called loup-garou. To him, Jake had simply grown bored with running his Bourbon Street bar, the Green Gator, and wanted a career change. At least half of the Gator's day-to-day operations already had been turned over to his bartender-slash-manager, Leyla.

Finally, Ken didn't know I was a wizard, the sentinel for the greater New Orleans region, and not an FBI consultant as my handy little badge proclaimed.

What Ken Hachette *did* know was that neither Jake nor I had any business at his crime scene. "You realize how much hot water I'll get into if my boss hears about this?"

The mist muffled Jake's silky-sweet Mississippi drawl. "We're here. Might as well let us take a look. I need the experience looking at scenes, and DJ knows a lot about the Axeman. The real one."

Yeah, I knew a lot about the famous serial killer who'd rained terror all over the city back in the early part of the twentieth century—I'd learned most of it over the past twenty-four hours from the Internet. It's amazing what turns up when you Google *Axeman of New Orleans*. There were better ways to do research, more accurate ways—even magical ways. But this had been a last-minute gig and even a research geek like me knows when to take a shortcut.

Ken unwrapped a stick of sugarless gum and rolled it up before popping it into his mouth. Then he folded the wrapper into a small, neat square and stuck it in his coat pocket. His face, the color of a deep, rich caramel, glistened with mist, and he pulled a handkerchief from his pocket to wipe it off. Who carried handkerchiefs? In our limited acquaintance, Ken had struck me as the type of man who might iron his boxer shorts and arrange his sock drawer by color.

The anti-DJ, in other words.

"Yeah, okay. Come on. Don't touch anything." He untied the yellow crime scene tape that stretched across a wrought-iron entry gate and waited until we walked inside. Much of the lower Quarter was residential, and surprisingly large Creole-style homes lay nestled behind the narrow street entrances.

We crossed the slate pavers of an elegant courtyard edged with a jungle of banana trees and palms, and waited while Ken untied yet another length of yellow tape, this one barricading a set of French doors.

"Who was the victim?" I closed my eyes while Ken fiddled with the tape and pulled out a key to unlock the house. I might be a wizard, but I had enough elven genes from both of my parents that I'd won the freak lottery and ended up with some elven magic in my repertoire—part of which was the ability to sense the presence of preternatural energy. The aura of anything inhuman that might have been out here in the courtyard, however, had dissipated into the mist.

Warped as it sounded, I was praying for a nice, ordinary, human serial killer. I'd barely recovered from an attack and near-drowning three weeks earlier at the hands of a psycho nymph, not to mention cracked ribs courtesy of overzealous merman CPR. Breathing remained a painful chore, and I really, really wanted Axeman Deux, as the media had dubbed the killer, to be Ken's problem.

The detective rattled off the details in short, clipped phrases. "Joseph Isaacson. Age fifty-seven. Owned a shipping-container company that does a lot of business with the port. Divorced. Lived alone. Same MO as the other attacks."

The copycat murders had started two weeks ago, and tonight's was the third death. These attacks shared a lot with the original ones committed in 1918 and 1919 by a never-identified serial killer the newspapers had named the Axeman because of his chosen weapon. The assaults came late at night, death resulted from hard blows to the head with an ax while the victims slept in their beds, and the bloody weapon had been left propped against a door or kitchen counter at the scene as a gory souvenir.

We entered the French doors into a parlor that could have served as a ballroom back when this place had been built in the early 1800s. It had been decorated in tasteful shades of cream, tan, and ivory, which made the puddle of blood next to an end table all the more gruesome.

Jake knelt next to the blood and I followed his gaze to the droplets trailing crimson across the room and into a back hallway. How was the loup-garou inside him handling the blood? Jake had been withdrawn for the last few weeks—since he'd almost lost control on our one and only attempt at a real date, and again after my near-drowning.

Nothing could kill a budding romance like having a guy threaten to go furry while you're making out on the sofa or stare down at you with flat yellow eyes and bared teeth as you lie helpless on the ground.

Physically, Jake hadn't changed a lot since being turned loup-garou three years ago. His wiry runner's frame was more muscled, but he still had the laid-back exterior, the amber eyes, the sun-streaked blond hair, and the dimples. But the loup-garou tended to be violent loners, and Jake's control over his wolf was shaky. He'd never embraced what he'd become. We still flirted with each other a little, but in the last couple of weeks it had become hollow, as if done from habit rather than from heart.

"The ax was propped against the table here." Ken squatted next to Jake and pointed at a small cherry end table with delicate legs. "The bedroom where the body was found is down that hall. This ax was the same as the others."

"Any fingerprints?" Jake asked.

"Plenty—but nothing that matches anything in our databases. He's not being careful about what he touches. He's taunting us."

I didn't like the sound of that. It could be a sloppy or arrogant human killer with no police record . . . or a prete who knew nothing about forensics.

They stood up, and Ken pointed to spots where little cardboard placards had been placed by the crime lab team. "Look in those areas and see if you can find anything we missed."

"Good idea." Jake's eyes lingered on the pool of blood before he turned away and began canvassing the room.

Had Jake's voice sounded a little shaky, or was I looking for trouble? My former cosentinel Alex Warin, an enforcer for the wizards and Jake's new boss on the DDT, thought this low-stress assignment would be a good test for his cousin. Alex was supposed to be on this field trip instead of me, gauging Jake's reaction to a bloody scene.

When Alex had been called away to investigate a merman-weregator problem in one of the river parishes, I got drafted—thus the late-night Axeman research.

I was partly here to see if the murder had any prete connection, and also to see how Jake handled himself.

There hadn't been anything to indicate preternatural involvement, but any copycat crime pushed my paranoid button these days. Since the borders between modern New Orleans and the Beyond had dropped last month, any old prete could wander into town without the fear of being escorted out of the modern world by the New Orleans sentinel—namely, me.

That included the historical undead, famous former citizens given immortality in the Beyond by the magic of human memory. I wanted to make sure Axeman Deux wasn't the real Axeman, come back in undead form to resume his murderous ways.

I had more than a passing acquaintance with all the trouble that could be caused by a member of the historical undead. The undead pirate Jean Lafitte had initially come to my house to shoot me. I'd visited his hotel room on business, only to find him interested in pleasure. We'd shared boat rides, he'd tried to impale me with a dagger, I'd accidentally set him on fire with the ancient elven staff I call Charlie, and we'd ventured back to 1850 to have a dinner date at Antoine's before getting assaulted by an elf.

Yeah, it's a complicated relationship.

While Ken and Jake looked at spots where the police had found minute bits of evidence—hair and fibers that could have come from either the victim or the killer—I pretended to study an antique vase and reached out with my senses.

I usually wore my mojo bag, a pouch of magic-infused herbs and gemstones that blunts my empathic abilities, but I'd left it off tonight. Whatever was here, I needed to pick up on it, whether it was residual energy from the Beyond or the fact that the blood scent made Jake's mouth water. Can I hear an *ick*?

I ignored the wonky energy of loup-garou and filtered out the other sensory details: the quiet voices of the men as they talked about the crime, the drip of water off the leaves of the banana tree outside the doors, the iron-rich scent of blood, the muddy odor of wet concrete. There was nothing else here except human energy.

That could be attributed to Ken, but it also didn't rule out the historical undead, whose energy read mostly human. By spending time around Jean Lafitte, I'd learned the slight variation between the auras of regular humans and that exuded by the famous immortals.

At least my time with the pirate hadn't been for nothing.

"Okay if I go back to the bedroom?" I approached the guys, who were enthusiastically discussing carpet fibers.

"Sure," Ken said. "Just don't—"

I threw up my hands. "I know, don't touch anything."

He smiled at that, and it took a decade off his face. "Alex has said that to you a few times, I bet."

Laughing, I walked down the hallway, avoiding the blood droplets on the polished wooden floors. I'd met Ken shortly after Katrina, when Alex and I had just become cosentinels and were posing as a couple. I'm not sure he'd ever learned our true relationship. Not that I could even define it these days. Friends on the way to being . . . something . . . maybe . . . or not.

Yeah, that relationship was complicated too.

I didn't need to follow the bloody path to find the room where the murder had occurred; the stench of death led me to the second door on the right. The overhead lights had been left on, and thank God my stomach was empty so I was spared the humiliation of barfing at Ken's crime scene.

A duvet covered in intricate gold and brown embroidery lay in a heap at the foot of the bed, exposing a bare mattress. The sheets and pillows were missing—probably covered in blood and brain matter and taken by the cops. The top third of the mattress was soaked a deep crimson, and the spatter of red on the wall resembled some horrible Rorschach test.

I went through my ritual again, filtering out extraneous sensory data, focusing on the room. Death, especially violent death, leaves behind a signature, but it was fading.

The human aura was stronger. The place had been covered with cops. But underneath it all, like the high-pitched whine of a mosquito that's flown too close to one's ear, the not-quite-human energy of a member of the historical undead swept across my skin.

Damn it. This wasn't going to be Ken Hachette's case. It was going to be mine.

2

We left the crime scene a few minutes before eight a.m., led out by a grumbling Ken. I was hungry, sore, and edgy.

"We're gonna stop and get breakfast—want to come?" Jake asked Ken. "My treat. A thank-you for staying up all night."

The detective unlocked his sedan, which in daylight was a coplike shade of beige. I'd bet the interior was very, very neat. "No, thanks. I gotta sleep a few hours and then hit it again. You never know when this nutcase will be back. I need to figure this thing out. Somehow."

He didn't sound hopeful that the figuring out was imminent. If the killer turned out to be the real Axeman, neither was I.

The Quarter remained misty as Jake and I walked toward Bourbon Street and the Green Gator, but the streets had already begun to stir. Shop owners hosed down the sidewalks in front of their businesses, the smell of strong, bitter chicory coffee drifted out of café doors, and delivery trucks blocked the narrow streets while their drivers hauled in another day's worth of French bread and beer. The cars trapped behind them erupted into periodic bursts of horn-blowing. It all felt comforting and normal after the past few hours.

We stopped at the Old Coffeepot and got takeout orders of *pain perdu* for me and steak and eggs for Jake, then strolled on to the Gator. The bar was closed, so we'd be able to talk about the Axeman crimes without worrying about anyone overhearing words such as *undead* and *preternatural*.

My injured ribs ached, and by the time we got to the Gator, I was hobbling like an arthritic grandmother. Make that an arthritic grandmother with tonsorial issues; in the damp weather my hair had puffed up until I felt a blond-woolly-mammoth hair day coming on. Not a look I ever achieved intentionally.

Like most French Quarter bars, the Gator only closed a few hours a day, between four and ten a.m. We had about ninety minutes before Leyla and the early shift workers arrived to start prepping bar food and putting bowls of peanuts on the tables. Gloom had settled in the corners of the long, rectangular room, even with the overhead lights turned on.

Jake opened the massive green hurricane shutters on the outside of the front window to let in some light. He stopped at the bar on his way back to the table where I was spreading out our food. "You want a drink?"

I'd kill for coffee, but didn't want to wait for it to brew. "Soda's okay. Whatever's easiest and caffeinated."

I opened the first Styrofoam container and grimaced. The steak part of Jake's steak and eggs had barely left the cow. The red slab of beef looked way too much like the crime scene we'd just left.

My "lost bread," on the other hand, was perfect. French bread grilled, then deep-fried, floating in butter and syrup.

I'd be in such a sugar coma my sore ribs wouldn't prevent me from sleeping like they'd done most of the last three weeks.

"Learn anything at the crime scene?" Jake took the seat opposite me at the table, setting a soda in front of me and a glass of amber liquid over ice next to his tartare and eggs. It smelled like bourbon.

I focused on my breakfast and bit my tongue so hard I was surprised I didn't swallow a piece of it. I wasn't Jake's mother; I wasn't even his girlfriend, although we'd tried to make that work. I sure wasn't his keeper. If he wanted bloody beef and bourbon for breakfast, it was none of my business.

Unfortunately, the crime scene we'd just left *was* my business.

"I felt an energy signature that made me suspect Axeman Deux could be the real guy," I said. "You know—the real Axeman from 1918, one of the historical undead."

Jake dug into his steak. "Well, sunshine, I know just the guy to fill you in on the comings and goings of famous dead guys."

I sighed. "Jean Lafitte's still got his suite at the Hotel Monteleone and I could call him—he's learned to use a telephone very well." I knew this because he'd developed the bad habit of calling me at ridiculous hours with grand business ideas such as charging pretes admission to go in and out of Old Orleans—with him taking the pirate's share of the profits. The man needed a hobby.

There were other members of the historical undead I could contact for gossip and information, however, so I might find another source.

"I'll handle it later," I said. "What did you make of the crime scene? Anything different from what the cops found?"

Jake nodded and took a sip of his drink. "I scented something the police didn't catch, and I think it supports your theory. At least my goddamned sense of smell came in handy for something."

He reached in his pocket and pulled out his cell phone. After punching a few keys, he held the phone out to me. "Scroll through the photos of the shirt. I found it stuck way down under a sofa cushion but couldn't figure out how to get it past Ken. He took it as evidence."

I scrolled from photo to photo while Jake went back to the bar for napkins. The images weren't very good quality but were clear enough to show a white shirt stained red over much of its front, presumably from heavy blood splatters. In one shot, the shirt had been spread out.

"It looks huge," I said when Jake rejoined me at the table.

"Belonged to a big man, for sure. Which Ken says the victim wasn't."

The sound of liquid over ice drew my attention away from the photos. I frowned as Jake refilled his glass. He'd brought a half-empty bottle of Four Roses to the table, his favorite bourbon for as long as I'd known him. He'd leaned on alcohol too hard after coming home from Afghanistan but, again, I went through the litany of reasons for keeping my mouth shut.

Jake was oblivious. "Notice the collar? There's a couple of close-ups."

I scrolled through two more shots and looked at the blood-soaked band collar. The shirt also had a bib front, which wasn't a style one often saw in men's clothing these days.

"Looks vintage." I glanced up at Jake. "So, what, the Axeman comes over from the Beyond, hacks this shipping guy to death, then either trots back across the border half naked or brings along a handy change of clothes?"

Jake shrugged. "Hell if I know. When you were reading up on the Axeman, did you see anything about clothes?"

"No, but I'll have to take another look now that there's a possibility it's the real Axeman." I tried to will my tight shoulder muscles to relax. "Damn it. I really wanted to have a few quiet days until Thanksgiving."

Since the borders with the Beyond dropped last month, life's chaos factor had gone viral, and my body ached from both fatigue and stress. Now we had the new DDT office, for which Jake and Alex were the only agents so far, and I'd been promoted to sole sentinel of South Louisiana. The Congress of Elders, grand poobahs of the wizarding world, were in hot negotiations with the major prete leaders about the balance of power as the Interspecies Council was solidified. God only knew what further chaos was in store.

My last case, involving a sociopathic killer nymph and a horde of territorial mermen, paled beside the prospect of a serial murderer from among the historical undead. "The thing that sucks about this, if it is the real Axeman, is that he's immortal." I used my fork to submerge the last bite of my *pain perdu* under a tsunami of syrup. "If I kill him, he just fades into the Beyond, rebuilds his strength, and pops right back over the border." Kind of like a psychotic jack-in-the-box.

Jake pointed at me with his fork. "Arrest him and have him banned from re-entering modern New Orleans. Case closed."

"Yeah, eventually." Visions of red tape danced in my head. The Elders wanted something as mundane as a business lunch justified in triplicate. "Banning a member of the historical undead from New Orleans will take a ream of paperwork and an act of the Interspecies Council, which isn't fully formed yet. All the Elders and species representatives will have to meet, and they'll all have to sign off on the warrant. The Axeman could chop up half of the city by then."

Personally, I thought any of the historical undead with a criminal record should have been automatically banned from the modern world as soon as the borders dropped. But since New Orleans' most famous undead citizen was a certain French pirate with a list of crimes a fathom deep, that wasn't likely to happen.

"How about we make it too painful for the Axeman to stay?" Jake tilted in his chair, balancing it on its back legs. "I'll go to the scene and track him, then let my wolf take over and kill him. The historical undead can't turn loup-garou, but it'll hurt like hell while his system rejects the virus, or so I hear. If I kill him every time he comes back, pretty soon he'll quit coming."

What a bad idea, on so many levels. We didn't need a loup-garou vigilante. "You're forgetting one thing. He could kill you. He's immortal. You aren't."

Jake stared out the window for a few seconds before turning back to me with a cold smile. "Yeah, it's easy to kill me, isn't it?" He sipped half-finished drink number three. "One silver bullet and I'm dog food."

A pang shot through my chest that had less to do with my cracked ribs than with pure heartache at hearing such despair and anger in his voice. I desperately wanted to help Jake, but I didn't know how to breach the walls he'd put up around himself.

"How much did the blood at the crime scene bother you?" I watched as he chewed enthusiastically on a bite of steak, and hoped the question would open the door to a real talk.

"It made me hungry." He speared the last chunk of rare meat and held it up, giving me a steady, pissed-off look. "Did it make *you* hungry?"

I swallowed hard. Was Jake's control unraveling or was he just trying to push me away? "Did Ken seem curious as to how you knew the shirt was there when the cops missed it?"

"Give me at least one ounce of credit." Jake finished his last bite and shoved his Styrofoam container away. "You think I don't know why you went this morning since Alex was gone? The two of you wanted to babysit the wolf, see if I'd lose control and rip off Ken's head, or start lapping up puddles of blood. Well, I didn't."

I tamped down my own angry response. The last thing I wanted to do was accelerate his darkening mood.

Stacking my breakfast container on top of his, I took them both to the big trash can behind the bar. I stopped and looked back at him, a slow realization sinking in. When Jake was turned loup-garou he'd changed——but I hadn't. Seeing him sit there, staring into another newly filled glass with a simmering temper that had flared in a heartbeat, revealed a hard truth.

I'd been naïve. Jake would never again be the easygoing, flirtatious guy I'd met three years ago. Until the people who cared about him accepted what he was now and stopped hoping he'd go back to what he used to be, he couldn't accept himself. And that comment about the silver bullet scared me. He'd thought about dying.

I wasn't sure if I could pull him out of this downward emotional spiral, but I had to try.

Jake raised an eyebrow when I walked behind the bar, grabbed a glass, and returned to the table. I poured myself a finger of bourbon and sat across from him. I might not be Jake's mother, girlfriend, or keeper, but I was his friend.

3

I took a sip of the bourbon and blinked a couple of times. My eyes watered, and heat rushed all the way down my gullet to create a noxious mix with my *pain perdu*.

Jake shook his head. "You're such an amateur."

I had no intention of starting a drinking contest. I just wanted to get his attention. Now I had it, and the anger still wafting off him sent chills through me.

I took a steadying breath and dived off the cliff. "I care about you, Jake—wolf and all—and I'm sorry for pressuring you to be something different." His lack of response propelled me to keep talking. "Tell me what I can do to help, even if it's just to leave you alone. Talk to me."

He stared at his glass, then over my shoulder at the street outside, everywhere but my face. My empathy allowed me to feel the war within him as his pride battled his need to open up, and as the wolf battled for dominance over the man.

When he finally looked at me, his eyes weren't the soft amber I'd hoped to see. They were hard and calculating. "You care about me, do you? Wolf and all?"

"I do care." He was calling me out. "I just realized I'd

been asking you to be someone you aren't. I'm sorry it took me so long to see that. It wasn't fair."

His smile was cold. "So you think we can be friends?"

We'd have to start from scratch, but we could do it. "I know we can."

He slid his chair around the table until it was next to mine, and I stifled the impulse to put more distance between us. "What about more than friends?"

How much truth-telling did I want? An image came to me unbidden: Jake standing over me on that pier last month in his wolf form, teeth bared. "I—"

"Don't bother to answer the question, sunshine. I can feel your heart speed up without touching you—did you know that? And it's not speeding up because you want me. It's because you're afraid of me. Do you have any idea how that makes me feel?"

Probably not very good, but how could I make myself *not* fear him? How could I slow my heart rate or the rush of adrenaline into my muscles? "No," I whispered.

He leaned closer, close enough for his body heat to mingle with mine. "Your fear excites me. It makes the wolf want to come out and play."

With some effort, I forced myself to look him in the eye. I'd always insisted to Alex that Jake would never hurt me, but a few grains of sand had been falling from the hourglass of doubt for a few weeks. Now they'd sped to a fast trickle. Jake wouldn't hurt me intentionally, but Jake wasn't always in control.

He leaned back in his chair, his point made. "Well, at least you're not looking at me with that poor-bastard-what-are-we-gonna-do-about-Jake expression. I'm sick of seeing it, from you and Alex both. You want to know why I drink? It's because of that look. I'd rather see fear on your faces than pity, and the more I drink the less I care."

My own anger sparked. We might have screwed up, but we'd been trying to help him. "Then tell us how to do better. Help *me* do better. What do you need from us?"

He rested a hand on my forearm and squeezed a little tighter than necessary. "I don't need a goddamned thing from either one of you. Just leave me alone and stop watching every move I make." He looked at me with yellow-gold eyes that had an odd, flat refraction. Wolf eyes. His nostrils flared as he inched closer.

Jake was about to lose control, and I didn't want to be alone with him anymore. He was scaring the hell out of me, and the wolf part of him liked it.

Tamping down a surge of panic, I pushed my chair back, but his hand remained clamped to my arm as if glued. I tried to slow my galloping pulse without success as he slid his chair even closer.

Pulling my arm to his face, Jake inhaled deeply. "Your heart is pounding so hard, it vibrates through my whole body. I can almost taste it." His voice was a rough whisper against my skin.

"Jake, stop it. I've got to go." I stood and tried to tug my arm away, but he gripped it harder and stood as well, pulling me against him and sending a sharp stab of pain through my rib cage.

"What's wrong, DJ? You scared?" His words, carried on hot breath sweet with whiskey, tickled across my cheek. Jake's eyes were completely gone now, replaced by something cold and alien. "You should be."

Damn it, the wolf was in control. I couldn't read any emotions but anger and aggression. "Let me go. Now." Panic surged through my system and I couldn't stop the overflow of magic that shot from the fingers of the free hand I had pressed against his chest.

He jerked away with an inhuman snarl and a nip at my forearm still clutched in his grip. A burn raced across it as I jerked it away.

We stilled, the moment carved in ice as we both looked at my arm. He'd broken skin. A small scratch, three or four inches long with a deeper jag at the end. Not serious enough to need stitches, but deep enough for the blood to well up and start a slow drip onto the scuffed hardwood floor of the bar.

Deep enough for a little of the virulent loup-garou DNA to mingle with my own.

Deep enough to change my life forever.

Jake took a step backward.

"I'm fine." I grabbed a napkin from the table and dabbed at the wound with trembling fingers.

Jake hadn't spoken. When I looked up, his eyes were wide, his gaze fixed on my arm. Terror and arousal roiled inside him as Jake tried to regain control. The wolf wanted to feast, and the man wanted to flee.

"It's all right." I pressed the napkin against the cut, as much to get the blood out of his sight as to stanch the flow. My voice quavered. "No big deal. Just a little scratch."

"I . . . God." Jake shuddered and backed away.

He whirled and walked behind the bar, pulled a pistol from beneath it, and stuck it in the waistband of his jeans, underneath his sweater. I could see his hands shaking from across the room.

He paused to stare at me one long, soul-cracking second, his eyes gone back to amber and filled with unspoken regret, before walking out the front door and slamming it behind him.

Jake's footsteps were absorbed into the daily noise of Bourbon Street, and I was alone.

4

The crack in the plaster ceiling began next to the base of the light fixture and zigzagged a path to the corner of the room. I studied the lightning-bolt pattern, wondering how much pressure would be needed before the crack became a crevice and the whole ceiling came tumbling down on some unsuspecting fool's head.

I had no idea how long I'd lain on the bed in the vacant apartment across from Jake's on the second floor of the Green Gator, staring at the potential ceiling disaster hanging overhead. The symbolism didn't escape me.

Finally, I rolled to my feet, clutched my ribs, and walked to the bathroom with Jake's bottle of Four Roses that I'd brought upstairs. I took a sip, coughed at the burn, and took another. Then I walked to the sink, used the rest of the bourbon to clean the scratch on my arm, and tossed the empty bottle in the trash.

Alcohol wouldn't kill the virulent loup-garou strain of lycanthropy, but the pain it caused on the open wound awoke my brain from its fugue. No point in freaking out; too many variables were unknown. When I had answers, I'd panic.

I had no idea if a wizard had ever become loup-garou. As a natural shapeshifter, Alex was immune—he'd been attacked by the same loup-garou as Jake. Ditto for Jean Lafitte. If shapeshifters and the historical undead were immune, perhaps wizards were too. Or maybe my elven DNA would protect me.

Otherwise . . . Otherwise was a horror show. How would it feel to change form? Would the Elders consider me too dangerous to live if I shifted into an uncontrollable wolf who could do magic?

They'd taken a chance on Jake because he'd been human when he was turned—and because Alex pled his case and agreed to be held responsible for his cousin's actions. Jake didn't know that. Take my elven skills, which already made the Elders nervous, and make me a rogue wolf who could absorb the negative emotions of others? They'd either turn me into a weapon or put me down like a rabid stray.

Part of me was worried about Jake. Part of me cared where he'd gone and how this would tear him apart. Part of me was concerned that he was probably driving around drunk and upset. On some level I made note of those things, but mostly I felt all my fretting over Jake the last few years had been wasted time. We'd still come to this.

Leyla wouldn't arrive for at least another half hour, and I didn't want to explain why I was here and Jake wasn't. She was used to opening up, so I put the key to the apartment back under Jake's mat, left her a note that Jake might not be coming in, made sure the front door of the bar was locked, wrapped a clean towel around my arm, and exited the back, which had a door that would lock behind me. A tiny court-yard served mostly to store big green trash cans on wheels and give delivery drivers a way to get to the kitchen without having to walk through the bar.

The long, narrow alley between the Gator and the adjacent building could induce claustrophobia on the best of days. By the time I emerged into the gloom of the open street, hyperventilation was imminent. I walked to where I'd parked my SUV around the corner from the Gator and drove home on autopilot, my thoughts a swirl of blood-covered axes and loup-garou scenarios.

Two vehicles were parked behind my house in the small lot I shared with my new neighbor: a spotless black Mercedes convertible and a big, beefy black Range Rover. Alex, who was now a two-vehicle household all by himself, had moved into the little green shotgun next door to me last month.

Jake wasn't the only chicken in town; I wasn't ready to face Alex.

Instead, I eased my Pathfinder's door shut with a soft click and hurried to my back entrance. Sebastian, the chocolate Siamese I'd inherited from my father, lay in wait, ready to trip me when I walked inside. It was his hobby. When I stopped and leaned over to pet him, he meowed at me suspiciously and streaked out of the kitchen.

Nothing like an affectionate, welcoming pet to make a girl feel loved.

Upstairs, I cleaned the small cut again and wrapped it in a bandage, reflecting on the overflowing medicine cabinet in my bathroom. Before Hurricane Katrina had turned New Orleans into what was arguably the world's most active prete hot spot, I'd never taken so much as an aspirin or had a sprained ankle. Now I had tape for my ribs, glue and bandages for cuts, instant ice packs, painkillers . . . and the borders between the modern city and the Beyond had officially been down only a few weeks.

The cut burned and throbbed, and I could imagine my body beginning to change in an explosion of morphing cells and respooling DNA. This tiny wound should already be covered with a Band-Aid and forgotten, but instead my arm felt heavy and alien. How much was mental, and how much physical? There were no answers, only an avalanche of questions.

I stretched out on my bed, curling up under my grand-mother's old-fashioned patchwork quilt that doubled as my bedspread, the elven staff in its usual spot poking out of a deep vase on my nightstand. Some people slept with teddy bears or pets. I had Charlie, an ancient stick of wood the elves called Mahout.

My muscles ached from the stress of being up all night, the crime scene, and the disaster with Jake. I needed sleep, but my brain writhed with useless what-ifs.

What if I'd walked out when Jake became argumenta-tive? That might make me a bad friend, but it would have been a smarter thing to do. Why did I have to try and *fix* everything?

What if I'd come home and simply reported Jake's drinking to Alex, letting him deal with the situation? He loved Jake, no matter how much they fought. But Alex saw life in black and white, and Jake's current world was painted in shades of gray. I found it comfortable living in a world without absolutes, but it drove Alex crazy. I'd have done neither of them any favors by ratting on Jake without first trying to help.

What if I shifted at the next full moon? The thought filled

me with terror, but I had to confront it. I rolled over and dug my cell phone out of my pocket, clicking on a browser app and finding a November lunar calendar.

Life as I knew it could be over in ten days. Happy Thanksgiving.

In my dream, a man called my name, softly at first, then in a shout. He needed a big serving of shut-the-hell-up.

I cracked one eye open, discerning a bear-shaped hulk standing in my bedroom door. The elven staff was in my hand and pointed toward the bear without my realizing I'd grabbed it.

"DJ, put the staff down." The bear spoke in Alex Warin's deep baritone.

Groaning, I sat up and rubbed my eyes with my non-staff-wielding hand. Even my freaking eyeballs hurt. Then the horror came back to me. *What the hell was I going to do?*

As soon as I stuck the staff back in its holder—a vase that had begun its life in the late 1800s as a pattern glass celery dish—Alex stepped inside the room and glanced around. Seeing nothing amiss, he walked to the bed and looked down at me, a suspicious frown etching a little worry line between his eyebrows. His unkempt dark hair—always on the shaggy side—made me suspect he'd gotten home late and just rolled out of bed himself. He had the makings of a scruffy midday shadow, which pushed my sexy-as-hell buttons.

He pinned me with a decidedly unsexy glare. "Well?"

Loaded question. He looked like a man who'd arrived here with a purpose, but surely the need for an update on a crime scene wouldn't have put that intense look on his face. "What's up? I was sleeping. How's Denis Villere?"

Denis was the most cantankerous merman I'd ever met, and he liked me almost as well as I liked him, which was not at all. As punishment for causing part of last month's merman drama, his clan had been consigned by the Elders to an isolated corner of the Atchafalaya Basin. They were already stirring up problems with the local weregators.

"Denis sends his love." Alex sat on the edge of my bed. "But I'm not here about that. Jake called."

Oookay. Time to tread carefully. "What did he say, exactly?"

"Not a damned thing. 'DJ needs you at the Gator.' Nothing more, and then he hung up on me. I get to the Gator and Leyla says you left a note for her saying Jake might not be in."

Alex stretched across the bed, propped on one elbow. Those long-lashed eyes that could simmer like melted chocolate and turn me into mush—not that I'd admit it to him—hardened into squinty orbs as he gave me a once-over.

I kept the hem of my left sleeve grasped firmly in my fist and under the quilt. "Like what you see?"

He reached out and put a hand on my left shoulder. The warmth of his skin seeped through my thin sweater. At six-three and at least 240 pounds of solid muscle, he had ample body heat to share even without his shapeshifter genes.

I could pretend he was getting romantic, but I knew better. He was trying to intimidate me, and it wouldn't work. Alex wasn't going to find this scratch on my arm until I figured out how and what to tell him. I wouldn't lie, but truth can be couched in all kinds of creativity.

Faster than I could track his movement, he slid his hand from my shoulder to my left wrist and jerked my arm from beneath the quilt.

"Gotcha." He shoved up the sleeve of my sweater before I could say *traitor* and unwrapped the bandage.

"Not deep," he muttered, running his fingers along the scratch. "How'd you do it? Was it . . ." His voice trailed off, and he lifted my arm to his nose. My efforts to pull away were as effective as trying to extract a stick from dried cement. He dropped his head and touched his tongue to the cut.

"Stop that—it's gross. Seriously." I twisted my arm out of his grasp, ready to give him a lecture about canine behavior when he wasn't in his pony-dog shifted form. Damned shapeshifters and weres. They can scent anything. It's a freaking invasion of privacy. I needed to start bathing in cheap perfume. Might make me reek like a Friday night slut, but having a good shifter repellent would be worth it.

Unless I became a loup-garou. The thought left me breathless, as if I'd been zapped with my own elven staff. Alex picked up on that too.

His expression destroyed any attempt I might make at smart-assery. The shaky network of defenses I'd built around myself in the three hours since Jake walked out also crumbled. Alex's face blanched beneath the remains of his summer tan.

Nothing scared Alex Warin. Ever.

"I'm going to kill the son of a bitch." His voice shook, and his features morphed from fear to fury with the force of a Category five hurricane. I'd never before considered Alex, Mr. Steady, as capable of mercurial emotions.

"*Are* you going to kill him, Alex?" I sighed and swung my legs off the edge of the bed, my earlier exhaustion back in triplicate, my ribs and arm throbbing in sync. "Consider what you're saying and whether you mean it, because we have to be careful. Jake's life is at risk. Your career and family are at risk. My . . . well, my everything is at risk."

Alex blew out a breath and moved to sit next to me. "Better tell me what happened. Everything."

I spilled it, from the drinking to the walkout, including my own role in unintentionally accelerating things. Alex stared at the floor, doing a poor job of shielding his emotions. He was scared, furious, and worried. I didn't have to absorb his feelings; they mirrored my own.

"Did we put too much pressure on him?" I asked, then answered my own question. "Of course we did, especially me. I thought if I pushed hard enough, believed hard enough, tried hard enough—I could make him into the man he was before the loup-garou attack. That wasn't fair to any of us."

Alex spoke in harsh tones, but the hand he reached out to take mine was gentle. "This is not your fault. We protected him as long and as well as we could."

I wiped the heels of my other palm across my cheeks, scrubbing away a few hot tears. Self-pity wouldn't help me decide my next move.

I got up and grabbed Charlie. "Come on downstairs. We've got another problem." Might as well further brighten Alex's day by sharing our newest encounter with the historical undead.

We spent the next couple of hours bouncing around ideas on the Axeman case, trying desperately to avoid the loup-garou issue. We were both exhausted but knew the NOPD was incapable of containing a historical undead killer even if they caught him in the act. He'd eventually fade into the Beyond. Jean Lafitte was strong enough to remain in modern New Orleans indefinitely because he was so well remembered—not only the pirate himself, but his name.

Names have power in the preternatural world and the Jean Lafitte Wildlife Refuge, Jean Lafitte National Park, the Lafitte Blacksmith Shop Bar, Lafitte Boulevard, and the town of Jean Lafitte on the north shore of Barataria Bay—they all kept him fueled.

The Axeman didn't have a park, bar, boulevard, or town. He could come into the modern world for a while but would eventually fade into the Beyond until he built up enough metaphysical strength to return.

I did a little math on the notepad I kept in the kitchen for shopping lists while Alex rummaged in my refrigerator.

"How long's this pizza been in here? Which one's the newest?" He held up three cardboard boxes.

"The one on top's from a couple of days ago. The others are probably science experiments." I needed to clean out my fridge. Whenever I had a couple of hours where something wasn't trying to kill me or I wasn't trying to keep one prete from killing another.

Ignoring Alex's banging as he dug out a cookie sheet and reheated the pizza, I consulted a calendar on my phone and wrote down yesterday's date, when the last murder occurred. Counting back to the second murder, I hit six days, then another eight days to the first.

"Eight days elapsed between the Axeman's first killing and the second, but only six between the second and third." I stared at the figures. "It makes sense, I guess. More people are mentioning his name and reading about him with each attack, so he gets stronger and can come back sooner. The more he kills, the stronger he'll get."

Alex sat across from me while he waited for his pizza to heat. "So you think maybe four days and he can attack again?"

I shook my head. "No way to tell. Maybe sooner. The more attacks there are, the more people will talk about them—and him."

I looked at the locations and sketched out a map of the French Quarter, ten square blocks of prime real estate on high ground alongside the Mississippi River that, so far, had survived everything man or nature had thrown at it.

"You mapping out the attack locations?" Alex got up to plate his pizza and then took the chair next to mine.

"Yeah, look at where they fall, and look at the most active open portal between New Orleans and the Beyond." I drew a big star over the gardens behind St. Louis Cathedral, near the end of Pirate's Alley. This was the most central route in and out of the Beyond, via the no-holds-barred preternatural border town of Old Orleans.

"That solves the question of how the Axeman is getting around." Alex picked pieces of pepperoni off his pizza slice. He considered them too unhealthy, so I ate them.

The Axeman could easily have walked to all three attack sites. "I think we need to get some help from our contacts within the historical undead and see if anybody's heard anything."

Alex chewed and gave me an indecipherable look. "I wondered how long it would be before you called in the pirate."

Jean and Alex had learned to coexist, sort of, but they'd never be more than antagonists who tolerated each other's presence as a necessary evil.

Alex was off base this time, though. "Actually, I was thinking of Louis Armstrong."

5

I figured summoning Louis Armstrong from the Beyond would be a good diversion from worrying about whether my newly developed low-grade fever had anything to do with the loup-garou virus. It was probably the result of running around in the damp air early this morning. Or so I told myself.

Alex insisted on staying while I did the summoning, and I didn't argue. Last time I'd tried it, I'd been trying to get my father and had instead called up a pissed-off voodoo god who wanted to kill me and steal my powers.

I didn't want to summon Louis Armstrong and end up with something dangerous. If I wanted to flirt with danger, I'd ring up Jean Lafitte.

Just because Alex was present didn't mean he was attentive. While I rolled up the area rug in my library, freeing an open space on the hardwood floor and groaning from the pain the activity caused my ribs, Alex ignored me and stretched out on the sofa with a graphic novel on the Axeman I'd found online.

Last week, he'd helped me etch three perfect, concentric

circles into my library floor while I apologized to all the previous owners of my century-old home for defacing it.

Digging the broom out of the upstairs closet, I gave the room a quick sweep to make sure no dust bunnies interfered with the ritual. Sebastian got shut out of the room for the same reason.

I sprinkled a trail of unrefined sea salt along the outermost circle, then went in search of summoning totems. A biography of Louis went outside the circle at the north point, and a photograph of him on the south. East and west, I placed my iPod scrolled to "What a Wonderful World" and a pen he'd left in his room at the Gator when he'd come across as my spy after the hurricane.

After walking the circle to make sure nothing was out of place, I knelt and flicked a small knife across the pad of my thumb, squeezing until a big dollop of red fell on the lines. For now and forever, the sight of blood would bring Jake to mind, and not in a good way.

I shook off the thought and focused instead on Louis Armstrong, envisioning his face as I spoke his name.

Sometimes, if the object of a summoning is antagonistic or reluctant, it will take a while for the person to materialize. Louis popped up within thirty seconds, wearing a tuxedo and a huge smile.

I broke the circle and hugged him, which shot pain through my rib cage, and Alex hauled himself off the sofa to shake hands. Louis looked a lot less stressed than the last few times I'd seen him.

"I been thinking about coming to visit you all, but didn't know if it was the right thing to do." Louis followed us downstairs and joined us at the kitchen table, the immaculate black and white of his tux and dress shirt out of place in the kitchen of my hundred-year-old house with its scuffed floors and the vintage chrome-and-red Formica table I'd found at a yard sale.

I poured Louis a soda while Alex filled him in on how the city had recovered since Katrina. A long, slow haul. We'd been told after the hurricane it would take a decade to recover. At the time, I'd thought it was an exaggeration; now, not so much.

"How's Jake doing? Been seeing him in Old Orleans every now and then and he seems to be okay." Louis sipped his Coke and got that glazed-over look in his eyes that only sugar and carbonated water can bring.

Alex and I exchanged raised eyebrows. Jake had been going to Old Orleans?

"Where did you see him?" Alex asked. "Have you seen him today?"

Louis shook his head. "Nope, not today. Off and on the last six months, I guess. He comes in and listens to me play, mostly at the place called Beyond and Back. Listens to the other musicians. Has a few drinks." He shrugged. "Nothing unusual."

We pondered that news a few seconds. "Does he meet with anyone over there?" I asked. "Seem to have any friends?" I hoped Jake was building a life for himself, even if it wasn't one he wanted to share with me or Alex.

Louis fixed me with a rare frown. "You aren't trying to get Pops to spy for you again, are you? I wasn't good at it, and I won't do it again, especially if you're wanting me to spy on Jake."

He might have been the world's worst spy ever, in fact,

but I wasn't asking that of him again. I liked the idea that if Jake was hanging out in Old Orleans—the free-for-all zone just across the physical border from the modern city—he had somebody watching his back, even in a passive way.

"No spying," I said, and smiled when Louis visibly relaxed. "But there have been three attacks here in New Orleans that look to be the work of one of the historical undead. A serial killer known as the Axeman. We wondered if you'd heard anything."

Louis leaned back and frowned. "I remember when the Axeman was killing folks all over town—was just after the first world war. I was playing in a jazz band with a steady gig on a riverboat, sailing up and down the Mississippi and playing all the way to the parishes and back. Got married 'bout that time." His mind seemed to float into the past for a few seconds.

"What do you remember about him?" Alex asked.

"He was evil." Louis looked at Alex and then at me. "Lots of folks didn't even think he was a human—thought he was a devil of some kind. Other folks thought it was a mob thing, you know, 'cause so many of the people he chopped up were Italian."

I'd read both theories and thought both were bunk. Not that I didn't believe in demons—or the Mafia, for that matter. But the Axeman had liked to play sadistic games with the authorities and the newspapers of the day. Demons didn't send bizarre letters to newspapers claiming to be demons, as the Axeman had. But it was exactly the kind of stunt that would be pulled by a batshit-crazy human.

"Have you heard anything about him in Old Orleans?"

I asked Louis. He could keep his ears open. Technically, that wasn't spying.

"No ma'am, but I can tell you how to protect yourself," he said.

I hadn't considered myself a target, but I'd play along. "What's that?"

"Get one of my records." Louis smiled. "That Axeman, he loved him some jazz. Even said in one of his letters to the *Picayune* that he wouldn't attack nobody while they were playing jazz. Made business real good for us at the time."

Somehow I didn't think distributing jazz CDs to everyone in New Orleans to play twenty-four/seven would solve our problems. "If you hear anything, will you let me know?"

"Sure thing. Pops'll keep his ears open, long as he don't have to spy." He paused, his mouth widening in a sly smile. "You got one of those . . . what did you call them . . . cell phones? I'd sure like another one of them."

The cell phone had worked fine after Katrina, when Louis was living in that vacant apartment over the Gator. Somehow, I doubted anyone offered cellular phone service in Old Orleans. But if the man wanted a phone, I'd get him one of those no-contract specials with some minutes on it.

6

Sleep wasn't happening, and it wasn't just the Axeman bothering me.

My muscles ached, and my limbs twitched under the covers with nervous energy. After flailing around my bed until my legs were entombed in a knot of sheets and blankets, I extricated myself and slumped into my library-slash-workroom.

Here, I stashed my magical gear and the spell and potion ingredients that comprised the stock-in-trade of Green Congress wizards, the ritual magic-makers of the wizarding world. The bottles, jars, and containers—most from my collection of Early American Pattern Glass—sat on their floor-to-ceiling shelves, organized and meticulous in a way only achieved by the truly obsessive-compulsive. Cinnamon, mint, and ginger scents swirled in a comforting mélange, and I took solace in the order of it.

Speaking of demons, Sebastian, an evil minion of Satan with crossed blue eyes, grabbed his rubber rat and fled the room. He lived under the mistaken impression I coveted the slimy thing.

I paused next to the worktable. If I turned loup-garou I

might want to eat rats. At least one or two days a month, I'd probably want to eat Sebastian. My funk reached the status of utter and epic.

Books consumed one wall of the library: magical histories, textbooks on fables and lore, and grimoires—spellbooks filled with magic both legal and black as evil. Along with Sebastian, my elven genes, the staff, and the gutted shell of a house in Lakeview, the black grimoires were my legacy from my father and mentor, Gerry.

I spent an hour pulling out anything that might address the issue of wizards' immunity to werewolf viruses, but found conflicting information. Enough to keep hope alive, but not enough to offer relief.

I didn't dare log onto the Congress of Elders' secure online database and do a search. Big Brother might be watching. Probably Adrian Hoffman, the Speaker of the Elders. My translation: PR flack and receptionist, although I guess he had to have decent wizarding skills to even hold that position.

I would never be a fan of Hoffman's, and held him at least partially responsible for the rampage of the killer nymph last month, a debacle that left me in the hospital. Had he done a background check when I'd asked, or given any credence to the red flags raised by my elven abilities, my merman friend Rene Delachaise wouldn't have lost his twin brother, and Tish Newman, the closest I'd had to a mother since my own mom died when I was six, would still be alive. She'd been murdered on my front porch when the killer couldn't get inside to me, and part of me would forever lay the blame at Hoffman's feet.

I felt Tish's absence like a physical weight now. She could

always ground me, give me perspective, provide moral support. We'd buried her only a month ago, and the memory of her death, violent and unnecessary, hurt worse than my ribs. Until she was gone, I hadn't realized how much I loved her, and maybe had taken her for granted.

So, yeah, Adrian Hoffman wasn't my favorite person, and since he'd been publicly chastised by the Elders for not doing the background check on the killer as I'd asked, the feeling was probably mutual. If he found out I'd been exposed to the loup-garou virus, my life value would sink to the price of cheap Mardi Gras beads, Jake's life would be forfeit, and Alex might as well open a chain of fitness centers.

I sat in the armchair by the window and stared into the branches of the live oaks outside. Horns blared and car stereos rumbled from the buildup of Monday morning traffic along Magazine Street.

Why couldn't I have psychic skills instead of empathic? I could get my hands on that shirt Jake had found and tell where the Axeman was—maybe even tell when he'd strike next. I would know the outcome of my loup-garou exposure and could either forget it or send myself into a full-blown panic.

Holy crap. I might not be psychic, but I knew who was.

I hurried to the desk and flipped open my laptop, logging on to the Elders' site and clicking until I had the wizard directory. No Yellow Congress wizards had lived in New Orleans before Katrina, which had been fine with me. They excelled at mental magic, often telepathy and divination. I absorbed too many emotions from other people through my empathy to not be freaked out by the idea of someone else being able to read me—not just my emotions, but my thoughts.

However, all kinds of folks interested in the city's renewal, both human and wizard, had flocked here since the storm, so we might have one now. Finally, I found one name with a New Orleans address. A familiar name.

I'd met Adam Lyle, a Houston psychiatrist, during a hare-brained foray to the post-Katrina temporary morgue. I'd been desperately looking for Gerry, and Adam had been working the morgue as a volunteer—they'd needed help so badly, even a psychiatrist was welcomed. Guess he'd decided to stay.

Phone numbers had been removed from the database after a group of young Australian Blue Congress wizards had dreamt up a pyramid scheme last year, calling wizards and posing as Elders. The only contacts listed now were email addresses.

I clicked on Adam's link and dashed off a quick note. I re-introduced myself and posed a hypothetical question I'd supposedly been asked at a party and couldn't answer: whether a wizard exposed to a virulent strain of lycanthropy such as the loup-garou could be turned. If so, what signs should one look for, and would a Yellow Congress wizard be able to tell if the change would occur without waiting for the full moon?

It made sense that if a thought-pattern change had occurred from human to garou, a Yellow Congress wizard might be able to detect that through psychic skills. Of course if it were possible, I'd have to put a lot of trust in Adam Lyle. I'd worry about that later.

My Green Congress colleagues were geeks; we were

almost always scientists or engineers—or risk-management experts. Adam should have no trouble believing this was a subject we might discuss at a cocktail party.

Relieved I'd done something proactive, I flopped on the sofa to watch the last dregs of the local morning news and mainline caffeine, still wearing my favorite Gryffindor pajamas. I closed my eyes and tried to feel anything in my own body or energy field that had changed. I still had the low-grade fever, but nothing else. If I were giving off were-wolf vibes, would I be able to tell? I didn't feel my own wizard's energy, so probably not.

About nine, the back door rattled a few seconds and I was halfway off the sofa when I heard the dead bolt slide back and keys jingling. I relaxed again. The only other person who had a key to my house was the guy slamming cabinet doors and pouring himself coffee. "It's me," Alex said as an afterthought.

I'd given him a key to my house shortly after Katrina, when I'd needed a bodyguard. The immediate danger passed, but he never gave the key back and I never asked. Didn't mean anything. At least that's what I told myself. It must be true or I'd at least sit up and try to look presentable.

He came into the living room with a cup of coffee and one of his cardboard-coated-in-wax protein bars. Unlike me, he was neatly dressed, pressed, combed, and presentable.

"I called Ken to ask if he'd heard from Jake and he said there'd been another attack—made the TV news yet?" He shoved my feet far enough off the sofa to sit down on the other end. Sebastian raced in, dropped the rubber rat on Alex's lap like a sacred gift, and purred in contentment. Traitorous wretch.

"Nope—is it the same as the others? Was it in the Quarter? How the hell did he come back after one day? Can you get me into the crime scene? Has Ken heard from Jake?"

Alex stroked Sebastian and scratched behind his ears. "No news on Jake. I'll be able to get into the scene after the NOPD lab guys are done, as a courtesy, but I doubt I'll be able to get you in. Ken won't fall for the 'Axeman expert' thing twice. And you tell me—how can he come back this soon?"

I sat up, holding on to my ribs to keep them from falling out. "I guess all bets are off on his return time because of the media attention he's getting. They're even reading original newspaper stories on the air. He's probably strong right now."

Alex bit off a piece of chocolate-flavored wax and wiped a crumb from what I called his winter fighting clothes—black pants, kick-ass boots, and a black long-sleeved T-shirt. In summer he changed to short sleeves. When running, he changed shoes. The man was easy to shop for.

On TV, the anchor launched into a story on the upcoming holiday lights display at City Park with no news on the Axeman. Alex turned sideways on the sofa to face me and rubbed my ankles. "Did you get any sleep?"

"Not for lack of trying." I put my cup on the coffee table and told him about Adam Lyle and my email. "I'm out of ideas."

Alex stretched, a flex of taut muscle that distracted me more than anything I'd come up with on my own. "I bet even if your wizard DNA doesn't protect you, the elven-wizard combination will."

"How quickly would I feel something? Does it mean anything that I have a fever?" I'd been so jumpy since the argument with Jake, I didn't know if my problem was heightened loup-garou senses, fear, or paranoia. Maybe all of the above.

"Not sure. I've dealt more with werewolves than loup-garou. Everything's amped with them. Don't forget, Jake healed so fast after his attack that a Blue Congress guy had to go in and doctor his medical records. He even had to cast a confusion spell on the medical team."

I eased my sleeve up, baring a forearm that still showed a scratch. Lighter and scabbed, but still there. "No fast healing. It's a good sign, right? And my ribs still hurt like a sonofabitch."

Alex reached over and squeezed my shoulder. "No clue, DJ. Jake was seriously torn up and had more virus in him from the get-go. Scratch like yours, you might not be able to tell anything till the full moon."

"Great." I slumped back again. "You go by the Gator?"

He slouched next to me, stretching out long black-clad legs and propping his feet on the coffee table. "Yeah, it's locked tight and doesn't look like he's been home. The ledger from last night's sales is still propped against the door to his apartment. I left a note for Leyla that Jake was called out of town unexpectedly and to keep running things as normal."

"I bet he went to Old Orleans," I said. Their hometown of Picayune, Mississippi, was full of nosy relatives, and Ken would ask too many questions.

"It's probably a good place for him right now." Alex slid an arm around my shoulders and pulled me against him.

He was warm and safe, and I wished we could stay like this all day.

"What are you going to tell the head of the enforcers about Jake?" The enforcer chief, who also had FBI connections, had helped get the DDT set up. He'd have to know if half of his two-man investigative team was off radar.

"I'm not going to volunteer that Jake isn't here. With headquarters in Virginia, I can cover for a while." Alex rubbed his eyes with his free hand. "But if I'm asked point-blank, I won't lie for him. Not anymore."

I prayed Jake would come back before Alex had to report him AWOL. With a loup-garou it would mean an immediate death sentence, and I wasn't sure Alex could live with that, however brave and fed up he sounded right now.

"But this does mean it's time to tell Ken about the Division of Domestic Terror." Alex got up and began to pace. "With Jake gone and this Axeman case getting bigger, we need help."

The Elders had already approved the move, but Ken was a hundred-percent human and reasoned his way through problems like a cop. He didn't realize things like wizards existed, much less that his buddy Alex could turn into a pony-size dog and that Jake was a rogue werewolf with control problems.

But having someone inside the NOPD would be more than helpful. Alex and Jake thought Ken could handle our wacky world, and I tended to agree. I didn't know him that well, but he struck me as serious and levelheaded and not prone to drama. "When do you want to talk to him?"

"Tonight. He's coming to my place at nine when he goes

off duty, and I'd like you to be there," Alex said. "If he makes me go furry to prove we're not lying, you'll have to keep him from running."

Fabulous. I'd done such a good job at keeping Jake from running away, why not go oh-for-two?

7

I'd become so engrossed in the local NBC affiliate's special on the Axeman that I jumped like a cat with his tail on fire when my cell phone blared its new Zachary Richard ringtone. I'd spent most of the day doing Axeman research and was skittish from trying to figure out the mind-set of a psychopath.

"Crap." I knocked the phone off the coffee table and had to lean over to get it, which in turn squeezed my sore ribs. Zachary got off a full chorus of "Big River" by the time I'd slapped a hand on the phone, picked it up, saw an unfamiliar number, and punched *talk*. "DJ's orthopedic ward, how may I help you?"

"Open your back door. I have dinner."

Dinner sounded good.

I'd ended the call and shuffled halfway to the kitchen before realizing I had no idea who I'd be dining with. Male voice, but not soft enough for Jake. The right timbre, raspy and deep, but not Southern enough for Alex.

The kitchen was dark, and I glanced at the wall clock as I flipped on the lights, opened the kitchen door, and stared at Quince Randolph. He lived catty-cornered across Magazine Street in an apartment above his landscaping business, Plantasy Island.

I didn't like him because unlike every other human I'd met, alive and historically undead, he gave off no emotional signature whatsoever. Which meant he either had been trained to shield his thoughts and emotions, or he wasn't human. I tolerated him only because my best friend, Eugenie, had convinced herself he was The One. What was The One doing at my house at six p.m. with dinner and minus his girlfriend?

"Where's Eugenie?" I gazed past his shoulder at her house directly across the street. No sign of her. "Is she on her way?"

He pushed past me with a big plastic bag and two bottles of beer—Abita Amber, my favorite. He was tall and lean, built like a swimmer, with broad shoulders and a touch of muscled lankiness. Not to mention pretty as a girl, with shoulder-length, wavy hair the color of honey, and too-alert eyes a bluish-green.

"Quince, seriously, what are you doing here?" I didn't remember making plans, but the last twenty-four hours had probably killed a few brain cells.

"This is just for us—and call me Rand, remember?" He pulled cardboard cartons and Styrofoam containers from the bag. "From Five Happiness. You like Chinese, right?"

I loved Chinese, and the rich, savory aromas set my stomach to rumbling. I hadn't done more than graze on junk since yesterday's sugar-infused breakfast. Still . . .

"Rand!" I shouted, and he finally stopped fiddling with

the food to look at me, pretty mouth turned up in a questioning smile. "Why are you here without Eugenie?"

I hated mysteries. Never liked *Matlock* reruns, didn't watch detective shows, avoided whodunits. Okay, I'd watch *CSI* for the gross-out factor and had gone on a *Law & Order* jag when we'd first started investigating prete cases, but I got over it.

Not understanding Quince Randolph annoyed me. I was almost sure he wasn't human, but not sure enough to come right out and ask him. Another damning bit of circumstantial evidence: He always wore peridot jewelry. Peridot is a beautiful stone, but it can be spelled to hide a prete's native energy and, face it, your average guy doesn't constantly waltz around in peridot earrings. Plus, he just flat gave me the creeps.

"No big mystery," he said, smiling as my eyes widened. Coincidence about using the word *mystery*, right? Had to be. "I wanted Chinese tonight and Eugenie doesn't really like it. So I'm eating with you." He walked toward me and I stifled an inexplicable urge to back away.

His smile wilted when he got close, and his gaze flicked downward.

"What are you look—"

He moved fast, reaching down to encircle my left wrist in a firm grip. He lifted my arm, pushed up my sleeve, and studied the scabbed-over scratch.

"What the hell are you doing?" I jerked out of his grasp and walked around him to the table. The food smelled like twelve kinds of heaven. Maybe even good enough to eat with the wackadoodle. Who surely couldn't be human, or he wouldn't have sensed my injury. I didn't think he was a shifter, though, unless it was some exotic animal I'd never encountered. Maybe he was fae. I needed to research them. I'd never met a faery, but I bet they were pretty like him.

"How did that happen?" His gaze remained riveted on my arm.

"Scraped it on the back fence when I took out the trash last night," I said. "Stupid of me. I should've turned on the floodlights."

"You're lying." He raised his gaze to meet mine.

Enough already, freak show. "What *are* you, Rand?"

He smiled and handed me a pair of chopsticks in a paper sleeve. Maybe I'd poke those pretty eyes out. "I'm hungry." He sat down at the table, cracked his chopsticks, and dug into a carton of steamed dumplings. "I got you the fried pot stickers."

I loved pot stickers, which he obviously remembered from the one time I'd accompanied Eugenie and him to dinner. I'd expected to feel like a third wheel, but instead he'd been inappropriately attentive to me, and by the time we left, Eugenie was almost in tears.

Which is why this wasn't going to happen. I still held my cell phone, and I punched Eugenie's speed dial. When she answered, I invited her to dinner. "It's Chinese, not your favorite, but you and Rand can play with the chopsticks and keep me company."

She laughed. "Sounds good to me. Got to finish up Mrs. Reese's perm and then I'll be over. I'll call Rand."

I looked at the offending party, who sat at my kitchen table watching me with a bemused expression. Jerk. "I'll call him. Just come over as soon as you finish."

I pulled the carton of pot stickers in front of me and

slipped my own chopsticks out of the sleeve. "Take off your earrings," I said, popping a fried dumpling in my mouth and chewing. He wore peridot studs in both ears.

Smiling, he propped his chopsticks against the side of his carton. "Sure, I'll take off anything you want." He maintained eye contact while he reached up and removed one stud, then the other. He laid them on the table.

"No, hand them to me." More direct contact might help me figure him out.

"Whatever you want, however you want it." I ignored the double entendre as he reached across the table. He didn't know what I wanted. I wanted to know what he was, and then I wanted him to leave. I'd keep the food.

A pulse of magic swept up my arm when our fingertips touched. I curled the small gold and peridot studs inside my fist and pulled my hand away. Wizard's magic—they'd been bespelled to hide what he was, as I suspected. I studied them a moment, the anger I'd been tamping down since the incident with Jake boiling to the surface. "Where'd you get these?"

"Bought 'em on eBay," he said without a hint of humor.

"Give me your hand." Touching ramped up my empathy and ability to read aural energy. Afterward, I'd want to know what he was up to. If he'd had a wizard bespell peridot for him—or even if he'd bought bespelled gems on the black market—he was going to a lot of trouble to stay hidden. These days, with no restrictions on any species moving into New Orleans as long as they could mainstream with humans, what good reason could he have for hiding?

He slid his hand into mine, wrapping long fingers around my knuckles and stroking my palm with small circles of his thumb. I ignored his pathetic stab at intimacy and searched for his energy signature. And got exactly nothing. Maybe he had something else pierced with a bespelled peridot, something I couldn't see.

"You're frightened of something," he said, frowning and squeezing my hand, his eyes dropping back to my arm. "What happened to you? How did you really get hurt?"

Holy hell. Was he reading *me*? I jerked my hand from his and rubbed it on the leg of my jeans. "Rand, what are you?" I thought back to my classes on the dominant species in the Beyond. Elves were empathic, and so were some types of fae. I'd almost bet he was one or the other. But why hide?

"No one who would ever hurt you," he said. "I—"

Whatever he was about to say, it was lost. I hadn't heard the door open, but Eugenie stood framed in the doorway, looking from Rand to me and finally at the floor. Damn it. This wasn't what it looked like, namely her best friend holding hands with her boyfriend, but I couldn't exactly tell her I was trying to identify his species. Unlike Rand, Eugenie *was* human.

"I was just looking at the cut on DJ's arm." Rand's lie came out as smooth as whipped butter. "Says she cut it taking out the trash, but I think she probably should have a doctor look at it."

It almost killed me to see tenderhearted Eugenie go from jealousy and hurt to quick acceptance and concern for her friend DJ. "Let me see."

I held out my arm, and she studied the wound. Deeper on one end, where a loup-garou fang had entered, then more shallow where it had scraped. "I dunno. Rand might be right—it kind of looks like it's getting infected." I looked at the angry red skin surrounding the scab. It burned and throbbed, but I suspected it would be unlike any infection a local doctor had seen.

"I'll keep an eye on it." I pushed a container of fried rice toward her, and she made a face. Eugenie had changed a lot since meeting squeaky-clean Quince Randolph the Mysterious Hippie Plant Guy Who Now Might Be an Elf or a Faery. No more weird hair colors, no new celestial tattoos, no partying on Saturday nights, no fried-food pig-out tours of the neighborhood restaurants.

He'd killed a lot of her spirit, and for what? I swear, half the time he didn't seem to even like her. Currently, the son of a bitch was watching her like a teenager in history class during a lecture on Edwardian politics, detached and bored.

Eugenie cared about this guy, and he was going to break her heart. I might not be able to stop that, but I'd do my best to make sure he didn't use me as his weapon.

8

Stuffed full of Chinese food, I limped next door to Alex's house, unsure whether the sick churning in my gut came from too many pot stickers, fear of impending furhood, anger at Quince Randolph for complicating my friendship with Eugenie, or dread over unveiling the real facts of life to a nice human cop whose worldview was about to implode.

Preternatural roulette—a fun game for the entire family.

I walked up the steps of the raised cottage, knocked on the front door, and walked in without waiting. Alex owned a true shotgun house, with the living room opening into the dining room, which opened into the bedroom, which opened into the kitchen. One could literally fire a shotgun from the front door and the shell would go straight through the house and exit the back door. The only break in the line was a long, narrow bathroom off the bedroom.

The house, built around 1900, reminded me of a cute little dollhouse, with intricate old millwork and a hearth in every room except the kitchen and bathroom. I'd never tell Alex his house resembled a Victorian dollhouse, however. He'd only recently finished painting the interior walls in manly earth tones. He'd feel emasculated by *cute*.

Once inside, I spotted Ken standing in the kitchen near the back door—he waved at me. "Want a beer?"

"Sure." The idea of alcohol kind of made me ill after the Jake incident, but the encounter with Quince Randolph had unsettled me. He'd all but admitted he wasn't human. Question was: Why was a faery or elf hiding his species and hanging out with my friend Eugenie?

Alex and Ken met me in the dining room, and we sat at the heavy (manly) wooden table with our beers. Over the mantel hung my housewarming gift, a framed autographed poster of Sir Ian McKellen as Gandalf—an in-joke since I'd given Alex's shifted canine version the name of Tolkien's wizard back when I thought he'd been a normal dog.

I hoped the only Gandalf we saw tonight was the one hanging on the wall, but suspected Ken would want solid evidence that everything we told him didn't amount to absolute nonsense. I'd need to do magic tricks, and Alex would have to bark and fetch.

"How come this feels like an ambush?" Ken took a sip of beer and shifted his steady regard from Alex to me and back again. He was an angular man of medium height, his shrewd eyes a warm greenish brown. Even in his posture he was neat, precise, and orderly. Unlike everything in the prete world.

Alex thrummed his fingers on the table—his nervous tell. "You remember a while back I talked to you about a new FBI public-threat division based here in New Orleans?"

"Yeah . . ." Ken gave me a curious stare, probably

wondering why I'd be part of this conversation. "I still might be interested in being the NOPD liaison if we can get it cleared through channels. Is that what this is about?" When he said "this," he swirled a finger to indicate the three of us.

"Right." Alex sipped his beer. If I didn't have a dawning suspicion that most of the explaining was about to get dumped in my lap, I'd laugh at his discomfort. "Consider the channels cleared. Paperwork's done. We're a go, starting now, and there are things you need to know."

Ken propped his elbows on the table and hunched forward—about as demonstrative as I'd ever seen him. "What do you mean 'paperwork's done'? My request for a change of duty hasn't been filled out, and the process can take up to a month or two."

"Well . . ." Alex looked at me, which made Ken look at me.

My former partner was so dead.

"What Alex is saying, and doing it badly, is that this new unit has top priority among high-ranking officials," I said. Yeah, like the Congress of Elders and the FBI's double-secret enforcer unit. "The usual channels get bypassed. It's a done deal unless . . ." Unless Ken had a nervous breakdown or got so distraught that I had to modify his memories and send him home with a few missing hours. I had a vial of memory-erasure potion in my jeans pocket just in case.

I pushed my chair back, unprepared for this conversation. "We need some chips. You got any chips? I'm going to run next door and get some."

"Sit down." Alex grumbled a curse under his breath.

"Okay, you're both acting like freakballs," Ken said. "Spill. And nothing personal, DJ, but how does this concern you?"

I swore if I did turn loup-garou in two weeks, Alex's throat would be the first one I'd rip out. Mr. Macho, picking at the label of his Turbo Dog beer. More like Turbo Wuss.

"Here's the thing, Ken." I shot one last glare across the table. "I'm here to help explain some things about the special nature of this unit because I'll be working closely with you guys."

"As a risk-management consultant?"

Ah, yes. My fake human occupation, which Ken still thought was true. "Um, not exactly."

"Just tell me straight out if this has something to do with insurance-claim investigations. Because if it does, you can forget it." Ken's brows formed chevrons of confusion over his eyes.

I searched for the right words. "Sometimes, you've had cases where things didn't add up, right?" I asked. "Where something defied explanation, or where you wondered if maybe things exist in this world beyond what you're able to see?"

He gave me blank cop face. "What in God's name are you talking about?"

I sighed. "Hell, Alex, take off your pants and call Gandalf."

Two shapeshifts by Alex later—plus some nifty magic tricks from me, including a narrow thread of fire intended to travel from the elven staff to the dining room fireplace but which instead burned a small corner off Alex's antique mantel—and Ken's hands shook. I could tell because he'd taken out his pen and was flicking the ballpoint in and out, in and out, in and out.

Alex hadn't bothered fully dressing after Ken demanded he shift to his enormous dog alter ego the second time. He'd pulled the jeans back on and stayed barefoot and barechested. Which I found inappropriately distracting. But damn.

"One more thing we need to tell you," Alex said. "The reason we had to do this tonight involves Jake. He's in trouble."

Ken had been staring into space, slightly openmouthed, but now his jaw clamped shut and he focused on Alex. "What about Jake? Please don't tell me he turns into a dog too."

I gave him a tight grimace. "No, a wolf. As in big and bad and would eat your grandmother with little provocation."

"Holy Christ." Ken finished his beer in a single swallow and crossed his arms. He stared at the table a moment, seemed to reach some conclusion, and nodded. "Tell me where Jake is, and what he needs."

Hearing those words, I relaxed. Jake had been right. Ken would flounder over this revelation for a few days but he would adjust.

"Remember right after Katrina, when the wild animal attacked Jake?" Alex asked.

Ken nodded. "And when he recovered, the injuries he brought back from Kabul, the ones the doctors failed to fix, disappeared almost overnight. You tellin' me his recovery was something preter . . . preternatural? Because, man, I thought it was weird at the time."

"The attack came from a loup-garou, a wolf that carries a virulent form of the werewolf virus." I considered how much to tell him, and decided he didn't need to know how magic had turned normal lycanthropy into loup-garou. "He's had problems adjusting—his temper gets away from him. The wolf controls him sometimes instead of the other way around. He isn't handling things well, and he's . . . he's missing."

I didn't want to go into more detail. Jake would be embarrassed and angry we'd brought Ken into this at all.

"Missing. Then we need to find him." Ken pulled a notebook from his pocket and wrote JAKE at the top of the first blank page. Thinking like a cop. "He saved my life over there, you know. And not just mine."

"Not quite so simple." Alex's voice was a stark monotone. "Jake lost it with DJ yesterday. He freaked out and took off. He's not answering his cell and hasn't been back to the Gator. He's drinking—a lot."

I cleared my throat. "This ax attacker doesn't appear to be human, and with Jake off radar we're going to need your help with the investigation."

Ken set his bottle back on the table with a thud. "What do you mean, he doesn't appear to be human? Wait. I need another beer." He pushed out his chair and walked the length of the house to the kitchen, giving Alex and me a chance to exchange nods.

"That wasn't too bad," I said with a sigh. "He's going to be fine."

9

Things had not been quiet in the Crescent City overnight. Besides the usual gang shooting or two, a young woman had fallen from the third-floor balcony of an unoccupied building in the lower French Quarter a block off Esplanade. Sometime in the early hours of morning, she'd been found in a cold, drizzling rain, blood from a head wound the shape of an ax blade pooling on the concrete beneath her. The bloody ax had been propped against the doorjamb of her bedroom.

The local TV station reran its hour-long special on the original Axeman and dug up a New Orleans history expert, who pointed out that the ax attacks weren't exactly like the famous series of assaults and murders that occurred during 1918 and 1919. The original Axeman, he said with great authority, had been much less brutal, often using a straight razor to cut his victims' throats and then going to work with his ax. Furthermore, he rarely arrived with his own ax, but used the one belonging to the victim.

Sorry, professor. Not this time, or at least not so far.

Willem Zrakovi, head of the Elders for North America,

wanted to talk to me at eleven, so I fed Sebastian, wrapped my ribs, pulled on a skirt and jacket appropriate for a business meeting, and drove to my office. I had no idea of the agenda, but if Zrakovi considered the matter important enough to warrant a special trip to New Orleans from Boston, I probably didn't want to know.

Unless Jake had turned himself in or gotten in more trouble, no way Zrakovi knew about the loup-garou curse hanging over my head. And he wouldn't hear it from me.

Tchoupitoulas Street traffic moved light and fast on this gloomy Tuesday morning, so the drive took me less than five minutes. Located near the end of a strip shopping center that backed up to a Mississippi River wharf, my official place of business at Riverside Market resembled a box. Dark green industrial carpet, white Sheetrocked walls, and a sign on the door sure to drive away any shoppers who might wander over from Stein Mart or Walgreen's: CRESCENT CITY RISK MANAGEMENT. In case anyone needed to discuss genuine insurance-risk issues, mild magical wards around the door made plain-vanilla humans suddenly queasy and ill at ease.

I brewed a pot of caramel-drizzle coffee and fired up my office computer. A jolt of adrenaline washed through my veins when I saw the email from Adam Lyle. I sipped the sweet, rich brew and stared at the subject line a few moments before clicking it open.

Dear Ms. Jaco—or may I call you Drusilla?

I hadn't told him my real name—I don't tell anyone DJ stands for Drusilla Jane, no offense to Great Aunt Dru, and

I'd registered my email account under *DJ*. But I was the local sentinel, so his knowing my name didn't mean he'd been checking up on me. No point in being prematurely paranoid. There would be plenty of time for that.

Nice to hear from you again——I've been meaning to call and see if you'd like to do lunch sometime

Only if he doesn't try to read my mind.

and I promise not to read your thoughts.

Ha-ha. A Yellow Congress comedian.

I had to chuckle at your question about wizards being infected with the loup-garou or other were virus——I have a couple of Green Congress friends and this is exactly the type of debate they get into at parties themselves.

Yeah, yeah. We're proudly geekish.

I can assure you that wizards are NOT immune to were viruses,

Oh, shit.

and the cases I've read about were very sad indeed. Not surprisingly, the Elders cannot allow a werecreature with magical abilities to wander free, so a wing of the wizarding mental facility at Ittoqqortoormiit is set aside for them as long as they've not injured anyone.

That the Elders had asylums for crazy wizards was news to me. And what the hell was an Ittoqqortoormiit?

As for the other part of your question, the answer is no—a Yellow Congress wizard, even a strong healer, would not be able to tell if a wizard would turn after exposure to a virus such as loup-garou.

Well, crap on a stick.

Much depends on the individual makeup of the wizard, and I've heard of a few cases where wizards were exposed but never turned— although only a few. But all I or another Yellow Congress wizard would be able to tell is whether or not exposure had occurred. We can make psychic connections and tell what a person is thinking, but do not have such specific gifts of divination.

That was of no help whatsoever, except . . .

As you know, I'm a psychiatrist. While in medical school, I did a rotation in hematology. One of the things I did as a private project, just out of curiosity, was to look at werewolf blood alongside that of a human. There is a distinctive curved-cell signature in were blood that doesn't occur in humans or wizards. So I suppose a blood test could theoretically tell a person whether or not changes were occurring on the cellular level if that signature were present, although I'm not sure at what point after exposure the blood change occurs. This is not widely known, so you might use it to stump your friends at the next party!

Call me about lunch!
Adam Lyle

My heart thumped. A blood test. I could find out and maybe, just maybe, this would all be over and we could move on.

I shot off a quick reply to thank him and suggested a date after Thanksgiving for lunch. By then, I'd either be really thankful for my fried turkey or tearing into a raw bird with claws and teeth, spitting out feathers.

Next, I Googled Ittoqqortoormiit.

Awesome. It was a remote outpost of Greenland with an average daytime temperature of six degrees, which usually occurred in late July. Nine months of the year, the town of less than 500 rarely got above zero. My future could take place in a home for insane and homicidal wizards, with possible field trips to hunt muskoxen. On the plus side, I'd be so hot-natured the absurd temperatures might feel pleasant.

Adam's email had left me depressed and craving pralines, so I made do by adding cream and sugar to my coffee. While waiting for Zrakovi to arrive, I logged on to the Elders' secure database and clicked on the supplies tab. I was a Green Congress wizard; ordering a good microscope wouldn't look suspicious.

I ordered it, paying extra for overnight delivery to the transport in my library. I thought about calling Alex, but no point in telling him until I knew something, especially since he and Ken were going over past cases this morning to show our newest coworker how the enforcers operated (a three-word summary: aim, shoot, kill). Afterward, they'd be devising a plan to investigate the Axeman Deux crimes without tripping over the NOPD.

My next contribution to the Axeman investigation would

be talking to Jean Lafitte, so I'd left a message for "John Lafayette" at the front desk of the Hotel Monteleone that I needed to see him as soon as possible. New Orleans' most famous pirate—arguably *the* most famous citizen in her long, storied history—had ensconced himself in the Eudora Welty Suite, paid for with what appeared to be an unending supply of gold he'd either stashed away during his human lifetime or accumulated doing illicit business deals between modern New Orleans and the Beyond. I figured the less I knew about Jean's business, which also seemed to involve my merman friend Rene Delachaise, the better.

The buzzer over my office door sounded, and I looked up with a smile for Willem Zrakovi. I liked him. He was bureaucratic and prone to arrogance like any wizard at his level, but also fair. When Gerry had gone rogue, and then died as a consequence, he'd not only been kind to me, he'd given me a promotion.

Unlike the man walking in the door behind him. My smile faded at the sight of Adrian Hoffman. They made a real Mutt-and-Jeff pair. Zrakovi was short, dark-suited, and able to blend in with a crowd of downtown bankers having lunch at the Palace Cafe. Hoffman was tall, handsome, and smooth. He looked like Montel Williams after he'd visited an expensive French Quarter jewelry boutique, his shiny shaven head only out-blinged by the diamond studs in his ears. Except I'd never seen Montel Williams wear such a sour expression.

Zrakovi shook my hand and introduced Hoffman as if we'd never met or, more likely, as if we might need to get off to a new start. Determined to play along, I stuck out a hand and he shook it with a brief smile. Good. We were both going to play nice even though tension and annoyance wafted off him in equal measures, partly because of me and partly because he didn't like New Orleans.

Admittedly, my hometown wasn't to everyone's taste unless they liked air the consistency of cream soup, funny accents, and a penchant for having parades for every conceivable holiday as well as some that were fairly inconceivable. The last parade I watched honored Naked Bike Ride Day. I was still having nightmares.

I pointed them to the chairs at a small round conference table, my curiosity piqued. I'd assumed Zrakovi wanted to talk about getting me a research assistant—he'd mentioned the possibility a couple of times before—or maybe he'd gotten wind of prete involvement in the Axeman Deux murders.

Hoffman's presence confused me. Zrakovi had dragged him here for his dressing-down in front of me and Alex in my hospital room last month, but I hadn't talked to him since. I'd thought the man rarely left Elder Central, aka Edinburgh.

Zrakovi took a cup of coffee, grimaced at the first sip, and politely refrained from commenting. Nobody shared my love of flavored coffees, which meant more for me. Hoffman sat to my left, stiff and expressionless.

"Let's get to it then," Zrakovi said, setting his cup on the table. "We need to discuss the elves."

I stifled a groan. Freaking elves. I hadn't considered that being the subject of his visit.

"I haven't been using the staff," I said. Not much, anyway. Just a couple of small fires easily contained, and a little char on Alex's mantel. "Do the elves still want to meet with me?

Oh, and can you think of any reason an elf or faery might be living in the city and masking his species?"

I had enough elven DNA to be claimed by Mahout, the ancient staff of the Fire Elves that I'd found in Gerry's attic after Hurricane Katrina. He hadn't been able to use it, but it ramped up my ability to do physical magic until I was the equal of a Red Congress wizard—well, a Red Congress wizard with poor control over her powers. It also quickly drew the attention of the elves, who had thought the revered relic no longer existed.

As soon as they figured out Mahout was the staff I had, they'd begun asking to meet with me. After Zrakovi consulted with the other Elders, he'd ruled that since the staff had claimed me, I had no obligation to return it. Yet they still wanted to talk.

"I've set up a meeting between you and the head of the Synod, Mace Banyan, the Monday after Thanksgiving." Zrakovi picked up his coffee cup, frowned at it a moment, then set it back on the table. "I'll be attending as well. We'll discuss what limitations, if any, they want placed on your use of the staff, but frankly I'm not inclined to give them any concessions. It isn't as if you're chasing down elves with it."

I hated Mace Banyan, whom I'd met only once. He had tried to scramble my brains when he caught me unawares during a dinner date with Jean Lafitte in the Beyond last month—at least it felt like brain-scrambling. I had no idea what he wanted, but I was sure only Jean's threat of violence had gotten me away unscathed. Now I figured what he wanted was Mahout, aka Charlie.

Of course, this meeting might never take place. By the week after Thanksgiving, I could be ensconced in a locked ward in

Ittoqqortoormiit—unless my combination of wizard, loup-garou, and elf DNA was determined too dangerous to live.

"Sure, where and when?" I might as well be optimistic about the wolf thing until I began sprouting whiskers.

"I suppose we could meet here"—Zrakovi glanced around at the bare walls—"although the ambience is a bit . . . generic. Maybe get someone to decorate for you if you aren't inclined to do it yourself. Elves can be odd about their surroundings. Two p.m."

Well, excuse me for having a life. "I've been kind of up to my neck in mermen lately, with no time to worry about office decor." I kept my expression neutral, but a faint smirk crossed Adrian Hoffman's lips. What was his role in this? "Will Mr. Hoffman be attending the meeting as well?"

"No, Adrian's here for another reason." Zrakovi beamed from Adrian back to me, either oblivious to the tension between us or, more likely, willfully ignoring it. "He's going to instruct you in elven magic and help you hone your use of the staff."

Wha? No!

"Is he an elf?" I refused to look at the man. Instead, I addressed my question to Zrakovi in a calm manner at odds with my inner screaming banshee.

"Adrian did his master's levels in elven magic, which has made him a valuable consultant for the Elders," Zrakovi said. "He's quite the expert. We're lucky he's available to teach you."

"Yeah. Lucky." I turned to Hoffman. At least now I knew how he'd made himself valuable to the Elders. "You'll be staying in New Orleans for a while, then?"

He finally looked at me directly. "I leased a flat for a

month. That should be sufficient time to give you the basics. You asked about an elf or faery hiding in the city—have you met one?"

Adrian seemed genuinely interested, and I guess if I'd studied for master's levels on a species as elusive as the elves, it would be exciting to think one of them might be in our midst.

"I'm not sure. There's a guy who moved into my neighborhood a month or two ago, and he's wearing peridot jewelry that I was able to tell had been bespelled by a wizard—probably a black-market buy. So he's hiding what he is."

Now that I put it into words, the whole notion that this crunchy-granola nursery owner was an elf or faery in disguise sounded paranoid.

"Why would you think he was an elf? And how were you able to tell the jewels had been bespelled?" Adrian frowned at me, and Zrakovi leaned forward with interest.

"I can sense the energy that comes from people and objects. Each species gives off a slightly different energy signature." This was not a wizard skill, and Adrian's contempt for my ability to read auras was a major factor in the deaths last month. From the sour look on Adrian's face, he hadn't forgotten.

Zrakovi leaned back and gave me an assessing look. "Reading auras is an elven skill and is one of the reasons I wanted the two of you to work together to see what other abilities DJ has inherited. Adrian, I believe you're going to find our DJ a very interesting student."

Adrian locked his annoyed gaze with mine. "I'm sure."

10

There was nothing I could do on the loup-garou front, so I spent the next few hours working on the Axeman case. I charted the latest two attacks, which both fit within the walking-distance radius. But attacks four and five had come so soon after the third that I had to wonder if the Axeman had just killed on one big spree instead of coming back each time from the Beyond. He'd probably be strong enough by now to stay for long periods, and every kill would make him stronger as more people talked about him.

With Ken now willing to smooth the way, I walked each of the crime scenes, reaching out with my senses to see if I could again sense that bit of energy from a member of the historical undead. Nada. It didn't hang around long enough.

Next, I went to the Historic New Orleans Collection and did some research on the Axeman I couldn't get from the Internet. He had left clothing behind at a few of his original crime scenes, so Jake's find was consistent with the original killer. The professor on TV had been wrong. What really made the Axeman's latest spree different is that he'd grown more efficient at killing—several of his victims in 1918 had survived.

I'd discussed the Axeman case with Zrakovi and Adrian before they left, but thanks to my sort-of friendship with Jean Lafitte, I knew more about the historical undead than they did. Zrakovi planned to call a meeting with the nascent Interspecies Council and ordered the paperwork that would confine the Axeman within the Beyond for the rest of his miserable immortal life . . . once we'd caught him. But the Council had yet to decide how many votes each species got, or how the balance of power would break down. They could be tangled in bureaucracy forever.

Unfortunately, with the historical undead, the death penalty wasn't an option, and if my calculations were accurate, the Axeman could kill again as early as tonight. He could do a lot of damage before the Interspecies Council got its act together.

By midafternoon, I was out of ideas and full of nervous energy that finally sent me out of doors, catching up on yard work I'd neglected all season, raking the small, crunchy leaves from the live oaks into piles a kid would love to play in.

"Need help?"

I ignored the voice and counted to ten, hoping it would go away. Instead, Quince Randolph knelt next to a tall pyramid of leaves I'd erected and took the lid off the big green trash can he'd brought with him. He began scooping up armfuls and piling them in the can. "You should compost this down. It would make a good mulch for flower beds. Plus you need more color in your landscaping."

"Whatever." I didn't know what mulch was, didn't care

enough to ask, and had such a brown thumb that flowers never survived my gardening efforts. Rand wore a chocolate-brown sweater almost the same color as mine, with jeans in a similar wash. With our comparable shades of long blond hair, we resembled grown-up Bobbsey Twins, except he was prettier. Freddie and Flossie do New Orleans. "Are you here for any particular reason?"

He squinted up at me against the soft afternoon sunlight. "I just want to get to know you better."

Uh-huh. I was about to get to know Adrian Hoffman better. That constituted enough challenge for one week. "Tell me what you are, and then we'll know each other better. I'm betting elf or faery." I was kind of betting elf—it might explain his interest in me although, thankfully, he'd never shown any inclination to plunder my brain.

He grinned. "Go to dinner with me and I might tell you."

I noted the return of his peridot earrings. Big liar. Super-big cheater. "Where's Eugenie?"

A flash of irritation spoiled his perfect features a half second before he answered. "Working. Can we—"

Whatever he planned to ask, my answer would be no, but he didn't get a chance because a clomping noise reached us from the direction of Prytania Street. Rand and I both were stricken speechless at the sight of Jean Lafitte sitting like royalty in the back of a gold-and-white French Quarter tourist carriage. It was being pulled by a light gray mule wearing a hat festooned with fake flowers and driven by a smiling guy who had no idea how many daggers his undead passenger had hidden on him.

The ornate carriage rolled to a stop, and the mule flicked an ear at the passing traffic. Those animals pulled tourists around the French Quarter all day, and it would take more than an impatient Toyota driver to rattle one of them. The carriages were also ridiculously expensive if one commissioned a ride outside the Quarter.

Then again, Jean Lafitte was loaded. The driver probably had a reason to smile.

Jean exited the carriage with extraordinary grace for such a large man. He was tall, powerfully built, black-haired, cobalt-eyed, a shameless flirt, and talked with a raspy French accent that made me swoon even though he was technically dead. In other words, I had a bit of a problem with Jean Lafitte and my own common sense being present at the same time.

Jean said a few words to the carriage driver, then turned to prop his hands on his hips in a broad piratelike stance, giving Rand a disapproving visual once-over. The mule backed up a few awkward steps before pulling the carriage into my driveway. God help me, I hoped Alex didn't get home in time to see this. I'd never hear the end of it.

"Do you wish me to rid you of this intruder, *Jolie*?"

Rand stood and faced the pirate, and I had to give the man—thing, elf, faery, whatever—credit for going toe-to-toe against Jean without a flinch of hesitation. "If she wants me to leave, she just has to say so."

Seriously? "Okay, I'd like you to leave." I leaned on my rake, half hoping Rand would refuse so Jean would bully him. I wouldn't let the pirate hurt him, of course, but it might be gratifying to watch a little heavy-handed persuasion.

Rand hefted the big can of leaves. "I really do need to talk to you soon, Dru." He gave Jean a disdainful smirk before striding back across Magazine Street.

Did he just call me Dru? I shot daggers at his back as he

disappeared into Plantasy Island, swinging the load of leaves as if it weighed nothing.

"Any idea what he is?" I asked Jean, who'd followed my gaze.

"*Non.*" He turned back to me. "I received your telephone message. We must speak, Drusilla. It is urgent."

Good Lord. I couldn't handle any more bad news. "Yeah, I need to talk to you too. Come on inside. Is the carriage waiting for you?"

"*Oui.* I cannot stay as long as I might wish."

This must be serious. Jean had been here more than thirty seconds and hadn't made a pass at me, tried to broker a business deal, or issued a half-baked smarmy comment. Either he was losing his touch or, more likely, whatever he had to say was catastrophic. Life seemed to be following that path these days.

He followed me through the back door and we settled at the kitchen table, facing each other. He looked even more odd sitting there than Louis Armstrong had, his energy too big for such a small space. At six-two he stood an inch shorter than Alex and probably had twenty or thirty fewer pounds of muscle, but still his presence seemed to exaggerate his size to overflow whatever space he was in. The man reeked of power.

"You want a Coke?" If the undead Jean Lafitte was going to sit at my kitchen table, I could at least be a good hostess.

He frowned. "*Qu'est-ce que c'est Coke?*"

I had a few real Cokes in the fridge for Eugenie, who considered corn syrup less poisonous to one's system than the chemically sweetened stuff I guzzled. I poured some over ice, handed it to him, and set the bottle on the table. "You'll love it."

He sipped cautiously, then smiled. "*Sucre.*"

"Exactly. Sugar and bubbles."

He sipped again and smiled more broadly. "As always, *Jolie*, you know how to lighten a man's heart. I should have come to visit you sooner."

There was the Jean Lafitte I knew. The charming devil.

"Why does your heart need lightening?"

"Ah, yes." He set the glass down. "I must speak to you about the most unfortunate incidents that have befallen our city. I assume that is why you called me at my hotel?" His dark blue eyes crinkled. "Or might I hope you called on more personal matters?"

I returned his smile. I couldn't help myself. I needed therapy. "Sorry, but it was about the Axeman murders. I believe it's one of your historical undead."

He sipped the Coke again and narrowed his eyes as he studied the glass. I wondered if a black market for Coca-Cola among the prete population of Old Orleans would be forthcoming. Louis Armstrong said Jean had made inquiries about supplying certain bars in the Beyond's version of a Weird West border town with modern alcohol and cigarettes. Since most of the denizens of the Beyond weren't likely to drive drunk or get lung cancer, I figured it was good for business on both sides of the border.

He poured the rest of the soda into his glass and examined the empty plastic bottle. Yep, definitely a business plan in the making.

"You can figure out how to smuggle Coke to the Beyond later. Is the attacker the original Axeman?"

He set the bottle down and nodded. "*Oui*, you deduced this much, which is good. I have not been able to discover his true identity and he has proven skilled at remaining hidden. I have made arrangements to leave the city for a short time, to see if I can capture him in Old Orleans and turn him over to your Elders."

I had to smile. "The infamous Jean Lafitte is going to help the authorities?" Definitely not standard pirate procedure.

He grinned. "Ah, but you must understand, *Jolie*. If this vicious *criminel* is not apprehended, his activities could interfere with my ability to conduct my affairs or cause your Elders to place limitations on when the historical undead might come into the modern world. I might not be able to once again ask you to dine with me."

Uh-huh, because that had turned out so well the first time.

"There is another, more urgent reason for me to discover and apprehend the Axeman, however. One of which you might be unaware."

A reason more important to Jean than business or romance had to be extreme. "What is it?"

"There is talk in Old Orleans that the Axeman is no longer acting alone, that he has now fallen under the control of one of your kind. Toward what purpose, I do not yet know."

I was lost. "What do you mean, one of my kind?"

He got up from the table and paced, muttering in French. "How to explain. The Axeman is no longer acting on his own counsel. He is being controlled by someone else, a"—he paused and muttered again—"what do you call a person who can manipulate *le morte*?"

"Manipulate the dead?" I frowned at him a few seconds before a horrible understanding dawned. "You mean a necromancer? A necromantic wizard is controlling the Axeman?"

I'd never heard of it happening, but I didn't see why it

couldn't. Necromancers could raise zombies, but zombies were ordinary dead people who acted by the will of their resurrector. They weren't sentient like the historical undead. Would necromantic magic outweigh free will in a member of the historical undead? I'd had a good grounding in preter-naturals through my education with Gerry, but somehow this situation had never arisen.

Jean correctly interpreted my dumbfounded expression and sat again. "*Oui*, just so. I wanted to be certain you were informed of this before I left the city, and to inquire if you would accompany me."

I looked up at Jean. "Go to Old Orleans with you to try and catch the Axeman? I think that's a good thing for you to do, but I'd be more effective on this side of the border." For many reasons, not the least of which is that I had possibly added a necromantic wizard to my most-wanted list. I had no proof, but could see no advantage Jean would gain by lying.

"I will learn what I can about this *necromancer*"—he said the word slowly as if committing it to memory—"and will provide you with any details I learn."

The whole necromancer scenario didn't add up for me. I couldn't see the purpose of it. "You said the necromancer was *now* controlling the Axeman—does that mean he wasn't always controlling him?"

"*Oui*, that is my understanding of the matter. The killer was simply coming across the border as I do, although with dark purpose. I come only with the purest of intentions, as you know."

Pure intentions and pure greed. "Certainly," I said. "So what changed?"

"When in Old Orleans this past evening, seeing to a possible shipment of goods, I heard talk of a wizard who had enabled the Axeman to reenter the modern city more quickly than he might otherwise do."

So he could kill more people? How would that benefit a necromancer?

I rubbed my eyes and fought off a sudden wash of heat, then chills, then overwhelming exhaustion. Maybe it was loup-garou DNA making another change, or maybe I'd simply reached my limit for bad news between the Axeman attacks, Jake, loup-garou viruses, elf lessons, and now a freaking rogue necromancer. A wizard. One of my own people.

"Are you certain you will not go with me, Drusilla? You could stay at my home in Barataria. It is a fine big home, and you could be at peace there."

Peace. I barely remembered what that felt like. "I can't go with you, Jean. I hope you can help solve these crimes from the Beyond, but it's my job to stay here and catch whoever's doing this."

Jean nodded. "I suspected such, although I hoped to change your mind. And now I must ask another thing. May we move to your receiving parlor?"

I stared at him a few seconds before figuring out he meant my living room. "Sure, I'll receive you."

We walked into the front room and sat on the sofa. He turned sideways to face me, our knees touching. Any other time, his hands would be wandering where they shouldn't. Now, they twitched on his thighs.

He searched my face, then nodded. "You have been exposed to the loup-garou curse. Do you yet know if you will transform?"

Air left my lungs with an audible *whoosh*, and I had trouble drawing in anything to replace it. My chest tightened. "How did you find out?"

"I met your friend Jacob earlier today in Old Orleans as I sought answers about the Axeman. He described the events of Sunday morning. I am very angry at Jacob for endangering you and being so weak as to flee. In my time, such a man would have been hanged or set adrift."

Jean reached out and took my hand. His was warm and comforting, which was just wrong. "You did not answer, Drusilla. Will you change?"

I shrugged. "I'm going to test my blood tomorrow morning and might have an answer. Otherwise, I won't know until full moon week after next and . . ." I didn't want to put this fear into words but he had to know what was at stake. "Don't tell anyone. The Elders would kill Jake. They might very well kill me."

There, I'd said the words, and they felt like truth. If Jake had told Jean, did anyone else know? My only hope was secrecy.

"No one need die," Jean said. "I have agreed to give Jacob asylum until your situation is settled. However, he must face punishment for his behavior as would anyone under my protection."

My gaze strayed to the scar that traced across his left jawline. Jean Lafitte had been a brilliant and charming man, but *Le Capitaine* also had a reputation as a strict master. His men did not break his rules twice. They didn't live to repeat their mistakes.

"Don't hurt him." I couldn't stand it if Jake was injured again because Jean had some nineteenth-century notion of appropriate manly behavior.

"Jacob will not be damaged. I give you my vow."

Somehow, I believed him. But Old Orleans operated under constant nighttime, with a steady full moon. Weres could literally run wild twenty-four/seven. "Are you sure he'll be safe?"

"I assure his protection, Drusilla. You need worry only for yourself. It will land me in good stead with his cousin your enforcer, *oui*? A favor owed by an enforcer is always of value. But I ask this of you. If you do change, do not put yourself in the hands of the wizards, who will use you or worse. Come to me."

I stared at him, realizing with dismay that this had been the best idea I'd heard so far. Better to be a wolf-girl with Jean in Old Barataria, an outpost of New Orleans' mirror city in the Beyond, than an inmate in a Greenland institution, hunting muskoxen. Jean was immune to the virus, and immortal. He might be the only one I couldn't kill.

"But I . . . well, thank you." Jean had an angle. He always had an angle. Helping Jake might earn him a favor from Alex, but I'd be a valuable bargaining chip in his dealings with the wizards. I knew their secrets but would be outside their jurisdiction. I'd get to live, so it would be a win for me too.

Until I thought of leaving my life in New Orleans behind—leaving Alex behind—and that twisted my gut into tight knots.

"When will you go?" I couldn't think about what might be coming or why the thought of saying good-bye to Alex brought with it physical pain. I needed to focus on this case, which had just gotten uglier than I'd imagined.

"This very evening," he said. "My hotel suite is paid until

the new year, so I will return to it as soon as I am able to capture the Axeman or I learn the whereabouts of the necromancer." He stood up. "I should leave now and prepare for my departure."

I nodded and followed him to the door. The carriage driver had turned the rig around so the mule faced the street, ready to roll. Jean turned, took my hand, and pressed it to his lips. *"Au revoir, Jolie.* Are you certain you will not accompany me? You do still owe me the remainder of our dinner date."

No more dinner dates for this girl, not anytime soon. I had enough drama in my life. "We'll finish our dinner date later."

A good word. *Later* might mean next week, or it might mean in another lifetime.

Jean paused on the bottom step, carrying the empty Coke bottle he'd snatched off the table—ever the entrepreneur, even in a crisis. "If I might make a suggestion, Drusilla, you should speak with my old acquaintance Etienne Boulard about your necromancer."

"The Regent of Vampyre?" I knew Boulard had moved to the city as soon as the borders dropped, but I didn't know he and Jean were acquainted. Like all Regents, he was responsible for keeping the vampires in his territory under control. As far as I knew, he was successful at it. They ran a French Quarter bar and, ironically, a thriving company that offered vampire tours of the city.

"I've been to L'Amour Sauvage a couple of times just to see what it looked like, but never saw the Regent. Why would Etienne Boulard know anything about the Axeman?"

"Before Etienne was turned vampire, he was a wizard

who could do this necromancy," Jean said. "He can no longer do magic as he once did, but he can perhaps provide you with information."

"And what's in this for you?" I hated to question Jean's motives, but then again, Jean always had a motive.

His smile was cold. "The sooner this necromancer and his Axeman are dealt with, the more quickly life shall return to normal," he said. "The idea of a wizard controlling the historical undead is disturbing to me, *Jolie*. I did not like to be controlled in my mortal life, and I do not wish to be controlled now."

11

An average autumn in New Orleans lasts about three weeks, from late October until mid-November. We enjoy the brief respite from humid misery while we can.

The first hint of winter hung in the mist as my feet thudded along the jogging path around Audubon Park—the first day I'd tried to run since fracturing my ribs. The pain set my pace somewhere between a walk and an amble, but the normalcy of returning to my early-morning routine kicked up a few endorphins and left me to ponder the future without panic.

I was trying not to obsess over the loup-garou thing, without much success. The full moon loomed like a dam, a flood of worry and fear building up on one side and a lit stick of dynamite wedged into a weak spot on the other. In nine days, the fuse would either fizzle or blow my world apart. No matter what I focused on or however much I tried to ignore it, that deadline traveled alongside me, heavy and shuffling.

And the necromancer business had me stumped. I'd made an appointment to talk to the vampire Regent tonight, but

I simply couldn't think of any reason a wizard would waste time controlling an undead serial killer. Although if Jean was right that the necromancer had just gotten involved in the last day or two, the wizard might have a target the Axeman hadn't gotten to yet.

But if you're a necromancer and you want to knock off an enemy, why not raise any old zombie and give it a kill order? Why a sentient dead guy with an ax fetish, unless you wanted to kill someone specific and have it passed off as just another Axeman murder? After all, if it weren't for Jean's ability to monitor everybody else's business as well as his own, we would have no idea a necromancer was involved.

After my run, I drove back to my house to see if the microscope had arrived. I hobbled upstairs, tripping over Sebastian twice, and stopped in the library door, my heart pounding. A large box sat in the middle of my permanent transport.

I don't know how long I stood there, frozen in place. But I finally walked to the circle, broke the plane, and dragged the box into the middle of the room.

It took a shaky forty-five minutes to get the microscope unpacked and set up, and another half hour to work up my nerve. Praying, I used my silver summoning knife to slice into my finger, placed a drop of blood on one slide, topped it with another, and clamped them firmly together.

Squinting into the rubber-rimmed eyepiece, I looked anxiously at the slide through my right eye, then my left. Everything looked fuzzy, so I dug out the instructions again and finally got the thing focused.

I stared through the eyepiece again, holding my breath

and then slowly letting my lungs empty. All the components in the blood sample were round. Nothing was curved or oblong.

I searched for "blood under microscope" on my laptop and looked at the assortment of images, which looked a lot like mine. A wash of relief spread through me. I'd check again in a few days. Hell, I might check every day to look for any sign of change. But so far, there was nothing like what Adam Lyle had described.

Maybe I was off the hook. And I'd have good news when Alex arrived in an hour or so for an update on the Axeman case. I wanted to hear his thoughts on the necromancer angle, plus he needed to know that thanks to Jake he was joining the Owe-Jean-Lafitte-a-Favor club, of which I'd been a member for the past three years. I doubt Alex would have the same repayment options Jean had offered me.

In retrospect, I wasn't surprised that Jean had offered Jake asylum, or that Jake had accepted it. Unlike Alex, Jake found the pirate interesting. He didn't care that Jean had the hots for me, or that I sort of returned the feelings for a variety of convoluted reasons. After all, Jean might leave me. He might lie to me and use me. But he couldn't die on me.

Which is more than I could say about Alex, and the thought of leaving him to live in the Beyond brought on the tears I'd been holding at bay for days. When had my former partner—the one I'd decided was too good a friend to risk losing by adding benefits—become a guy I cried over? I was not a crying kind of girl. An hour ago I'd have thought I was experiencing loup-garou hormonal surges, but now I attributed the tears to stress.

Screw that. I put the microscope away, splashed cold water

on my face, and re-taped my ribs. On my way downstairs, my cell phone vibrated with a text message from Alex, and my heart sank as I read the word *Axeman* followed by an address only a mile or two from my house. This would be the first attack outside a comfortable walking distance from the Quarter, but if a necromancer was behind it, he could be driving the freaking killer around. The whole game had changed.

I climbed into my Pathfinder and drove toward the Irish Channel address in the text. A couple hundred years ago, the channel had been settled by Irish immigrants who worked on the docks of the nearby Mississippi River. Today, it was a typical New Orleans neighborhood, which meant charming and full of old, interesting architecture, enormous live oaks whose roots pushed up the crumbling sidewalks, and insufficient off-street parking.

Red and blue lights strobed from half a dozen police cars gathered a block ahead of me. I threaded my trusty old SUV along the narrow street, squeezing between an ambulance and a fire engine. Spotting Alex's Range Rover around the corner on a side street, I turned off and parked behind him.

Rooting through my glove compartment, I finally dug out my fake FBI badge—then realized I had nowhere to put it. Cropped black running tights and a red T-shirt did not give me a pocket, belt, or collar, and I didn't want to go into a crime scene carrying a purse. Finally, I found a small notebook in the backseat and clipped the badge and a pen to that.

I shouldn't call the badge a fake, anyway. It was real, because "real close" is how hard you'd have to squint to find the tiny word CONSULTANT printed at the bottom.

After locking the car, I strode purposefully toward two

officers standing like sentries in front of a small Victorian cottage, its clapboards painted a mint green and gingerbread trim all in eggshell. Only in New Orleans were food-colored houses considered not only normal, but desirable. I'd been thinking about replacing my merlot-and-cream color scheme with something like sage or mocha.

The officers, wearing the black uniforms of the NOPD, didn't appear nearly as sweet as dark cocoa, with plastered-on scowls and eyes in constant motion. Ken had said the Axeman Deux attacks, with no leads or motive, had made the cops edgy. Having another one happen this soon wouldn't help.

I got within four feet of them before the older cop, a buzz-cut, middle-aged bulldog of a man who screamed ex-military, settled his cold gaze on me, eyes widening slightly when he realized I wasn't just out for a morning jog or being a nosy uptowner.

He placed his hands on his hips and adjusted the heavy belt loaded down with a gun and a baton and a pair of clinking handcuffs before sauntering onto the sidewalk to meet me. The belt-jiggle was obviously cop-code for "look what's coming," because his companion stayed in the yard but turned a full 180 to watch me approach without a word being exchanged.

"Morning, officers." When feeling insecure, flash badge. I held mine in front of me like a tiny leather-encased shield clipped to my spiral notebook. "I'm here to meet up with Detective Ken Hachette and my partner, agent Alex Warin. Sorry"—I waved in the general vicinity of my clothes—"the call came while I was running."

Officer Buzz-cut took the badge. "Ms. . . . Jaco?" He

pronounced it "Jock-O" instead of "Jake-O," but I didn't bother to correct him—we weren't destined for a lengthy relationship.

I waited while he examined the badge. He couldn't question its authority, but he didn't have to like it, either. Local cops didn't like feds poking around in their murder cases. Female feds? Even worse. He thrust it back at me with a scowl and a blatant look-see at my assets. I'd have kicked him in the nuts if I thought he wouldn't arrest me and enjoy it.

"Back bedroom of the house." He yelled over his shoulder at another officer who'd come out to stand on the porch. "Heads up, Matty—legs incoming. Oops, *fed* incoming, I meant to say."

I gave him a saccharine smile, made a show of squinting at his badge number as I slowly wrote it in my notebook, and nodded at the other officer.

The scent of blood hit me before I cleared the front room. Ken sat on a sofa facing the door, talking to an elderly man whose fear and sorrow soaked into my skin. I'd done my grounding ritual this morning, so only the strongest emotions reached me.

Ken knew how to keep his mind a blank. Thank God for the U.S. Marines and the police academy. Note to self: wear your mojo bag while jogging; you never know when you might have to jog over to a crime scene.

"Alex is in the back bedroom, checking out the scene before our guys go in to bag and tag," Ken said. "Tell him they're gettin' impatient."

"Straight back?" I pointed down the hall, and at Ken's nod, approached the source of the heavier blood scent, thick and rich and meaty. Everyone says blood smells like copper, but to me it reeks of iron and rust, earthy and viscous.

The metaphysical chaos hit me before I reached the door: the wonky tingle of Alex's shapeshifter aura, the lingering energy of violence, plus the light undercurrent of not-quite-human energy that told me a member of the historical undead had been here. And mixed with it, the buzz of a wizard's magic—like a necromancer would leave behind. I'd not felt it at any other crime scene.

I held my breath, pulled the neck of my shirt over my nose to blunt the blood scent when and if I did have to breathe again, and tiptoed into the room. No one was inside but Alex. He squatted next to the bed, studying his surroundings and ignoring my presence. He was focused, engrossed, a man engaged in his calling.

I stared past him at the bed and had to close my eyes, fighting for control of my heaving gut. Thankfully, I hadn't eaten this morning. Sheets stained the color of raw meat were dotted with clots and chunks I wanted to pretend I hadn't seen. Blood spattered the lampshade on a nightstand, the pale green walls behind the bed, the hardwood floor.

I had to clear my throat a couple of times before getting words out. "What can you tell?"

"Not much." Alex stood and walked to the other side, getting another angle on the scene and, unfortunately, giving me a clearer view of the mattress.

"I'm assuming nobody lived through that."

He knelt next to the nightstand and disappeared from view as he checked under the bed. "Still alive for now. Critical condition, though."

Being careful not to touch anything, I walked into the

postage-stamp-size half bath off the bedroom, trying to get a break from the blood. An old-fashioned white iron pedestal sink sat adjacent to a low white toilet. I gazed in the plain, unframed mirror, and a ponytailed blonde with dark circles under her eyes gazed at me. Blood had even spattered the mirror.

I turned back to the gore, watching for a few seconds as Alex contorted to examine every nanoparticle of the bed without touching anything. "What's different about it? Where did he leave the ax?"

He stood up and shook his head. "He didn't—and that's what's different about it besides the location being outside our French Quarter radius. We've combed the house and the grounds and the ax isn't here. Blood droplets led out the back door, so he must have taken it with him. I'm wondering if it could be a copycat."

The ax was the killer's calling card, so not leaving it fell way outside his normal pattern. But the energy signatures told a different story.

"No, it isn't a copycat," I said, and Alex stood and looked at me for the first time.

"Tell me how you know."

I glanced into the hallway to make sure the forensics team was still keeping its distance. "I can still feel the aura of the historical undead here. Plus a wizard's magic, which I'll explain when we get somewhere more private. Who's the victim?"

"A *Times-Pic* reporter," Alex said. "So you know this is gonna get played up. This wizard's magic—it's important?"

"Yes, but I don't want to get into it here." I turned to

study the woman's dresser. A couple of rings and a bracelet looked real enough, but robbery hadn't been the motive in any of these cases, so the culprit wasn't a necromancer in need of cash.

I scanned the rest of the cluttered dresser top. A small packet of tissues. Bottles of perfume—what I thought of as pop-culture scents, named after people like Beyoncé and Britney. A spiral reporter's notebook. A couple of lipsticks lying atop a page of lined notebook paper.

Good grief. Blood spatter had even gone on the wall behind the dresser, except . . . "Alex, come here."

I pointed at the wall, where the numeral 25 had been written in blood. "What does that mean?"

"We don't know." Ken walked into the bedroom and stood next to us, studying the wall. "There was a number at the last crime scene too. It's one of the details we aren't releasing to the media. We always hold a few things back to help us filter out crackpot leads and confessions."

"What was the first number?" I didn't remember reading anything about the Axeman leaving numbers back in the good old days.

Ken flipped through his notebook. "Fifty-seven."

Fifty-seven and twenty-five. A chill washed over me. I lived at 5725 Magazine Street.

Alex cleared his throat. "DJ, that's your house number."

Ken and I looked at him, then at each other. "Gotta be a coincidence," he said, but he was frowning. "Right?"

I looked back at the number. "Right."

But maybe I'd amp up the security wards on my house, just in case.

12

If zombies and ghouls took over Disney World, with creative direction from Satan, the theme park would resemble the corpse of Six Flags New Orleans. I parked outside the main gate and squeezed past rusted, twisted turnstiles and purple-painted, crumbling offices covered in graffiti.

Six Flags had never been profitable. Folks who come to New Orleans for vacation aren't usually looking for a Louisiana-themed amusement park in the eastern part of the city, far from the Quarter. Plus, underneath the Cajun kitsch, the place was, well, Six Flags. When Katrina hit in 2005, the park sank under six feet of water for more than a month and never reopened.

Years later, here it remained, a distorted, hellish sideshow in the middle of swampy soil. It was tied up in a terminal case of litigation, its rusting roller coaster reaching toward heaven like a monument to the fates of nature and indifference.

The perfect place, in other words, for some discreet lessons in elven staff usage. Or so I'd thought—the site was my bright idea. Now I wasn't sure. It was eerie, even in the weak sunlight that had finally broken through the clouds, and my nerves had been on edge *before* learning the Axeman had left bloody numbers at his last two crime scenes that added up to my street address. Were they left under the instructions of the necromancer?

My logical mind said it was a weird coincidence. My panicky, spiraling-out-of-control imagination whispered that maybe I was a target. Except I didn't know any necromancers, and while I'd pissed off a few people in my day, I don't think I'd made any mortal enemies.

I wandered past the sculpture of a headless merman next to the roller coaster, which looped and twirled through the sky like a demon sculptor on hallucinogens had carved a statue of rusty metal. Stephen King should set a horror novel here.

A creaking noise sent shivers down my arms and made my fingers tingle, but when I spun around, only the wind revealed itself to me, moving the swinging chairs of a Looney Tunes ride like they were being boarded by a horde of ghost children.

In a burst of creative irony, I'd left Adrian Hoffman a message to meet me by the entrance to the Jean Lafitte Pirate Ship ride, which during better days had taken passengers on a short lagoon trip. Now it looked as if Jean himself might have abandoned it during his human life. Even the water in the murky faux-lagoon had a rusty tinge.

My first task was to set up an open portal for my *teacher* since he'd told me during our meeting with Zrakovi that he wasn't comfortable driving in the U.S. Apparently, we uncouth Yanks insist on driving on the wrong side of the road. If I'd been a responsible, mature adult I'd have offered to pick Adrian up, but obviously I wasn't.

I set my backpack on the "dock" and retrieved a baby-food-size jar of iron filings. I also had a sizable cache of premade potions and charms in marked vials as well as the elven staff. Lately, the motto *Be Prepared* was more than a Boy Scout slogan.

I turned in a circle, searching for the best transport spot. Something not likely to be disturbed by the photographers, gangbangers, and "explorers" who risked arrest to wander out here and take photos or add to the urban art. The land belonged to New Orleans, so the city council wanted to curtail access. They worried that people like graffiti artists (or stray wizards) might fall on a rusty pirate sword or trip over the merman's missing head and sue them.

For the transport, I found a tangle of weeds next to the entrance to the Gator Bait ride that would give Adrian a great view of the sign when he arrived. On it, a bright green gator in a king's red cloak and a crown drove an airboat and waved, although the storm-broken sign beneath him now read GATOR BA_T.

The spot was overgrown enough to camouflage the transport so we could keep it open, but not so overgrown that we couldn't get in and out easily. I used trails of iron filings to create a large interlocking circle and triangle inside it. Taking the elven staff from my pack, I touched it to the closed transport, muttered a few directives in my South Louisiana version of the ancient wizard Celtic language, and shot enough energy into the figure to fuel the site indefinitely. Once this educational adventure ended, I'd break the transport line and close the connection.

I had plenty of my own native physical magic to power a transport, so using the staff was a bit of overkill, but I figured the first thing Hoffman would do was order me to quit using Charlie until the post-Thanksgiving elf meeting. Might as well wield it while I could.

I took my pack and returned to a bench near the pirate ship entrance, my mind fixated on the Axeman and his necromancer. If the necromantic wizard was planning to direct the Axeman to a specific target or targets, how could we figure out who it was beforehand? We'd been able to find no link between the two targets where numbers had been found.

And the numbers had to be significant. Just on the off chance it was my house number, I typed a reminder into my phone to download a few jazz CDs. Couldn't hurt.

I'd met Alex for lunch at my house before heading to Six Flags. First, I had to share my good news from the blood test. Alex broke into the rare smile that cracked apart his enforcer façade and revealed the sweet, decent guy he so rarely showed anyone. I'd seen it a few times, but never quite like now. He didn't say anything, but pulled me into a hug so tight my ribs ached. And I didn't care.

I didn't know how Alex felt about me. I wasn't even sure how I felt about him. But something was growing between us, and I was glad a fur disaster wasn't going to ruin it.

Although he hadn't said he was worried about Jake, the sag of relief in his shoulders when I told him his cousin was safe told me more than words. He didn't even complain about being in Jean Lafitte's debt.

Once we finally focused on the Axeman, Alex had reluctantly agreed the numbers were probably a coincidence. Once he heard the necromancer angle, however, he helped me gather the supplies to walk the circle around my house, burying packets of magic-infused herbs and stones at regular intervals and reinforcing my security wards.

Before I left for Six Flags, Alex had also called Ken and asked for extra patrols around my neighborhood.

He'd even offered to come with me to Six Flags, but I needed to learn to work with Adrian on my own. We would never be best buddies, but I did want his respect. I didn't think I could earn it arriving with backup for what was supposed to be simple elf lessons. Right now, the rest was paranoia. "Keep your phone nearby," I'd told him when I left. "I'll call you if there are any problems."

Instead, he'd decided to stay at my house all afternoon and make sure an ax-wielding bad guy didn't show up. He also planned to call the Elders for a list of locally registered necromancers. When I got home, we'd divide the list and start tracking them down, and then—

"Could you possibly have picked a more disagreeable place to meet?"

Heh. I wiped the grin off my face before turning to greet my new mentor. Wearing a charcoal-colored, tailored suit that probably cost more than a month of my salary, Adrian stood ankle-deep in the patch of briars. He held a briefcase and a scowl.

"Sorry." I tried to appear contrite. "I wanted a spot where an open transport would be camouflaged."

He gave me a look that would freeze habaneros and high-stepped out of the brush. "I half expected you not to be here. I heard on the television news that another ax attack had occurred. Do you still believe it's the historically undead Axeman at work?"

"I do." I gave him a quick rundown while we walked to

a bench located near the Lafitte Pirate Ship ride, ignoring his expression of derision at the information from Jean about a necromancer's involvement.

"Well, obviously the local Regent of Vampyre is the culprit and Lafitte is covering for him." Adrian assumed an I-smell-turnips expression. "Nasty creatures, vampires. Totally self-absorbed. We should never have allowed them open access to our world."

In my albeit limited experience I'd found the vampires to be among the most self-regulated of all the species, and I'd never heard a whisper of complaint about Etienne Boulard or any of his people. Vampires were extremely practical. After all, they knew following prete law kept their favorite snack food—i.e., humans—close at hand.

"Have you met our local Regent?" Except for one sample tour with Eugenie, my visits to L'Amour Sauvage and the Tour Blood offices had only exposed me to his human minions. Tonight, I had an appointment to meet the Regent himself.

Adrian's upper lip curled. "Of course not. Why on earth would I want to meet a vampire?"

Maybe because he was one. A few minutes in Adrian Hoffman's company could suck the soul out of a banana. "I'm going to talk with him tonight at his bar. It's not far from your apartment. Why don't you go with me? I'd like to get your reactions and compare them with my own."

Yeah, I was sucking up, and he fell for it. "That would be most . . . interesting. Yes, I'll go." He almost smiled.

Good. Sucking up done. Now for the real show. "What are we doing today?"

I expected a bunch of dry lectures on elven history and

lore, but he surprised me. "Show me what you can do." He sat next to me on the rusty bench, crossed his legs, and waited for me to perform like a trained seal.

The thing I'd most like to do was point my elven staff at him and set him on fire, but such an act would probably hurt my opportunities for career advancement. "Can you be more specific?"

He rolled his eyes heavenward as if asking the Almighty to spare him from idiots. "What elven skills do you claim to have? We'll start there. Next time I'll test you on some other skills known to be elven."

Wait, this might actually be helpful. My mouth dropped open involuntarily.

He sniffed. "Unless, of course, you've highly exaggerated your abilities."

What a jackass. "Fine. I can do hydromancy. I can—"

"Show me."

I sighed. "It's daylight. And we're outside." The ideal time to do hydromancy was at night under a full moon and, failing that, indoors in a dark place.

"You've a reputation for being *creative*." His tone left no doubt as to what he thought of creativity: Out-of-the-box thinking sat atop the undesirability scale alongside horrible things like genocide and polite behavior.

"Some people consider creativity an asset." He wanted creative? I'd show him creative. I studied the area around us, grabbed my pack, and walked toward the long midway, filled with a couple dozen dilapidated wooden structures tricked out like French Quarter buildings. Before the hurricane, they'd sold overpriced Cajun- and voodoo-themed souvenirs. The sign leading into the area read PONTCHARTRAIN BEACH, a lakeside amusement park in New Orleans that had been closed years ago. The name had a certain irony now.

The storefront on the end had once been bright yellow, with orange window and door trim and sage-green shutters. Designed to mimic a Creole cottage, the building more resembled something a colorblind do-it-yourselfer had painted using clearance-bin paint from Home Depot, then left to rot for several years. The windows gaped open, and graffiti covered the front. In bright red, VENDETTA; in black, ROACHERY.

Shuddering, I stepped through the open doorway and picked my way around shards of glass and empty display cases, dodging a rodentlike skeleton the size of a terrier and taking shallow breaths to protect my lungs from the chalky smell of dried mold spores—a scent I remembered too well from the post-Katrina city. Gerry's entire neighborhood of Lakeview had reeked of it for a year.

I knelt in the darkest corner. Not pitch-black, but dark enough to work. My skin jumped and twitched and itched with the feet of imaginary spiders and roaches and God knew what else crawling inside my clothes. At least I hoped they were imaginary.

"What in bloody hell are you doing?"

I started at the sound of the petulant voice coming from the doorway. Adrian had been following closely until I reached the building.

"I'm going to do some basic hydromancy and I need darkness. Come closer—just past the giant mutant rat carcass. I can't do it any closer to the door."

Glass crunched under his feet, and he muttered curses at me all the way across the room. A pair of dust-covered, fancy loafers came to a stop about a yard to my left. Had the man thought he was dressing for a garden party?

The creak of his knees as he squatted echoed in the dark, and the crackle and whisper of something crawling nearby made the little hairs on my arms prickle. We needed to get this done and get out of here.

I felt around in my backpack and pulled out my portable hydromancy kit. Unzipping the leather pouch, I removed a small black-glass bowl, a flask of holy water, and two cones of patchouli incense. If I did the ritual at home, I used mimosa leaves, but the incense was more portable.

I looked up. "You got a match?"

"Did you not even inherit enough of your father's Red Congress magic to light incense? What a pity. He was a powerful wizard."

I hoped he didn't see my teeth gritting in the gloom. I could light incense; I just saw no need to waste my energy reserves.

"How well did you know Gerry?" I touched a finger to the incense cones and sent enough physical magic into each one to ignite the ends. My father, whom I'd known only as a mentor until he went missing after Katrina, had been a strong Red Congress wizard, warrior class. I'd inherited very little of his physical magic and Adrian was right—that was a pity.

"I knew him too well." I imagined the wizard assuming his most condescending expression, which would match the tone of his voice. "He squandered more talent than most wizards ever have. He was arrogant and unwilling to follow the rules or respect the traditions of wizardry."

Adrian would hear no argument from me. Gerry had

raised me since I was six. I loved him and I missed him. But I wasn't blind to his faults. Willem Zrakovi had expressed much the same opinion.

I poured the holy water into the bowl and sat back on my heels. One final element. "You have a pen? Or anything small that I can use for a focus?"

Fabric rustled as Adrian dug through his suit coat and handed me a fountain pen. A really nice one, judging by its sleek casing. Exactly what I'd need to help me stage a little magic show he'd appreciate.

"Okay, keep your focus on the water," I said, and closed my eyes. In my left hand I clutched his pen while my right index finger touched the surface of the water. I used a little more of my native magic to shoot a small burst of energy into the bowl, keeping Adrian's face fixed in my mind.

I heard a sharp intake of breath and opened my eyes. He squatted next to me and peered into the water at the image of himself as viewed from above. I shifted my finger to different sections of the water's surface, and the view of his image shifted in correlating angles. I twirled my finger more deeply into the bowl and the image zoomed in on his horrified face.

"Enough." He reached out and pulled my hand from the water. The image vanished, the chain between me and the magic broken. "Give me my pen."

I handed it to him without comment, and he stood up. He was shaken, broadcasting fear like a human or a young wizard who hadn't learned to put up mental shields. After a few seconds I felt them slam into place, but too late. My little demonstration had surprised him. In theory, Adrian knew I could do hydromancy, but he hadn't realized I could use it on him.

"You realize that is regulated magic." His smooth exterior slipped back into place.

"Of course." Anything the Elders couldn't do themselves tended to go on the "black" list of illegal or regulated magic. I poured the water onto the incense cones to douse them, then returned the bowl and bottle of water to my pack. "Okay, your first show-and-tell is over." I stood up and motioned toward the door. "After you."

We walked back into the sunlight, blinding after the darkness of the store. Squinting, I took a lungful of clean air. "Want to return to the bench?"

He shouldered past me and returned to our former perch, where he'd left his briefcase. I slung my pack over my shoulder and followed.

Once we were seated, he crossed his arms and met my eyes for the first time today. "What else can you do?"

Guess we'd finished hydromancy class. "Well, Gerry and I were able to communicate through dreams." A truly awful thing I didn't want to try again. "Never happened with anyone else."

Adrian nodded, looking thoughtful. "My understanding is dreamsharing only works between people who have a blood bond. The skill's probably dormant now that Gerald's dead."

Anger leapt up, hot and sharp, followed by a blur of tears. I glanced away so he wouldn't see them. I'd accepted Gerry's death, mostly. But grief has a way of slapping you silly when you least expect it. Sitting here, surrounded by so many reminders of what had happened during Katrina as if three years hadn't passed, and listening to this jackass talk about Gerry's death so callously . . . it hurt.

"What else?" asked Mr. Oblivious.

I choked on a lump of grief. "The empathy and energy recognition."

He laughed, a sly, silky flex of vocal cords and throat muscles. "Ah yes, the famous ability to read auras and emotions."

Yeah, the famous empathy and energy recognition he'd ignored, which cost some lives and got him publicly chastised by Zrakovi. "Despite your disregard for them, my empathic skills are valuable," I said, my tone flat.

"They could be," he said. "But they're a tool, and like any tool they have to be taken in context."

I swiveled on the bench to face him. "Well, it told me how my hydromancy display—a minor example of that skill, by the way—made you uncomfortable."

He nodded. "But how do you know I wasn't thinking of something else that made me uncomfortable?"

He was right. I didn't know. "Okay, I'll give you that one. But knowing what emotions are driving an adversary's actions can be a powerful weapon, regardless of their source."

His brown eyes narrowed. "And am I your adversary, Drusilla Jaco?"

I gave his question serious consideration. I was angry at Adrian Hoffman and we'd never be friends—maybe not even friendly acquaintances—but we were fellow wizards. "No, you're not my adversary. We differ in our methods, we certainly have different temperaments, but in the end we're on the same side and that's what matters."

His face relaxed, and the man actually smiled. "So, shall we agree we'll never be chums, get through this exercise as pleasantly as we can, and then go on our way?"

"Great idea." I had enough to deal with between the Axeman and the loup-garou crisis without adding political warfare. "So, that leaves the staff."

I pulled the ancient weapon out of my backpack, its carved sigils glowing under my touch, and enjoyed Adrian's naked admiration. He'd never seen the staff, and if he'd spent his academic years studying elven magic, he'd probably be itching for a closer examination.

I held it out to him. "This is the staff known by the elves as Mahout." I'd leave off the Charlie nickname.

His face was reverent, eyes shining like a sugar addict in a praline factory. He better be careful, or I might decide to like him.

"This is amazing." His voice held reverence but his heart held jealousy—which I was able to tell with my useless empathic ability. "How did the claiming happen? You found it among Gerald's belongings, yes?" He ran a finger over the sigils, which had stopped glowing as soon as he touched them.

"I found the staff in Gerry's attic after Katrina. I knew from his journals he'd never gotten it to work for him, but it began glowing the instant I picked it up. It began following me from room to room, although it's never come right to my hand except once when I summoned it using wizard's magic. It really amplifies my physical magic."

The staff did other things too. It ramped up my hydromancy and just about any other kind of spell or ritual I'd tried, but I didn't volunteer that. I didn't like the way Adrian caressed it, almost possessively. He might as well be Sméagol cooing over the One Ring and muttering "preciousssss."

I held out my hand. "I'll give you an example."

He laid the staff across my palm but didn't let go until I finally pulled it away. My aim was notorious, in a bad way, so I searched for a broad target. The side of the Jean Lafitte Pirate Ship ride looked unmissable. I took a deep breath, pointed the staff at the skull and crossbones painted on the ship's hull (which Jean would never have permitted lest he be seen as a real pirate instead of a "privateer"), and channeled a bit of magic through it.

"Holy Mother of God!" Adrian jumped to his feet as a stream of red fire flew from the tip of the staff and burned a hole in the side of the ship about six feet to the left of where I'd been aiming. He'd never know the difference.

An acrid, smoky odor wafted our way as flames began to lick along the hull of the rotted vessel.

"I suggest you put that conflagration out." Adrian crossed his arms. I'd really shaken him this time.

"Um, well, I haven't gotten to the 'undo' lesson yet." I'd been working on a flame-retardant charm but hadn't perfected it enough for it to work on something as large as the pirate ship. The vial was in my pocket, but the ship would burn down to water and then the fire would be automatically doused. No point in wasting good magic.

Adrian snorted and ran toward the edge of the small boat landing, chanting and twisting his fingers in front of him like he was speaking to the fire in sign language. The flames flickered, then died, leaving a charred, gaping hole.

Adrian fisted his hands on his hips and stared at the ship a few moments before turning back to me with an assessing look.

I gave him one right back. "You're Blue Congress?" I'd never seen magic like his. It differed from Gerry's brute-force Red Congress magic and my own methodical rituals. Blues were artistic, creative—a congress I'd never have pegged for Adrian. His magic was poetic, almost delicate. "That was beautiful."

He looked back at the ship. "Normally, that spell would restore a magicked situation to its previous state, but it apparently doesn't quite work with elven sorcery. Let's try something else. Just don't burn anything down."

I followed him down the midway, dodging the patches of weeds that had sprung through cracks in the concrete. He came to a stop near a giant clown's head lying on its ear, red mouth gaping in a curve like a parenthesis, blue eyes goggling at us. Mr. Happy was the size of a Volkswagen Beetle and made me shudder. I freakin' hated clowns. They weren't as bad as zombies or elves, but close.

"Shoot the clown, aim for his right eye, and put as much of your own power into the shot as you can," Adrian said, moving to stand behind me and, theoretically, out of harm's way.

"Why would I want to do that?"

"Because I want to know your maximum power with the staff and how inaccurate your aim is." Okay, so maybe he *had* realized I'd been going for the skull and crossbones and not the middle of the pirate ship hull.

I held the staff up and aligned it with the clown's big, blue right eye. The eyeball was easily three feet wide, but the staff seemed to kick left so I adjusted my aim a few feet to the east.

Gathering as much physical energy as I could summon

without a concentrated buildup, I fed it all into the staff, and the ropes of flame came out wider, brighter, and faster-moving than anything I'd produced so far—so much that I jerked my arm a little to the right.

The flames went wide, hitting a wooden equipment shed behind the clown head. It whooshed into a massive bonfire, the likes of which only a pile of dried wood could produce.

"You. Are. A. Menace." Adrian elbowed me aside and started his hand motions again, muttering and weaving a spell I hoped would dampen the fire, which had spread to an adjacent building with fast-growing flames. It seemed to tamp briefly, then flared again.

Damn. His magic wasn't working. I scrambled in my right jeans pocket and pulled out my flame-retardant charm. Thumbing off the top, I ran toward the burning buildings.

Adrian grabbed the back of my sweater as I passed him, pulling me to a halt. "What in bloody hell are you doing?"

"Trust me." I wrenched free of him, got as close to the fire as I dared, and tossed the charm. Adrian came to stand beside me, and we both watched in awe as a plume of bright purple smoke shot into the air so high it briefly dwarfed the roller coaster. Too much Chinese beautyberry in the mixture, maybe.

On the positive side, the buildings were no longer burning. They simply crackled and turned black, sending occasional plumes of purple smoke skyward.

"You might wish to adjust that recipe a bit." Adrian and I stood and watched the purple geysers erupt. They were kind of pretty, sparkling magenta and violet as the sunlight hit them.

Adrian spun in alarm as the distinctive whoop of a siren sounded in the distance. "It's the constabulary. You're going to get us arrested for arson."

"Holy crap." I raced back to the bench for my backpack and hooked fingers through the handle of Adrian's briefcase. "Let's go."

"The transport," he shouted, running for the patch of weeds. I set my backpack and his briefcase inside the transport next to him, rummaged in the backpack a split second, and pulled out one of my premixed camouflage potions. I couldn't leave my SUV here for the cops to tow away.

"You're going to get us arrested, you stupid woman! Leave the vehicle!" His voice had risen about three octaves and I'm sure at some point I'd think his falsetto was funny.

Not that he'd be able to hear me laughing. As I turned to answer him, he disappeared. The SOB had taken the transport and left me—and he took my backpack.

Cursing, I sprinkled the camouflage potion in a circle around my Pathfinder so I wouldn't have to steal it out of impound later. Damned hysterical Blue Congress wizard. Like waiting another thirty seconds for us to transport together would have killed him. Now I'd have to track him down to get my stuff back.

I ran into the transport just as blue flashing lights turned in at the entrance to Six Flags. In the distance, I heard fire engines on their way. Behind me, purple flares continued to shoot almost as high as the Jocco's Mardi Gras Madness roller coaster. I had no idea what the fire department would make of it.

Just before time and space compressed around me, taking

me to the transport nearest Adrian's apartment, I spotted a pair of NOPD officers running breakneck toward the enormous, grinning clown with purple smoke drifting from behind its head.

13

I sat on a bench near the French Market on Decatur Street with my cell phone, squeaky-clean tourists giving me wide berth on their way to drink hurricanes and soak up the New Orleans ambience. Probably thought I was a gutter punk, between the jeans I'd ripped the knee out of scrambling away from the clown fire and hair that was more pony than tail.

My backpack, retrieved from Adrian's apartment after I'd tracked him down, leaned against my leg, the elven staff sticking out the top. It completed the picture of what the New Orleans Chamber of Commerce would not want to show off about our fair city: eccentric and possibly dangerous locals of questionable mental health.

Alex answered on the first ring. "Toxic purple smoke being reported at Six Flags. What did you do?"

If it weren't true, I'd resent his assumption that I'd caused the incident. "A spell went a bit south. And it wasn't toxic."

He chuckled. "Where are you?"

"Outside Aunt Sally's on Decatur. My SUV is still at Six Flags."

"On my way." He hung up without a good-bye.

A half hour later, I spotted Alex's Range Rover inching toward me down Decatur and hefted the pack over one shoulder. There was no place to pull over, so as soon as he stopped, I quickly opened the door and scaled the half-mile incline into the passenger seat.

Alex had bought the Range Rover when he got the job as DDT director, since his Mercedes convertible wasn't suitable for transporting massive amounts of concealed specialized weaponry. Whether it used prete ammo or premium unleaded, the man liked his toys, and damned the price of gas. A pickup truck like Jake's wasn't cool enough and, besides, Jake had one so it wasn't suitable.

I slammed the truck door behind me. "What a horrible day."

"I thought every day you got to commit arson was a good day." Alex stared straight ahead, eyes focused on traffic, but his mouth twitched.

"Go ahead and laugh. You can't help yourself."

The twitch turned into that crease at the corner of his mouth, just on the left side, that was about the sexiest thing going. Plus it felt good to share a joke, even if it was at my expense.

"Other than the fire, how'd the lesson with Adrian go?"

Better than I'd expected, overall. "He's still a pain in the ass, but I think we'll get through it okay. Too early to tell whether it will actually help me manage my elven skills. Today, I mostly showed him what I could do."

"Like start fires?" Alex laid on his horn, scaring the crap out of a small flock of tourists wandering across Decatur.

I groaned. "Adrian got a firsthand view of my little aiming

problem. It undid all the brownie points I'd earned showing him my other skills. I think the hydromancy freaked him out."

"He underestimated you," Alex said, turning down Esplanade and heading away from the river. "We've all underestimated you at one time or another."

This was the closest he'd ever come to admitting he'd been wrong not to take me or my magic abilities seriously when we first met after Katrina, which left me pathetically warm and fuzzy. "How'd things go with Ken today?"

"We should have done this a long time ago—set up the DDT unit and brought him in. He's the perfect liaison with the NOPD. He doesn't care if the department gives him shit. He just ignores them."

Good for Ken. "He's not freaked out by"—I fluttered my hand between Alex and me—"us?"

We finally escaped the Quarter and began winding along a back route to New Orleans East to avoid the interstate glut. "He's good."

"Mmm-hmm." I might or might not have said more. Truth was, I passed out and didn't awaken until Alex bounced his truck over the rutted entrance to Six Flags. I'd done enough physical magic to wear me out.

"Where are you parked? Oh, never mind." Alex squinted across the lot near the turnstiles and navigated to within three feet of the Pathfinder.

"You can see it?"

"Sort of—only because I knew what to look for." He took the keys out of the ignition and looked at me a little too closely. I had an annoying urge to comb my hair. "You fell asleep pretty fast. Have you been tired a lot the last couple of days?"

I unbuckled the seat belt. "Just a lot going on and too little sleep. Plus, I used a hefty dose of magic today."

I opened the door and got out, digging my keys from the backpack and using the staff to break the camouflage charm on the car. I didn't have enough juice left to do it on my own.

"Walk around with me a few minutes and give traffic time to clear out. I want to check out your latest handiwork. You've become quite the arsonist." Alex sat on the top of the fence and swung his long legs over while I struggled through the turnstile. I caught up with him near the clown head, which no longer smoked. It held small pools of water, like the ruins of the buildings at its back, and stank like a dirty ashtray left outside in the rain.

"Impressive. Your fire-setting skills are improving." He sat on one of the carousel swings nearby, testing his weight against the rusted chains before shifting all the way back.

"Let me give you the guided tour." I did a game show hostess presentation. "Behind Door Number One: the now-half-sunken Jean Lafitte Pirate Ship—only half sunken because Adrian used his pretty Blue Congress magic to undo some of the fire I set." I twirled dramatically. "Behind Door Number Two: the great Smoking Bozo, which I was trying to blow apart when I hit the building behind him."

Alex didn't smile. In fact, he frowned.

"Hey, you gotta laugh. I don't do my *Price Is Right* impression for just anybody."

His voice was quiet. "How are your ribs?"

I laughed. "They're—" Shit. The world tilted, and I had to rest a hand on the clown head to stay upright. "They don't hurt at all." My ribs had still been sore this morning and had healed in the last four hours—to the point I'd forgotten about them?

I needed to take another blood test.

Alex didn't say anything. He didn't need to. I took the swing next to him and plopped down, daring it to dump me on the ground. I eased the left arm of my sweater up to look at my unmarked arm. "Did you know that when a wizard turns werewolf, the Elders lock him or her up in an institution in Greenland?"

"You don't know for sure," he said. "Maybe you just turned a corner with the ribs and they quit hurting."

He was grasping at wolf whiskers and we both knew it. "Jean Lafitte told me to come to the Beyond if I shifted, so the Elders wouldn't be able to use me or lock me up, or kill me."

Alex stopped his gentle swinging. His stillness, the sudden quiet, felt heavy and profound. "You aren't leaving. I . . . you can't leave."

He reached his left hand out to take my right and tugged me toward him.

I had to deal with this. We had to deal with it. "Alex, we just—"

His mouth landed hot on mine, and the world shrank to the two of us. My palms absorbed the heat of his shoulders, and I closed my eyes to block out everything but his big hands circling my back, his breath hot on my lips, my neck.

I pulled away. His long-lashed eyes, rich, dark brown, were half focused on my mouth at first, but finally his gaze rose to meet mine. His voice sounded hoarse. "Come home with me."

I kissed him again and bent to pick up my backpack. "This

is the wrong time for the wrong reason," I whispered. The waterfall of tears was threatening to start again. I wanted his warmth and his comfort—needed them. But not out of pity.

He focused on the ground, his jaw clenching and unclenching as if he were biting back words. Finally, he stood up and looked down at me with pain-filled eyes. "You're wrong about both the time and the reason. Just think about it."

We walked back to the parking lot in silence, the setting sun burning orange and blue and promising another ending. I was sick to death of endings.

It's just as well we drove home in our respective vehicles so we didn't have to talk. I knew Alex was afraid for me, and he was desperate. Afraid for Jake, too, because whatever became of me impacted both of us. I couldn't be sure if he asked me to go home with him because he wanted us to see whether things were real between us, or because he was afraid it was our only chance to be together.

Maybe both.

He reached the parking lot behind our houses ahead of me and was waiting next to his truck. When I climbed out of the Pathfinder, he took my hand and squeezed it. "We do the blood test together this time."

I nodded. The trip through the kitchen, up the stairs, and into the library felt like a gallows walk. I felt oddly calm, and even though I realized it was probably shock, I welcomed the lack of feeling. It helped me pull a clean slide out of the box, slice my finger, let the blood drop onto the glass, and cover the first slide with a second.

But I couldn't do anything with it other than stand there,

looking down at it. My whole future could rest on the red smudge between those two thick rectangles of glass.

"Here, let me." Alex took the slide from me, fiddled with the microscope to turn it on and get the slide into the right position. Finally, he took a deep breath and leaned over, closing one eye and squinting into the eyepiece with the other as he focused the image.

"What do you see?"

"Lots of circles, kind of pinkish in color."

That was good. That was normal. My heart sped up. Maybe the rib thing was a false alarm.

"Anything else?"

"Some brown curvy things, kind of like commas with wide tails." He looked up from the microscope. "Is that bad?"

I nodded. That was very, very bad.

14

Adrian Hoffman's expression told me he was a vampire club virgin, just in case his earlier vamp snark had left any doubts. His eyes bugged out like an anthropologist who'd just uncovered an exotic cultural artifact, and his wizard's energy buzzed with equal parts fear and excitement. We weren't even inside the club yet.

I had little patience and no desire to share his feelings. I'd done a long grounding ritual—part meditation, part magic—to keep my empathy under control before leaving the house. I'd be able to absorb what was useful but didn't have to take it all in like a radio receiver.

My own nerves were bad enough, but the daze that had come over me this afternoon had yet to break. For now, it let me ignore the results of the blood test. I'd even been calm enough that Alex had agreed to go home.

Nine p.m. had barely come and gone, yet the line of people waiting to get into L'Amour Sauvage already stretched down Chartres Street. It wasn't the normal tourist crowd of bug-eyed Midwesterners and shitfaced college kids. Very upscale clientele, well-dressed and broadcasting sexual vibes. These people didn't realize the sexually charged atmosphere luring them in had been intentional foreplay, designed to get them in the mood to become vampire dinner. From what I'd heard, they'd enjoy it plenty and remember nothing.

Adrian fit in perfectly with his tailored black suit, crisp, open-collared white shirt, and a tasteful diamond stud in his ear. I was back in jeans and a black sweater, but I had at least showered and washed the ashes out of my hair.

I fingered the small bag of magicked herbs and rubies in an amulet I wore around my neck, the better to avoid picking up horny vibes and doing something like coming on to Adrian or a vampire. Either of which would be a bad idea on so many levels.

I led Adrian to the front of the line, ignoring the grumbles of the waiting dinner entrées. The sommelier—er, greeter—was tall, pale, and gorgeous in an androgynous sort of way. He lifted one perfect brow. "And you are moving to the head of the line because . . .?"

"Because I have a meeting with Mr. Boulard." I held my sentinel badge up discreetly, and Pretty Boy looked suitably alarmed. In case that hadn't worked, I had the FBI badge in my purse.

"Hold on." He punched a number in a cell phone, spoke a moment, then clicked it shut. "Go on back. Look for Terri—tall redhead. She's Etienne's assistant and will take you to him."

I'd rather go home. I'd done my research and the Regents of Vampyre were powerful, plus Etienne was a former wizard who'd lost all his magic upon being turned vamp—except the ability to control the dead.

Fortunately, the Regents took seriously the job of policing

the undead subjects in their territory. No feeding off unwilling humans. Memory modification required. No enthralling humans unless to keep the peace. No turning humans without prior permission from the Interspecies Council. Unless Etienne Boulard had decided to create a little mayhem by bringing back the Axeman of New Orleans.

Jean Lafitte considered him a resource, not a suspect, however, and the vamps had a good setup here. Boulard wouldn't want to risk it.

"I feel as if I'm being judged on my suitability to be someone's dinner." Adrian stuck close to me as we edged past Pretty Boy and entered the darkened club. A closed door to our left had a sign that said "Tour Blood. New Orleans' Only Genuine Vampire Tours." Eugenie had talked me into going on one of their nightly specials, and she seemed to think it was great fun.

The inside of L'Amour Sauvage was pure class—dark woods, walls the color of a fine merlot (or a pint of O-positive), polished floors. Candles flickered atop tables, and chairs were upholstered in an expensive-looking fleur-de-lis tonal pattern. The tall redhead stalking toward us looked equally expensive.

She was also vampire, which surprised me. I'd expected Etienne to have a human factotum, although I guess he could have a variety of flunkies in different species.

"Terri Ford. You must be the sentinel." She held out a hand to shake and I clasped it, unsure what I'd feel. Turned out that vampire energy, like that of the historical undead, was similar to human, but with an earthier edge. She was curious about us, and hungry. Luckily for me, she'd dropped my hand and had her appetite focused on Adrian.

"Who is your handsome friend?" Terri had been a Southerner in her human life; her accent still dripped honey. She held on to Adrian's handshake and within seconds had him glassy-eyed and practically drooling—and I don't think there had been any illegal enthrallment.

Adrian introduced himself before I could intervene. "You are much too lovely to be a vampire," he said, probably insulting her deeply.

"And you look absolutely delicious." She dragged the last word out an extra few syllables.

Oh, please. I poked Adrian in the arm. "We're here on business, remember?"

He glanced at me briefly before returning his attention to Terri. I took a few steps away and paused when I realized he wasn't going to follow. I should have acted like a real sentinel and stayed with him, but I was tired, getting shaky over my blood-test results, and not inclined to babysit a horny guy who'd apparently changed his opinion of vampires.

Neither Adrian nor Terri acknowledged my pending departure, so I turned and left them to make their own dinner plans. It couldn't be that hard to find Etienne's office. Maybe Adrian could get some useful information from the assistant while I talked to the boss.

As I walked through the crowded club, multiple pairs of cold, dark gazes settled on me, assessing. The vampires emitted wisps of hunger that flowed over my skin but never settled. Had I been human, I suspected those feelers would have been absorbed, getting me in the proper mood for snacking—or whatever.

I should just write "AB-Neg/Wizard" on my forehead.

All wizards had the same blood type, which made transfusions handy as long as other wizards were nearby. Would my blood taste different from that of another wizard since I seemed to have some elf? And loup-garou? If a vamp fed from me, would he turn furry alongside me at the next full moon? I had no intention of finding out.

I made my way to the back of the club and stuck my head in an open, unmarked doorway. There were restrooms directly in front of me, then a dark, narrow hallway that stretched left and right with a closed door at each end. Which one looked as if it might house a vampire Regent?

I tried the door to the right, but it led into a small courtyard that opened on Conti Street. I doubled back, stopping to make way for two giggling women headed into the ladies' room. Once I got closer, I knew the door on the other end of the hallway had to be the inner sanctum. The wood was intricately carved with vines and scrolls, and the doorknob was ornate brass.

I knocked twice, turned the knob, and walked into the office of one of only three vampire Regents in the country. South Florida and San Diego had the other two. Vamps liked warm weather. Guess it made them feel more human even if they couldn't go outside and enjoy the sunshine without frying.

A large wooden desk sat empty, its polished surface covered with several small, neat stacks of paper and a box that looked like a depository for invoices and receipts. A typical office, in other words, not so different from Jake's office at the Green Gator except it had nicer furniture.

"Can I help you?"

I whirled to find a section of the room that had been

blocked by the door. A man and woman sat on a black leather sofa, looking at me with polite interest.

Before I could answer, Terri swept into the room behind me with Adrian on her heels. "I'm sorry, Etienne. The wizard got away from me." I wasn't sure it was possible for a vampire to be breathless, but Terri came close. "This is the sentinel who wanted to meet with you, and her associate Mr. Hoffman, who works for the Elders."

The man rose, and I felt the power before he got within a foot of me. "Never mind, Terri—obviously, you found Mr. Hoffman distracting." He had the deepest blue eyes I'd ever seen, his irises almost black. I'd always thought Jean Lafitte's eyes were a dark blue, but where they were cobalt Etienne's were navy. He was as easy to read as any other former human. He was angry at Terri.

Something of which she was well aware. "Again, I'm sorry, Etienne." She looked ready to grovel.

He waved her away and turned creep-eyes back to me. His power battered at my mind, but I was too experienced at slamming my mental doors to fall for that trick. He was playing with me. "Don't try mind games. They won't work, and I'll give you a citation."

He spiked a brow and chuckled. "My friend Jean hasn't exaggerated your spirit, Ms. Jaco. I am Etienne Boulard."

I didn't remember offering him my hand, but suddenly he had it, lifting it toward his lips. He kissed the back of it in that courtly, old-world-French kind of way. Somehow, despite his name, I hadn't expected him to be French, although his accent had been Americanized over the years—however many years he'd been around.

I wanted to ask how he knew Jean, but the woman who'd

been sitting on the sofa with him rose and put a hand on his arm. She was of average height and had hair such a pale blond it appeared almost white. She also had blue eyes—cold, unfriendly, freeze-the-leaves-on-the-trees blue—and an unreadable energy signature.

I scanned her for peridot jewelry, but saw nothing. All these pretes without magical auras were making me jumpy.

Her voice was sandpaper on silk. "Etienne, I'm going. Please give serious thought to what I said."

He nodded. "Terri, show our guest out, please, and leave me alone to get acquainted with our sentinel. Mr. Hoffman, would you like to join us?"

Adrian had remained silent until now, watching Etienne with wary eyes. He lifted an eyebrow at me, and I gave a slight nudge of my head. I'd rather he stay with me so we could compare notes later.

"I would, if you don't mind, Mr. Boulard." Adrian closed the door, shutting his new friend Terri outside.

Etienne walked behind his desk, sat in his leather chair, and leaned back with his arms crossed. He had blond hair stylishly cut and moussed, and the commanding presence I'd expect from a Regent, even though he wasn't a particularly tall or muscular man. In fact, except for the power he exuded, he looked like a downright ordinary businessman in a gray suit.

"Thanks for seeing us tonight." Adrian and I took the seats across from him, and I cast around for how to broach the subject of the Axeman.

"It is no problem—we should've met before but, as you can see, business has been good since we opened the club. Between that and discussions over the Interspecies Council,

I've had my hands full." He unfolded his arms and leaned forward, propping his elbows on the desk. "I assume you're here to talk about these Axeman murders, yes?"

"Jean Lafitte suggested you might be able to give me a lead."

He nodded, and I felt him trying to get into my head again. I wondered if he were trying the same thing with Adrian, but imagined the Blue Congress wizard would have been throwing a tantrum if he had been.

"Your skills at blocking your thoughts are very strong." He gave me an appraising look. "And you seem immune to enthrallment. Why is that?"

"Good training." Like I was sharing the whole elf thing? "I'm Green Congress; my father was Red Congress."

"Ah, yes, I heard of Monsieur St. Simon, but never met him. My condolences on your loss."

Oh, this guy was good. Steering me off topic with small talk. "Back to the murders. We believe it's the work of—"

"A necromancer, yes," he interrupted. "Jean and I discussed this. And as I am a necromancer, I understand why you'd wish to speak with me."

Okay, that had been easy enough. "We had been searching for the Axeman himself, but obviously if he's now being controlled by a necromancer, this is of real concern to the wizards and the historical undead as well."

While I'd been enveloping Six Flags in purple smoke, Alex had done his research on local necromancers. Other than the vampire sitting across the desk, the Elders knew of only one other in New Orleans.

"It concerns me as well," Etienne said. "After all, a necromancer also could control my vampires, and I can assure you our Council of Vampyre would not tolerate that. So I will do anything within my power to help you."

"Necromancers are required to be registered." Adrian spoke up for the first time. "It should be relatively simple to narrow down the suspects. Your assistance would be appreciated, however."

"Here's what I need to know." I crossed my legs and faltered as Etienne's eyes tracked the movement like Sebastian's did when he spotted an interesting bug crossing the porch. He usually followed up the stalk with the pounce and eat. Thank God I'd worn jeans. "Normally, one needs a summoning name in order to call a member of the historical undead to the modern world, and the Axeman's name was never known. Would the necromancer be able to call him without the name?"

The vampire pulled a small cigar from his drawer. "Do you mind?"

Yes, actually, but I shook my head. Fortunately, it was mild and smelled like the rich tobacco Jean used, and had probably been smuggled in by the pirate. Etienne blew a ring of smoke into the air, drawing my attention to his mouth. I could see the very tip of his fangs, and wondered how it would feel to feed a vampire. I'd never know, at least not willingly.

"He was likely summoned simply by that name—the Axeman—since that's how he is remembered in the city's history." Etienne took a puff of his cigar. "So, if it were my business to discover who the necromancer was, I would begin with the Axeman himself."

Interesting. If Etienne was right, I could summon the Axeman as long as I could catch him when he was in the

Beyond, and could coax him to reveal the name of the necromancer. I'd had good luck placing magic-infused rubies inside a summoning circle, which compelled the person inside the circle to answer questions truthfully.

If I could pull that off, we'd be done with this whole thing in time for a normal Thanksgiving. Except for the turning-wolf-at-the-full-moon issue.

If the Axeman were spending most of his time in the modern world, fueled by his own renewed fame and the necromancer, however, a summoning wouldn't work. Still, it was worth a try.

I pulled out the small notebook I'd stuck in my bag and looked over my list of questions. "Can a necromancer control a member of the historical undead the same as any other undead—a vampire, for example, or a zombie?" He'd sort of answered, but I wanted him to elaborate.

Etienne's cell phone rang with a generic, salsa-themed ringtone. He glanced at the screen, then set it aside. "I don't know firsthand, never having tried to control one of the historical undead. I imagine it would be more difficult than a zombie, however—more like controlling a vampire. A sentient being is more apt to"—he struggled for the right word—"*fight* his instructions if they are actions with which he disagrees, so I imagine the necromancer would find it more difficult to maintain control. So you're probably looking for quite a strong necromantic wizard."

And if Etienne was innocent, that left only one other local necromancer, a Green Congress wizard who owned a French Quarter new age shop.

"Would you be willing to provide us with your where-abouts at the time the attacks have occurred?" Adrian had been watching Etienne closely and guarding his thoughts. He seemed to put less credence in Jean Lafitte's trust of the vampire's innocence than I did. It was a fair question.

"Of course, Mr. Hoffman." Etienne flashed fang again, and this time I thought it was more scowl than smile. He was growing impatient. "I am here at L'Amour Sauvage every evening from nightfall onward except for trips into the Realm of Vampyre, which I believe covers your attack times. You are welcome to question any of my staff, vampire and human alike, to verify my whereabouts, however."

We might need the Regent's help again, so I thought we'd gotten enough information for tonight. At least I knew there was a possibility of summoning the Axeman without a proper name. "Thank you," I said, rising to leave. "By the way, how long have you known Jean Lafitte?"

Etienne grinned, and I had a fascinating glimpse of the full fangs. They looked very sharp. "I met Jean as a young man when he was building his empire in Barataria and I owned a riverside plantation through which he smuggled his goods upriver to Vicksburg. After I was turned, I offered to turn him vampire as well. He would have been even more powerful—but he didn't wish to be under anyone's control, then as now."

A friendship of more than 200 years. Holy cow. No wonder Jean trusted him.

Etienne rose and opened the door leading back into the hallway. The three of us walked together into the club, which had grown even more crowded. Terri sat in a back corner table with the pale blonde who'd been in Etienne's office earlier. They both rose when they saw us, and the blonde faded into the crowd.

"Perhaps I could offer you a drink before you leave," Terri said. She spoke to both of us, but only had eyes for Adrian, who practically preened.

"Who is she?" I gestured toward the departing blond woman.

"Lily? Just a new acquaintance who wishes to do some business with Etienne."

And she was neither human nor vampire. "*What* is she——?"

But Terri's focus had shifted to Etienne. He had walked away from us toward a scene unfolding at a table in the opposite corner. A dark-haired young woman was fangs-deep into the neck of what looked like a college boy, who was having a public orgasmic experience and attracting a lot of attention.

Etienne touched the vampire on her shoulder, and even from halfway across the room I could feel his power swell. Every vamp in the place fixed eyes on him. The girl immediately pulled out her fangs, sealed the wounds, and sat back in her chair, looking dazed. Etienne spoke to her in words I couldn't hear, and she gave him a fearful look before walking past us toward his office. The power level in the room dipped, and a wave of relaxation swept over the vampires. The humans hadn't seemed to notice anything.

"Glad it's her and not me." Terri watched the boneless college boy as Etienne grasped his chin and forced his glazed eyes to focus.

"He's erasing the kid's memories?"

"Definitely, and will be on the lookout for anyone else who might have seen too much. The boy will go home, fall asleep, and won't have a clue. But Dani will be punished.

We have rooms upstairs for feeding. Nothing's allowed down here." Terri shook her head. "Stupid cow."

Enough vampire weirdness. Adrian was watching Terri with hooded eyes, so I poked him for the second time tonight. "Are you ready to get out of here?"

He frowned and blinked at me. "You hurry along. I think I'll stay a bit longer and do some . . . research. Besides, Terri promised to treat me to the special house Bloody Mary." Adrian smoldered at Terri, and just like that I ceased to exist.

If Adrian wanted to drink a Bloody Mary that probably had blood in it, followed by a fine dining experience in one of the upstairs rooms, it was no concern of mine. Maybe he'd be too tired for an elf lesson day after tomorrow. Plus, I'd have leverage. If I'd learned anything from Jean Lafitte, it was that knowledge led to power.

15

I considered stopping for ice cream comfort on the way home, but decided against it. I didn't want to be a chunky loup-garou, something to consider since I'd be running around wearing only a fur coat. There was an outside chance I might not shift, but from what I'd been reading it was probably inevitable. The virus was active in my system. I was healing fast. Running a fever. Feeling excellent.

Alex's lights were on in his little shotgun when I parked out back and made my way into my darkened kitchen, using my new password to get past my enhanced wards: *Galadriel*. A famous elf queen.

Sebastian barreled into my shins about halfway to the light switch, so I stopped and dumped some cat food into his bowl. He was only affectionate at mealtime.

I took a shower, made myself a cup of cocoa, and turned on the upstairs TV, but couldn't settle down. Maybe it was all the sex in the air at L'Amour Sauvage or maybe it was loup-garou panic, but my mind kept going back to Alex and that kiss at the park.

We had done a lot of flirting in the years since he'd come

blasting through my front door—literally—right after Katrina. The attraction was intense, but we'd always held back from seeing where a relationship could take us. We'd even talked about it, about how it could hurt our friendship and our working partnership—both of which I cherished. I was so afraid of screwing it up, of losing him, that changing the status quo terrified me. As long as we'd been cosentinels, Alex wasn't willing to stir the pot, either. Since he'd been moved to DDT duty, though, his whole vibe had changed, and given my circumstances, I couldn't help but consider what he meant to me.

I'd clean the house instead. I mopped the kitchen and put Sebastian's bowls in the sink to wash. The bowls had come from Gerry's house, where I'd grown up sheltered and clueless as to how to have a relationship. My experience with men consisted of a meaningless fling during college at Tulane and one disastrous affair with another wizard right after I'd made Green Congress. Pathetic, in other words.

Gerry had taught me many things about magic and self-preservation and thinking on my feet. He hadn't taught me a damned thing about being a mature adult who could care for someone and be cared for in return.

I gathered the dish towels that needed washing and took them to the guest bathroom, where I had a compact washer and dryer. From the window, I could see Alex's house. His lights were on, and I saw a shadow move behind the shade in his dining room.

When Alex walked into a room, women watched him, and he wasn't oblivious to it. Jake said his cousin had been quite the womanizer when he worked at the FBI field office in Jackson, but I knew he hadn't done much dating since moving to New Orleans. Just enough for me to admit I wasn't nearly experienced enough or sophisticated enough for somebody like Alex Warin.

But if I turned loup-garou, I was going to lose him anyway. I'd be too dangerous.

Tears threatened again, and I sucked them down even though it felt like a stone in my throat. I shook out way too much washing powder for my light load, but poured it in anyway. In a week, what would it matter if I had clean dish towels? Why was I wasting my time cleaning?

I had to be brutally honest with myself. If I only had a week or so until the full moon, how did I want to spend it? Not crying, that was for sure. Not cleaning house. What would be on my pre-werewolf bucket list?

I wanted to wear boots and go out dancing to zydeco music under the stars, in one of those little river parish towns like Lutcher or Paulina.

I wanted to spend time with Eugenie doing stupid girl stuff like going to the mall and playing at the makeup counter.

I wanted to lie on the grass in the mild autumn sunshine before I moved into a lifetime of night in the Beyond or incarceration in Greenland.

I wanted Alex.

My heart rate sped at the admission, and all the fear flushed to the surface. God, what I would give for Tish to still be here, to help me sort through these alien emotions. She and Gerry had been together so long, and somehow they'd made their relationship work. Why hadn't I asked her about it before it was too late?

Losing her last month, having her murdered because the

killer couldn't get to me, was still raw. But Tish had liked Alex. If I only had a few days left before the virus took hold, Tish wouldn't want me to spend them alone. She wouldn't want me to go into a hazy future wondering what I'd missed by being afraid.

I had a bad habit of overthinking things. I should just go to him. The worst that could happen was I'd humiliate myself and have to move to the Beyond with Jean Lafitte, which I was considering anyway.

Sometimes, when there's nothing left to lose, you have to stop thinking and take that hard first step.

Or at least that's what I told myself as I brushed my hair with hands that shook, fumbled with the buckles on my boots, and reached for my keys. *Don't overthink. Feel.*

I had a sense of unreality as I walked out the front door and locked it behind me. Crowds sat at the outdoor tables at Marinello's Pizza across the street, laughing and clinking glasses despite the chill in the air. I tripped at the end of the sidewalk when I noticed Rand at the table nearest the door of the restaurant, sitting with a book and a glass of wine. He wasn't reading, but watching me intently. At least I only pinwheeled once and hadn't fallen on my butt.

Quince Randolph, king of the creepy nonhuman stalker types, was not on my bucket list. I tossed my hand up in a casual wave and turned left toward Alex's house. Traffic crawled along Magazine Street, even on a Wednesday night, and my heart took on the rhythm of a hip-hop song blaring out of someone's open car window.

I paused at the bottom of his front steps. Was I going to do this? I didn't *have* to do anything. Just go in and have a beer. He might be busy, after all. The man wrote reports for the Elders like it was going out of style. Or he might have Leyla in there, or another woman.

Spurred by the gentle sound of a clucking chicken inside my head, I rang his doorbell and swallowed hard when I heard footsteps crossing his living room.

And there he was, as big and solid and sexy as the day I'd met him, but more than that. I hadn't known then what a good man hid beneath the sometimes-Neanderthal exterior. A kind man. A kind man wearing a pair of low-slung jeans and no shirt, with abs to get lost in and hip bones flashing temptation. I was so in over my head.

"You just gonna stand out there all night?" He moved aside and I had no choice but to go in. He closed the door behind me. "What's wrong? You look—"

"A beer," I said. "I look like I need a beer. Or were you busy? Is someone else here? I can come back another time." I turned back toward the door. This had been such a bad idea.

"Don't leave." He gave me a puzzled look and walked toward the kitchen. "Nobody's here. I downloaded some new music—something you'd like, in fact."

I stopped in the dining room and smiled at the achingly sweet voice of Zachary Richard. "I didn't know he had a new CD out."

My first real date with Jake had been to see Zachary Richard. That was also the first time Jake had almost lost control of his wolf while he was alone with me. Now, with the clarity of hindsight, I saw that I'd put so much pressure on him to adapt it was no wonder he snapped. Alex and I both had been guilty of it.

"It's an older one—found it online." Alex returned with

two bottles of Abita and handed one to me. "So what's up? How'd the meeting go with the vampire?"

"The vampire meeting went okay."

"It went okay? That's it?" He watched me for a second, brown eyes intense. "DJ? What the hell's wrong with you? Do you want to talk about the blood test?"

I jumped when he put a hand on my arm. "No."

He reached over and took the beer out of my hand, set both bottles on the table, and pulled me into the living room. "Sit down and spill it. I've never seen you this nervous."

No kidding. *You're at the top of my pre-loup-garou to-do list* was a little flip. *I want to fall into your arms and forget everything else* was melodramatic. I had no idea whether *I love you* was true or not. "You remember the question you asked me this afternoon at Six Flags?"

He frowned. "You mean about how you set the clown on fire?"

God, how dense was this man? I punched him on the arm. "Later. On the swings. I changed my mind."

Understanding dawned on his face, followed by surprise and a chaser of amusement. He thought I was joking. "Really?"

"Go for it." Before the words left my mouth, embarrassment baked my face from the inside, and his dark eyes softened from laughter to heat.

"Why the one-eighty?" His voice was low and silky, and his gaze dropped to my mouth when I bit my lower lip. This was too damned awkward. What had I been thinking?

"Well, if you're going to talk it to death, never mind." I got up with every intention of marching back to my house and dying of humiliation—it would solve a lot of problems.

He reached out and grabbed my arm before I got out of grabbing range, and pulled me onto his lap.

"Shut up." He cradled my jaw in his hands and touched his lips to mine. His body heat enveloped me, and my heart adjusted its rhythm to keep time with his, or the other way around. That wonky shapeshifter energy had gone into hyperdrive, buzzing over my skin and tightening my nerve endings.

I slid my hands from his shoulders to his hard chest, feeling a mark I'd never seen on his right pec—because I was always chastising myself for looking. A crescent shape faintly lightened his skin, and I ran a finger over its raised edges.

"What's this from?" It was too perfectly shaped to be accidental, plus shifters can heal just about any kind of flesh wound without scarring.

"Enforcer's mark," he mumbled, his lips worrying at my neck and his fingers under the hem of my sweater.

"So when you—"

He stopped nuzzling and lifted my chin to force me into eye contact. His intensity sent a rush of heat right to my gut, and farther south. "Are we going to talk about work?" His voice was rough.

Struck mute, I shook my head, and in a movement too fast to track, he reached up, fusing my mouth to his. A soft moan came from one of us, I wasn't sure which. One hand twined in my hair and the other stroked the bare skin of my back as his lips and tongue made me forget . . . whatever it was I'd been thinking about.

His light evening stubble scratched delicious heat across my neck as he got up with barely an effort, pulling my legs around him. He walked us to the bed and lowered me not so gently, pausing long enough to ease off my boots.

"Are you sure?" Alex's eyes were glazed and hungry, his breathing ragged.

I sat up and hooked my fingers under the hem of my sweater.

He stayed my hands. "My job." He pulled it over my head slowly, then pulled down the straps of my bra, following his fingers with his mouth. "So. Damned. Beautiful." His voice rumbled against my skin.

"Yeah, you are." My fingers eased down his chest, across the ridges of his belly, and rested on his hips a few moments before reaching for his jeans. He pulled back to help.

"Nope. My job." I laughed, pushing him to his back and taking charge like I knew more than I did. He didn't seem to mind a little clumsiness, raising his hips to accommodate me. Nope, he didn't mind a little clumsiness at all.

Jeans and socks and underwear hit the floor at some point too, but I lost track of everything except Alex's lips and heat and his busy, talented hands—at least until my brain kicked in briefly. "Wait," I gasped, "do you have, you know . . ."

"Ungh." He rolled off the bed and disappeared into the small bathroom. Cabinets opened and closed with frantic slams. "Aha."

He reappeared with a box of condoms and pulled one out. Plenty more remained in case we got overly enthusiastic. Not that I was worried about disease—shifters can't carry diseases as far as I knew. But the last thing I needed was a wizard-elf-loup-garou-shifter kid baking in the oven. Ye gods.

The break had given us a chance to catch our breath, but the heat hadn't dissipated. He caught my wrists and pinned them over my head on the pillow with one hand, shifting his weight, and we began to move in tandem.

He groaned and slowed his movements—agonizingly slow. "You doing that on purpose?"

I bit his ear. "Don't stop," I gasped. "Doing what?"

His voice was strained. "Your magic's buzzing all over my skin. Feels so . . . ."

Must not have felt too bad, but I couldn't ask because he hit a spot that wiped out all rational thought.

16

Early morning sun slanted through the blinds and backlit odd shapes across my closed lids. I snapped my eyes open. Alex was propped on an elbow, watching me like a cat sitting outside a fishbowl. Alert, patient, predatory.

"Morning," I croaked, then a smidgeon more awake. "Do I smell coffee?"

He narrowed his eyes and waited a few seconds. "Hmm. Fascinating. No running away or making excuses for last night yet. It's a good sign."

I reached over and pulled him to me for a kiss. "Just one question. Was that pity sex? Because of the loup-garou thing?"

He rolled me on top of him. "Yeah, it'd be a pity if we didn't do it again." After which the man proved he was right. That would have been a pity.

Later, I showered and went on a clothes hunt. I found last night's sweater and jeans, but my underwear had gone truant. Alex's bedroom had gotten a direct hit from a sartorial hurricane. I was absurdly pleased with myself. It would be my first walk of shame, crawling home wearing last night's clothes, even if there was no one else to witness it.

By the time I finished dressing, Alex was in the kitchen and pouring coffee, wearing a black sweater and a pair of jeans worn light in all the right places. His back was to me, so I leaned against the doorjamb and watched him a few moments, waiting for fear and regret to make an appearance. It was my MO, after all.

So far, my only regret was that it had taken us this long. A rare moment of peace, a dash of happiness, and one fine butt.

"Stop leering." He turned to hand me a mug, appearing pretty damned pleased with himself as well. You'd think we'd been the first people to discover sex.

"I don't leer, I admire." I took the mug and sipped cautiously. Plain medium-roast. I'd have expected no less of a man who considered putting ketchup on his fries thinking outside the culinary box.

He treated me to that sexy little crease next to his mouth and kissed me. And kissed me again. Then the smile faded, taking his happy thoughts with it. He was shielding. "We need to talk about what happens next week."

So much for the whole happiness and feeling-at-peace thing. Only I could spend the night with the sexiest man to ever come out of Picayune, Mississippi—no, make that the whole state of Mississippi (sorry, Elvis)—and barely have time to enjoy the afterglow before he had to get all serious and bring up my impending furmageddon.

I took my coffee into the dining room and sat at the table. I'd either take my chances with the Elders or I'd run, and I knew which path straight-arrow Alex would recommend. He could get me snowshoes for Christmas so I could go muskoxen-hunting, assuming there was a way to actually get to Ittoqqortoormiit without being zapped there in a transport.

I exhaled. "We know the virus is active, and I'm almost certainly going to shift next Thursday at the full moon. What else is there to say?"

"We need to talk about you getting your stuff together and your ass to Old Barataria before Thursday." His voice was hard and businesslike. He'd been thinking about this awhile. "I want you to do it. Go to Jean Lafitte."

I'd frozen with the coffee mug halfway to my mouth, which was hanging open so far it could have caught flies, as my grandmother back in Alabama liked to say. "You *want* me to go to Jean?"

Alex hated Jean. Jean hated Alex. It was a perfectly equitable arrangement.

For the first time since this unfortunate conversation began, a hint of expression—disgust—stole across his face. "Of course not, and if he lays a finger on you I'll kill him." He paused, no doubt realizing Jean was immortal and his threats were ridiculous. "Okay, I can't kill him. But I can dry up all his little business arrangements between the Beyond and New Orleans. He won't be able to make a dime."

That would hurt Jean a lot more than a bullet.

"Then why . . .?" I didn't finish the question. There was no point in asking why. Alex might be a by-the-rules kind of guy, but he didn't trust the Elders to come up with a solution that didn't involve institutionalization in a far corner of a cold, lonely place nobody could begin to pronounce. Or death by enforcer.

God, would they order Alex to kill me and Jake both? Was that what frightened him?

He rolled his head from side to side, popping his neck. "Set up a transport for me and I'll come as often as I can. The Elders don't have any jurisdiction in Old Orleans or any of its outposts, and Lafitte will protect you if they send someone after you. I have to give him that much credit." Albeit grudgingly, judging by his tone.

I'd pretty much come to the same conclusion, and Alex's words filled me with relief. I'd been so afraid that if I took the run-like-hell option, I'd never see him again.

"Here's something I've been wondering about, though." I'd been worrying about it ever since Jean suggested I hide out in the Beyond. "Let's say I go into the Beyond on Tuesday. The full moon here isn't until Thursday night, but there's always a full moon there. Won't I shift immediately?"

Alex drained his coffee cup and set it on the table. "No, Jake and I talked about him living in Old Orleans after he was turned awhile, before he decided to try the enforcer route. We did some research. The full moon in the Beyond isn't tied to the one in the modern world, so weres and garous can change at will there—or not change. We just need a cover story to tell the Elders. You learn to control it, then you come back and do your job. Take full moons off and go into the Beyond for a day or two."

That sounded so easy, but the first time I came across a prete who could sniff me out as a loup-garou, I'd be turned in and Ittoqqortoormiit wouldn't be an option. If I went into the Beyond, I'd have to stay. We'd figure the rest out later. "Agreed," I said.

"Good. That's settled." Alex got up to replenish his coffee cup and glanced out the dining room window. "What the hell does he want?"

"Who?"

"Eugenie's boyfriend, that Randolph guy. He's on his way over here, coming from your house." Alex headed toward the back door. "You ever figure out what he was? Still think he's not human?"

"I know he's not human. I'm thinking elf or faery." I set my mug down with a thud. Talk about romance killers: first the loup-garou talk, and now my neighborhood stalker.

Alex opened the door, and I heard the low pitch of voices.

"I gotta go with Randolph a few minutes. Stay here." Alex went into his bedroom, and I followed the sound of dresser drawers opening and closing. He came out strapping on his shoulder holster with his bigass Smith & Wesson, then stopped to pull on his shoes.

"The Axeman again? What's Quince Randolph got to do with it?"

"Stay here." He walked out the front door and shut it behind him with a rattling slam.

Wait. Who did Alex Warin think he was, anyway? One night of bucket-list sex—okay, a night and a morning of amazing bucket-list sex—did not give him the right to be bossy. I had to murder that instinct before it became a habit.

I scrambled into my boots and strode out the front door, looking catty-cornered across the intersection at Plantasy Island. An Uptown matron struggled out the door carrying an oversize exotic plant with yellow-and-green-striped leaves, but there was no sign of Alex or Rand.

Digging my keys out of my jeans pocket, I walked next door and climbed my front steps, glancing across Nashville Avenue at Eugenie's house. The OPEN sign was on the door to her Shear Luck salon entrance, so she probably had a customer.

A window-rattling thump sounded from inside my front parlor, and I heard male voices. They were in my house? Dread stealing through me, I tried the front door and found it unlocked. "What are you—"

I tripped over something just inside the door, and it took a moment for me to realize it was my overturned sofa. I looked around, trying to understand what I was seeing. My house had been trashed. The mirror over the mantel was shattered, and broken glass glittered across the hardwood floor. Furniture lay overturned, stuffing spilling out like billowy cotton. A hole had been gouged in the plaster wall, exposing wires and lathing. My freaking ceiling fan even had a blade broken in half.

"You should have stayed next door." Rand stood in the doorway between the back parlor and the kitchen. I heard Alex's footsteps—at least I hoped they were Alex's—going up the stairs to the second floor.

"Who did this?" My first instinct was to blame Rand, but after a second's thought I knew it wasn't him. He'd been trying too hard to get in my good graces for some reason, and he also was too much of a tree hugger to risk broken glass and overturned furniture ruining my antique hardwood floor.

"Come here and you can see who did it." He stepped aside and I edged past him into the kitchen. "Look by the door."

I had no desire to touch the ax embedded blade-first in the wall next to my back door. It was covered with crusty red-and-black gunk that I had no doubt was from the

Times-Pic reporter still clinging to life in a local hospital. "He came for me last night and I wasn't here," I whispered, looking around. The kitchen was intact. "He just tore up the living room to make sure I knew he'd been here."

What might have happened if I hadn't gone to Alex's last night? Could I have fought him off? Gotten to the elven staff in time? Been trapped in my second-floor bedroom? I'd been in such a hormonal frenzy when I went to Alex's I'd forgotten to set my security wards. They'd probably have kept him out.

"Where's Sebastian?" I looked under the kitchen table and atop the cabinets, and finally spotted him on the fridge, glaring at me from between two cookbooks. As soon as I spotted him, he yowled at me and ran out of the room. At least I knew he was safe.

Rubbing my arms to try and smooth out the chill bumps that had taken up residence, I approached the ax. The handle was smooth, light-colored wood, and a wide black stripe around the base matched the ones from the other crime scenes.

Ken had discovered that both of the big-box home-improvement stores had sold out of axes—about two dozen total. I doubted the Axeman had been shopping, so I'm betting it was the necromancer. He'd paid cash, however, so there was no way to trace the sales until the NOPD studied the security-camera footage—and hoped the ax sales were made recently.

I reached out to touch the ax, then drew my hand back.

"You might as well go ahead," Rand said, making me jump. He'd moved close behind me. "We all know the finger-prints on that ax handle aren't going to match anything the police have."

Sticking my hands in my pockets to keep from touching anything, just on principle, I turned to face him. "And how would you know that?"

Rand's expression was serious. "You know damned well he isn't human, and he's targeting you for some reason. Do you know why?"

I stared at him. "What *are* you?"

He reached out with his right hand and twirled a lock of my hair around his index finger. I grabbed his wrist and tried to push it away, but he was strong—and an emotional void, as usual. "I'm somebody who doesn't want to see you hurt."

"Not good enough." I grabbed his wrist again and fully opened my mind to his. A big freaking empty hole.

He frowned, morphing his pretty face into a picture of concern. "You're really worried about the loup-garou change. You're healing too fast and it's taking hold. I can help you."

A chill washed over me. He'd known the Axeman wasn't human and he knew about the loup-garou exposure. What the hell was he? What did he want? Quince Randolph could read me like my thoughts were running across my forehead on a ticker tape, and I could get nothing from him.

"Get out of here." My voice rasped. "Until you're ready to tell me the truth about being an elf, get out." He had to be an elf.

"We'll talk later, when you're not so upset." Rand gave me a final, almost tentative smile before opening the back door. "I'm not your enemy, Dru."

17

I spent the rest of Wednesday trying to clean my living room—thankfully, the only place the Axeman had left his calling card. I'd felt his residual energy in the room when I first went into the house, but it had dissipated quickly. I'd also driven to the Quarter to talk to the new age shop owner and necromancer, but his store was closed until tomorrow morning.

Because he'd been busy directing the Axeman to kill me? Why me? Why would I be a target for a necromancer?

Alex and Ken were running background checks on all the victims and trying to find a link between them and me. I thought they were wasting their energy. The necromancer hadn't been in charge of any attacks before the numbers of my house appeared—just a taunt, apparently. They should focus on the wizard with the target on her back. The killer had missed me once but he'd be back—unless I could summon him first.

I also had downloaded hours' worth of jazz and had it playing in a nonstop loop on my iPod, with speakers attached so it could be heard in every room.

My sixth construction-size trash bag overflowed with white, cottony stuffing that had been ripped out of my living room furniture before the Axeman chopped off the arms and legs. Probably what he'd planned to do to me, which should scare the crap out of me but I was too pissed. It wasn't like I could call my homeowner's insurance company and file a claim, and I didn't make the money Alex and Jake did since they had the "high-risk" jobs and I didn't. Yet, exactly who was being stalked by a psychotic ax murderer? Oh yeah. That would be the girl with the low-risk job. The high-risk guys were noodling through computer data files.

"Son of a bitch." The bottom of my trash bag caught on the wrought-iron railing that ran along my back steps, spilling broken glass and furniture stuffing all over the sidewalk.

I fetched a new bag and squatted beside the mess, picking up glass shards and setting them aside.

"Rand told me someone broke in and wrecked your house." Eugenie knelt next to me and began picking up trash. "I'm sorry. Not just about this. About everything."

I stopped her hand halfway toward the trash bag and squeezed it with mine. "I'm sorry too. Nothing is going on with Rand and me, I swear to God. I care about you too much, and I care about Alex too much."

I didn't add that I thought Rand was a slimeball of undetermined preternatural parentage. She was definitely not ready for that conversation.

"I believe you. And I'm glad you finally realize what all the rest of us knew about you and Alex." She sat on the stoop above the trash, while I swept the last bit of furniture fluff into the bag, and nudged a broken candelabra off the stoop with her tie-dyed sneaker.

I set the bag aside and took the seat on the step below hers. "Do you ever wish we could go back three years, before the storm, and just have things the way they were?" Life had been so simple then, in retrospect, and the things I thought were life or death were nothing of the kind. My biggest concern had been how I could prove myself to Gerry so I could get bigger assignments. Well, now I had them.

"It wasn't so much better," Eugenie said. "My shop is doing more business now than before Katrina. And I met Rand."

That was a subject best avoided. "Yeah, I guess. Life just seemed easier then."

She reached down and hugged me. "It might help if you'd talk to me, DJ. You think I don't know there's a lot of stuff going on in your life that you're keeping to yourself? That you aren't able to do things with me anymore? That you're always stressed out? Especially the last couple of months. You lost Gerry and Tish both. I wish you'd let me help you—by listening, if nothing else."

I swallowed a lump of guilt. I had been so consumed with my own post-hurricane dramas that I hadn't given a lot of thought to how it might look from the viewpoint of the woman who was supposed to be my best friend. When was the last time we'd gone shopping or seen a movie?

"I'm sorry, Eugenie. There are just—"

"I know, I know." She smiled. "Things about your job you can't talk about. Just remember I'm here when you can."

I could start by listening to her. "What's going on with you and Rand?"

She sighed. "Who knows? He can be sweet one minute

and an hour later he's just . . . not there. I don't know where his mind gets off to. He's a very deep thinker, you know?"

"I guess." He might be a deep thinker in ways neither of us could imagine.

"His ears must have been burning." Eugenie pointed, and I looked toward the street. Rand's long legs ate up the distance across Magazine and Nashville, bringing his bright, smiling self to my doorstep way too soon. Just when Eugenie and I were starting to finally talk to each other, here came a major source of contention.

"You have some big furniture pieces that need to come out, don't you? I'll get them." Rand tossed a paper sack on the steps next to me, pushed past us, and disappeared into the kitchen.

"Yeah, hello to you too, and thanks for asking before you went inside," I called after him. Presumptuous jerk.

"See, he can be so thoughtful." Eugenie propped her elbows on her knees. "But he didn't even look at me. Sometimes I don't think I even know who he is."

This conversation was dipping further into the pool of surrealism. "You really haven't known him that long." I measured my words. "You guys went from handshake to full tilt almost overnight."

She laughed, flipping a strand of auburn hair out of her eyes. "We can't all be you and Alex, with three years of foreplay."

"You had foreplay for three years?" Rand stood behind us in the doorway, holding the sofa. The whole sofa. Without straining. "Let me get past you and set this on the curb, then I want to hear about three years of foreplay."

I would not be discussing foreplay with Quince Randolph.

And who the hell could walk around carrying a sofa—even one without arms or legs? I doubt Alex could have managed that.

Rand settled the sofa skeleton next to the street, then arranged my collection of trash bags next to it.

"Looks like you're about done except for sweeping it out." He ran fingers through his hair and pulled it back into a tail very similar to mine, binding it with an elastic band from his pocket. "When you decide on your new furniture, let me know and I'll bring you some plants from the shop."

"Aw, that's so sweet." Eugenie was hopeless. "Isn't it, DJ?"

"Yes. Sweet." Rand and I exchanged meaningful looks. Mine said: *I don't know what you are up to, but I will.* His said: *I love a challenge*—or so I imagined it, since I couldn't read him.

Rand settled on the step below Eugenie and leaned back against her knees, which gave her a chance to begin trying to weave his thick hair into a braid. She was a hairdresser; she couldn't help herself.

"You spent the night at Alex's." Rand jerked his head away from Eugenie's clutching fingers, which stopped braiding once his words sunk in.

"You what? Did you . . . How was . . ." Eugenie huffed at the questions she wanted answers to but wasn't willing to ask in front of Rand because she knew damned well I wouldn't talk.

"How was it you happened to know my house had been broken into?" Alex and I had wondered about that this morning after Rand left. The doors weren't standing open. He either saw the Axeman go in or out, or had been snooping around and looking in my windows. I voted for number two.

Rand smiled at me and paused a moment too long. Oh God help me, he was going to say something outrageous. "I came by with some beignets, hoping we could share breakfast. When you didn't answer the door, I got worried and looked in the window."

"You were bringing her breakfast?" Eugenie's surprise and hurt flared around her aura, and I winced. Damn him.

"I knew she liked beignets, so I picked some up from Café du Monde after I went to the market this morning." Rand's gaze held steadily to mine as he nudged the paper sack. I wanted to rip his eyeballs out and chop them up for Sebastian to eat.

"I need to go." Eugenie stood up and almost tripped on her way down the steps. Rand reached out to steady her, but let her go as soon as she regained her balance. She turned to look at him, uncertainty in her eyes.

"You need to leave too, Rand," I said. "Maybe you and Eugenie can have dinner." If he could read my moods as well as I suspected, he'd know I meant it, as well as my underlying message: Hurt her, and he'd have to deal with me.

"I'd like that," he said, grinning, before he turned to follow Eugenie across the street.

I wasn't sure which he meant: He'd like dinner, or he'd like to deal with me.

18

I wouldn't be able to talk to the other local necromancer until tomorrow morning, so rather than sit around and imagine horrific loup-garou scenarios or, worse, pack my bags for a life in the Beyond, I decided to try summoning the Axeman. Ever since Etienne had suggested it last night, I'd been thinking about how best to do it.

I'd strengthened the security wards on my house again, jumping at every gust of wind, then wandered from room to room to make sure the new window glass remained reinforced and the curtains closed. As if sensing my discomfort, Sebastian twined between my ankles at every turn, clingy and skittish.

After Katrina, Alex had left a couple of small grenades at my house and I had them locked in the bottom shelf of my library cabinet along with the really strong painkillers and a few particularly dangerous potions ingredients. Now, I removed them and gingerly set one on my worktable. After much inner debate, I put the other behind a vase on the mantel of my front parlor. Alex had assured me they were the best things for destroying zombies. The Axeman wasn't a zombie, but he still might need destroying.

Alex had been called to Monroe on a DDT case, to take down a vampire who'd ignored warnings to shut down his gaming operations. He'd exposed his fangs to a roomful of gamblers and had been turned in by none other than Etienne Boulard, his own Regent. With Alex out of town and Jake gone, that left Ken Hachette as my primary backup. As much as I liked Ken, he didn't have enough experience to handle the Axeman or a necromancer.

Still, I'd vowed not to charge into any more dangerous situations alone, so I pondered my backup options. Louis Armstrong would be no help in a fight if the Axeman escaped, although I guess he could play some jazz. Jean Lafitte would be more useful if things turned violent, but I needed someone who was straightforward and agenda-less.

I called my favorite aquatic shapeshifter, Rene Delachaise.

Two hours later, the merman arrived on my doorstep carrying a big plastic bag. "Hey, babe."

We hugged a long time. It had been less than a month since his twin brother, Robert, had died at the hands of a nymph we'd all trusted—the same woman who'd killed Tish. He'd saved me from drowning, fishing me out of the river and administering the CPR that cracked my ribs. And we'd done a power share that left us living inside each other's heads for about seventy-two hours, which, freaky as it was, had led to a deep mutual respect. Rene was a good man.

"You doing okay?" I stepped back and took a look at him. Like most mers, Rene was of short-to-average height, about five-nine, but he was shapeshifter strong. He had a wiry, tanned body, a thick South Louisiana accent, dark liquid eyes that showed the stress of the past month, and an impressive set of tattoos that spread across every bit of his skin I'd seen—and I'd seen a lot. Like most shifters, Rene had no body issues.

"Some days are better than others." He retrieved his bag from where he'd set it on the floor inside the front door. "How 'bout you?"

I could think of Tish some days without crying now, and could remember more good times than bad. "Yeah, same here."

"I brought dinner. Just caught these yesterday." He led me into the kitchen and pulled a big plastic bucket out of the bag, along with a pile of old newspapers. In the bucket was a mountain of shrimp and new potatoes, both boiled with enough cayenne to clear out my sinuses for a month.

He spread the newspaper on the kitchen table and dumped the shrimp and potatoes out on it. "Is this a social call, babe, or you come up with some crazy shit for us to do?"

I pulled a couple of beers out of the fridge and set them on the counter. "Hey—the power-share thing was crazy but you've gotta admit it was fun."

"Yeah, you right." He grinned, reminding me how it had felt to be in his head while he swam through the marshy waters near the mouth of the Mississippi River. "It was nuts. Want to try it again?"

"No way." We settled in at the table and began eating the shrimp and potatoes with our hands. "But I do have another adventure you might find interesting."

"I knew most of that," he said after I'd filled him in on the Axeman case. He pulled the tail off a fat shrimp and popped it in his mouth. "The pirate's been staying in the Beyond trying to find the killer, but he ain't showed up. So

Jean Lafitte thinks he's in N'Orleans most of the time now. Jean, he's still nosing around trying to find out what wizard is pulling the strings."

Rene and Jean had been business partners for quite a while now, so it made sense he'd be keeping up.

I washed down a red-hot potato with my beer. "I'd hoped Jean had found something. When you see him, ask him if he can figure out why I'd be the target." I shared the information about the numbers at the crime scene, and the Axeman's arrival at my house. "You notice I don't have any furniture in my living room? He broke it all."

"So, what're we doing tonight, babe? Furniture shopping or huntin' down the Axeman?"

"Neither." I smiled. Rene liked anything that might lead to a good fistfight, and he was surprisingly open-minded for a mer. As a species, they tended to be surly and pigheaded. "We're going to summon the Axeman. Bring him to us."

Rene frowned and scratched at his goatee. "And why would we want to do that, exactly?"

"If I can get him contained in my circle, I might be able to force him to tell me the name of the wizard that's controlling him." Chances were, the Axeman didn't like being controlled any more than Jean Lafitte would, so I hoped he wouldn't resist.

Rene shook his head, but his mouth tipped up at the edges a few seconds before he started laughing. "You are one crazy chick. What you need me to do?"

"Provide moral support." We put away the plates and walked toward the stairs to the second floor. "Maybe kill him if he escapes the circle." *Kill* being a relative term when it came to the historical undead.

Rene followed me up the narrow staircase. "I can do that."

Only the strongest circle for this one. While Rene lounged on the sofa and did dramatic readings from a book on merpeople lore, I gathered iron shavings, unrefined sea salt, and ash, and carefully filled in the etched circles. Red candles for strength and gold for power rested at the four compass points.

Also around the circle I placed items associated with the killer. The ax he'd left in my house after ransacking the living room. A photocopy of a letter the Axeman had allegedly sent to the *Times-Picayune* in 1919.

Esteemed mortal, it began, *They have never caught me and they never will. They have never seen me, for I am invisible, even as the ether that surrounds your earth. I am not a human being, but a spirit and a demon from the hottest hell. I am what you Orleanians and your foolish police call the Axeman.*

It went on and on in that vein. I shook my head. You couldn't make up stuff like this.

To my collection, I added a photo of one of the 1919 murder sites, a house on the Westbank of the Mississippi River. And, finally, Alex's graphic novel about the infamous Axeman of New Orleans.

Since I couldn't use a real summoning name to force him into being truthful, I placed two rubies inside the circle on which I'd worked a truth-inducement charm.

I laid the silver ritual knife on the worktable in my library and looked at my setup. It just needed a little of my blood as a summoning medium, and I'd be good to go. I'd have to decide whether to use my own physical magic to fuel the ritual or mix my magic with that of the elven staff.

I turned to Rene. "You ready?"

He laid the book aside and walked around the circle to study what I'd done. "Where do you need me?"

"Anywhere as long as it's not close enough to accidentally break the plane of the circle. If he gets out, we have to catch him."

Rene hopped on my big worktable, dangling his legs off the side. "This is as close as I'm gettin', babe. Unless I need this." He pulled a pistol from inside his shirt, released the safety, and laid it on the table beside him.

"Let's hope you don't need it."

I knelt next to the circle and cut yet another finger. At least I didn't have to worry about scars from cutting the same finger over and over. Thanks to the freaking loup-garou virus, I was healing everything in a few hours. Rene had sensed it in me almost immediately but had promised to keep his mouth shut, and I trusted him.

Once the blood hit the circle, I closed my eyes and called on the Axeman to come forth.

"Holy shit."

I opened my eyes at Rene's soft curse and stared at the Axeman of New Orleans. He had been in the Beyond; we'd lucked out.

He was well over six feet, and broad. His black suit coat had wide lapels and reached to his thighs. A black fedora cast a shadow over his eyes, but they had no light in them, no life. They weren't the eyes of a dead man; they were the eyes of a monster.

He took off the hat and gave a slight bow, revealing dark

hair slicked straight back from his forehead. "Greetings, esteemed wizard. I was most distressed to have missed you last evening."

I just bet he was. "Why are you trying to kill me?"

He grinned at me. His teeth were crooked and yellowish black. Serial killers in 1918 couldn't afford dental care, apparently. "I am not trying to kill you."

"You have to answer me truthfully. The stones bind you to the truth."

He looked down at the rubies and kicked one of them with the toe of a dainty-looking button-top shoe. It bounced against the invisible plane of the circle and landed on the wooden floor with a clatter. "I spoke the truth."

Interrogating an uncooperative prete was a thankless task.

Rene jumped off the table and came to stand beside me. "Why are you trying to attack her?"

The Axeman examined his new questioner with great interest. "You are not human or wizard. What are you?"

"I'm the guy who's going to kick your ass if you don't answer my question."

I bit my lip to keep from smiling. I knew there was a reason I liked Rene. He couldn't kick the Axeman's ass and he knew it. But it didn't keep him from antagonizing the guy. And if called upon to do so, he'd try to kick the guy's ass until he couldn't kick any longer.

"I have been ordered to attack this one, perhaps to kill, but I don't know why. Ours not to reason why; ours but to do or die." He treated me to another big, grotesque grin. Great. We had an undead serial killer quoting Tennyson.

"Who ordered you to attack me?" Here was the real question.

The Axeman frowned. "I know not his name."

Okay, it was a man. That didn't help much. Both Etienne and the new age shop owner were male. "What does he look like?"

I hadn't met the new age necromancer yet but if Axeman said dark hair, it let Etienne off the hook.

"I have not seen him. He remains hidden from my sight when he summons me."

I paced outside the circle, thinking. "Is your summoner a vampire?"

The Axeman blinked. "I do not know."

I huffed in frustration.

"When you gonna attack again?" Rene asked.

The Axeman didn't answer. Instead, he looked up as if hearing a voice, then looked back at me with animation in his eyes for the first time. "I'm being called."

He disappeared. Just like that. One second he was there, the next he was gone.

"What happened?" Rene walked around the outside of the circle as if the Axeman might be hiding. "I thought he couldn't leave on his own."

That made two of us. "I'm guessing the necromancer summoned him again, and it pulled him out of my circle." I released his name anyway before breaking the plane. No point in leaving an open door for him to return.

Rene propped his hands on his hips. "Does that mean the necromancer's magic trumps yours?"

It sure looked that way.

19

Rene insisted on sleeping in my guest room since Alex wasn't due back until noon the next day, so we stayed up half the night playing poker. By the time it was over, he owed me five pounds of oysters and a ride in his shrimp trawler. Gerry had taught me some things well, and how to play a mean seven-card stud was one of them.

Rene also insisted on going with me to visit Jonas Adamson, the only registered necromancer in Southeast Louisiana besides the vampire Regent. He ran a shop in the lower French Quarter and publicly claimed to be a witch. Witches were minor mages who got little respect in the wizarding world, so for a wizard to proclaim himself a witch—even for commercial reasons—was incomprehensible.

I found a parking place about four blocks from Peaceful Easy Feelings. It was starting to feel like winter, which in New Orleans meant wind and bone-chilling damp. Around us, people snuggled inside sweaters and jackets as they hurried along the streets. Rene the aquatic shapeshifter and DJ the soon-to-be-loup-garou wore short sleeves and thought the wind felt refreshing. Damn it.

A bell chimed over the door when we entered the shop, and a middle-aged man dressed in an embroidered hippie-gypsy purple tunic looked up from behind the counter. "Be with you in a minute—just look around." He resumed a conversation with a young woman asking about the different ingredients and cost of an herbal concoction to banish negative spirits from a house she was buying.

Rene and I wandered the narrow, crowded aisles, studying the assortment of candles and pouches of herbs that promised everything from cash windfalls to true love to fertility. I saw nothing that warded against ax-wielding dead guys, pending wolfhood, or creepy prete neighbors.

I hadn't told the necromancer I was coming. Not so long ago I would have considered it a breach of etiquette to drop in unannounced. Call me jaded, but now I figured the less warning people had, the less time for them to devise lies and subterfuges. They might slip up and be honest.

"Any of this stuff real?" Rene held up a sexual potency tonic.

"No way. It's illegal to sell real magical potions and spells and, besides, I lived inside your head for a couple of days, remember? You don't need any help in that area." Sex and money and food—welcome to the life of a merman.

He took a step closer to whisper. "Never done it with a wizard, though, babe."

I elbowed him in the ribs and laughed. "Don't even think about it."

Since Mr. New Age wasn't paying any attention to us, I picked up a few of the herbal pouches and held them to my nose, deciphering the scents. Some of them—love potions, pouches to attract wealth, and Rene's sexual potency tonic—were obvious fakes unless our necromancer had stumbled upon some secret not yet known to wizardkind.

I sniffed at a pouch that promised protection. I could isolate the bergamot, eucalyptus, heather. Common herbs. No aura of magic came from the pouches.

"Can I help you find something?"

New Age Guy came from behind the counter and approached us with a friendly lift of the eyebrows. The goodwill faltered as he got closer. "Have we met?"

I glanced around to make sure no one else was in the store. "Are you Jonas?"

"Yessss . . . And you are?"

I held out a hand, which he looked at a second before shaking his head. "Sorry, I don't do handshakes. Nothing personal. Too many germs."

Too bad. I'd found handshakes a harmless way to do empathic mental pat downs of new acquaintances. "No problem. I'm DJ Jaco, the sentinel for the region. I need to ask you a few questions."

His wizard's energy and nervousness spilled out unchecked. "I've had this shop open for almost six years. Your predecessor cleared it with the Green Congress. I don't sell anything illegal here."

I held up my hands. "Wait, wait, wait." I didn't give a crap what he sold in his shop to gullible tourists unless the potions were real. Then we'd have to talk. Later. "I want to ask you some questions about necromancy."

Jonas's eyes widened, and he turned to Rene. "And you are?"

The mer crossed his arms over his chest, which highlighted

all the smooth muscle packed into those wiry limbs. "I'm her bodyguard."

I rolled my eyes. Rene was having way too much fun.

Jonas seemed to accept my having a bodyguard as perfectly normal. "Let's go in the back."

He flipped the OPEN sign on the door to CLOSED, thumbed the dead bolt forward, and led us behind the checkout counter and through a curtain of shiny, clinking black and gold beads. Sort of half goth, half New Orleans Saints.

We walked through a storage room filled with stacked boxes stamped with RARE EARTH SUPPLY INC., but in the back of the room, nestled behind a partition, I spotted a small worktable filled with jars and bottles. It looked not unlike my own workspace, where I mixed real potions and charms. Jonas's aura had relaxed since learning I wasn't there to talk about his shop inventory, but I'd bet most of Jean Lafitte's gold he was selling real potions to human clients and using the new age shop as a front.

We entered a small office about the size of a walk-in closet, with barely enough room for the institutional metal desk covered in peeling green paint and two straight-backed chairs. My bodyguard propped himself against the doorjamb with his hands in his pockets and his surliest expression while Jonas and I took the chairs.

"What can I tell you?" Jonas sat in one chair and pointed me to the other. "First, I have to say I was so excited to hear our new sentinel was Green Congress. It's about time!" His hazel eyes blazed out of a pale face that had spent too many days inside, his hair a cloud of thinning orange-red that jarred with the purple tunic.

Buttering me up wouldn't help him when I came back to

investigate his potions sales and ingredient purchase records, but for now I agreed with him wholeheartedly. It *was* about time the Elders recognize that not only Red Congress wizards could be sentinels, the old gits. There were a handful of Greens and Blues working as sentinels around the world, but I was the first non-Red in the U.S. Physical magic was faster and the Elders equated that with power.

"Thanks, but I'm here to talk about necromancy—namely to ask if you know of other practitioners in the area, maybe someone new who hasn't registered yet."

"Doesn't work that way. Once registered, always registered." He held up a forearm sporting a tattoo of an N inside a pentacle inside a circle. "The only other necromancer I know of in this area is the new vampire Regent."

I studied his tattoo. "This is some sort of tracking charm?" I knew necromantic wizards were required to register with the Elders, but hadn't realized they were tracked.

"Yes. I could move anywhere in the world and they'd know about it. I wouldn't have to reregister. Of course"—he leaned toward me in a show of conspiratorial Green Congress fellowship—"most necromancers don't register. Unless they're caught raising a body, who's going to know?"

Holy crap. There could be necromancers living on every corner. I should have realized this. After all, I used elven magic all the time without the Elders knowing it.

"So why register at all?"

He smiled and leaned back. "Only registered necromancers get official jobs. I get called by the Elders to help with dispute cases—you know, when they need a corpse raised to answer a question or clarify a point. There's money in it, although the Elders are tightwads. Most necromancers register so they can have an extra source of money. I love running this shop, but at least half my paltry income is from official necromantic jobs and I still can't make ends meet."

I'd bet my own paltry income that my salary wasn't much more than his. I asked for Jonas's whereabouts during the past two Axeman attacks, but he had ready answers and I didn't pick up any unease coming from him. He could be good at shielding, of course, but I couldn't think of a plausible reason he'd be summoning someone to kill me.

On the way out, Rene bought the sexual potency tonic, holding it up and grinning at me. "Just in case you change your mind," he said, slipping the vial into his pocket.

If Jonas had had a Find the Hidden Necromancer tonic, I'd have bought a bottle myself.

A quick po'boy lunch and an hour drive to New Orleans East later, I parked the Pathfinder outside a back fence to Six Flags, figuring the front parking lot might be too high profile since the fire.

Adrian Hoffman sat on our same bench with his arms crossed, tapping a foot impatiently and staring at a series of targets lined up along the entrance to the Cajun Nation arcade. They looked like shooting range targets except they were made of metal instead of paper—steel or aluminum, maybe, in the shape of a person. He must've had the Elders' handy-dandy supply house up all night packing and delivering those babies.

The building behind them was plain cinder block, unadorned except for gang tags in varying degrees of obscenity. Fireproof. Adrian was prepared for me.

The sun still hadn't made an appearance, and my nose

grew numb in the cold, damp air. I did not want to be here, but learning to use the elven staff more effectively seemed like a good idea given my priority on the Axeman's hit list.

Which I tried to explain to Adrian, without much success, when he wanted to know why I was ten minutes late. "He's after me specifically," I said. "Can't the Elders help find the necromancer who's controlling him? It has to be someone unregistered."

"We have only the undead pirate's word that there is even a necromancer involved, and I consider Jean Lafitte far from reliable." Adrian brushed off a leaf that dared land on his camel-colored sweater, which had to be cashmere and perfectly matched his slacks.

"No, we have more than Jean Lafitte's word for it." I filled Adrian in on the summoning. "The Axeman admits someone's trying to control him, and I'm his target."

Adrian crossed his arms and studied me with a frown. "He gave you no more information on this wizard's identity? Or why he'd want to kill you?"

"Nothing. Do you have any ideas?"

He shrugged. "Obviously, you've inherited your father's talent for alienating people. I'd suggest you go through your list of enemies."

What a jerk. "I'll do that. Thanks for the suggestion." I'd worn my Tulane sweatshirt because it was roomy enough to accommodate the latest in wizard weaponry. I'd adapted a Velcro-fastened belt of the type joggers used to stash money and keys so it would hold a variety of premade potions and charms. I'd loaded it with the Axeman in mind, but I might have to use it on Adrian.

Instead, I decided to try talking to him again. Adrian

could help me if he'd drop some of his attitude. He was older and his skill set was different.

"Look, I'm the Axeman's target, so this has gotten personal." I told him about the numbers on the wall at the crime scenes and the trashing of my living room. The longer I talked, the deeper his frown etched into his features.

Adrian sat back on the bench, staring at the roller coaster. "You realize that if the Axeman was summoned by this necromancer while you had him in a circle, that means the necromantic wizard is more powerful than you."

Yeah, well, thanks for pointing that out. "Unfortunately, yes, at least when it comes to necromancy versus summoning. Anyway, I'm at a dead end and thought you might have some ideas."

Adrian shook his head. "This is outside my realm of expertise, but let me talk to someone at headquarters. Maybe we can come up with some ideas. In the meantime, the best thing you can do is learn to use your elven magic more effectively."

I nodded and pulled Charlie out of my backpack. "Let's do it."

Adrian reached beside him for his briefcase, snapped it open with authority, and pulled out a sheaf of papers. "First, I want to talk about the political structure of the elves and some of the skills you don't seem to have." He thrust half of the papers at me with a rattle.

Great. The Axeman wanted to slice my head open; Adrian wanted to make it explode with political minutiae. I looked at the top sheet on the stack and stifled an eye-roll. The man had made a freaking elven organizational chart.

"Terrific," I said.

"And then you can practice with the staff." He looked pointedly at the blackened, half-submerged hull of Jean Lafitte's Pirate Ship. "Which you obviously need."

"Obviously."

"If you'll refer to the first sheet, you'll see the top hierarchy of the elves, along with the individuals who currently hold the seats of power." It was official; he was going to bore me to death. Except when I took a grudging glance at the sheet I noticed the name at the top: MACE BANYAN, chief of the Elven Synod.

He was the one who wanted to meet with me so badly, the same one who'd popped up in 1850 New Orleans like an evil genie when I'd gone into the time-travel portion of Old Orleans for dinner with the pirate. Mace had touched me under the guise of shaking hands, and I would have been on the ground within seconds, my mind broken under a tidal wave of memories and images from my past, had it not been for Jean's intervention. That elf had some serious skills.

"Who are these names below Mace Banyan, and why is his name on here twice?" I studied the org chart more closely.

"The elves are divided into four clans or tribes, according to their magical specialties." Adrian warmed to the subject; he'd have made a good professor, much as I hated to admit it. "There has been little intermarriage between clans, as nearly as I can tell, so the bloodlines have remained remarkably pure."

He held up his own chart, identical to mine except larger. We should have met at his apartment so he could have popped up a slide show. "Each of the clans represents one of the elements and has a clan chief. Mace Banyan, in addition to being head of the Synod, or ruling council, is also chief of the Awyr, or Elves of the Air. The other clans are the Ddaear, or Elves of the Earth; the Dwr, or Elves of the Water; and the Tân, or Elves of the Fire. I've heard they're the smallest clan by far, but it's rumor—the elves don't advertise their politics."

My eyes started glazing over. "So, I can study this all later, right?" Or was he planning a pop quiz?

He sniffed. "I suppose your attention span is too short to absorb more than the barest of basics in one sitting."

Damn straight. "So, from your vast knowledge about elven magic"—Adrian nodded solemnly, the snark flying right over his shiny head—"which clan do my skills best fit?"

He thought a moment and looked back at me. "Let me ask about a few more of your skills, and I might have a better idea. Given that the staff Mahout claimed you, and you wield fire with it, my first instinct would be to guess that your dominant clan is the Tân."

Fire elves. That made sense. I wondered if that dominant gene came from Gerry or my mom, who'd given up her Green Congress skills to live as human just as her mother had done.

Adrian put the papers back into his briefcase. "Shall we continue?"

I put my own sheaf of elven bureaucracy in my backpack. "I'll look through the papers tonight and write down any questions I have."

"Fine. Let's go through a few other elven skills." Adrian moved the briefcase aside and turned to face me on the bench. "Can you discern health issues—if you touch a person, can you tell if they're ill or have a pending health crisis?"

That was an elven skill? "No, I can't do that. Can all the elves do that?" Thank goodness Zrakovi hadn't set up the elf meeting until after the full moon, when I'd be gone. Otherwise, Mace Banyan would know about my little fur problem and use it against me.

Adrian folded his arms over his chest. "Not all elves can do that—chiefly the earth elves. You've said you and your father could communicate through dreams. Have you been able to communicate telepathically with anyone while awake?"

"No. I can only read emotions and energy signatures," I said, earning a look of confusion. "It's the thing I was talking about at the office last week. Every species has a unique energy field—I can feel them and tell what species someone is, most of the time." Quince Randolph being an annoying exception.

Adrian frowned. "So you can identify a species by the *aura* they project?"

I nodded. "It's how I was able to tell that murdered professor whose body we found last month was a wizard—there was still enough of an energy signature on him that I recognized it. And how I knew the Axeman Deux murders were being done by the real Axeman. The historical undead have a slightly different aura than a human or another undead species like vampires."

He frowned. "So you can tell I'm a Blue Congress wizard by the energy I give off?"

His interest surprised me. Of all the elven skills I had, energy recognition was helpful but hardly exciting. "No, I can tell you're a wizard, but not what congress you're in or what your unique abilities are." Too bad, because that *would* have been useful.

"What about the emotions—you claim to be empathic?"

"I *am* empathic, and those abilities are ramped up by touch." I reached out and rested my hand on his arm. He flinched but didn't jerk it away. "I can tell you are uncomfortable with me touching you, and that you're worried about something . . . and that you feel love toward someone." Interesting.

I smiled at his look of alarm. "Don't freak out. I can't tell what you're worried about or who you love—only the emotion. I'm not psychic."

He stared at me a long time before finally moving on. "Can you do memory acquisition? Touch someone and pull memories from them?"

I shuddered at the sensation of Mace Banyan scrambling in my head. "No, but that's a trait of the air elves, right?"

He raised an eyebrow. "Yes, although it's the water elves who are most adept at it. How did you know?"

I told him about my brief encounter with Mace Banyan in the Beyond.

"Interesting," he said, eyeing me curiously. "What did it feel like?"

I tugged down my sleeves to ward off a chill that had nothing to do with the weather. "It felt like my brain was being run through a food processor, set to liquefy. It hurt."

Adrian digested that for a moment, then abruptly stood. "Let's work on your staff skills."

I set my backpack on the bench, pulled out the staff, and walked over to inspect the targets. They were about six feet tall, metallic silver, and in the shape of men and women—sort of like the little universal symbols on the doors of restrooms. An etched X marked the rough location of heart and brain. "You got these from central supply?"

He nodded. "The enforcers use them with trainees. The metal targets are good for using incendiary ammunition like one would use on a zombie—or for wizards who have poor aim with elven staffs."

Yeah, because there were so many of us.

"Pay attention," Adrian snapped, taking a spot about four feet away from the figures. "Start from here. Once you're accurate at this range, you can move farther back."

For the next hour, I practiced aiming the staff and shooting small ropes of flame at the targets. Adrian complained about the size and fury of my flames, insulting my lack of power, but I wasn't about to waste energy on target practice when I needed to plan an escape to the Beyond.

Finally, I managed to hit the heart four times out of five from close range. The head remained a problem, being a smaller target, but I'd had enough. The lack of sleep, plus the physical magic used to channel the staff, left me with a pounding headache and muscles that felt like they'd been squeezed through a wringer. Not to mention loup-garou changes, since I'd worked up an unladylike sweat and had pushed my sleeves up to my elbows.

Adrian was sort of droopy himself. "I need to go to Edinburgh on business for a few days, so after our lesson tomorrow we won't meet again until next week. But you should come out here and work over the weekend. You need the practice." He helped me drag the targets into the shelter of what was left of the Cajun Nation building. They'd probably be covered in gang tags by tomorrow, unless they'd been stolen.

But he was right—I needed the practice. The fire from my staff was going to be my best weapon against the Axeman if he managed to catch me. Correcting my aim was just going to take practice.

Lots and lots of practice.

20

Alex got back from his DDT run well before dark. In case I had missed him slinging gravel when he rammed his monster truck into the driveway, he'd shown up ten minutes later, striding through my back door like the leader of an invading Mongol horde. "Dinner's at my place. Pack up a few days' worth of stuff."

If I'd known sex was going to make him so domineering, I might have rethought that bucket-list thing. Then again . . . "Where am I going?"

He picked up the staff and handed it to me, and I followed him into the living room, watching as he stared at the cheap plastic lawn chair parked in front of the TV.

"I brought it in from the yard so I'd have a place to sit." Like I should have to defend my décor under these conditions.

He shook his head. "Take the staff. You're moving in with me, at least until we've caught the necromancer or it's time to make a run for the Beyond." He turned to give me a little half smile that made my toes curl. "I'll make it worth your while."

"Yeah? How are you going to do that?" Good Lord, he just had to bat those chocolate-brown eyes at me and I started simpering like a high school girl. Totally pathetic.

He gathered me in his arms and kissed me, in case I'd forgotten exactly how he could make it worth my while. I wrapped my legs around his waist only to keep from falling. Really.

Sanity returned midway between his mouth's journey from my earlobe to my collarbone. We couldn't have a relationship if I hid things from him—especially things he thought were dangerous. We'd been rehashing that same argument since the day we met.

"Wait." I unwound my legs and settled to my feet. "I need to tell you what happened today. I summoned the Axeman."

Alex rested his chin atop my head, his arms still wrapped around me. That meant we were touching, so I picked up his frustration even though he was shielding.

I stepped back. "I know you want to protect me, but that can't be your full-time job."

"Actually, it could be a full-time job." He stuffed his hands in his pockets. So much for the romantic moment. "I know you follow your heart and I admire that about you, but you take too many chances."

I considered what he was saying. "Would it make you feel better if I told you I had backup with me when I did the summoning? And when I went to interview the necromancer this morning?"

"Jean Lafitte?" He looked only slightly mollified.

"No, Rene Delachaise."

Alex smiled. "Yes, that makes me feel better. Good choice. I like Rene."

Crisis averted for now, but I had a feeling this subject would bite us a few more times before we figured it out.

"Come on, I'll fill you in." He followed me to the kitchen since I only had the one white plastic chair. We spent the next hour catching up and debating theories.

The phone rang while I was dragging out leftover shrimp and potatoes to reheat. I'd set my cell on the lawn chair, and I heard Alex's voice rumbling in the living room.

He had answered my phone without asking. This being-a-couple thing kind of made my shoulder blades itch, but I sure didn't want to leave it behind to live in the Beyond. And I didn't want to run away to save myself while the Axeman and his wizard buddy continued to prey on my city. There had to be a solution to both problems.

"Quince Randolph wants to talk to you." Alex returned to the kitchen and thrust the phone at me, frowning.

I gave him a frown in return. "Can't it wait?"

Broad shoulders up, broad shoulders down. "He says no."

Oh good, a chance to chat with Mr. Creepy. I set the plate down and took the phone. "What's up, Rand? I'm busy."

"Sorry to interrupt." He didn't sound at all sorry. "Can you come over to the shop? I need to talk to you. Just for a few minutes."

"You want to talk, you can come here. You know how to walk across the street." Unfortunately.

"I can't leave the store untended. It's important. You wanted to know what I am, and I decided it's time you did. But I want to show you, not tell you over the phone. It won't take long."

Oh, Moses on a mountaintop, as my granddad used to say. "Fine, I'll come now, but I can't stay more than ten minutes. I have plans." Which didn't involve him, whatever he might be.

I ended the call before he could respond and stuck the phone in my pocket.

"What the hell does he want?" Alex loomed in the doorway to the living room.

I finished arranging the leftover potatoes on the plate and shoved it in the microwave. "He says he'll show me what he is if I come over there now, so I'm going. Take this out when it's done? I'll be back in ten minutes."

"I'm going with you." If Alex frowned any harder, his face would crack open.

I started to argue that Rand might not talk to me if Alex were there, but I rethought it. Hadn't we just talked about me taking too many risks? And besides, if Rand was an elf, I didn't want to be alone with him in case he turned into Mace Banyan Jr.

"He might not tell me if you're there, but let's try it." I turned the microwave off and left the potatoes in there.

"I'll stay in another room if he wants privacy, but he needs to know he can't just snap his inhuman fingers and have you hop-to. If you run into trouble, yell or whistle and I'll be there in two seconds."

That sounded like a good compromise, and we'd avoided another argument. Maybe we *could* do this couple thing.

Darkness fell early since we'd gone off daylight saving time, and the late rush-hour traffic was heavy on Magazine, forcing us to cross at the light. I looked at Shear Luck as I walked past, and my annoyance at Quince Randolph swelled.

He was coming between Eugenie and me, and seemed to

be doing it deliberately. I resented it. I needed to stop by her house tomorrow and make her talk to me. Try to make her understand that I not only wasn't involved with her man, I didn't even *like* him. Without revealing anything about wizards or other species or creepy stalker vibes, of course, which was a bigger problem. Eugenie knew I was shutting her out of big swaths of my life—bigger swaths than she could imagine.

"We had good luck telling Ken the truth about us," I told Alex. "Maybe it's time to clue Eugenie in about our world. She'd think it was cool."

Alex rested a hand on my shoulder as we waited for the light to change. Possessive, but nice. "I don't know. She might think it was so cool she'd get herself in trouble. The thought of Eugenie in a room with Jean Lafitte is just scary."

He had a point. But I was going to give it serious thought. The Elders wouldn't like it, but I'd never used their approval as the ultimate gauge for what I should and shouldn't do. I was Gerry St. Simon's daughter, after all.

The light at Magazine and Nashville turned, and we crossed the street to Plantasy Island. I'd never been in the shop, my own gardening efforts being limited to a few pots of herbs for potions and charms. I loved flowers but couldn't grow them.

A bell sounded over the door when I pushed it open, Alex right behind me. The front of the store was stuffed with cuteness. Metal sculptures, fancy scrolled flowerpots, garden flags, even an entire wall of ceramic gnomes representing different occupations. I paused, staring at Attorney Gnome with his pinstriped hat and scales of justice. Who came up with these things? Plus they cost seventy-five bucks each.

"There you are, Dru." Rand emerged through a wide door in back. Behind him I could see a large, leaf-filled space. "And . . . Alex."

Was it my imagination, or was he less than thrilled to see my backup?

"Stop calling me Dru—that's my great-aunt. Alex and I were about to have dinner when you called." I peered around him. "How do you get enough light in there to grow anything?"

"I replaced the back walls and roof with greenhouse glass. It's retractable when the weather's good, but it's too cool right now." Rand glanced behind him. "Wait a sec."

He disappeared through the greenhouse door for a moment, then reemerged with a terra-cotta pot holding three white lilies with wild purple spots on them. "For you, something unique."

Alex mumbled something under his breath, and I'd lay odds it wasn't a comment on Rand's thoughtfulness. I took them reluctantly, wondering what he'd expect in return. I also wondered how he managed to work around dirt all day in his pristine white sweater. It should have made him look washed out but instead gave him the appearance of some pretty Russian snow prince. "Thanks."

"Toad lily," he said. "One of the few things that blooms here naturally this late in the season."

"Pretty," I said, "but we have dinner plans, so let's talk about what you are."

"So impatient." He shifted his gaze to Alex. "I'd really hoped to speak to you alone."

Alex crossed his arms and gave Rand his enforcer stone-face. "I'll wait out here and you guys can talk in the greenhouse."

Rand responded with his own crossed arms and pouty face. Good grief. "Alex can study the garden gnomes. We'll talk in the greenhouse. Take it or leave it." I gave Rand my bitchy wizard face.

"Fine. Let me close up." Rand locked the front door and dimmed the front lights. "Give us a few minutes, Alex."

Grunting in his best monosyllable, Alex settled into a chair behind the counter and picked up a landscaping magazine. I set down my toad lilies, met his gaze over the top of the magazine, and smiled. We made a pretty good team when we worked at it.

"Come on, it's time for me to answer some of your questions." Rand rested a hand on my shoulder and propelled me toward the back, closing the door behind us. Alex would probably ease it back open within seconds.

The lights of the city streaked gold across the greenhouse glass, giving the whole thing a glittery feel. The air was clean and crisp, probably from the small sprayers that cut on and off to keep the plants green and healthy. I took a deep breath.

"The plants give off all that oxygen—nice, isn't it? Come this way." Rand walked ahead of me toward an ornate gazebo that took up an entire corner of the cavernous greenhouse. Painted white, it had Victorian-inspired wooden trim and two benches inside. He sat on one, and I took the bench facing him.

"Okay, Rand. Give it up."

He reached up and removed the peridot studs from his ears, then tugged a gold chain from beneath his white sweater. At the end of it hung a gold-and-peridot tree. He handed them to me.

As before, the buzz of wizard's magic made my palm tingle. "Where did you get these? And don't tell me you bought them on eBay."

"Black market—they're easy enough to get. Even wizards need a supplementary source of income these days."

"You still haven't told me what you are. Elf? Faery?" I eyed him for any physical changes with the removal of the peridot. Apparently, his prettiness was real. If anything, his blue-green eyes were richer and brighter than before. I still didn't read any aura from him that was identifiable, just a light, unfamiliar magical charge.

"You haven't figured it out?" He grinned at me. Even his teeth were perfect.

"Give me your hand." Maybe I could tell more if I touched him.

A flick of an eyebrow in an expression almost triumphant spread over his face before he settled into an easy smile. He stretched out his arm and took my hand. His fingers wrapped around mine, but still I felt only that light energy.

He grasped my hand harder, closed his eyes, and spoke softly in an odd, musical language I couldn't understand. The room spun, and the greenhouse slipped into a soft fade. I opened my mouth to scream, but the sound came out soft and breathy as time and space squeezed my lungs.

The gazebo was a freaking transport.

21

Holy crap—I'd been tricked and kidnapped like I was a rookie. I'd never hear the end of it.

One second I sat in a gazebo in a Magazine Street shop, and now my boots were planted on an area rug in a large octagonal room. It had what architects called an open floor plan, with lots of blond wood to give it a modern, urban feel. Bright floodlights outside the floor-to-ceiling windows illuminated what looked like the edges of dense forest. It was already nighttime here, which probably meant I was either in Europe or Asia, or somewhere in the Beyond. My bets were on the Beyond.

A fire popped and crackled cheerfully in the middle of the room from a central fireplace surrounded by rugs and conversation areas. Deep, cushiony armchairs beckoned in greens and browns. In the back, where the windows ended, lay a short hallway and a small but functional kitchen. The place smelled of pine.

"What the hell have you done?" I jerked my hand away from Quince Randolph and glared at him. I was going to make his life a living hell when I got out of here. Making me look boneheaded was the quickest way to bring out my vengeful streak. And I had a long memory.

"Want something to drink?" He walked into the kitchen area, looking pleased with himself.

"Where are we? Why are we here?" My voice hinged on hysteria, louder and higher-pitched than normal.

"I thought it would be easier to explain things this way."

I was going to kill him, that's all there was to it. If I could sprout fangs and fur right now, he'd be so much dead, bloody meat on the polished hardwood floor. We'd see how pretty he was then.

I willed my voice to reflect a calm I didn't feel. "Explain what? Didn't it occur to you that I might listen better if you hadn't *kidnapped* me?" And right under Alex Warin's nose. He was going to be so royally pissed.

Rand cocked his head. "You wanted to know what I am."

"What you are is a flipping sociopath." I stomped to the only visible outside door, which had been inset in one of the huge windows that looked out on an ocean of treetops. From what the floodlights illuminated, the land looked hilly. We definitely weren't in pancake-flat Southeast Louisiana anymore.

I turned the doorknob and pulled, but it wouldn't budge. Frowning, I grasped the knob with my right hand and tried to send a pulse of physical energy into the lockset, willing it to turn. A feeble, tingling force of will skittered from my hand and dissipated. I don't have a lot of physical magic, but that had been pathetic, even for me.

But wizard's physical magic didn't work in the Beyond. Crap.

I rounded on Rand. "Let me out of here, you lying, peridot-wearing sonofa—"

He assumed a contrite expression I didn't buy for a minute. "Don't be mad, Dru. You're in Elfheim. You'd already guessed I was elf. My Synod just wants to talk to you a few minutes, and then I'll take you home. I promise."

Freaking elves. I should have known. I tried to blast a shot of physical energy into the fireplace, just a pulse to stoke the fire, and when that didn't work, willed every bit of magic I could muster. Nothing, damn it. Why oh why hadn't I stuck one of those grenades in my pocket?

"Alex is going to kill you, you know. You can't go back to New Orleans. And I have friends in the Beyond who can take you down." I'd hire Jean Lafitte to kill him. If I could just get out of here. Jean would probably do it for free.

I studied the floor, but our transport wasn't visible so it had to be hidden under that big area rug. I wasn't sure exactly where we'd landed, but it was somewhere between the door and the round dining table.

I walked to the edge of the rug and threw it back to see the universal transport symbol. Rand made no move to stop me as I stepped into it. I knelt to activate it and send myself home . . . and then remembered I had no magic.

"You'll need me to get you back anyway. It's locked without our transport phrase." Rand's voice was annoyingly patient. "Just wait and talk to them. It won't take long."

"They can wait until the Monday after Thanksgiving, when we planned." I picked up a heavy wooden stool from the kitchen bar and tested its weight. Turning it upside down, I grasped the legs and hefted the whole thing back to swing it like a baseball bat. If I could break the window, I'd be out.

I might be short, but I'd jogged with Alex every day until

the rib injury and was highly motivated. I could outrun Quince Randolph.

"Please don't break the window. You'll make a mess, and there's really nowhere for you to go."

I whirled at the sound of a different voice and at the man it belonged to. An urbane guy in his mid-to-late forties, medium height and slender, with salt-and-pepper hair and a short, dark beard. Deep brown eyes glittered cheerfully above high cheekbones, his face lean and tanned. He looked like he'd walked out of the pages of *GQ*—or a past version of New Orleans.

I spoke through gritted teeth. "Mace Banyan."

The head of the Synod eyed me with an infuriating expression of detached amusement. "Drusilla Jaco. Welcome to Elfheim."

Like I'd chosen to visit. "Why the secrecy? Why kidnap me and piss off the Elders? I'd already agreed to meet with you."

"Call me Mace," he said, ignoring my questions. He walked into the kitchen and pulled several wineglasses from an overhead rack. Six glasses. Awesome. The rest of the Synod must be on the way.

He pulled a bottle of red wine from beneath the counter, popped the cork with practiced skill, and poured three glasses half full. He handed one to Rand, who took a seat on a stool at the bar. Mace held the other out to me.

I shook my head. "No, thanks. You've already kidnapped me. Why shouldn't I think you'd poison me as well?" Okay, they were drinking the same wine, so it likely wasn't poisoned, but I was through giving Rand—or any other elf—the benefit of the doubt. Plus, Mace Banyan scared the crap out of me. I remembered our first meeting all too well.

"You might as well relax, Drusilla." Mace leaned against the kitchen counter, a picture of relaxed arrogance. "We're just going to get to know you better, and then you can go home. We've saved a lot of time and political maneuvering by having Rand bring you to Elfheim."

I gave Rand my surliest look. Words weren't needed. He shrugged and looked cute.

Some pretes were easy to type. Vampires were pale, had an unmistakable air of world-weary resignation, and projected emotions like humans. Mers and werewolves and other shifters were full of buzzy energy.

Not elves. I tried to find any similarity between Mace and Rand, something that should have tipped me off besides Rand's lack of aura. Even with no peridot, their energy was like a whisper across skin. Rand was tall, Mace was of medium height. Rand was bright and shiny like a silver Mardi Gras doubloon; Mace was dark and suave, but looked prone to brooding. No pointy ears. Brown eyes versus blue. Stylish, charcoal sweater and slacks versus crunchy-granola sweater, jeans, and long hair.

I should give myself a break—there was nothing about Quince Randolph to set off my radar, except for his weird preoccupation with me. I'd even suspected he was an elf; I just hadn't suspected he was a kidnapping elf.

I rethought the wine and snatched the glass off the counter. Rand laid his hand over mine. "It'll be okay. Everyone promised to behave." He spoke softly, his eyes on Mace. The Synod leader had strolled to the far side of the room and was looking out the window with his back to us.

"I was going to meet with the Synod in just over a week anyway." I spat the words at him. "What is the hurry?"

"There are political considerations which are none of your concern." Mace turned away from the window. "It has become important that we understand the scope of your abilities and your use of our ancestral staff."

As Mace spoke, a crackle of power sent a ruffling shiver across my scalp. Forget that whisper-across-skin thing. They could turn it on and off. Mace oozed power of a kind I'd never encountered, and my fear of him jumped another notch. How can you fight what you can't understand? One touch from him a few weeks ago had almost incapacitated me and had freaked out Jean Lafitte. Jean was *immortal,* plus he'd seen some dangerous things in his day. Whatever unsettled him had to be bad.

"No doubt Elder Zrakovi will be unhappy about our methods, but we wanted this meeting on our terms," Mace said. "We'll learn more by talking to you alone."

So this was partly about me, and partly to show the Elders they couldn't call the shots? Willem Zrakovi would take this kidnapping very seriously. If Mace Banyan wanted to get the Elders' attention, he'd definitely have it. But what was so urgent? I'd been using the staff for three years.

"You're an arrogant jackass." My anger overtook my fear, and I ignored a hiss from Rand to be quiet. "You underestimate the Elders. If your political considerations are serious enough to pull this kind of stunt, you might get more than you expect. And you"—I turned and stabbed a finger in the air at Rand—"should be ashamed of your part in this."

I met Rand's gaze, and his voice sounded in my head. *They won't hurt you. Stay calm. Don't antagonize him.*

My breath caught in my throat. How had he done that? Did I imagine it?

I tried to think something back at him—*how did you do that?*—but he just frowned and blinked.

"What are you doing?" Mace's voice wasn't in my head, but across the room. He spoke sharply to Rand. "Can you communicate with her?"

"Of course not," Rand said, his voice smooth and easy. The elf was a good liar. "She's just a wizard with a few minor elven skills. You'll see."

"Yet Mahout, one of our most revered relics, claimed her." The cold brilliance in Mace's eyes was at odds with the easy smile on his lips.

The elves wouldn't dare hurt me, or at least I told myself that. Doing any real damage would end a centuries-long truce between the wizards and elves. Unless, as Adrian Hoffman kept telling me, I just wasn't that important.

Or unless they were *trying* to break the truce. Tucking that thought away to consider once I got out of this mess, I focused instead on not hyperventilating. Suddenly, my lungs had trouble drawing air, and a headache began a steady rhythm behind my eyeballs.

"Lighten up on her, Mace." Rand's voice was soft. "You can't influence her emotions. She's one of Vervain's—and mine."

I could tell the second Mace's gaze left me, and I took a deep breath. He'd been trying to control my emotions?

Mace and Rand had some kind of stare-down I couldn't interpret. "She might be one of Vervain's, but she's not one of yours yet," Mace finally said. "Don't forget your place."

I sat in one of the armchairs across from the sofa where

Mace had taken a seat and banged my cell phone on the end table to get their attention. I'd been trying to get a signal but it was dead. Guess Verizon couldn't hear me in Elfheim.

"Wait just a damn minute, both of you." It wasn't like I couldn't hear them talking about me. "What do you mean, I'm one of yours and Vervain's?" I asked Rand, and then turned to Mace: "You can influence a person's emotions?"

"You don't need to know more about our skills—you know too much already." Mace went to pour more wine. He needed a serious attitude adjustment, and I had just the staff to do it with. If it even worked on elves. Not that I had it with me.

"Reading and manipulating emotions is an elven skill," Rand said, coming to sit on the arm of my chair. I wasn't sure if he was being his flirty self or was there to protect me from Mace. I suspected the latter, which made me both grateful for his presence and even more furious at him for bringing me here. "But it only works with members of other species, and within our own clans. Your skills seem to be aligned with my clan, the Tân."

Fire elves, just as Adrian had suspected. "And Mahout was the staff of the Tân."

"Yes, it—"

"Silence, Quince Randolph," Mace snapped. "We don't discuss Synod business in front of wizards." Mace said *wizards* much as I might say *toad spawn*.

I looked up at Rand. "You're not Synod, are you?" The Tân chief's name had been Vervain.

Mace came to stand in front of us. "No, he's not, and he'd do well to remember that."

Rand rested a hand on my shoulder, and I felt myself

relax involuntarily. Mace couldn't manipulate my emotions, but Rand could. He'd hidden his power when he was spying on me in New Orleans and pretending to care about Eugenie, and that thought was enough to help me shrug away from his hand and welcome my anger back. I was tired of this crap.

"Ask your questions, and then let me go home," I said. "The wizards have been nothing but cooperative. I'll ignore the fact that you've taken me against my will."

Mace's smile gave me chills. "Don't be impatient. The other Synod members will be here shortly."

Reclaiming his seat on the sofa, he reached over to a side table and pulled a thin cigarette from a carved wooden box. As he lit it, the smell of lavender and olive filled the room. "Would you like one? They're quite mild."

I shook my head. "No, and if you're using the herbs in your smoke to calm me down, that's not going to work either." Tricky, smooth-talking, kidnapping elf. I'd match my Green Congress herbal knowledge against his any day.

It looked like I was about to have my meeting with the elves whether I liked it or not. I looked at my watch. Forty minutes had passed since I left Alex sitting behind the counter at Plantasy Island, assuming time in Elfheim ran parallel to the modern world. He'd probably been raising holy hell for at least a half hour and had already called the Elders. No way repercussions from this weren't going to be ugly.

Mace raised his chin and looked at the ceiling. "The others are almost here." I couldn't hear anything but the crackle of the fire.

I assumed *the others* were the three remaining clan chiefs. "What is it you hope to accomplish tonight?" Did they want the staff? To know what I could do that they'd consider elven magic?

Mace took a drag on his happy smoke. "We've been watching you for a long time, the first wizard with enough elven blood to hold some of our magic. You're woefully unskilled, of course, but that might be just as well considering the quality of instruction you would have received from the wizards. Have you had any at all?"

I pondered my answer. Would the Elders want the elves to know they were trying to teach me to use my elven magic, or that Gerry had encouraged me to use it my whole life? Probably not. "None to speak of. This is all about the staff? Because it claimed me?"

A darkness crossed his face, and his expression sent a spear of unease through me. Those refined manners could dissipate in seconds.

"One of our ancient staffs should never have fallen into wizard hands. The fact that it claimed you as its master is"—he clenched his jaw so hard it could have cracked nuts—"unacceptable."

I smiled at him, seeing a solution. I loved the way the staff enhanced my magic, but I'd survived without it before and could do so again. Long before I lit a flame at Six Flags and burned down a good chunk of the protected wetlands in Plaquemines Parish, I'd set a table in the Napoleon House banquet room on fire (I'd been aiming at Jean Lafitte), exploded a goodly number of ancient crypts in the Beyond's version of St. Louis Cemetery No. 1, and had done lots of damage to my own house.

"No problem," I said. "Just send me home, I'll return the staff to the elves, and our business is finished. I'm sure you're too busy to worry about me, and I have a necromancer to find." And a life that doesn't involve sinister, cigarette-smoking elves and their pretty flunkies.

"Once a staff has claimed you, you cannot give it up while you still live," Mace said, his voice flat, the threat understood. Rand reached out to give me what was no doubt a comforting touch, but at my glare, he pulled his hand away.

There was more going on here than just the elves wanting to reclaim Charlie. *Political considerations*, Mace had said. Maybe it had something to do with the Interspecies Council, but those negotiations were far, far above anything a wizard on my level would know about.

"If you don't want the staff, what *do* you want?"

"We first verify your lineage, to see if you really are of Vervain's fire elves," he said. "I understand you can use hydromancy but that's not specific to any clan. I've seen no sign that you hold any of the skills unique to my airfolk or Lily's water elves, but that remains to be seen."

"How did you know I could do hydromancy?" It wasn't a skill I advertised since the Elders didn't like it.

"We have ways."

The number of people who knew I could do hydromancy was limited, and unless he pulled it out of my mind, Quince Randolph wasn't one of them.

"Who talked to you?" I leaned forward in the chair. Other than Alex and Jake, no one outside a small group of wizards—including Zrakovi and Adrian—knew of my skills. Although Gerry could have told people I didn't know.

A woman's voice, whisper soft, spoke from behind me and sent a wave of tingles over my skin. "We keep track of these things." I stood and turned, fists clenched. Couldn't elves just knock on the door like civilized people instead of this scary appearing-out-of-nowhere shit?

In this case it was two elves. I stared at the woman who'd spoken.

"You." It was the tall, pale-haired woman who'd been in a tête-à-tête in Etienne Boulard's office. And she'd been sitting with Etienne's assistant Terri when we came out of our meeting. Had Adrian been running his vampire-besotted mouth and telling people things they didn't need to know?

"I am Lily," she said, and I fought the urge to hide my hands behind my back. I couldn't pinpoint where the impulse came from, but I really, really didn't want to touch her. Still, if I could salvage any relationship with these people I needed to try. I forced myself to take her hand, and a light tingle of energy rushed over me before I jerked it back.

"Fascinating," she murmured. Lily's hair, pulled atop her head in an elaborate updo, set off her pale blue eyes. Now *she* was an elf, or at least what I expected an elf to look like. She hadn't seemed so exotic in the dim lights of L'Amour Sauvage. Then again, maybe she could assume some kind of glamour in public. Or maybe she'd been wearing camouflage jewelry of some kind. Rand had been even prettier once he stripped off the peridot.

A short, dark-haired man with swarthy skin and charcoal eyes came to stand beside her. He too held out a hand for me to shake. I wondered if the elves had a secret handshake and if they were waiting to see how long it took me to figure it out. It was all terribly polite for a kidnapping.

"I am Betony, of the people of earth," he said, and turned to Mace. "She is definitely one of Vervain's—look at her."

I wasn't one of anybody's, thank you very much. "I'm a

Green Congress wizard. That's the only cult I belong to."
Well, it felt like a cult. And it was better than an elven clan,
which probably had its own Kool-Aid.

"Then let me greet her." I looked around for the source
of the voice and saw a woman rising from a chair in the
shadows of a darkened corner I would have sworn was empty
a moment before. The elves must have their own type of
transports.

She was petite, a bit shorter than me in my overpriced
designer boots. Her rich blond hair ran in a braid down her
back, and while her skin was smooth, an old wisdom dwelt
in her blue-green eyes—very similar to the color of mine.
And Rand's. How whacked was that?

Her demeanor was more imperious than the others, not
arrogant like Mace, but regal. She held herself with detach-
ment, showed less curiosity. I couldn't read elven emotions
but I got that much from the set of her jaw and the tilt of
her head. She was older than the others.

"You're Vervain?" I held out my hand to get the secret
handshake over with.

She nodded and smiled, and the difference it made in her
face was dramatic. Years dropped away, and her cold beauty
melted into something warmer and prettier. How much of
it was illusion? I got no uncomfortable vibes from her touch,
just warmth.

"You're right, Rand. Her dominant ancestor was of our
clan." My elfnapper had retreated to the corner chair now
that his chief was here. The suck-up merely nodded.

I looked back at her, fascinated—we were sort of cousins
forty-thousand times removed. I spared a moment of sadness
for Gerry that, as enamored with the elves as he'd been, he

hadn't ever met one. They rarely left Elfheim, and for many years the Elders had let people believe the entire species was extinct. "Both of my parents had elven blood. Can you tell which of my parents was dominant?"

Vervain smiled. "We might be able to tell."

"So what do we do now?" I asked. "This family reunion rocks it, but I'd like to go home."

"Sit here." Mace pointed toward a round table, and I reluctantly followed the others. There were five chairs and six of us. Rand sat in an armchair a few feet away, his eyes glued to me, face tense. His posture and tight expression told me he was uneasy, which in turn made me nervous. The irony that my stalker seemed to be my only potential ally in this funhouse wasn't lost on me. Although if I got home in one piece, I planned to rip him a new one.

Mace took the seat to my left and Betony to my right. The two women settled across the table. I waited expectantly. This was their show, and I figured I'd do well to keep my mouth shut, although remaining quiet wasn't one of my stronger skills, elven or otherwise.

"What we must do, Drusilla, is learn about you, about your skills, in order to determine exactly what of our magic you have inherited, and how you've used it," Mace said. "It seems clear you are of Vervain's people, but it's vital we be sure. Looks can deceive."

"Questioning her will take too long, and wizards are notoriously clever at twisting the truth," Lily said. "We need to do a regression."

"No!" Rand's voice was just short of a shout, and we all turned to look at him. He leaned forward, fingers turning white from the pressure he exerted on the chair's wooden arms. "That wasn't what we agreed to."

"What's a regression?" I might as well have been talking to myself, for all the attention the elves paid me. But if Rand didn't want this regression thing to happen, it had to be bad.

"You will learn your place, or you will leave," Mace told him just as Vervain murmured, "Peace, son."

Son? Was she Rand's mother?

"Very well, we will learn what we need to know using the old methods." Mace turned to me. "Then, we'll talk about how we might be of service to each other, if you're still able."

22

I was still pondering the words *old methods* when he got to the part about *if you're still able*.

"What do you mean, *if I'm still able*?" If I'm able because I might be too stupid to understand deep and mysterious elven things, or if I'm able because I might be unconscious—or dead?

My heart fluttered as I pushed my chair back. I'd been angry tonight. Alarmed. Concerned. Surprised. But this was the first time I'd felt physically threatened.

Mace grasped my arm. His grip wasn't rough, but it also wasn't yielding. "How easily this goes depends on how willingly you allow us to know you." Mace looked around me at Betony, and the dark-haired man gave a brief nod and locked my other arm in a firm grasp. Mace had said *know* as if it should be epic and biblical. Vervain extended an arm across the table and grasped my arm above Mace's hand.

Holy crap. They were all touching me. Nothing had happened yet, but I knew what was coming. Whatever mind-scramble Mace Banyan had tried on me last month, he was going to do again—with help.

I tried to wrest myself free, but they only gripped harder. "Don't struggle, Drusilla," Mace breathed into my ear. "Let us know you." Definitely a capital *Know*. His voice grew muted, but I was able to hear one more sentence: "Quince Randolph, if you move an inch closer, I will have you lashed."

The room grew brighter and I fought for every inch of calmness I could muster. "I'll tell you whatever you want to know." My surroundings seemed to melt and run like a warped Salvador Dalí painting. "Just ask your questions, and don't touch me. I'll tell you the truth."

Suddenly, cool hands brushed my temples from behind and Lily's soft voice whispered across my mind. "Calm down, you stupid wizard. Stop fighting."

I sank back to the chair with Lily's voice in my head and her light energy flowing over my skin. Why had I been struggling? It was warm and peaceful here, and when Mace picked me up and carried me to the sofa, I looked in his brown eyes and smiled. He smiled back.

Why had I ever thought he was scary?

On some level, I knew there was something I should be doing, something else I should be remembering or feeling, but I couldn't seem to focus. I hadn't felt this relaxed and peaceful since Katrina had thrown my world into disarray.

I felt them around me, occasionally touching me, remaining close. Then in a wash of gray, the room around me disappeared and I found myself sprawled instead on a half-rotted pier next to the river. Rene Delachaise was doing CPR and sending lances of pain through my abdomen from his compressions, but it worked. I coughed out a lungful of water and rolled to my side, where Rand stood in the semi-darkness at the edge of a clearing, watching me.

"Wait . . . interesting. There's something recent we need to see," a male voice said.

A heave and sickening swirl of my surroundings jerked me to the barroom at the Green Gator, frozen in fear as Jake and I looked at the scratch on my arm, the weight of an unknown future heavy on my heart.

I relived the scene four times—four fights with Jake, four scratches, four initial moments of terror, then finally the scene faded to the front porch of my house, where I skidded in the slippery coating of blood. Tish lay nearby, her throat cut in a perfect red line, killed because of me. Her face was so clear, so nearby, I reached out to touch her cheek, but my hand passed through it.

The night around me grew darker, and I found myself stumbling through New Orleans' oldest cemetery, in the Beyond. It was the night of the real full moon, the cemetery dimly lit with a stoked bonfire. The voodoo god Samedi stood before me, a giant figure with a skeleton painted on his dark skin and the glint of death in his eyes.

On some level I knew he wasn't real, knew this had already happened, but the fear washed over me as it had the first time I lived through it, right after Katrina. Gerry lay dying, and Jake had fallen nearby, a huge red wolf sinking white fangs into his thigh. I looked for Alex and couldn't find him. He was hurt, out in the dark somewhere. Jean was injured too, after trying to help me. All my fault. All of it.

I scrambled around on the dark ground, looking for the elven staff, and when I got it, I pointed it at Samedi and shot red ropes of fire at him, sending him back to his corner of the Beyond, his strength destroyed.

Another gray mist came and went, and ropes of fire flew from the staff as I wielded it in a long, candlelit room with a large wooden table down the center. I was injured, and I faced Jean and some of his men. Alex lay motionless on the floor nearby after fighting with one of the Baratarian pirates. Had he been killed? My anger fueled the fiery ropes from the staff, which wrapped themselves around another of Jean's people. I watched him die and be absorbed back into the Beyond, and felt a sense of satisfaction as Jean's expression changed from anger to grudging admiration.

The mist faded, and I jolted back to reality. The room spun like a drunken top, but I remembered where I was—in Elfheim. I had to get out or I might not live through this. I struggled to sit up, but hands held me immobile. Once again, I felt Lily's cool palms on my temples, and the world grayed.

I stood upstairs in Gerry's house after Katrina. Black, oily sludge oozed from the carpet on the first floor, and I stared at a voodoo symbol painted on the wall in blood. Gerry was missing, and the Elders suspected me of helping him go rogue. Alex, a stranger who worked for the wizards as an enforcer, descended the stairs from the attic, holding a box containing an old wooden staff. I didn't know what it was. Sparks flew from its tip when I touched it, and it glowed with a golden energy. I decided to take it home.

Other scenes flitted by, in and out of the gray mist, some in fast-forward, some slowing down as if I needed to relive them in slow motion, each second agonizing because I knew the punch line of each scene, and they were never funny. Using hydromancy as a teenager. Scrying in a frantic attempt to find Gerry after Katrina. Being brought into dreams by Gerry before he died, then learning how to dreamwalk myself using the staff.

It always came back to the staff.

I curled on my side as I was jerked back and forth in time. Lessons with Gerry. Using the staff to trace odd rifts in the Mississippi River back to the Styx. Early runs as sentinel. Every time I fought through the mist and pain, clawed my way back to consciousness, Lily's cool hands would rest on my forehead, and my ability to fight evaporated.

But unlike the first flashbacks, the more recent events that seemed to transport me away to relive them, older memories razored through my mind at random, as if etching themselves into my aura. Or maybe the cuts were already there, and now they were exposed and raw.

Oh, God, I hated these creatures. I tried to pull away from them and wrap my hands around my head as if I could physically keep them out. My face was wet and I tasted blood. Had they hit me? Was an aneurysm like the one that took my mother also ready to take me?

And behind it all, a plea: God, don't let them go all the way back.

Another cooling touch, and the gray fog settled over me again. I was six years old and sat in the backseat of the old Plymouth as my grandfather parked in front of Gerry's house. My grandparents were getting rid of me, foisting me off on a stranger I'd never seen, and I was petrified.

The drive had gone on for hours, and I'd cried most of the way, bunching my hands up in my stiff pink Sunday School dress, begging them to turn around so often that my gran yelled at me to hush. Why did they want to get rid of me? I'd tried to be good, to do what they wanted. I'd tried to make them love me but I always knew how they felt, that Gran was afraid of me, that Grandpa stayed away from home so he wouldn't be ashamed of what I was.

Today, in the car, driving over long bridges and past towns with funny names, they were relieved someone was going to take me off their hands.

Blinded, I struck out at the hands touching me, and realized on some level that the voice crying in long, ragged sobs was mine. But the disconnect was too great, like my brain and my body were separate now, and I didn't have control over either one.

I was five, and heard a sound in my parents' room. I couldn't sleep, so I padded down the hall and pushed open the door. Mommy lay on the floor, clutching her head, and Daddy (only he wasn't really my daddy, was he?) leaned over her, his face white as the paper in my kindergarten notebook. He cried and called her name. Carrie. Her name was Carrie.

I cried out, and when he saw me, he sat heavily on the bed, like a balloon whose air had been released. I tried to run to Mommy but he reached out and pulled me away. She was dead and, without her, he was afraid of me too. My magic grew out of control. I broke the vase. I broke Mommy's mirror. I broke and broke and broke.

The gray screen that was my mind went blank, and I knew on some level that I'd returned to a place more than twenty years later and a world away. There was shouting and movement around me, but nobody touched me. Maybe if I curled up tighter, they'd forget about me, leave me alone.

I remembered nothing more. Just darkness, and blessed silence.

23

The soothing, steady noise of a ceiling fan droned above my bed. I burrowed deeper into the pillow, wondering why my muscles ached. Faint voices drifted from downstairs. Had I left the television on?

Someone shifted next to me and whispered, "Dru? Wake up. We have to talk."

I frowned and slit my eyes open to see Rand sitting on the bed next to me, his white sweater smeared with blood. Why was he here, in my house, in my room? Had something happened to Eugenie?

It all came back then, and I scrambled away from him, looking around for some sign of the Synod members. Snatching the staff from its holder and pointing it at Rand, I eased off the bed and edged toward the door.

"Where are they?" The end of the staff wavered with the shaking of my arm, so I grasped it two-handed, sending sparks out the tip.

"They're not here—Mace doesn't like to leave Elfheim. Don't shoot that thing at me." Rand eased off the bed with his hands up and sat in a chair in the far corner of the room. "Just listen to me a minute before you leave."

The fear dissipated, replaced by its bully classmate, anger. "Go to hell. This is all your fault." My voice was hoarse, and I vaguely remembered screaming as I saw my mother die again and my grandparents give me away. Tish dying. Gerry dying. Rene's brother dying. Jake's life destroyed. So much death. So much loss. I couldn't stop shivering.

"Let me help you." Rand stood up and started toward me, but I held the staff up again and its sparks sent him back to his chair.

"I swear to God if you come anywhere near me, I will fry you." I hadn't been sure the elven staff would work against an elf, but he seemed to respect it.

"They were just supposed to ask you questions, I swear. I would never have taken you to Mace if I'd had any idea he'd try something like a regression. I fought them to get you out of there."

I'd never felt so violated. They'd stripped away my will, torn my memories from me, made me relive things I'd spent years putting behind me, seen private things no one else had any right to. "I'm never going to forgive you for this. Never."

My head pounded, and the room spun in a way that made me queasy. "What are you doing here? Who's downstairs?"

"Sit on the bed before you fall. I promise I won't come near you." Rand gripped the chair arms as if to convince me he wasn't moving. "It's important that we talk and there isn't much time."

"Who's downstairs?" I asked again.

"Alex and one of your Elders. Why do you think my face looks like this?"

I opened my mouth to scream for Alex, but closed it again after taking a closer look at Rand. His lower lip was cut and swollen, a bruise was already purpling on his jaw, and he'd have a black eye within the hour.

"Alex did that?" Good for Alex.

Rand touched a finger to his lip and winced. "He was tearing up my store when I brought you back."

A new panic arose. "Did you hurt him?"

"No, I didn't fight him." Rand started to rise, then thought better of it and settled back in the chair. "Look, we don't have long. If he catches me up here, he'll try to kill me and I'll be forced to defend myself this time. None of us wants that."

I stared at him, wondering what he could do that I hadn't seen. Whatever it was, I didn't want him doing it to Alex. "What *do* you want?"

"I want us to be bonded to each other. It's a short ritual, a blood exchange."

Was he flipping insane? "If I do anything with you involving blood, it will be because you're injured." My voice got louder as I talked, despite Rand's gesturing for me to talk softly. "I want you out of my house. Out of my life. Out of Eugenie's life. If you or any of your Synod members come near me again, I will kill you with your clan's sacred staff."

Rand's gaze on me was steady and intense. "Do you know yet if you'll shift to loup-garou at the full moon?"

The question surprised me and dampened my anger. "What?"

Then the enormity of the question slammed into me. The whole Synod knew I'd been exposed to the loup-garou virus. They'd watched the scene with Jake over and over like a viral Internet video. It was ammunition, and I had no doubt they'd use it. The elves could have me destroyed without Mace Banyan breaking a fingernail.

I shuffled to the bed and sat heavily, leaning against the headboard and closing my eyes. What a disaster. If Mace Banyan did nothing until the full moon, I had one week of my life left. Or he could already have gone to the Elders, in which case Willem Zrakovi was downstairs deciding my fate.

"Answer me, DJ. It's important for us to talk about this before Alex comes up and finds me here." Rand leaned forward in his chair but didn't make a move to come closer.

No point in pretending now. "I don't know for sure, but a blood test has shown the virus is active in my system. I'm already healing fast, which means it isn't dormant. It's virtually assured that I'll shift. The Synod knows I've been exposed, so what are they going to do about it?"

Rand nodded. "Mace will use it to destroy you; he's furious that our staff claimed you, and you have a lot more of our magic at your disposal than we realized. You haven't begun to even discover it yet. This whole thing was set up to see if you were powerful enough with the staff to pose a threat to us, and he's convinced you are."

I shook my head, not understanding. "How can I be a threat to him? To any of you?"

Rand fidgeted in the chair, and I got the impression he'd be pacing the floor if I hadn't been clutching Charlie. "Think about it. If the elves and wizards ever break their truce, the wizards would be at a huge advantage if one of their own could do elven magic."

"Then why are you telling me? If I'm a threat to the Synod, I'm a threat to you."

Rand studied me a moment before answering. "You're not a threat unless the elves and wizards end up in a war, and I don't want that. I actually don't think Mace does either, but he still finds you a threat and your loup-garou exposure makes it easy for him to get rid of you. If the Elders don't lock you away or kill you themselves, he'll find a way to goad you into losing control so the Elders will be forced to act."

Damn. I couldn't wait until next week to move to Old Barataria. I needed to go tonight. I got to my feet and opened the top drawer of my dresser, pulling out clothes and throwing them on the bed. "Get out of here. I have to pack."

Rand was across the room and grasping my wrist before I realized he'd moved. "If you bond with me, you won't shift."

I wrenched my arm away from him and backed up a step. "What kind of crap are you trying to pull on me? Why would I believe anything you say?" I might be impulsive, maybe even naïve at times. But I wasn't stupid.

Rand's blue eyes were almost glowing. "Elves can't become loup-garou. If we bond with a blood exchange, it will counteract the virus. You won't shift, DJ. Mace's threat will be neutralized."

I shoved the pile of clothes out of the way and sat on the bed again. I'd only thought things couldn't get worse. There had to be an angle. "So Mace wants you to bond with me so he can blackmail me into siding with the elves?"

Rand's chuckle held no trace of humor. "Mace would kill me if he found out I'm trying to bond with you."

I looked at the elf, hate and despair and hope mingling in an ugly stew. Elves apparently didn't heal quickly like shapeshifters or weres. If anything, his blackening eye looked worse. I, on the other hand, was feeling stronger by the second. Can't keep a good loup-garou down. "What's in it for you?"

He sat beside me on the bed, shifting farther away when I waggled the staff at him. "Political leverage. My mother is dying, and I will ascend to chief of the Tân, a full member of the Synod. Our clan is the smallest and therefore has the least power. Mace wants to reduce our Synod vote by half. But if I have a connection to the wizards, he won't dare move against me or my clan."

I rubbed my eyes. "I don't want any part of your political crap, and bonding yourself to me doesn't mean the Elders would back you in a Synod power struggle. Forget it."

Rand inched closer. "It will work, and it's good for both of us. You'll be in a stronger position with your Elders as a liaison with the Synod. I'll secure my clan's position in the elven hierarchy and have an alliance with the wizards that would make Mace think twice about ever breaking the truce between our people. And you won't turn loup-garou and either be killed or spend the rest of your life in hiding."

I sighed and closed my eyes. Crap on a freakin' stick. I couldn't even think about the political fallout right now. "Well, doesn't that sound like candy and unicorns? Look, I don't trust you. I'm not agreeing to anything without finding out exactly what this bonding entails, so I need time to think about it. I need to do some research."

Rand gave an impatient growl. "We don't have time. The closer you get to the full moon, the more the virus takes over your system and it will be harder to counteract." He touched tentative fingers to his eye, which had almost swollen shut. Alex's knuckles were probably bruised. "Not to mention the wizards won't let me anywhere near you again, not in time to make this work. It has to be now. I'll tell you whatever you want to know."

Yeah, and I might believe him. Or not. "Okay, what does the bonding mean? You say it gives you political clout, but how?"

He hesitated, which ratcheted up my suspicion level. "It's a sacred union among my people. You'd be given the rights of any full-blooded member of my clan, plus a high standing from being bonded to a member of the Synod once I ascend."

The last elf lesson with Adrian seemed like a month ago instead of a day, but I remembered him saying the elven clans had remained pure. "Tell me this isn't like a marriage because if it is, the answer's not only no, but hell no."

Rand studied the hem of his sweater and didn't meet my eye. God, I'd nailed it. "We'd be mates. But it's not a marriage like you're thinking about."

Right. "Does it involve an exchange of vows?"

He shrugged. "It does."

Uh-huh. "Does it involve a physical consummation?" Because I would never have sex with Quince Randolph. Not. Ever. Happening.

He smiled, which cracked his busted lip and sent a trickle of blood onto his chin. Served him right. "No, except for a small exchange of blood."

"Can we bond until the loup-garou business is over and

you've gotten your political benefit, and then undo it?" Elven divorce court was probably about as entertaining as the scene I'd just endured.

Rand pressed the hem of his sleeve against his lip to stop the bleeding. "Um, well, no. It's permanent." Recognizing the disgust on my face, he spoke faster. "Look, I'm offering you a way out. You can keep your life here. You won't turn loup-garou. You keep the staff. You keep your job. And I know you and Alex are involved. Do you want to leave him?"

God, no, I didn't want to leave him. I wanted to be able to live my life here, not hide out in the Beyond and meet with Alex in stolen moments, if I could even trust myself not to hurt him. Look at the problems Jake was having. I didn't want Alex to start fearing me the way I'd begun to fear Jake.

Tying myself to Quince Randolph for the rest of my life—even in some bonding of convenience—made me ill. I had to consider it, but needed more time.

"I'm sure there's more," I said. "What about my elven skills. Will they change? Will you get power from me?"

"You'll get more from it than me in terms of skills," Rand said. "I won't pick up any wizard's magic, but if we're bonded you'll be immune to our mental influence, even mine. Your empathic and aural skills will be stronger. As for me, well, I'll be able to communicate with you mentally— the way I did in Elfheim, only you'll be able to talk to me as well."

Oh, great. Rand would be able to annoy me from a distance.

Encouraged by my silence, he kept yapping. "This can

be a good thing, Dru. You can stay here in your house. You can see your friends. You don't have to give up your life to either the Elders or the call of the moon."

Speaking of friends . . . "You'd have to break things off with Eugenie because I don't want to see her pulled in the middle of a mess she can't possibly understand. She cares about you, and you've just been using her as a way to get to me. And break up with her in a way that doesn't hurt her or make it look like it has anything to do with me."

"Then you'll do it?"

I closed my eyes. I'd be stuck with some sort of contact with Quince Randolph for the rest of my life, which was disgusting. On the other hand, at least I'd have a life. I'd have my job. I'd have a future in New Orleans. I'd have the possibility of a future with Alex. The Elders might even get some political stability from it with the elves. In the end, maybe it was worth the trade-off. It wasn't like I had to live with the guy. Maybe I'd never even have to see him again.

Besides, with Mace Banyan and the Synod aware of the loup-garou exposure, what choice did I have? Put up with the pest, die nobly, and sign Jake's death warrant as well, or be consigned to the Beyond forever . . . if the Elders didn't find a way to force me back under their control.

Crap. This was too big a decision to have to make in this short a time, but Rand was right. Alex, if not Zrakovi himself, wouldn't allow Rand to get this close to me again. "What do we have to do?"

Rand reached in his jeans pocket, pulled out a small, ornate silver knife, and lifted my arm to make a small incision near where the healed scratch from Jake had been. He lifted my bleeding arm and dropped his mouth to the cut, drawing my blood into him. I tried to pull away but he held it fast, sucking on the wound. What did he think he was, a freaking vampire?

He leaned over, his mouth just above mine, and whispered, "With your blood you are bound to me." He kissed me softly, lingered over it, and I elbowed him in the gut as hard as I could. The metallic taste of my own blood was vile, and I had no sympathy as he doubled over in pain. I still had the growing strength of a loup-garou.

He smiled up at me, his eyes a glaze of glassy blue. He'd gotten off on that. Just gross me out already. "The kiss is part of the ritual. Now, you."

I still had time to back out. Alex would be furious but I was doing this for him as much as for me. For us. For Jake.

I nodded, and Rand flicked the knife across his neck, just over the collarbone. I started to point out how much more intimate this was going to be and insist he cut his arm, but, really, I just wanted it done.

He tilted his head toward his shoulder, baring his neck. I pushed his hair aside and hoped I could do this without barfing. *I don't want to be loup-garou. I don't want to give up my life to live in the Beyond and hide from the Elders. I don't want to be put down like a rabid dog, and I sure as hell don't want to be locked up in Ittoqqortoormiit. If I shift, Mace Banyan wins.*

I touched my tongue lightly against the blood trickling down his neck, and was surprised to find it tasted rich and sweet and most un-bloodlike. I put my lips over the cut and sucked in a tiny bit, trying not to think about what I was doing.

"Say the words," he whispered.

I had to think a few seconds to remember what words he

meant. "With your blood I am bound to you," I said in a flat tone. I wanted him to know I certainly did *not* get off on it.

He smiled. "Now, kiss me."

Ick. "Do I have to?"

"Yes."

Fine, whatever. I leaned in and lightly touched my lips to his, then shoved him as hard as I could when he tried to slip an arm around me. He slid off the bed with a tumble and landed hard on his fine elven ass. If Quince Randolph thought being bonded to me would be a day in the park, he had a few surprises coming. "I hope that hurt."

"It did." He grunted as he climbed to his feet.

I stood up too fast and had to catch myself on the night-stand to keep from falling over. The energy that had been building in my muscles disappeared, and the achiness returned with a vengeance. The cut on my arm continued to bleed. I was no longer recovering like a loup-garou. Hallelujah.

"Now get the hell out of here, Rand. Go home. Think up a way to gently break it off with Eugenie. And keep your freaky Synod away from me."

"I'd suggest you listen to her unless you want your ass handed to you again." The low, hard sound of Alex's voice preceded him in the doorway by a half second. He must've heard Rand hit the floor. "Eugenie's downstairs now. I'd rather not kill you in front of her, but I will. Don't doubt it."

"Talk to you later, Dru." Rand limped past Alex and disappeared into the sitting room. A few seconds later, his boot heels echoed on the stairwell.

I guess some part of me—the part that sneaked an occa-sional romance novel home from the grocery store—wanted

Alex to rush over and hold me, make sympathetic noises, and generally make me feel safe. I didn't remember going back to Rand's in the transport, but I vaguely recalled Alex carrying me across the street and up the stairs of my house. Taking off my boots. Washing blood off my face from the nosebleed I always seemed to get around the heavy use of elven magic. Talking to me in a gentle drone.

Now he stood framed in the doorway with an expression I could only describe as bovine. As in the angry bovine being teased by the clown right before he spears the cowboy's butt with his horns.

"Don't you dare blame me for getting kidnapped by elves." I stood up and waited for the wave of dizziness. The room swayed on cue.

"I don't blame you." Alex pushed himself off the doorjamb and wrapped his arms around me. "I'd kill Quince Randolph if I wasn't afraid it would start an interspecies war."

I rested my cheek against his warm chest and his grip on me tightened. This was what I needed.

"What did they do to you?" His voice was soft. "What did I just walk in on?"

I didn't think I could go through it all, not yet. A lot of the experiences I'd relived, especially from my childhood, weren't even things Alex knew.

I spoke into the dark fabric of his shirt, keeping my eyes focused on one little loose thread next to a buttonhole because I knew if I closed my eyes, I'd see death and loss. "They took control of my mind, my thoughts, my memories. I was helpless to stop them. If I'd been there much longer, I don't think I'd have lived through it."

Alex's arms tightened around me, and standing this close, his fear and anger and sorrow were impossible to keep out. "It's over now. What they did had to be illegal, and I'm going to make sure Zrakovi doesn't slide it under the rug. They have to pay."

I pulled away from him. "There's something else I need to tell you—about why Rand was here."

Alex led me to the bed, and we sat facing each other. "Trying to make excuses for tricking you into a transport, I'm sure." His jaw clenched. "Tricking both of us."

I shook my head. "No, it's more than that." I explained the bonding, the loup-garou angle, the elves' bureaucratic maneuvering, Rand's suspicion that Mace considered me a political liability. "So I did it," I said. "The loup-garou nightmare is over."

Alex hadn't moved. He hadn't spoken. I felt the distance between us growing. "Did it ever occur to you that you might talk to me before making a decision like that? Did it not even pass through your mind that you're not the only one this affects? Jesus." Alex ran his hands through his hair and stood abruptly.

"Wait." I stood too fast and stumbled until the room stopped spinning. "I don't want to be tied to Quince Randolph, but I also don't want to spend the rest of my life running. The elves know about me, Alex. They know I'm carrying the loup-garou virus, and they know Jake caused it. Mace Banyan could destroy us all. If this neutralizes him and puts the whole issue to rest, we can get on with our lives. Rand's a minor nuisance by comparison."

"Shit." Alex sat on the edge of the bed with a slump of shoulders. "How did they find out?"

I sat beside him. "They saw it when they were plundering through my head—watched the whole scene with Jake more than once, like a freaking movie. Rand thinks Mace plans to let the Elders kill me, or set me up in some way so they have no choice. Then the elves can get their staff back."

"Why not just give it to them?"

A question I wished I could answer. "I tried, but there's something more going on with them I don't understand. I think the staff is just an excuse. Something political that Rand's involved in. Maybe some power play within the Synod."

I had to make him understand. "I don't want to leave you here and live in the Beyond like I've done something wrong. I don't want to be like Jake, afraid of who I'm going to hurt. I don't want you to end up being afraid of me."

Finally, the tears came. I tried to stop them, but the levee had broken, flooding me with so much hurt and anger and fear I thought I might drown in it.

Alex pulled me against him. "I get why you did it, but I don't like the idea of Quince Randolph in our lives. I don't trust him."

"Neither do I, but we'll figure it out." We had to.

He held me but didn't say anything more. We were touching but I felt the gap between us and didn't know how to bridge it.

"DJ, I'm doing my best here, but . . ." Alex shook his head. "I don't know what I'm doing anymore. What's right, what's wrong, what's best for everybody. Nothing can just be simple with us."

With me, he meant. I swiped my palms across my swollen

eyes and stood up. I knew Alex was frustrated by yet another layer of my messy life, but as much as I'd like to fix it for him, I didn't have any answers.

"I'm going to take a shower." I turned and walked to the dresser, looking in the mirror at a woman whose face said she'd spent the last few hours in hell.

Alex cleared his throat, making me think he'd choked back a few tears of his own. "Make it a quick one. Zrakovi's downstairs."

24

More than an hour later, just after two a.m., I stood in the living room with Eugenie while Alex, Zrakovi, and Rand sat at my kitchen table—the latter only because Zrakovi insisted he stay. They were waiting for me to do some quick damage control with my best friend and send her on her way.

"Tell me what's going on, DJ." Tears shone in Eugenie's eyes. "I'm begging you. Look at Rand. He's been beaten up, and it's obvious Alex did it. He told me things weren't working out between us and he didn't want to see me anymore."

She tightened her lips as she looked over my shoulder at Rand. "The only thing Alex and Rand have in common is you, so tell me what happened."

I was going to hell for lying, no doubt about it. "Rand got mixed up in some of our business, that's all. And my boss from the FBI is here." I pointed through the kitchen door at Zrakovi, who sat at the head of the table in his business suit, his expression blank but his shoulders tense. "Let us talk and then I'll come to your house and tell you everything I can. I promise."

Eugenie looked at the floor, and the hurt in her eyes when she looked back at me broke my heart. "You always say that, DJ. Do you know how many times you've said, 'I'll tell you everything when I can'? And you never do. I know you have an important big-shot job. I know I'm just a hairdresser. But we're supposed to be friends."

God, I'd never made her feel inferior, had I? I didn't think of her as "just" anything. She was the funniest, most warm-hearted, most generous person I'd ever met. She didn't have a dishonest bone in her body.

But I did. Maybe my reasons were sound, but I had lied to her again and again. I closed my eyes because I was too chickenshit to look at her when my hollow "I'm sorry" came out. "I'll try harder. I really will."

"Trying's not enough." She pulled her shoulders back and gave me a fierce look before walking out, ignoring Rand. Any grounding ritual had long worn off, and there was enough hurt and anger floating around this house to drown in. I didn't know if I could ever put things right with her unless I told her everything, and my hatred of Quince Randolph—who would now and forevermore be a part of my life in some way—grew deeper.

I'd made what I thought was the best long-term decision for everyone and hadn't considered what the short-term fallout would be for Alex and Eugenie. Asking Alex his opinion before I made a decision hadn't occurred to me, and it should have. I'd tried to do the right thing for everyone and still screwed it up.

When I returned to the kitchen, Alex was seething at Rand, Rand had pressed a bag of frozen peas to his battered face, and Zrakovi thrummed his fingers on the tabletop.

Quince Randolph might not be the scariest elf on the block but only because he'd gotten his way so far. He was strong, devious, and God only knew what kind of powers he had. Eugenie thought relationships were all about love. In the prete world, love was an inconvenience or, at best, a perk. In the prete world, it was all about power.

I sat in the empty chair, wishing I could be anywhere else, except maybe Elfheim. "Can't we talk about this tomorrow?" My voice rasped like a three-pack-a-day smoker. I didn't remember many details of what my body had been up to while my brain was being plundered like one of Jean Lafitte's pirated galleons, but crying and screaming had been involved.

"No." Zrakovi sipped a cup of coffee someone had made, probably Alex. The Elder's usual laid-back friendliness had turned terse and somber. "I must know what happened. The full Council of Elders will convene in a few hours to decide on the actions we wish to take against the Synod. Start at the beginning."

I glared at Rand. "Please. Feel free to go first."

He gave me a tight-lipped smile. "Mace Banyan asked me to bring Dru—I mean DJ—to the Synod instead of waiting for the meeting you'd set up. They wanted to question her in Elfheim without any of you controlling her answers. No offense. It wasn't supposed to be any more than that. Just questions and answers."

Zrakovi turned to me, his expression leaving no doubt that a recap was nonnegotiable. I clutched my coffee mug and went through it in monotone. I didn't leave out any details, even the most private ones about my mother or how I'd trashed my parents' house when she died using raw, emotion-fueled physical magic more powerful than any I'd been able to duplicate since.

Gerry always said it was because I got in my own head too much, a detail I didn't share.

"Mostly, they wanted to see anytime I'd used elven magic, how I'd discovered my skills, and anything that . . ."—tore me up emotionally—"was particularly painful in my life," I said. "I don't know why they needed so much detail."

"To see how much of a threat you pose, gauge how much of our magic you can do, and watch how you react under stress," Rand said, ignoring a look from Alex hot enough to boil water. "But they broke the agreement I had with them by performing a regression. A regular human wouldn't have survived it. Maybe not even a regular wizard." He turned his good eye to Zrakovi. "I'm sorry. I got Dru out as quickly as I could, and will be punished by the Synod for it."

Rand had more layers than a Vidalia onion. He was positioning himself to be the go-to elf for the wizards, and he thought bonding with me would strengthen that position. He was already working his political angle. In his own way, Rand was more devious than Jean Lafitte, only without the charm or the French accent. At least Jean had his own, albeit skewed, sense of honor.

Alex spoke up for the first time, his voice tight and angry. "Is regression legal? It's a mental version of rape. They imposed their will on DJ by force, took away her choices, did things to her without her consent. They should have to pay for it." He turned eyes of dark brown fire to Rand. "All of them."

Zrakovi leaned back in his chair, fingers steepled in front

of him. "I need to check precedent. The elves have had little to do with other species until now, so it might not have been an issue that has ever arisen, at least not in recent memory." He pierced Rand with a forbidding look. "If it isn't illegal now, rest assured I will be bringing it up before the Interspecies Council and asking for sanctions."

I sipped the now-lukewarm coffee and wondered what sanctions would be considered fair trade for what I'd endured. Maybe dragging the Synod members behind Rene's shrimp trawler through gator-infested waters? That would certainly make me feel better.

"Also, Randolph left out an important part of his story." Instead of dissipating, Alex's anger level continued to rise. "About talking DJ into bonding with him."

Rand's jaw clenched and I choked on a gasp. Alex had lost his freaking mind. Zrakovi obviously didn't know I'd been exposed to the loup-garou virus, which was the only reason I'd agreed to the bonding. Once he knew, he'd easily deduce Jake's involvement. The Elders would eventually learn it from the elves, but not tonight. We needed time to figure out a way to protect Jake.

"It was a preemptive move, for political reasons," I said, giving Alex a warning look.

"I explained to DJ that my clan is in jeopardy," Rand said quickly. "Our numbers are small, for a variety of reasons. Having an alliance with her will give us leverage when I take my seat on the Synod, probably in a matter of months. In turn, it will strengthen the alliance between the wizards and elves. There are those among the elven people who would see our long truce broken, or at least compromised."

He rested a hand on Zrakovi's arm, and I felt the shiver of his will . . . He was using elven magic on an Elder!

I whipped my gaze to Zrakovi's face, looking for a sign of elven mind control, and kicked at Rand under the table. He jerked his hand back as the toe of my shoe made hard contact with his shin on the second try. He yelled in my head: *That hurt*!

Good.

"Interesting." Zrakovi shook his head, probably to rid his mind of elven cobwebs. "It could provide a bridge between our people, which we need since relations are already strained over border negotiations. What I don't understand, Drusilla, is why you agreed. Was Mr. Randolph forthcoming about what a bonding means in his world?"

I didn't dare look at Alex. "I understand it's permanent. But for us it will be a business partnership, not a m-marriage." The word would barely come out, and I wished my mental communication skills extended to Alex so I could remind him again why I'd done this. "It's merely a partnership of convenience."

The room's silence was palpable, full of weight and as electrically charged as a supercell thunderstorm. The screech of Alex's chair legs across the floor was jarring. "I can't deal with anything else tonight. DJ, I'll talk to you tomorrow. Willem, I'll be sending you a report on the Axeman case tomorrow as well."

The back door slammed before I could think of words to stop him. He knew my reasons were sound, that it was the best of all horrible options. I needed to give him time to cool off and think things through, and trust in his feelings.

"We're going to have to revisit this, to talk about the

implications of a wizard-elf bond, but I have to deal with the kidnapping and regression first." Zrakovi pushed his chair back. "DJ, I'll let you know what measures the Elders will take against the Synod. Mr. Randolph, while I appreciate that you brought Drusilla home at physical risk to yourself, she would never have been taken without your subterfuge. You'll be hearing from us soon as well, bonding or no bonding."

I turned to look at Rand, who'd settled back in his chair looking pleased with himself until Zrakovi's last words. Now his mouth settled into a horizontal line. His voice in my head was petulant: *I might need your help with him since you won't let me influence him.*

I turned away. Quince Randolph had come between Eugenie and me. He was threatening to come between Alex and me. If he thought I'd intercede on his behalf with the Elders, he'd bonded himself to the wrong wizard.

As soon as Zrakovi's feet sounded on the stairwell and his footsteps caused the ceiling overhead to creak, Rand broke the silence. "Are you okay, Dru?"

"Hm. Let's see. I've been kidnapped, emotionally violated, and forced by circumstance to bond myself for life to a treacherous, lying elf. Does that sound okay to you?"

"This is going to be a good thing—you'll see." Rand reached across the table to take my hand, but I pulled it away.

I left him in the kitchen and walked into the living room, looking around for Charlie. Sure enough, the staff had followed me from the bedroom and was propped against the wall near the guest room doorway. The only thing elves had ever been good for: making that staff.

"If you think this bonding thing gives you house

privileges, you're out of your elven mind." I left Charlie where he was and slumped into my white lawn chair. Life had been so simple a week ago. No loup-garou threat. No bonded elf. No undead serial killer. And I'd had furniture.

Rand sat cross-legged on the floor near my feet. "We need to talk. I want to clarify some of the things that will happen because of the bond."

A hysterical laugh escaped as I envisioned calling my grandmother in Alabama and telling her she had an elf in the family. She didn't even want a wizard in the family. "If you tell me that—oops—you were lying when you said this deal didn't have to be consummated physically, you can forget it."

Rand reached up and rested a hand on my knee. I reached down and zapped him with a burst of my magic. I could do that much without the staff.

"Ow." He shook his fingers, trying to jolt the feeling back into them. "I didn't realize you were so violent."

"We aren't in Elfheim any longer, buddy. Keep your hands to yourself." He'd think violent if he sprung any more nasty surprises on me.

"To answer your question, no more consummation is necessary—that's what the blood exchange was for. But sex will be amazing with us. You'll change your mind. One of the side effects of the bonding is increased attraction to each other."

Oh my God. He was delusional. "You're forgetting one thing. I hate you."

He smiled. "You're just angry right now. I think you're beautiful."

I looked at Rand. He was flat-out gorgeous, blackening

eye and all. "I think you're beautiful too, but it doesn't change the fact that I hate you. Go home. I need some sleep."

"Should I move in with you? Or would you rather move in with me?"

Oh, hell no. "Go home."

He ignored me. Again. "Tell me about the Axeman. Maybe I can help."

I stood up and walked around the living room, making my circuitous way to the guest room door where my friend Charlie waited. "Well, it looks like I'm his target now. He was acting on his own at first, but he seems to have come under the control of a necromancer. Can elves do necromancy?" I didn't have that many personal enemies, but every member of the Synod qualified.

Rand shook his head. "That's dark wizard's magic. Our magic has nothing to do with the dead."

No, they only dealt in mental torture. "Then I don't see how you can help. I do appreciate that you found a way to fix the loup-garou problem, but I'm done for tonight. Go home."

"I think I should stay here and protect—"

I grabbed Charlie and whipped around, pointing it at him. "Get the hell out of my house."

He rose to his feet in a fluid, graceful motion. "You wouldn't."

"No?" I fed energy into the staff and sent out a short blast of fire that melted one leg of my lawn chair. Adrian would have been so proud—that was exactly what I was aiming for.

Rand yelped and jumped aside. "Are you insane?"

I assumed my sweetest voice. "Get used to it, honey. Now, please go home."

He shook his head as he stalked to the front door. "Obviously, you need to calm down. If you need me, you only have to think something at me."

"Stay out of my head."

"Night, Dru."

And don't call me Dru! I shouted at him mentally after he closed the door behind him.

I shuffled into the small office/guest room, pulling aside the curtain to see if the lights were on in Alex's house. It was dark. With Jake absent, he might go to the Gator to unwind and calm down. At least I hope he calmed down.

Sebastian leapt onto the daybed and I sat next to him, scratching behind his black ears. He purred and head-butted my arm. I must be giving off a really pathetic vibe.

"Got good news and bad news, my friend." He fixed his crossed blue eyes on me and flicked an ear. "Good news is, I'm not going to turn into a wolf and have you for Sunday dinner. Bad news is, you've got a new daddy and he's an elf."

25

Damage control is hard to do from a deep freeze, and both Alex and Eugenie had me on ice. I'd left voice mails for both of them as soon as I woke up midmorning. Adrian had left a message that he was tied up in Edinburgh for at least another day, so I had time on my hands.

I was sick to death of thinking about the annoying elf across the street, and totally out of ideas on the Axeman case. The *Times-Pic* reporter was still in critical condition and hadn't regained consciousness. I wasn't sure what help she could be, anyway. I knew who the attacker was. I just didn't know the motive of his necromantic accomplice.

What I *could* do with my free morning was work on my skills with Charlie. I never knew when I might need to melt another lawn chair.

Two hours later, I parked the Pathfinder in my semi-hidden spot near the back side of Six Flags, with Rene Delachaise riding shotgun. Where the chaos of my life frustrated Alex, it amused Rene. Plus, he needed a distraction. Deer and small game-hunting season was in full swing, but he'd always hunted with Robert. He needed an escape from his grief over his lost twin.

So he'd readily agreed to hang out and play bodyguard again. While I hated being the little woman who called on the guy to protect her, it would be stupid to ignore the fact that I was being targeted by a maniac. Rene wasn't a big guy, but he was smart, strong, and enjoyed a good fight.

I left my backpack in the SUV and enacted a camouflage charm in case anyone drove by. We slipped inside the fence, and Rene whistled as he took in the surreal view. "First time I been out here, wizard. This is some crazy shit."

"That pretty much describes my life these days." I decided to practice first on Jean Lafitte's Pirate Ship, then move to the shooting range figures. Rene sat on a bench to watch.

Aiming at the P in *pirate*, I channeled a small burst of my magic into the staff and promptly fell on my butt on the concrete. A hole burned in what was now Jean Lafitte's irate Ship. If there hadn't been black smoke still pouring from the former P, I'd have attributed the thick red cable of fire that had zoomed from the tip of the staff to wishful thinking.

Rene walked over and pulled me to my feet. "That was pretty powerful stuff, babe. Is your magic getting stronger or is it because of your new husband?"

I'd told Rene about the bonding, figuring he'd be the person least likely to judge me. I'd been right; he laughed at me. A lot. Ridicule I could handle.

"The elf is not my husband, but yeah, I'm thinking the bonding has ramped up my ability to use the staff." Not only had I hit my target, but I'd used very little of my own physical magic. It had been a play shot. When I melted the chair last night, it hadn't been this effortless, but maybe the bonding had taken a few hours to kick in.

Now I could kick some serious butt with this thing. Although a lifelong bond with Rand seemed a high price to pay for butt-kicking.

Rene tensed. "We got company, babe. You know that car?"

A black sedan had stopped near the turnstiles, its windows tinted so dark I couldn't see who sat inside. Kind of conservative for gangstas; kind of upscale for cops.

Whoever it was, we weren't authorized to be here. "We better get back to the Pathfinder."

I turned toward the fence, but after a few steps realized Rene hadn't moved.

I turned to find him still watching the car. The passenger door of the sedan opened slowly, and a large, bulky figure emerged. It was a profile I'd seen a couple of days ago in my own library summoning circle. Except this time, the Axeman carried his ax.

"Shit, it's the Axeman." Rene finally realized we had a bigger problem than a trespassing fine. "Let's go!"

We took off, but the killer moved with surprising speed for an oversize dead guy. I shot at him with the staff, but my aim was back to its normal awfulness. I'd never practiced shooting over my shoulder while running for my life.

Rene, however, was better prepared. He'd pulled a pistol from somewhere, stopped, and wheeled around long enough to fire two rounds. The Axeman shouted in anger and clutched his upper arm, but didn't stop running.

"Come on!" Rene and I raced across the entrance to the midway, looking for a hiding place while, behind my eyes, a nonstop reel played of the blood-soaked bed in the reporter's house. My stomach cramped as fear mixed with the gumbo we'd had for lunch.

If we could make him look for us, I could zap him with the staff from a safe position. Rene could shoot him again to slow him down and give me a good target.

"Over here." Spotting an open door in the center of the flying chairs carousel, we darted for it and slipped inside. Rene pushed me behind him and tugged the metal door closed except for an inch so we could see out. The enclosure, once filled with the mechanical equipment that powered the ride, smelled of dried mold spores and rust, and I pinched my nose to avoid sneezing. My heart pounded so hard and fast it was visible in the erratic rise and fall of my sweater. If Rene was scared, he didn't show it.

I held the staff to the side so I could shoot around Rene, and stilled when the Axeman walked past, just outside our hiding spot. Rene had his gun cocked and aimed at the opening.

The Axeman stopped, and through the narrow slit, I saw his gaze roaming the park grounds where he'd last seen us.

I held my breath. He turned to the left, then right, then looked directly at us.

I didn't see him move. Suddenly, he was just there, ripping the metal door off its hinges and reaching inside, his fingers clutching for me over Rene—until the pistol fired again. The Axeman fell back, clutching his thigh.

Rene pulled me out of the machinery room. "Let's go."

We ran about ten yards before I turned and fired the staff. The Axeman had sat up and was staring at his leg wound, but managed to roll out of the way of my shot, falling between the seats that hung by heavy chains from the carousel's top.

An unholy screeching and explosion of smoke poured from the room where we'd been hiding, and the carousel creaked to life. I'd missed the Axeman but hit the flying chairs carousel. A warbling, tinny version of a jazzy old Louis Armstrong tune—I think it was "Basin Street Blues"—blasted from speakers at the top of the structure, and the carousel began to turn, the hanging chairs swaying around the Axeman as he stood up and stared at the ride, transfixed.

It was the music. That stuff about the jazz had been true. Why hadn't I put some of those downloads on my phone?

This was my chance, so I took careful aim and fired again. He turned just as the flames reached him, but howled in pain as they glanced off his arm. Most of the fire went into the carousel, but smoke rose from the sleeve of his coat. This time, the carousel ground to a stop and so did the music.

Rene and I ran again. At the pirate ship, I risked a look back. Shit. Who knew a guy that big could move so fast? He was halfway between us and the carousel, and gaining ground—until he took an abrupt left turn. Where had he gone?

As soon as we raced around the corner toward the Pathfinder, I had my answer. The Axeman had circled around us and now faced us from the other side. He was no mindless zombie; he'd positioned himself between us and the SUV.

"Who the hell sent you? Why are you after me?" I kept the staff raised and pointed, backing away from him. In my peripheral vision, I saw Rene backing off at a different angle, his gun drawn. I should just zap him, but I wanted an answer to my questions.

The Axeman stopped, his dark, slicked-down hair not moving despite the breeze. His lips parted, his voice a hoarse whisper. "I don't know why, only that you have to be taken care of before the other wizard will let me go on with my real work."

"Who's controlling you—what does he look like?" I took a step back and aimed the staff. If old Axel wasn't going to be more helpful than this, I might as well fire.

Just as I sent another burst of energy into the staff, Rene fired another round and caught the Axeman in the shoulder with a bullet, dropping him to the ground. My thick, fiery rope went over his head.

An explosion behind the Axeman stopped all of us, and I stared in horror as one of my SUV's side mirrors landed in the dirt near the killer's feet. The rest of the Pathfinder had burst into flames.

I raised the staff again, but the Axeman was already climbing to his feet—could nothing stop this guy? "Draw him toward the tunnel and I'll get behind him," Rene shouted, so I ran, slipping into the first darkened storefront of the midway, one I'd seen earlier while looking for a hydromancy spot. The back wall of the building had a big hole in it, and the haunted tunnel lay adjacent.

I tripped over something in the gloom of the store and fell to my knees. My hands landed on fur. Fur that squealed and ran across my fingers before moving farther into the shadows. Oh-my-God-rat. I'd landed on a freaking rat.

"Where are you, wizard?" The Axeman's voice rasped near the entrance, and the blade of his ax cracked through what was left of the wooden doorframe. I fumbled in my makeshift potions belt and pulled out one of my fire charms. So far I hadn't been close enough to the Axeman to use one of my premade concoctions, but that was about to change.

I scrambled to the back wall and propelled myself through the hole in the concrete structure, landing in the weeds behind the building. The staff rolled out of my hand, and I rolled after it, the whistle of air from the ax blade following me, along with chips of concrete. Through the opening, I tossed the open vial containing the charm, and heard a bellow of pain in response. Good. Something we were doing had to slow the guy down eventually. He had three bullet wounds and at least that many burns.

Yet I heard him shuffling again. Hoping I'd bought myself a few seconds, I ran perpendicular to the midway and headed for the Krewe of Kreeps train ride and its tunnel entrance.

I picked up a fist-size chunk of concrete and waited at the mouth of the tunnel until I was sure he'd climbed out of the concrete building and spotted me.

Stepping inside, I pressed my back against the wall to the right of the door and waited. If I could trap him inside the tunnel, I might be able to collapse it on top of him with the staff.

His footsteps slowed as they got closer, then he stopped outside the entrance, probably no more than three or four feet away. His labored breath sounded ridiculously loud.

I pressed my back against the interior wall, not daring to breathe. Finally, I heard him again. He walked inside the tunnel a few feet to my left and stopped.

Moving slowly, lest even a rustle of fabric give me away, I tossed the concrete chunk as far ahead as I could. When it hit a train rail with a clatter, the Axeman took off, running deeper into the tunnel. This was my chance. I slipped out behind him and stopped a few feet from the tunnel entrance, aiming the staff at the top.

My shot hit true, but the structure of the tunnel was metal and not wood, so all I got was a rain of concrete and rebar before I heard the Axeman scream in rage, followed by the thud of his footsteps growing louder as he returned to the entrance.

Where the hell was Rene? With no answer to that question, I couldn't strategize. I had to run. And the Axeman ran faster than me. Simple as that. I'd have to shoot him close-range with the staff. I stopped and turned, aiming Charlie and waiting for him to get within a few feet.

Rene almost beat me to it. The Axeman had gotten nearly within grabbing range when I hit the side of his jaw with fire from the staff and Rene caught the other side of his face with a bullet. The left side of Rene's face was covered in blood. Now, so was the Axeman's.

The killer fell toward me, his eyes wide and empty, and I threw myself to the side to keep him from landing on me. Instead, I fell on the staff. Charlie broke with a sickening crack.

But at least for now, the Axeman was fading back into the Beyond. I shifted to look back at the entrance to Six Flags and wasn't surprised to see the dark sedan had disappeared, probably with the necromancer inside.

Rene collapsed on the ground next to me, staring at the now-empty spot where the Axeman had fallen. "That was intense, babe."

26

I sat cross-legged on the ground near the carousel, assessing Charlie's condition. It wasn't a complete break, but enough to make it fragile, not to mention crooked.

"Put some duct tape on it," Rene said, looking over my shoulder. "It fixes anything."

"It's worth a try." I'd spent some time experimenting and found it still channeled energy, but the fire was weak and had a range of less than two feet. I'd prefer any would-be murderers didn't get that close.

My heart gave a lurch at the screech of tires in the main parking lot, and I scrambled to my feet, ready to run to the transport.

"It's just Alex," Rene said. "You called him?"

Actually, I hadn't. But there he was, running for us at a full sprint, the driver's side door of his truck hanging open.

As soon as he spotted us, he slowed to a trot, then a walk, his expression—and the emotions boiling off his skin so strongly they might as well be visible—a cocktail of relief and fear, with a chaser of fury.

"Shifter's pissed off," Rene muttered. He met Alex

halfway to the truck, stopped to talk a few seconds, then continued walking to the parking lot. Giving us privacy.

"Thank God." Alex jerked me into a hug, and I wrapped my arms around him, giving myself over to the aftershock I didn't realize I'd been holding back. His hand traced circles on my back till I finally stopped shaking. Neither of us spoke for a long time, and I calmed at the slow, steady beat of his heart beneath the soft fabric of his black sweater.

Finally, I pulled away enough to look up at him, but kept my hands on his arms like they were anchors. "How did you know I was here?"

Alex took a step backward, and I let my hands drop. "From Randolph. I guess one of the bonding side effects is he can tell if you're in trouble. He said he couldn't drive right now, so he called me. I'm glad he did. And I'm glad you brought Rene with you, but you should have asked me."

I wrapped my arms around my middle, suddenly chilled. "You were so angry when you left my house after the meeting with Zrakovi, I wasn't sure you would come. Plus, you weren't answering your phone. I wanted to give you some space."

He opened his mouth to respond but sirens—lots of them—were speeding our way. "We've gotta get out of here." He looked around. "I take it the smell of burning rubber and gasoline is coming from your Pathfinder? Where was it parked?"

I pointed at the smoke drifting from behind the fire-mangled fence and started walking toward his truck. "There's what's left of it. And yeah, I blew it up. I'll fill you in on the way home."

Ever practical, Alex insisted on driving to my spot behind

the park, where we all did a quick search to make sure my license plate and any other identifiable, unburned parts of the Pathfinder were collected.

"You realize that once again I've hidden evidence?" Alex grumbled, sounding more like himself. He drove, I sat in front, and Rene had stretched out on the backseat with the portion of half-melted dashboard that had my VIN on it. The cut on Rene's face, which he'd gotten when the Axeman backhanded him in the rat building, had almost healed.

"Before I met you I never hid evidence." Alex slung gravel as he turned onto a side road and wound his way back toward civilization. "Now, thanks to you, I've hidden bodies. I've lied to the police. I've falsified reports to the Elders. I've been cursed by a maniac nymph and turned into a pink dog. And let's not forget looking the other way when your friend Jean Lafitte stole a goddamn Corvette."

That was the longest speech I'd heard Alex deliver in a while. I bit my tongue and looked out the window, while Rene chuckled softly from the backseat. No point denying I'd been a bad influence on Mr. Straight and Narrow, but I hadn't forced him to do any of those things.

"Why couldn't Rand drive?" He had a van for hauling plants and some kind of boxy earth-friendly car.

"No idea. Don't care." Alex took a curve too fast, and I grabbed the edge of the seat. He'd sealed his emotions like the lid of a mason jar, but he didn't drive this way when he was calm. Thank goodness Rene was with us; it prevented us from fighting. I couldn't handle another argument right now, and we seemed to keep treading the same patch of ground.

"Tell me what happened back there."

I gave Alex a blow-by-blow of the Axeman's attack. He kept his eyes on the winding roads, but listened intently. "What was the make and model of the car that dropped him off?"

"I don't know. Looked new." I turned to Rene. "Did you catch what model it was?"

"No." He sat up and looked out the window. "Black or dark gray sedan, dark-tinted windows. *Really* dark tint. It didn't have a license plate on the front. Looked expensive."

Alex handed me his cell. "Call Ken—speed dial five—and tell him what happened." He'd gone into full enforcer mode, which seemed to calm him down. At least he wasn't driving erratically anymore.

When I got a little carried away telling Ken about how fast the Axeman could run, and that I thought he'd dropped his ax in the building with the rat, Alex snatched the phone from me, slammed it to his ear, and barked out the car description. "Put some feelers out. Sounds like a luxury rental so start calling the rental places and asking about their high-end stock."

He listened a few seconds then ended the call and tossed the phone in the center console. "Where the hell was the heir apparent while all this was going on?"

"Who?" Rand was the only heir apparent I knew of, and he'd apparently been tied up with a mulch emergency and couldn't drive.

"Hoffman," Alex said. "Where was he? Wasn't this supposed to be your regular lesson time?"

I shrugged. "He's still in Edinburgh. Said he'd be back tomorrow, but I thought I'd go ahead and practice with the staff. Why's he the heir apparent?"

Alex had wound back to the I-10 and merged into the traffic inching toward the city. "I did a little digging. You know how you said you never figured out how he got such a trusted spot with the Elders without being one himself?"

Alex had done a background check on Adrian Hoffman? No wonder I liked this man. "I thought he'd just ingratiated himself with his knowledge of elves. What else?"

"His father's the First Elder, and I heard he was really pissed at Zrakovi for chastising Adrian after what happened last month and then sending him to New Orleans."

"Ask me, he got off easy," Rene said, his voice rough with emotion. I wasn't the only one blaming Adrian for Robert's and Tish's deaths.

"No wonder he's such a pompous ass." I pondered this new bit of information. The First Elder sat at the pinnacle of the wizarding hierarchy as the senior Elder above the seven wizards representing each continent.

I kneaded my temples, which throbbed with the aftermath of the magic I'd done, not to mention the stress. "With the staff broken, there's probably no need for Adrian to continue these lessons unless he knows how to repair it." Or the duct tape worked, or wood glue. Although I supposed Adrian could fill me in on other elven skills and traditions. Like bonding.

I stared out the window at the ships as we climbed the high arc of the Industrial Canal bridge, crested the summit, and crept down the other side toward downtown New Orleans.

"You think the necromancer was in the car?" I'd been thinking about it and realized there was something I hadn't asked either Etienne Boulard or Jonas Adamson—the range of necromantic magic.

"Probably." Alex beat a rhythm on the steering wheel with his fingers. "But unless we get a break when Ken calls the rental places, there's not much we can do other than wait for him to come after you again. I assume he can't come back for a while since you guys killed him—well, killed him for now."

"Not necessarily." A normal member of the historical undead would take a while to regenerate enough power to come back across from the Beyond on his own, especially after such a violent dispatch. The necromantic magic threw everything into question, though. The magic could speed up or even override the normal regeneration process for the historical undead.

"Why don't we sit down tonight, grab some dinner, and strategize?" If I were going to be serial killer bait, we needed a plan. And Alex and I really needed to talk about personal stuff.

His jaw tightened—the only hint that he was still upset. "We'll sit down with Ken tomorrow at your office." His voice softened, even though we both knew Rene could hear. "Just give me a little time."

"Sure." Disappointed, I watched the shotgun houses of Mid-City give way to the shotgun houses of Uptown.

I wanted to fix everything and make it right, but if Alex needed time to think, I'd stop pushing. The current crisis had exposed a flaw that had been in our relationship since Hurricane Katrina, when he'd been forced to choose between helping me and doing his job in the way that made sense to him—with clean, clear decisions that fell within the rulebook. My life had no rulebook.

When Alex parked in the back lot between our houses,

he left me with a wave that felt more like a kiss-off than a kiss-you-later.

"Give him time." Rene patted my shoulder before climbing into his pickup. "Shifters and weres, most of us like things straight and simple. And nothing personal, babe, but you ain't either one."

"You don't seem to have a problem with it." Rene liked my chaos. He didn't even seem upset that it had almost gotten him killed today.

"Big difference between me and Alex." He grinned at me out his truck window. "You aren't my woman. Later, babe."

Great. Relationship advice from a merman who bought questionable sexual-potency tonics. Life had come to this.

The pungent, nutty smell of Thai food hit me as soon as I opened my back door. I looked at the array of takeout boxes on the kitchen table and followed the sound of a male voice into my front parlor. Rand sat on the floor, fondling my cat and talking to him in that weird, guttural language. The wretch (feline variety) gave me a cross-eyed, baleful look before yowling once and running away.

"You want a cat? He's yours. I inherited him and he's never liked me." I considered myself a dog person, Alex notwithstanding, and thought the fact that I ended up with a surly feline proved God had a sense of humor.

I threw my phone and keys on the kitchen counter, thankful I'd had them in my pocket instead of in my back-pack. It would take me hours to recreate all the base charms and potions I had in that pack. I kept the staff in my hand. With any luck, I could threaten Rand without him being able to tell it was broken.

"Tell me how you got in here, and then go home. I can't deal with you right now."

He looked up and froze when he saw the staff in my hand. "I picked up dinner—had to guess at what you might like." He frowned. "What happened to the staff?"

Of course the freaking elf would have perfect vision. "None of your business. How did you get in here?"

Rand followed me into the kitchen and leaned against the doorway as I dumped cat food into Sebastian's bowl and refilled his water dish. "Sebastian, you unfaithful ingrate— come here!" I yelled loud enough that Rand winced. "Dinner!"

"I got chicken pad thai, spring rolls, red curry. You want extra nuts?"

Good grief. The elf was dense as week-old bread pudding.

"Rand." I held up the Meow Mix-coated spoon. "I'd rather eat this than sit down with you. It has been a bad day. I don't want to talk about weird elven politics. I don't want to talk about the Axeman. I don't want to talk about bondage. Go home."

"Do you want beer or soda?"

I rinsed off the spoon and stuck it in the dishwasher, listening to my stomach rumble. And I did need to find out how he'd gotten past my wards. Still, it set a terrible precedent.

"Get out of my house." I glanced at the kitchen table. "Leave the food. I'll pay you for it later."

He got both beer and soda out of my fridge, and I walked to stand beside him. With a hard poke, I stuck the staff against his arm. "It might be cracked but it's still going to hurt like hell when I burn you."

He looked down at me, but his face lacked the fear I wanted to see. "Do it."

Damn it, he was calling me out. I wouldn't really shoot at him unless it was in self-defense, and he knew it.

"Fine." I jerked a chair away from the table and sat down. "Soda."

He slid a diet soda in front of me and took the other chair, looking from my ash-smudged cheeks to the tear in my jeans just above the ankle. I've had doctor's exams less thorough than Rand's visual inspection. If I had tires, he'd be kicking them.

He nodded. "You're okay, then."

"Except for the staff. And how did you get in my house?" I'd keep asking as long as he kept not answering.

"I jimmied your back lock; you need a stronger one. Your security wards don't work on me now. How did the staff get broken?"

Great. The person I most wanted to keep out of my house, other than the Axeman, and he knew how to pick locks.

"Something heavy fell on it." I held up the crooked, cracked piece of wood that glowed only faintly now. I didn't add that the heavy thing was me. "Think it would work with duct tape or wood glue holding it together?"

"Let me see it."

I hesitated.

"It won't work for me—only for its master." He held his hand out, and I reluctantly let him have it. Rand examined the cracked wood. "The core is damaged so glue or tape wouldn't work. Can you fire it at all?"

I poured my soda in a glass, trying to decide whether it would be safer to let Rand know my power boost from the staff was diminished, or to let him think nothing had changed. It all came down to whether or not I trusted him to be loyal to me rather than the Synod.

This would be his first test—and if he failed it, his last. "I can use it at maybe a quarter of its normal strength, and only at short range."

Rand held the staff up to the light and studied it more closely. "Since it's the staff of the fire elves, I should be able to repair it, with your permission as its master. I'll ask my mother . . . No, on second thought, better not mention it to her." He thought a few seconds. "I'll slip into Elfheim tomorrow and pick up what I need."

"You don't trust your mother?" I didn't trust his mother. I didn't even trust him. But *he* should trust her.

"Her, yes, but no one else." He handed the broken staff back to me. "I'll get what we need and we'll try to fix it tomorrow night."

Uh-huh. I'd believe that when I had a repaired staff in my hand, shooting ropes of fire at something—maybe him.

I sighed, hunger and anger and exhaustion fighting for dominance in my heart. I didn't have the energy to fight with him anymore, and if he really could repair the staff, it wouldn't kill me to eat dinner with him. "Go ahead and start eating. I need to wash up."

I dragged myself to the guest bathroom and scrubbed the smudges off my face. I thought about going upstairs and changing into clean clothes, but what the hell. It wasn't like I needed to impress the elf. I did stop to examine my motivations, to make sure I wasn't, even in some deep, prehistoric recess of my mind, spending time with Rand to get back at Alex for distancing himself from me.

But I wasn't. Alex's issues with me—with us—had nothing to do with the elf. He was just a symptom of a bigger problem we had to work through.

When I got back to the kitchen, I stopped and watched Rand for a moment, his back to me as he riffled around for silverware. He usually moved with a fluid, long-limbed grace—not that I noticed such things—but his actions tonight seemed stiff and minimized.

An overwhelming need to touch him set my fingers twitching. Not in a sensual way, but because I knew something wasn't right. It was that bonding crap.

Mentally cursing Rand and his entire troublesome species, I walked up behind him and tugged the hem of his sweater up to his shoulder blades, hissing in a breath as he stilled. Deep marks scoured his back, fresh cuts in a regular grid, a couple still seeping blood. He'd been whipped, and badly.

He'd said the Synod would punish him for defying them, but I couldn't take any pleasure in his pain. Not this. "Take off your sweater and sit down."

I didn't wait for an answer, just headed upstairs to my library and pulled out aloe, hawthorn, ground hibiscus—all magic-infused—and mixed them in a base of holy water. I'd used my healing potion on wizards and mers, but had no idea if it would heal an elf. All my premade potions had gone up in a fiery explosion this afternoon.

After carrying the potion back downstairs, I stopped at the kitchen door, speechless. Rand had taken off the sweater. Purple and turquoise bruises bloomed across his abdomen, and a burn mark in the shape of a lightning bolt had turned the skin over his right pec a bright red.

The brutality of it shocked me. No wonder he wasn't

moving well. "What in God's name have they done to you?"

He looked down at the wreckage. "It's our way. When the Synod feels it has been wronged, each clan exacts its punishment. Our mental magic doesn't work reliably on each other, so it's usually physical."

"This is because you bonded with me?" He might be taking it like a good elven soldier, but I was outraged. "It's barbaric."

He shrugged, wincing as his shoulders rose and fell. "They don't know about the bonding yet, except my mother. This is for taking you out of Elfheim before they were finished with the regression. I knew it was coming and decided to get it over with this morning. It's our way," he repeated. As if that explained everything.

If they'd done this because he disrupted their regression, what would they do when they found out about the bonding? I set the jar of healing essence on the table. "Sit down. Let me see what I can do."

He pulled out a kitchen chair, straddled it, and sat with his back to me. "I'm not sure what you can do, but I can't reach it to treat it and my mother isn't allowed to help me."

That just pissed me off even more. I hated freaking elves. "Who did this? It looks like you've been whipped."

"Mace. It's his favorite punishment—I think he gets off on the sound of the cane whistling in the air before it hits skin." His voice held more than a trace of fury. This kind of punishment might be "their way," but he wasn't as passive about it as he'd first sounded.

I pulled the band out of my own ponytail and snapped it

around his thick blond hair to get it out of my way. Dipping my fingers in the tincture, I willed a bit more magic into it and began to ease it across the stripes of raw skin. Rand sat still except for a couple of flinches. I'd have been crying like a girl and cursing Mace Banyan with every breath.

"He's done this to others?"

"He usually doesn't take it this far, but he wanted to make sure he left scars." Rand's voice took on a bitter edge.

I smiled as I watched the cuts begin to close within seconds of the tincture being applied. My wizard's healing magic worked perfectly on elves. "Then next time you see him, make sure you aren't wearing a shirt. Because your lack of scars is gonna piss him off."

"Really?" Rand tried to look over his shoulder.

I fetched a hand mirror from the guest bathroom and held it at an angle so he could see his unmarked back. "It's going to be red and sore for a few hours, but it won't scar. Turn around and let me see what else they've done to you."

He stood up, turned, and sat in the chair facing me. I couldn't help the fleeting thought that at least they hadn't touched his beautiful face, and would bet if Mace Banyan thought he could get away with marring Rand in that way, he would have. He still had a bruised cheek and a black eye, thanks to Alex, but he'd deserved those.

I focused on the burn first. "It looks like you've been branded. But your clan is the fire elves. Your mother did this?"

"Yeah. Don't heal that one. I want the scar. It's the mark of our clan chief, and my mother pissed Mace off royally by giving it to me as my so-called punishment. We were going to do it soon anyway."

"You said earlier that your mother was dying. Do you mind if I ask what's wrong with her? Is she sick?"

"Yes." Rand leaned back in the chair. "My father was Synod, but he was killed during a power-grab after Hurricane Katrina, when things were in such flux in the Beyond—and here too, of course. She ascended to his seat, but she's lost the will to continue. She wants to follow him into our Place of Ancestors."

I wasn't sure what the proper elf etiquette would be for such a thing, so I kept my mouth shut. A potted aloe plant sat in my kitchen window, a testament to my proclivity to burn myself when I made a rare attempt at cooking. I broke off a piece and squeezed the clear, thick juice over the burn. "This will at least take some of the pain while it heals."

Next stop, his stomach. Bruise city. "There's nothing I can do to help that—who did it?"

"Betony—earth clan. He likes to spar. Of course, it's better when you can fight back. The offender is restrained when it's a punishment."

Better and better. "I thought elves were supposed to be refined and gentle and nature-loving and all that." I'd obviously read too much Tolkien. Something else occurred to me. "Wait, that's only three. You left out Lily—what did she do?"

I hoped it wasn't too gross and didn't involve parts of Rand I didn't want to see but would feel an obligation to heal.

He laughed softly. "Oh yes, Lily. Hers was best of all. She had her guards throw me in the water elves' ceremonial lake and watched while I kept myself afloat as long as I could—which wasn't long with my hands tied behind my back. Then she watched me drown. At some point—probably the last-possible second—she resuscitated me. She did it twice." His eyes hardened into blue granite. "She crossed a line."

I didn't know what to say to that, either. All of them had crossed a line, including Rand. "Did you know it was going to be this bad?"

He stood up, moving the chair back to the table. "Yes, and I'd do it again, except maybe for the drowning part. Let's eat."

27

I spent Saturday morning at home with my security wards firmly in place and Rand under orders to never again enter my house without permission. Like that would work.

First, I replicated the basic charms and potions I'd lost in my backpack. Camouflage. Healing. Replenishing. Translation (because Jean Lafitte spoke four languages fluently—only one of which I fully understood—and sometimes I wanted to know what he was up to). Plus a few that weren't specifically outlawed but were considered a tad dark by the Elders: sleep charms, freezing charms, and one of my favorites, a confusion charm.

Next, I did more research on necromancers. There were geographic limitations—the necromancer could be no more than two or three miles from the person he was controlling. Which didn't prove the necromancer had been in the dark sedan at Six Flags, but supported it.

My transportation problem wasn't as easily taken care of. I couldn't exactly call the insurance company and tell them I accidentally blew up my Pathfinder with a shot from an elven staff. I hadn't reported it to the cops. Adrian was due back in town today, so maybe he could get me one through the Elders. They should give me a car to compensate for extreme hazard duty.

Alex had two vehicles but he hadn't offered to let me drive the Mercedes, and I'd be damned if I was going to ask him. Rand would probably let me use the Plantasy Island van or his little boxy car, but I'd be damned if I'd ask him, either.

Instead, I called a cab to take me to a car rental place on Canal Street. I was perfecting self-pity and martyrdom to an art.

A half hour later, I puttered toward home in the cheapest car available, a domestic model built from an old soup can that I had to pay extra for because it was the weekend before Thanksgiving. When my cell rang, I saw Alex's name on the screen and waited a couple of rings before answering so I could get my professional self in charge. He wanted time, and I was determined not to push him until he was ready to talk. Maybe he was ready.

"Hey, what's up?" I was the soul of professionalism.

He paused before answering, and I wondered if he'd expected me to be either crying or angry. "Can you meet me for lunch? Liuzza's? We need to talk about the Axeman case and decide what to do next."

"Half hour?" I was already near Mid-City, so no point in putting it off. We needed to talk about the case before the Axeman came after me again. I promised myself we'd only get into relationship stuff if he brought it up.

When I pulled into the tiny, crowded parking lot at Liuzza's, I was disappointed to see Ken's sensible tan sedan in the lot instead of Alex's car or SUV. This wasn't going to be lunch for two, but I could be patient. Alexander Warin couldn't hide behind Ken forever.

Liuzza's had been up to its aging rafters in floodwater after Katrina, but had rebounded with fresh paint, glass tiles, and wood paneling that still managed to make it look retro and well-loved. As I squeezed through the crowds milling around the door, I spotted Ken and Alex at a table in the far corner of the front room.

A few fried green tomatoes with shrimp remoulade later, we'd had a perfectly professional conversation. Ken had found only three places renting sedans with dark-tinted windows, including one in Baton Rouge, so he was going to each of them this afternoon to chat with managers and employees and look at rental records.

We needed something more proactive, though. "The Axeman will have to lead us to the necromancer—it's the only way we'll ever catch him." I pushed a shrimp around my plate. "And the only way we can get the Axeman to do that is draw him out, and either catch the person who drops him off or follow his trail back to his summoner. I'm looking for a spell or charm I can use to do that."

Alex nodded. "Agreed. We just have to figure out how to draw him out since we don't know where he's going to be until he shows up."

I pointed at him with my cocktail fork. "Wrong. We don't have to know where he is. We just have to make sure he knows where I am. I'm the bait."

"Oh no you aren't." Alex set his spoon down with a clatter. "We're not setting you up as a lure. We'll find another way."

Ken cleared his throat. "She's right, Alex." He nodded at

me. "The only way of controlling this guy is to be a step ahead of him, not a step—or two—behind. I don't like it either, but DJ's the one he's after, so she's the only one who can draw him out. We just gotta set the trap and be smart about it."

Alex tapped the table with his fingers. "You get in enough shit on your own without us creating more trouble for you to get into."

This was business, not personal, and he should know better than to mix them. "I'm in more danger not knowing when he's going to jump out from behind a bush and split my head open with a Home Depot special." I struggled to keep the anger out of my voice. "I'm the sentinel, I'm the target, and it's my call. You don't get to decide."

"We don't know how long it will be before he can come back." Alex's face looked as stony as Abe Lincoln on Mount Rushmore. "And even if we knew he was coming back tomorrow, how do you plan to get word to his summoner—post your schedule on the front page of the *Times-Picayune*?"

I probably wouldn't have to. "I've thought about how the Axeman could have known I was at Six Flags yesterday. Either the necromancer followed me or he knew my schedule with Adrian. Chances are, as long as I let a few people know where I'll be and then be there, he's going to show up."

Alex frowned, but he didn't argue.

"Did you find out how soon he can come back?" Ken asked.

I paused while the waitress delivered three steaming bowls of gumbo. "If this were a normal case, it would take the Axeman a couple of weeks to build up enough strength to return—maybe more. But the necromancer is a wild card.

The necromantic magic could compel the Axeman to return immediately. He doesn't need the strength to cross the metaphysical borders since he's not coming in under his own power."

Ken picked a crab claw out of his gumbo and held it up with raised eyebrows. Alex grabbed it.

"Once we get a rough timetable and plan the trap, who will you share your whereabouts with?" Ken picked out a couple of shrimp with a fork and scraped them into Alex's bowl. Why the man ordered seafood gumbo and then picked out the seafood was beyond me.

I thought about necromancers and the people who might know them. "Etienne Boulard and Jonas Adamson, of course. Adrian Hoffman. And I'll get Rand to spread the word among the Synod." That pretty much covered my least-trustworthy list, and Adrian was only there because he'd proven he couldn't keep his mouth shut. He was the only one who could have told Lily about my abilities in hydromancy.

Ken leaned back in his chair. "You really think there's a chance the elves are involved in this?" Then he shook his head. "Man, I cannot believe I just asked that question. The words that have been coming out of my mouth this week. Damn."

I grinned at him. It had been so long since I smiled it felt unnatural. "You've had a steep learning curve."

"Tell me about it." He hunched over his gumbo, but paused with the spoon halfway between bowl and mouth. "Seriously, though. You think the elves could be behind the Axeman?"

A day ago I'd have said no, that they were more into

mental than physical violence. The sight of what they'd done to Rand, one of their own, had changed my opinion. "They're not necromancers." My anger bubbled to the surface again, just thinking of Lily letting Rand drown and of Mace wielding his cane. "But the elves are beasts, and they know how to hire black-market magic. We'd be nuts to not consider them."

"Does that include Quince Randolph?" Alex's question was asked in a tone that caressed like velvet, but his expression hinted of razor blades and gunpowder.

We glared at each other until Ken cleared his throat and pushed back his chair. "I gotta . . . make a call, or answer the call of nature. Or see a man about a call."

I waited until he got out of earshot, then leaned close to Alex. "Okay, look. You know damn well I didn't"—I made quote marks with my fingers—"*marry* Quince Randolph. I wanted out from under the loup-garou curse. I didn't want to give up this job I've worked so hard for. I didn't want to give up my magic, which would happen if I moved into the Beyond. I didn't want to give you up. You were a big part of my decision."

Alex slumped in his chair and rubbed his eyes. "I'm sorry. Damn it, I know you didn't really have a choice. But Randolph's like your buddy Jean Lafitte—another example of the chaos that surrounds you. It swirls around you like a dust cloud."

Alex took a sip of his iced tea and avoided making eye contact. "As much as I want to be with you I don't know if I can handle everything, and everybody, that comes with it. And I don't like admitting there are things I can't handle."

"That's . . ." I closed my eyes and took a deep breath.

This had been the problem all along. He'd just finally verbalized it, and I didn't have any answers.

"Alex, I want to be with you too, but you're the only one who can decide what you can live with," I said finally. "You're an adrenaline junkie with a control fetish, and maybe I'm a chaos junkie who doesn't want to be controlled. I'd like to tell you I could change, but most of the crazy crap in my life is not stuff I go out looking for."

Yet chaos always found me, and I was Gerry St. Simon's daughter. I'd come to accept that I would always have a streak of rogue in me.

I'd been obsessively flipping a cardboard coaster as I talked. Alex reached out and rested his hand over mine. "Let's slow down and see where it goes."

Which was probably manspeak for *let's go back to being friends*. Maybe it was for the best. The highs of being together were amazing, but the lows hurt. Right now, it hurt a lot.

I nodded, pulled my hand away, dug my wallet out of my purse, and tucked a twenty under the edge of my plate. "Ken wanted to visit L'Amour Sauvage tonight and see some vampires. You want to go?"

Alex shook his head. "I have a meeting with the head of the enforcers, to fill him in on how Ken's doing. I'm hoping he doesn't ask about Jake."

God, Jake. I'd gotten so caught up in my own drama I'd forgotten him. I needed to get word to him, maybe through Jean Lafitte or Louis Armstrong, that even though I wasn't going to shift it wasn't safe for him to return. Not until the elves played their hand.

*

The lines stretching from the door of L'Amour Sauvage were especially long on a Saturday night, even the Saturday before Thanksgiving. I stood off to the side until I caught the eye of the bouncer, and he motioned me to the front. The grumbling masses would have to get over it.

I weaved my way through the well-dressed crowd. I'd made more of a stab at blending in tonight, or at least at sucking up to Etienne by respecting his dress code. I'd slithered into a curve-hugging red dress with a low back and high hemline, wore my hair down, and gave up my boots for a pair of ridiculous red heels.

Heels I almost fell out of when I rounded the end of the bar and came upon Adrian Hoffman in a cozy clutch with Etienne's leggy red-haired assistant, Terri. I'm not sure whose eyes widened the most.

"You're back," I finally coughed out.

Terri gave me a disconcerting, fangy grin. She wasn't supposed to flash those things in public. "Adrian couldn't stay away from New Orleans too long." She pronounced the city's name like a tourist—*New Or-leens*—but who was I to correct a woman with oversize canines?

Adrian, who'd also never pronounced the city's name correctly, clearly hadn't heard about the staff's untimely breakage. "I'd planned to contact you on Monday about resuming our lessons."

"The staff got broken during another Axeman attack yesterday." What would his reaction be?

A smirk. "You really are quite the menace. We'll continue, nonetheless. You have other skills that don't involve the staff."

Fabulous. "Call me Monday with our next class time.

Good to see you feel up to making regular blood donations now that you're back." And with that zinger, I turned and walked across the bar to the table where Ken waited, all buttoned up in a dark sports jacket and slacks.

"You ready to play spot the vampire?"

He scanned the room. "How can you tell who's vampire and who isn't?"

"It's hard unless they flash fangs at you, and most of them won't do that. Doesn't pay to scare your food supply."

I looked around the room, pointing out vamps of both genders. "They're pale—no sunlight, you know. Although most of the Midwestern tourists are just as pale. Vamps also tend to be very attractive. When they're changed it maximizes whatever physical potential they had as humans. The better looking they are, the easier for them to lure in potential blood donors."

Ken's eyes had grown wider by the second. "Isn't that one sitting with your wizard friend Adrian?"

I watched them a moment. Adrian looked kind of besotted with her. Good for him. Somebody should be happy. "Yep. Really, all you need to know is to not make direct eye contact, especially with Etienne. He likes to play mind games."

As long as we were here, why not drop in on our local Regent? "You want to meet him?"

Ken looked a little fearful, but nodded. "Why not?"

"Follow me." I walked into the hallway and slipped through Etienne's office door without knocking—the better to learn something. The post-Katrina influx of pretes hadn't done much for my manners.

The blond vampire had his back to the door, phone clamped to his ear. "I don't care—forget it. It's too risky to—" His posture straightened, his body stilled, and his voice lost its anger. His French accent, much lighter and more Americanized than Jean Lafitte's, assumed a friendlier, more neutral tone. "I'm sure you'll know what to do."

He ended the call and finger-stabbed a couple of buttons on his keypad, still facing the other way. I held my breath. "Terri, *ma chère*. Unless you wish to be locked in a coffin for a month, I suggest you leave your new plaything alone and keep any other *sorcières* and their human friends from prancing into my office unannounced."

I had never pranced anywhere in my life, and I doubt Ken had either. "How'd you know we were here?"

He clicked his phone shut, rose to his feet, turned, and prowled toward us. I had to force my feet to not prance away from him. Standing entirely too close, he lowered his head and took a long, leisurely inhale in the vicinity of my jugular. Ken tensed beside me, but to his credit, he hadn't yet pulled out a weapon.

"Wizard blood is so very tempting, and yours is especially interesting."

Yeah, obviously. "Sorry to drop in unannounced, but I was in the neighborhood."

He straightened and walked back to his desk with a laugh, but I could sense his tension. Something had our Regent out of sorts tonight.

I had enough crises without volunteering for more, though, so I sat in the chair facing his desk. "I have another question or two about necromancy."

"You should introduce me to your human friend first. I didn't know wizards had allowed humans in on preternatural business. It seems unwise." He'd fixed Ken with a vampirelike, unblinking stare, but Ken kept his eyes focused on Etienne's desk.

The detective was determined to be a polite cop, however. "Ken Hachette. I'm with the NOPD homicide unit as well as consulting on preternatural cases."

"Interesting." Etienne studied Ken a second before turning back to me. "What is it you'd like to know now, Ms. Jaco?"

"You grew up as a necromantic wizard before you were turned vampire. How did you first learn about your necromancy—who taught you how to use it?" Unless they pursued specialized fields like Adrian, attending formal schools, the majority of wizards obtained their educations the way I did, through private mentoring. Gerry and Tish had been my only teachers before college. But a specialized skill like necromancy might need specialized training with records I could use. It was a long shot, but worth a question.

Etienne laughed, and the soft glow from his desk lamp glinted on his fangs. "That was two centuries ago, Ms. Jaco. Rules were much more relaxed, and the Elders of my time did not try to exert so much control. We practiced our craft openly, and my father was likewise a necromancer. Today, your Elders are nothing but bureaucrats and politicians."

Couldn't argue with him there. I'd done enough research to know necromancy, like most wizards' skills, was inherited. So most probably learned necromantic magic from their parents or mentors. That had been no help.

"What's your relationship with Adrian Hoffman?" I wondered if he knew about Big Daddy Hoffman, king of all wizards. It would be easy to blackmail the First Elder by threatening to blab about sonny's new vampire habit.

Etienne waved a dismissive hand toward the door. "Terri

has a taste for exotic blood. She'll tire of him soon and send him along, although she does seem quite taken with him. You needn't fear for his safety. She didn't become my assistant by being careless."

I'd decided to tell Etienne about my encounter today. If he was behind it, he already knew. If he wasn't, he might prove helpful. Jean trusted him. "The Axeman tried to kill me today. I managed to kill him—well, send him back to the Beyond with some nasty burns and a few bullet wounds."

Etienne studied me over the expanse of his desk. "And you wish to know how long before he could be summoned again? How long you have before you must worry about him coming for another visit?"

Sharp vampire, but I guess Regents had to be. "Exactly."

He nodded, thinking. "This is all theoretical, of course."

Yeah, right. "Of course."

"But I don't believe, should your necromancer wish to recall the Axeman immediately, the normal recovery time would apply."

Much as I suspected. "But he was burned."

Back in our early days, when Jean and I were still trying to kill each other, Alex had shot him. It had taken Jean almost two weeks before he could build up enough strength to cross over from the Beyond again. And Jean was at least ten times stronger than the Axeman.

Etienne seemed to know what logic I was using. "He was burned, yes, and he might come back rather crispy"—he looked amused at the idea—"but he can come back at any time now if he is summoned and controlled by a necromancer. At least I would think so, not having attempted such a thing, of course."

His navy-blue eyes told me he'd probably done that and much worse, but if it wasn't during my sentinel-hood, I didn't care. "Well, that wasn't what I wanted to hear, but thanks. I guess."

It was time to set a trap for the Axeman.

28

Traffic was Saturday-night heavy, so it took me forty-five minutes to make it home from the Quarter, including a stop by Winn-Dixie for cat food. I also might have wandered down the candy aisle with all the other pathetic people who had no Saturday night plans. Chocolate would help in planning our Axeman setup.

Alex's truck was still gone when I parked behind the house, and Eugenie's place sat dark and empty looking. I hoped she'd found something fun to do tonight, and that someday we'd be close enough again to do things together. As for Alex, he was probably late returning from his meeting in Jackson.

"Sebastian!" I yelled, rattling the plastic grocery bag on my way in the back door. He didn't come running to attempt murder-by-tripping like he usually did. Probably napping. I couldn't remember how old he was. Seemed like Gerry had him forever before Katrina, when I inherited him. He usually had plenty of energy where food was concerned, though.

Dumping the bag on the counter, I flipped the lights on my way into the front parlor. It was one a.m., and the pizza place across Magazine Street was dark. I looked through the mail I'd pulled from the box on my way in—a water bill, a catalog of overpriced cheese and fruit, and a postcard from Maple Street Animal Clinic reminding me it was time for Sebastian's shots. Kiss another few hundred bucks good-bye.

I'd been slogging my way through a reread of The Lord of the Rings trilogy for the last week, so I figured I might as well see if I could get Sam and Frodo closer to Mordor, maybe even indulge in a few Sean-Bean-as-Boromir fantasies. There was nothing else I could do about the Axeman tonight. Grabbing the book off the coffee table, I started toward the stairwell. I'd get out of these blasted heels, drag out my PJs, read awhile, and get to bed before two a.m. for a change.

A creaking sound overhead stopped me cold. It was the squeaky floorboard in my upstairs sitting room, which lay at the top of the stairs. Sebastian wasn't heavy enough to make that floor creak.

I relaxed my shoulders and took a deep breath to slow down my heart rate, which had begun to jackrabbit in erratic spurts. My security wards were active, and no one knew the password, so I was being paranoid. I lived in a house that had been built in 1879. It settled. It creaked. When the wind blew hard, it moaned. I was just jumpy because of everything that had happened in the last few weeks.

The floor overhead creaked again, followed by a thump and the re-acceleration of my heart rate. Holy crap. That was not the sound of a house settling. I slipped out of the silly red heels, traded the book for my clutch bag, and tiptoed toward the back door. I'd drive my rental car to the Gator and hang out, see if I could find Rene or other suitable backup.

Chicken, yes, but better fearful and breathing than brave and dead.

I picked up the broken elven staff from the kitchen counter and, pausing on the back stoop, pulled my cell phone out of my bag and punched Alex's speed dial. Voice mail. I tried Ken next, as I walked gingerly across the gravel parking lot. He answered on the first ring.

"It's DJ," I whispered. "Somebody's in my house." Not only in my house, but walking heavily down my stairs. I ran toward my car.

"Where are you?" Ken asked.

"Trying to get in my car. Where's Alex?" I fumbled with the keys and dropped them in the gravel.

"Got held up in Jackson. Drive to my place now—stay on the phone with me until you get here."

Runs raced up my hose from walking on the gravel, and I winced from the rocks poking in my feet, but I had the key at the lock. "Okay, I'm getting—"

Something jerked my head backward, throwing me off balance. Almost suspended by a fist in my hair, I looked up into the horrific face of the Axeman. I think he was smiling, but since the flesh hung off his burned, blackened face in gobbets, it was hard to tell. He looked mad, as in both angry and insane.

I screamed, but it was cut short by a meaty fist connecting with my jaw. My lip was crushed against my lower teeth, and the cell phone hit the gravel. I could hear Ken's voice yelling through the phone as the Axeman slung me to the ground. I landed near the cracked staff and grabbed it.

"You hurt me. Your friend shot me." The Axeman dragged me across the driveway by my hair, back toward my house. His voice was as rough as the gravel under my scrambling feet. "You burned me."

Well, it wasn't like I'd been the one to chase *him* down. I panted for breath, and sharp pains shot into my abdomen. "Why are you after me? Who's summoning you?" Give me a freaking name.

"Wizard. I'll come back and kill him later. It's your turn first."

From the corner of my eye as we rounded the side of the house, I saw movement across the street in front of the darkened windows of Marinello's Pizza—some guy walking a dog. I screamed again just before the Axeman shoved me inside my open back door.

Scrambling to my feet, I dashed toward the front of the house, but the Axeman lumbered behind me in big strides.

Using my hair again, he slung me toward the guest room and stairwell. If I lived through this, I was going to shave my head, unless he tore out my hair by the roots.

All the while he dragged me up the stairs, I held the broken staff like a sword and shot weak tendrils of fire directly into him—the most I could muster with the damaged weapon. What I wouldn't give for one of the premade charms in my purse, lying on the ground in the driveway.

My legs had gotten scraped from being dragged across the gravel, so I left a swath of red along the stairs. The Axeman grunted whenever the staff touched him, but despite the tattered rags of his jacket starting to flame again, he didn't loosen his grip on my hair. Finally, I got a hand around one of the banisters at the top of the stairs and held on, but the wood splintered with a loud crack.

I used every ounce of magic I could summon and channeled it through the staff. With a roar of pain, the Axeman dropped me at the top of the stairs and careened to the middle of the room before collapsing to his hands and knees. Smoke rose from his burning suit coat.

I rolled to my side and stilled, panting. Sebastian crouched under the sofa table a foot in front of me, surrounded by blood, his crossed blue eyes wide and dazed. An ax lay next to him, its blade red with blood and hunks of chocolate-brown fur. I scanned his head and paws, which all seemed accounted for, but . . . "You chopped off my cat's tail! You sick son of a bitch. Why would you do that?"

Still clutching the staff, I struggled to my feet, snatched up Sebastian, and ran toward the stairwell with him tucked under my arm like a blood- and fur-covered football. The Axeman was still on all fours, smoking and howling.

I raced downstairs, tripping as I rounded the bottom of the stairwell where it went into the guest room. Sebastian wriggled free and darted under the bed.

I hesitated, but heard the Axeman moving again, so I ran for the front door, praying I could get away and the lunatic wouldn't take it out on my cat. It would take too long to track down my keys again in the dark driveway, so my only hope was getting to the coffee shop down the block where there would still be people out, topping off their evening with a latte. Surely the necromancer would have told his killer to avoid crowds.

I didn't even think about going to Rand for help or trying to call him mentally, not until I almost bowled him over at the bottom of my front steps. But like with the attack at Six Flags, he'd known I was in trouble.

He grabbed my hand and pulled me toward the street. "Come on, let's get back to my house."

I balked, trying to drag him toward the coffee shop. "We need to get to where there are people. He'll follow us."

"No, we—" Rand looked up, eyes wide, and shoved me to the ground. He landed on top of me just as an explosion seemed to bring the world raining down around us. Something landed next to my face, and I squinted through the smoke to see a brass box just like the one I kept on my nightstand to hold jewelry. It took a second for me to register that it *was* my jewelry box.

"Wait . . . what . . ." I reached out for it, and gasped when it burned my hand.

"Dru—we've gotta get out of here." Rand rolled off me, hauled me to my feet, retrieved the staff from the ground, and pulled me across Magazine Street, stumbling behind him even as traffic began piling up and sirens sounded in the distance.

I jerked my hand away from his and looked back at my house. Smoke billowed from the upstairs sitting-room window, creating a foggy, surreal scene as it settled over the streetlights. My vision blurred a few moments before I realized I was crying. Flames flickered through my roof, and another explosion sounded from the back of the house. My library, all of Gerry's grimoires and spellbooks. Sebastian.

Anger, hot and deep, boiled up in my throat, and with a scream of rage I started back toward the house. It was part of me. Everything in there was something I'd worked for, something I loved, all I had left.

The world tilted, and it took a second for me to realize

Rand had picked me up and thrown me over his shoulder like a sack of mulch. I screeched at him as I struggled, beating my hands against his pale sweater that seemed to glow in the light filtering through the smoke. But he ran as if I weighed no more than a potted plant, only setting me down when he needed to open his door.

I shoved past him to run back toward the street, but he caught me.

"You can't go back, Dru—look."

I was looking at the burning roof, but my focus was drawn by movement from the front porch. A dark, bulky figure stood in the open doorway, backlit by the flames. My whole life was burning up and that freak stood there watching us, holding his ax.

Rand took my hand and pulled me inside Plantasy Island, closing and locking the door behind us. "Come on—upstairs."

"No, are you crazy?" I fought through the numbness that threatened to shut down my brain. "He can trap us up there, or set fire to this place and burn us out. And I have to see about my cat. He's going to kill Sebastian."

"The cat will find a way out, better than we could. We can barricade ourselves in upstairs, and I have another transport we can use if we need to." Rand's face was illuminated in golden light from the bonfire across the street.

I followed him up the narrow stairway. There was a landing at the top with three doors opening off it. In the middle one stood Vervain, Rand's mother and clan leader of the fire elves.

Her skin was glowing, and it had nothing to do with the fire.

29

Vervain seemed lit from within, as if her blood were molten gold. I gaped at her, the shock of glowing skin finally sending my overloaded brain into full meltdown. She reached out a hand and only Rand's presence behind me kept me from backing away on instinct.

"Don't be afraid, daughter. *Fod mewn heddwch.*" She touched my forehead and, almost instantly, my muscles relaxed and a calm, pure energy flowed through me. She continued to whisper in a language I didn't understand, until her final words: "Such pain."

A crash from below destroyed the moment—glass shattering, followed by hoarse bellows. "The Axeman cometh," I muttered, my feel-good elven vibes rapidly fading.

"Let's get inside." Rand propelled me forward, and we followed Vervain back into the room. Rand closed the door and locked it. I was glad to see a dead bolt instead of a flimsy doorknob lock. I barely had time to register a large, softly lit room decorated in earth tones before another crash came from downstairs.

"He's in the greenhouse," Vervain said. "Why would he hurt the plants?"

Was she bonkers? The man was an immortal undead serial killer fueled by the cold magic of a necromancer. He wasn't going to pet the azaleas and sing Grateful Dead songs.

Rand rested hands on my shoulders and turned me to face him.

"Are you hurt?"

I blinked at him. "My house is burning and my cat is in there." Sebastian and I had a rocky relationship, but I loved him. He was my last living link to Gerry.

Rand stepped back and looked at my legs, shrouded in strands of blood-soaked pantyhose. My feet had left bloody prints wherever I'd stepped.

I rubbed my eyes. "I'm okay."

He seemed satisfied that was true, and lifted my chin to look up at him. "Focus on what I'm saying. There's an open transport in the bathroom, right behind us. If we get separated, go through it. We'll follow if we can. Do you understand?"

I nodded and looked back at the glowing Vervain, whose attention was riveted on the door into the hallway. Rand handed the broken staff to me before moving to the far wall. I couldn't believe he hadn't lost Charlie in the chaos. He gripped a large chest of drawers around its top surface and dragged it in front of the door. Heavy footsteps sounded on the stairway, and my heart seemed to pound in time with their cadence.

"We should all go now," I said. "Why wait?"

"It goes straight into Elfheim, and we're giving Mace time

to cool down. If we can stop the Axeman here it'll be better." Rand's words tumbled out in a rush, and he flinched when the door into the room next to us crashed. "The transport word is *pobl-o-dân*. Say it."

I didn't trust Rand. I didn't trust Vervain. I sure as hell didn't want to run to Elfheim. But I didn't have any other options. "Poblo-don," I repeated, chanting it in my head. Whatever the hell it meant. "Poblo-don. Poblo-don."

The bedroom door shook in its frame, followed by a roar of rage that didn't sound even vaguely human. In an upper door panel not covered by the chest, the edge of a blade broke through once, then again.

You'd think when he burned down my house he'd at least have lost his freaking ax, but no.

Rand came to stand at my right, grasping my hand. "Vervain's magic is strongest. She wants to face him first."

The absurdity of this situation struck me, and I could hear Alex's voice in the back of my head, ranting, "Not a goddamn one of you idiots has a weapon except for a broken staff." I wished I had taken his advice to buy a gun. Instead, here Rand and I stood like unarmed fools, holding hands and hiding behind a glowing elven clan chief with a death wish.

The top part of the door caved in with a crash, and the Axeman stuck his head in the opening like a half-burned, demented Jack Nicholson in *The Shining*—except crazier.

With one great shove, he broke through the rest of the door, toppling the heavy dresser on its side and backing us all toward the bathroom. A woman's scream pierced the air, and in the chaos, I couldn't be sure it wasn't me.

I pulled on Rand's arm. "Transport—now!" I'd rather

face Mace Banyan and his whistling cane than let the Axeman grab me again. Obviously, my wards and fire from the broken staff hadn't been enough to slow him down. I had no idea what kind of magic elves possessed beyond mental assault, but the Axeman didn't have enough of his own mind left to care about self-preservation.

Rand gave me a hard shove into the bathroom and slammed the door, leaving me alone inside, holding the side of the pedestal sink. The staff had rolled across the tile and come to a stop near the tub. I grabbed it and then tugged on the doorknob but it wouldn't turn. Rand had to be holding it from the other side.

Poblo-don, Poblo-don. I glanced around, looking for a window, but there wasn't one. White tile, white tub and toilet, white towels. The man needed some serious color advice. But on the floor, in what looked like copper inlaid into the ceramic tile, was an interlocking circle and triangle. A quick touch to the transport symbol shot enough magical zing into my hand to tell me it was live. What wizard had Rand gotten to set up his own personal transport to Elfheim?

Another crash burst from the bedroom, and I heard Rand shouting in that strange, strangled-sounding language of theirs. As tempting as it was for me to jump in the transport and take off, I couldn't do it. Rand and Vervain were only facing the Axeman because of me and I wouldn't run away while they stood and fought.

I returned to the door and turned the knob. This time the door opened, and I stared into the room, my overwhelmed brain trying to make sense of the horror. Blood covered everything.

Rand was locked in hand-to-hand combat with the

Axeman, except they weren't exactly fighting. Rand was on his back on the floor, chanting his words, glowing like Vervain had been earlier, his hands locked around the killer's black-charred neck. The Axeman leaned over him, his face covered with blackened skin, blood, and dangling chunks of flesh. He screeched as if whatever Rand was doing hurt, but he wasn't letting go. Holy crap.

I scanned the room for Vervain, and the room spun when I saw her. I slipped out of the bathroom and ran to where she lay, but she was beyond help. Her head lay at an unnatural angle, neck obviously broken. Chunks of her body were missing.

Suddenly, everything stopped. Only the raspy breaths of the Axeman broke the silence, and I looked around at him. Rand lay at his feet, unmoving, covered in so much blood I couldn't tell where it was coming from. In the silence, I finally saw his chest rise and fall in a series of sporadic, shallow breaths.

I swallowed hard and held the pieces of the staff in front of me. I wasn't sure how much juice I had left, but everything I could muster would be going into that cracked piece of wood.

My feet skidded in the blood, but I skated toward the Axeman and thrust the staff against his chest, shooting all my magical energy into him. He screamed, a rasping, inhuman shriek that seemed to freeze me in place—until his arm hit my neck in a perfect clothesline, batting me across the room.

I landed facedown, my body skating across the blood-covered hardwood before hitting the footboard of the bed hard enough in the midsection to knock the air out of my lungs.

But for the moment, and I knew it would be a short one, the Axeman was down. He sat against the upturned chest of drawers, keening and rocking as he swatted at the flames engulfing his pants. I scrambled to Rand, grabbed two handfuls of bloody sweater, and, walking backward, dragged him into the bathroom.

Leveraging his long legs around the doorway, I managed to shove the door closed and roll him into the transport. There wasn't room for me to stand next to him and still be inside the symbols, so I made sure his hands and legs were in, then sat on him.

"Poblo . . . crap! Poblo-don. Poblo-don!" I screamed the words, looking up as the bathroom door crashed in, the Axeman falling with the force of his thrust amid the splintered pieces of wood.

The last thing I heard was the enraged sound of a killer whose prey had escaped.

30

Rand and I landed in the same cabin where the Synod had put me through their warped version of *This Is Your Life*. The open living area was lit only by a single, soft lamp on one of the end tables, and no flames flickered in the fireplace. We weren't expected, which was a good thing.

I rolled off Rand and lay on the floor next to him, trying to remember how to breathe and to summon the strength to assess our injuries. After I rested my eyes for a moment . . .

"Dru—wake up." Rand lay on his side, facing me, and cradled my cheek with a bloody hand. His breath rasped in and out like the bellows of an accordion, or like he'd run a marathon.

"Rand." My voice sounded like that of a sixty-year-old chain-smoker. "You look like hell." How long had I slept?

"We've got to leave. Mace will already be on his way. This transport is monitored so he'll know it's been used."

I groaned, and after two failed attempts managed to sit up. Everything hurt. Rand really did look awful. The lower front of his sweater, once a pale blue, was covered in such gore I couldn't tell what was flesh and what was wool. "How badly are you hurt?"

He shook his head, struggling to force out his words. "I don't know. But we have to get out of Elfheim."

Good Lord, they'd already whipped and beaten him black and blue, and with Vervain's death he had assumed her rank on the Synod. Not that I thought he'd taken time to consider that yet. "Let's just stay and deal with Mace. Why should we run?" We were in no shape to run.

He closed his eyes. "Because they might be involved in this. They might be behind it. I don't have proof, but my senses tell me it's true. It might not be Mace himself, but if it's one of the others he probably knows about it. He is not our ally."

Rand really thought the elves were behind this?

"Plus, Mace knows we're bonded. He found out somehow," Rand panted. "That's why my mother was in New Orleans. She'd come to warn me away from Elfheim until Mace cooled off."

I stared at him, my mind spinning through the possibilities. "But elves aren't necromancers."

He fought to keep his eyes open. "No, but we hire wizards all the time to do jobs that aren't legal. How do you think I got two permanent transports set up in my house in New Orleans? And who else sees you as a big-enough threat to want you dead?" He winced and pressed bloody fingers into his bloody stomach. "The wizards want to use your skills, not destroy them. Only the other elven clans, who saw you as a threat even before we were bonded, really want you dead. My money's on Lily if not Mace himself."

I thought again of Lily being in the L'Amour Sauvage office with Etienne—a necromancer. Even if he didn't do it himself, he might have given her a recommendation. Rand was right. No wizards hated me enough to go after me like this alone, but there had to be at least one greedy enough or power-hungry enough to help the elves.

Regardless, Elfheim was the last place I needed to be. "Okay, let's get out of here. Where can this transport take us? We can't go back to New Orleans. Not yet."

Rand winced and shifted position. "The transport here follows the geomantic lines. We can go to Old Orleans or one of its outposts, to Vampyre, to Faerie, or other places in Elfheim." Rand tried to get to his feet, but fell back with a grunt.

I managed to get up and held out a hand. With me pulling hard, he finally got upright, if slightly hunched over. He kept his left hand clamped on his stomach as if his organs might spill out if he let go. My own rib cage felt as if a water buffalo had trampled on it but at least I wasn't bleeding.

He couldn't take much more, and we needed to be gone. I located the transport by the heaviest bloodstains and hobbled into it.

Rand came to stand beside me, almost doubled over in pain. "Say *pobl-o-dân* and then the destination. Where are we going?"

I wrapped an arm around his waist and named the only place I could think of where I'd feel halfway safe: "*Pobl-o-dân*. Old Barataria. Grand Terre."

31

Transports were draining, even if a certain wizard hadn't already used up all her physical magic trying to fight off a homicidal undead maniac. Rand and I landed on a cold patch of ground in the pitch-black night, the sole illumination from the Beyond's ever-present full moon.

Its silvery glow revealed only that we'd come to rest on soft, damp soil, with high grasses around us. The crash of waves could be heard nearby, and the air was thick with the smell of salt and seaweed. This was Grand Terre, I assumed, but where on Grand Terre was another matter. Jean Lafitte probably wouldn't have an open transport too close to his home in the Beyond, just in case unwelcome visitors popped in.

I visualized the Louisiana coastline in my mind and tried to fix our position by the sound of the waves. Grand Terre and Grand Isle were the two biggest barrier islands due south of New Orleans. In modern times, Grand Terre was unpopulated except for a state-protected wildlife area, much of the island lost to erosion. In Jean's times it had been much larger, its land more solid. He owned a big house here and ruled a colony of up to a thousand pirates and other assorted riffraff I didn't want to stumble across.

Rand and I had collapsed where we landed, and didn't speak for a while. The black sky overhead seemed to hang low because of all the stars. Had there been more stars back in the early nineteenth-century slice of time Old Barataria was caught in? Or had city life just dulled the wonderment of them because we'd surrounded ourselves with so much fake dazzle?

Finally, I climbed to my feet. Sea winds ruffled through the tall grasses and whipped my hair across my face hard enough to sting. I shivered from the cooling air and realized for the first time that my sexy little red dress was mostly in shreds.

As the adrenaline drained, the damage reports started filtering from body to brain. My feet had been sliced up from running without shoes, and the dirt—or sand, or whatever combination of the two we'd landed on—stung them. My head throbbed. Breathing was torture. I touched tentative fingers against my rib cage and gasped from the knife-jab of pain. At least one of the ribs that had just healed was bruised again, if not cracked. I was a bloody mess but had no idea how much of the blood was mine.

To my right, I could see Rand struggling to sit before he gave up and flopped back down, panting. His pale sweater glowed in the silvery moonlight, covered with big, dark splotches I knew were literally bloodred. "Rand, you okay?"

"Not . . . sure." He wheezed on every exhale. "You got . . . staff? Can you start . . . fire?"

I sat next to him, feeling around where we'd landed, and finally raked my hands across the staff. "I have it, but I don't think a fire's a good idea—not until it gets lighter and we can see where we are." I didn't know how many undead pirates Jean had in Old Barataria, but being found by the wrong ones could be worse than facing Mace Banyan. Although hopefully they'd take us to *Le Capitaine* before doing anything fatal.

Rand coughed, and his breathing had a whistling undertone. I didn't like the sound of it. "I've never been to this part of . . . Beyond but I thought . . . always night." The sentence had cost him too much breath.

"Jean told me once that at dawn and sunset it lightens enough to see for an hour or two before it starts getting dark again. They never get sunshine, but they do get that kind of predawn and post-sunset grayness. When that happens we can see where we are. Till then, let's stay put."

Like either of us could go anywhere yet. Especially Rand, and I didn't have the strength to help him.

"Cold," he whispered, or maybe that's all the strength that remained in his voice. I shifted closer and curled up next to him, holding my breath until the pain of moving subsided. Too bad I hadn't had the foresight to bring a blanket from the cabin in Elfheim before we transported. While I was wishing for things, I wished that if I had to curl up in the outdoors, it could have been with someone else. Which was selfish, because if not for Rand, I'd probably be burned crispier than the Axeman. On the other hand, if not for Rand and his stupid elven Synod, the Axeman might never have been after me.

"Will Mace be able to tell where we've gone?"

Rand didn't answer, so I shut up and let him sleep or be unconscious. I didn't want to know which; there was nothing

I could do about it. I prayed we'd be able to find Jean, maybe even Jake, and one of them could get word to Alex.

My heart clenched at the thought of Alex. By now, Ken would have called him. He'd know I'd been attacked in the driveway. Ken heard me screaming. Would they realize it was the Axeman since he'd burned the evidence? Would they think to look in Rand's house and find Vervain's body, or would the elves find it first and do damage control? Would Alex think I had died in the fire? Had Sebastian survived, or was he cold and scared somewhere, bleeding to death?

I pondered questions that had no answers and, shivering, burrowed closer and sought warmth from the wrong man.

I congratulated myself for not screeching in fright when I woke face-to-beak with a brown pelican the size of an overfed bulldog. He appeared almost as startled as I, and hopped atop a log lying a few feet away, turning his back to me as if by not seeing me, I might not see him. I wondered if that would've worked with the Axeman.

Rand and I had curved ourselves into a spoon, and I was almost warm. Almost. I eased from beneath his arm and, holding on to my ribs, twisted stiffly to look at him. He didn't stir, so I poked him. "Rand." I spoke in a hissing whisper, not knowing if there were pirates about. Finally, he moaned and flopped on his back.

In the gray predawn light, I couldn't see what I looked like, but Rand looked like death personified. His skin had blanched almost as pale blue as the few parts of his sweater that hadn't been stained red, which was pretty much only the shoulders.

I took a deep breath, gently pushed his sweater up to bare

his stomach, and didn't see the bruises and cuts I expected. There wasn't enough solid expanse of skin to display them. "What the hell did he do to you?" If I'd had anything in my stomach to lose, it would've been gone.

Rand lifted his head enough to take a look, then dropped it back to the beach, even paler, if that was possible. "He had me on the floor, hacking with the ax. If you hadn't come after him with the staff again, he would've pulled my guts out. Like my mother."

I felt a stab of pity for him beneath my veneer of annoyance. I knew what it was like to lose a parent, suddenly and violently and right in front of you. Tish wasn't my mother, but she was the closest I'd had, and the sight of her lifeless body lying on my porch still haunted me, drifting into my thoughts late at night when things were quiet. And Gerry. I'd watched him die as well. "I'm so sorry about what happened to Vervain."

He closed his eyes, but not so quickly that I didn't see the hurt in them. "She was already dying. She'd be glad she went like that, fighting to save us and not just fading into the afterlife."

I didn't like Vervain. She hadn't done a thing to stop my mental abuse at the hands of the Synod—had participated, in fact. And what role she'd played in Rand's little bond-with-the-wizard project, I didn't know, although I was grateful for the end to the loup-garou saga.

But no one deserved that kind of death, and I had to admit she'd come through at the end, for Rand if not for me. She'd stood in front of us and taken the first hit of the Axeman.

"Does this mean you're Synod now?" I wanted to ask how old Vervain was, and what kind of afterlife elves believed in and how it related to the liberal interpretation of the Judeo-Christian faith I'd been brought up in, but that was the kind of leisurely conversation best saved for a time when we weren't so desperate and his grief so fresh. Not that I could pull emotion from him. Where Rand and emotions were concerned, I had to guess just like a normal person. It was really irritating.

"The Synod position falls to me now." Rand shifted a little, pulled a seashell from beneath his head, and tossed it aside. He might look worse than last night, but he wasn't wheezing anymore. "Doesn't mean Mace won't come after me—after us—until he formally acknowledges me as the head of my clan and you as my mate. Then he won't dare."

Now that we were talking, we'd aroused the curiosity of the pelican, who did a 180 on his log and watched us with bright eyes as if to say, "Daylight's wasting, people."

I'd address the use of the word *mate* later. Rand needed to be very clear on what our relationship was—and wasn't. But not now. "Do you think you can stand, or do you want to stay here while I look for help? We need to move while we can see."

"Any idea which way to go?"

I climbed to the top of a slight rise in front of us, toward the pulsing sound of the sea. Pushing the tall marsh grass aside, I tested each step to make sure I didn't hit anything I'd sink into up to my knees, or worse. During my adventures with the merpeople last month, I'd rolled around in enough wetlands mud to last a lifetime.

The Gulf of Mexico stretched before me, blue-black and churning. Just below the rise was a narrow strip of sand, and riding the waves to the east were two tall ships, their masts supporting sails dyed a deep blue, elaborate rigging outlined against the gray sky, cannons visible from their decks. The ships lay too far offshore for me to identify their flags, but I'd bet they bore the colors of Cartagena, from whence Jean claimed his marque. Basically, it gave him license to plunder Spanish ships and claim it as an act of war rather than the piracy it was, but I wouldn't be sharing that opinion.

"I say we walk east along the beach." I turned back to find Rand wavering on his feet. I was impressed to see him upright, although he still clutched his belly.

"Need help?"

"Just don't go fast." He hobbled behind me down the slope to the sand, which was hard-packed and made for easier walking. "Do you know where we're going?"

I pointed east. "I figure the ships are this way, so their master probably is as well."

"Why do you think he'll help us? Jean Lafitte is a common thief."

I realized the arrogant question had come from several feet behind me, so I stopped and waited for Rand to catch up. "Let me make this clear. Jean won't help *us*. Jean will help *me*. You're just part of the package, and if you're smart you won't mention anything about bonding. In fact, if you're really smart you'll keep your mouth shut altogether."

Jean had no claims on me, but I instinctively knew that however pissed Alex was about this whole ridiculous non-marriage, Jean would be equally so, and more apt to do something about it. Something that might involve a long-barreled, muzzle-loaded *pistolette*.

288 Suzanne Johnson

Jean had proprietary feelings toward me—not that I was his great love or anything. I think he considered me a desirable potential conquest with good political connections. Not so different from Rand, when I thought about it. The difference being, I liked Jean. Rand, not so much.

His face took on an obstinate, haughty, mulish look I was beginning to know too well and dislike intensely. "Lafitte needs to know you're mine now. When he comes back to the city, it's not appropriate for him to spend time with you."

I'd started walking again, but turned on Rand so quickly he stumbled and had to do a painful sand-dance to regain his balance. "I am not *yours*. I belong to nobody but myself. Got that? This farce of a bonding does not give you the right to say who I spend time with. In fact, it gives you no rights at all." If Alex, whose good opinion I cared about, couldn't dictate my friends or behavior, the elf sure as hell couldn't.

He managed to look pale and pretty and stubborn all at the same time, in a beat-up, bloody sort of way. "You saved me last night. If you'd really wanted out of our bond, you could've let the Axeman kill me."

Stupid, stupid elf. He'd known the night I refused to use the broken staff on him that I didn't have it in me to intentionally hurt anyone except in self-defense, much less let anyone die when I could stop it. "I would have done as much for anyone. It just happened to be you."

We trudged along in silence, the darkening sky causing me to speed up as much as Rand could keep pace. Ahead in the distance, fires burned and the sound of music occasionally seeped through the thunder of waves that sent tendrils of foam closer to our feet.

"*Qui êtes-vous?*" A man emerged from the inland shadows, a rifle and bayonet trained on us. He was short, swarthy, and had bad teeth. I knew this because he was grinning. Had pirate written all over him.

32

What does a half-dressed wizard, accompanied by an injured elf, say to an undead pirate on a fast-darkening beach in coastal Louisiana, circa 1814?

After staring at him a moment, I decided humor was best avoided. "Do you speak English? *Parlez-vous l'anglais?*"

"Bah." The man spat in the direction of our feet. "*Pas l'anglais.*"

I tried to conjure up some of the pidgin French I'd learned from Jean. "*Où est Jean Lafitte? Il est mon ami.*" Well, he was sort of a friend. Mostly.

"*Le Capitaine?*" Short and Swarthy treated me to an ebony-toothed grin, and did a slow visual crawl across my overexposed, bloody, dirt-encrusted body. He probably thought Jean had developed really bad taste in women, but shrugged and motioned with the rifle for us to go ahead of him. Rand wisely kept his big elven trap shut and stumbled alongside me, holding his stomach.

After what seemed like a half mile of walking in sand and mud, we approached a village of thatched huts and shanties, around which milled crowds of people. It was mostly men of all shapes, sizes, and colors, with a few women scattered in. No kids. The village seemed to go on forever, which confirmed my suspicion that Jean had quite an undead entourage in his little paradise à la Beyond. The historical undead seemed to exist in the Beyond at the height of their success or power in their human lives, which meant Jean would be in his early thirties, at the peak of his pirate command. None of them, other than possibly his brothers, would be famous enough to have much of a life outside the Beyond, but all the pirates lived here, fueled by his memories as he was, in turn, fueled by those of humans.

The silence of shock spread across the crowd, and all activity—mostly gator-skinning, dancing, fistfighting, and drinking—ground to a halt as our pirate escort herded Rand and me into a clearing. A carpet of reeds and grass covered the muddy ground, with trench-encircled bare patches serving as fire pits. I couldn't help but think of all the old movies I'd seen, where the hapless woman is captured and surrounded by tribal warriors—just before discovering the warriors are also cannibals.

Mr. Shorty spewed a stream of French that was way beyond my limited comprehension, then beat a retreat. Everyone else stepped back as well, drawing my attention to a man they'd left alone in front, facing us.

Crap. My heart bottomed out at the sight of our official welcoming committee of one. Dominique You was olive-skinned, hook-nosed, and allegedly Jean's half brother, although I could see no physical resemblance beyond a certain arrogance in his walk and a sharp intelligence behind his eyes. I'd hit him with my best confusion charm once upon a time, and he seemed to hold it against me.

After the War of 1812, when Jean had spurned his presidential pardon and gone back to pirating, Dom had gone straight and done well for himself. But he didn't share Jean's fondness for a certain blond wizard. Maybe I was such a bloody, ragged mess he wouldn't recognize me. I'd tell him my name was Adrian Hoffman.

"Far from home, are you not, Mademoiselle Jackal?"

So much for not being recognized. For some reason, Dom thought I was untrustworthy and a bad influence on Jean Lafitte, which was ridiculous. The man was an immortal undead pirate, for God's sake.

"We need to see Jean right away." I might look like something a bad gale blew in, but I wanted Dom to know I wasn't the naïve girl he'd first met in the weeks after Hurricane Katrina. He still scared the crap out of me, but I had the sense not to let him know it.

"And you have brought with you . . ." He studied Rand, annoyance puckering his face as if he'd bitten into a lemon. "*Qu'est-il?* What is he?"

Rand straightened and put more force in his voice than I'd have thought him physically capable of, with his injuries. "I am Elf."

I sighed. Rand sounded imperious, defiant, condescending, and antagonistic. Like an elf, in other words.

Dom snorted and turned back to me. "*Elf* is not welcome here, and neither are you, mademoiselle. I will give you a quarter-hour's head start out of respect for Jean, and after that"—he shrugged—"I care not what happens to you."

He turned to the crowd of men behind him, who were six shades of scary. "Prepare for a hunt, *mes amis*. The girl? She is the prize to whomever first finds her." Then he repeated it in French so they'd understand it. The English version had been for my benefit.

Nice. I could run or I could call his bluff, and my feet hurt too badly to run. He wouldn't risk Jean's anger by moving against us. I walked forward till we were inches apart and stuck the tip of the broken elven staff in his chest. "You might not care what happens to me, but Jean will. Do you trust all of those fine gentlemen behind you to keep secret what they do to me? Because if you don't trust them, you better forget your petty, vindictive game and take us to Jean." I poked him harder. "Now."

A dark flush washed across his features, and a low mumble wove through the onlookers. Did I know how to make friends and influence enemies, or what?

Several things happened at once, and it took a few seconds for me to sort them out. Dom wrapped a hand around my upper arm and jerked me roughly toward him. Rand stepped forward and began chanting elven gibberish. And a dark red wolf the size of a miniature horse prowled from the now-darkened beach into the firelight.

Everyone on two legs froze. The wolf continued forward until he stood alongside Dom, who loosened his grip on my arm. He stared at the beast a few heartbeats before throwing his hands in the air and pushing through the crowd. "You're the wolf's problem, then, and Jean's. *Tout est foutu.*"

Yeah, I knew that much French. The F-bomb was still popular in my world. I turned my attention to the wolf, who watched me with golden eyes both alien and sentient. Only once had I seen Jake in wolf form, but since this big, red loup-garou hadn't yet laid a fang on either me or Rand, I had to assume it was him.

"Jake?" I caught the wolf's gaze a moment, then looked down. I didn't know how much was Jake and how much was wolf, so I wanted to make no movements he'd see as threatening.

He moved closer to me, flames from the nearest fire reflecting in his eyes and giving them a red glow. I swallowed hard but kept my breathing even when he bumped my arm with his snout. I held out my hand, opening my palm to him.

"Dru, are you insane?" Rand reached across me and grabbed my outstretched hand. "That's a loup-garou, not a pet."

The wolf snarled and snapped, and Rand's skin began glowing as he muttered what sounded like curses in his consonant-heavy language.

Jake—wolf Jake—whined and backed away, shaking his head. Whatever Rand was doing to him, it hurt. I still hadn't quite figured out what the glowing and chanting did.

"Stop that." I stepped between Rand and wolf Jake. The elf still had his inner glow, but at least he shut up.

When had he picked up that glowing thing, anyway? It was awfully inconvenient that elven magic worked in the Beyond when wizard's magic didn't, because if ever an elf needed a good zap of calm-your-ass-down magic, it was Quince Randolph.

The wolf stretched out his neck and sniffed along my arm where I'd bled from God only knows what injury, then sat and cocked his head at me a moment before focusing on Rand. The black-tipped hair around his nose and snout bristled as his upper lip slowly curled upward, revealing the biggest, sharpest set of teeth I'd seen since I'd watched Rene skin an alligator.

"I don't think he likes you." I glanced at Rand, who was staring back at the wolf. He didn't get the memo about avoiding the dominance stare-down thing.

"It's mutual."

I'd rather talk to the wolf. "Jake, we need to see Jean Lafitte. Do you know where he is? It's urgent. You can fight with the elf later." Now we'd find out how much Jake's wolf understood, and how helpful he was feeling.

He stared past me at Rand a few moments longer, then turned and loped up the beach in the opposite direction from our transport.

"Come on." I stumbled after the wolf and heard the crunch of shifting sand as my *mate* followed.

We'd traveled at least another eighth of a mile beneath the once-again full moon before I saw the outline of a house rising from the higher land just beyond the beach. Soft light shone through its windows with a surreal glow. Pure French Colonial, as near as I could tell, with concessions made to the South Louisiana weather. It would probably be stunning in sunlight, with two stories and a gallery that spanned the upper floor. Spindly trees and lush banana palms grew up around it, dark and elegant shadows in the moonlight. From what I'd read, there were probably strategically placed cannons tucked away in several places, facing in all directions.

A raised wooden banquette stretched from the sand toward the house, and by the time Rand and I reached it, Jake's wolf was out of sight.

The verandah traversed the width of the house on the first floor, and double doors and floor-to-ceiling windows all along the front stood open to the sea breezes. Jean apparently needed lighter security in the Beyond than in his human life. Then again, he had his own personal loup-garou and lots of undead pirates at his disposal.

I looked up at Rand. "Stay here. Let me talk to him first."

The elf opened his mouth to respond, but thought better of it and settled for a nod and a disgruntled huff. Maybe he was learning.

Jean's living space was masculine and built for comfort. I passed a hammock on the verandah, which spoke of the West Indies, but the inside shone with a blend of island comfort and French wealth. Serious wealth. Oil lamps provided the lighting, and their soft illumination warmed the dark woods and rustic furnishings. Art filled the walls— nautical scenes, mostly. Furniture sat dark, heavy, solid. A fire blazed above the stone hearth, and the room smelled of the ocean and Jean's own scent of cinnamon and tobacco. I liked it.

"He's gone into Old Orleans, DJ. Should be back soon." I started as Jake emerged from a small door in the back of the parlor. He wore a pair of pants—probably Jean's, because they were too long and had an old-fashioned buttoned fly. No shirt, and his feet were bare. I was so glad to see him healthy and safe, I wanted to cry.

"You look like shit, sunshine."

"You look great." I hugged him, and he stiffened a little before eventually hugging me back.

Jake stepped back to give me a searching, hopeful look that broke my heart. "Thank God. I didn't infect you after all. Jean must have been wrong." His shoulders sagged and he closed his eyes, nodding. "Thank God."

"No, thank me." Rand stepped forward, the elven version

of testosterone on legs. "She *was* infected, thanks to you, and would be planning to shift and run for the rest of her life if not for me. I saved her."

Rand needed a gag, and if I had access to Mace's cane I'd beat him with it right now. "Stay out of this, Rand." More softly: "I'm okay now, Jake. As soon as some political stuff gets straightened out, you should come home." It was time we all moved on with our lives, whatever that meant.

An expressionless mask covered Jake's features as he tried to shut me out, but I could feel the despair filtering through his wonky loup-garou aura. I wanted to help him, but as usual, I didn't know what to do. I moved to hug him again, but he stepped back. *Don't pressure him. Don't put expectations on him.* I needed it tattooed on my forehead. If I'd learned nothing else from this ordeal, it should be that.

I began to notice other things. Fading bruises on his abdomen. A deep scratch across the side of his neck. "Who hurt you?" Jean had promised to take care of him. As fast as loup-garou healed, the fact he was still showing those injuries told me they were recent, and they'd been serious.

He ignored me and focused on Rand. "Aren't you Eugenie's boyfriend? What the hell are you doing here?"

Rand squared his shoulders. "I am a member of the Elven Synod, and Dru and I are bonded. This blood-bond allowed me to save her, as elves are immune to the loup-garou curse. If the shift didn't kill her, her wizard Elders would have, thanks to you."

I closed my eyes. Rand was such an ass. I liked him a lot better when he was half conscious or fighting for his life. "The little detail Rand omitted is that the Axeman was after us and we escaped through a transport that took us to

Elfheim, which was too dangerous for us. Long story. I don't want to go back to New Orleans without a plan to stop him, and I thought Jean could help."

Slow. No expectations. "I'm really glad to see you, Jake."

Jake was boring visual holes in Rand, his brows lowered. I didn't think he'd even been listening to me. "If you give me your blood, will it kill the loup-garou virus in me?"

Rand blinked. "I am bound to Dru. I can't bond with anyone else. Especially a man."

"It's that kind of bond? Sunshine, I'm surprised at you." Jake slipped into his easygoing, good-old-boy-from-Mississippi persona that didn't even begin to hide his disquiet. "Bet Alex is not a happy Boy Scout."

"It is *not* that kind of a bond." I hoped he could understand my words since I seemed incapable of unclenching my teeth. But Jake had brought up a point I'd been too self-absorbed to consider, and I was ashamed of myself. His stirrings of hope kindled my own. "Rand, if Jake were to bond with another elf, would that kill the loup-garou virus in him, or at least neutralize it?"

Rand chewed his lip and stared at the floor. The air seemed to get sucked out of the room while we waited. Jake's longing soaked into my skin so intensely it sent sharp pains through my head. I was still clutching the staff, and stroked my palms over it to soothe the ache. In previous trips to the Beyond, the staff had neutralized my empathic abilities. Broken, it only filtered out some. Jake was broadcasting like crazy.

"I don't think so," Rand finally said. "Dru was a given because she hadn't shifted yet, and the virus had just begun to change her system. You've been turned, what?"—he looked at Jake—"three years?"

Jake nodded. "More or less."

He shrugged. "I can't see it working. It might even kill you since the virus has changed your system completely. Plus, you'd have to find an elf willing to bond with you. It's a lifelong, unbreakable tie, and not a decision we make lightly."

Jake's eyebrow took a hike northward. "You're tied to this guy till death do you part?"

"No!" I shook my head emphatically. Not like he thought, anyway.

"Exactly," Rand said.

"That is most unfortunate for you, Monsieur Elf, since it hastens your death," said a voice from behind us—a deep voice, sexy and husky and decidedly French. I'd know it anywhere.

Jean Lafitte had come home.

33

Jean blew into the room like a hurricane gale, throwing a satchel on a chair and stalking to face our little group. He pinned me with dark blue eyes that softened when I finally met his gaze, then turned to Jake. "Jacob, please show our elven friend to the room we reserve for our most honored guests, and ask Marcel to bring what he needs in terms of bandages and clothing. Then find Josefin and send her to me with the things Drusilla will need for her *toilette*."

"Dru and I stay together." Rand moved closer to my side, and I rolled my eyes. That elf so needed a reality check.

Jean grinned at him. "That was not a request, Monsieur Randolph. The elves are accustomed to being *les tyrans* in the Beyond with their mental games, but you are in Barataria now. You would do well to remember you have no asylum here, but are tolerated on my forbearance. Jacob, do as I say."

For a moment, I didn't think Jake was going to respond. I didn't blame him. Rand might be able to help him get rid of the loup-garou curse, and Jean was being awfully pushy. I'd spent most of my time with the charming, flirtatious (if occasionally smarmy) Jean Lafitte, or his sneaky, devious alter ego. This was the cold, calculating, and extremely smart man who'd manipulated nations and commanded respect.

"Jake, you don't have to do anything you don't want to." I started to move toward him.

"Stay where you are, Drusilla. Jacob, do as I say. *Tout de suite.*" Jean's voice was hard, authoritative.

Jake gave a small nod and nudged Rand toward the outer doors with a grip on his upper arm. "You heard *Le Capitaine,* elf boy. Move it."

Rand jerked away from him. "Dru, give me the staff. I can work on it tonight."

I looked down at the cracked stick of wood I'd been clinging to like a lifeline for what seemed like a week. "I thought you needed supplies from Elfheim in order to fix it."

"Vervain's powers transferred to me when she died," he said shortly. "I can do it now."

Ah, yeah, Vervain's powers. That would be the glowing, chanting thing. I might as well let him have it. Its power had been so diminished I could do almost as much with my own native magic. I laid the staff in his open palm. If there was any chance he could fix it, might as well let him try, even though I didn't trust him as far as I could drop-kick him.

Once they'd left, I rounded on Jean. "You don't know what Jake's been through." I summoned up energy I didn't think I still had and put it behind my words. "I appreciate your taking him in but don't treat him like one of your lackeys. Why is he bruised?"

"I will treat him as he needs to be treated." Jean unstrapped the crossed leather belts slung across his hips and laid his bulky pistol on the table. "Jacob drinks too much and is dangerous to himself and to others, as you well know if you will only admit to it."

"Bossing him around like that isn't going to help."

"I beg to differ, *Jolie*. Of this, I know more than you—as hard as such a thing might be for you to admit." He treated me to a little smirk that drew my eyes to the strong jaw with the scar running across it, and neutralized my comeback. I needed to remember that my rational mind seemed to book a holiday whenever I was around this man . . . dead guy . . . pirate . . . and keep my wits on alert. I thought he was hot, and he wasn't above taking advantage of it.

I sighed. "What do you mean? You know more about what?"

"About soldiers and fighting men, Drusilla." He pulled out the elastic band he'd used to tie his dark hair into a short tail—a band he'd stolen from me—and ran his hands through his dark, wavy hair. My body ached and my heart was with Alex, but I wasn't blind.

"Jacob is a fine man, but he is confused by the things which have happened to him," Jean continued. "He also is a soldier, and soldiers who do not know their way need someone to lead them. Sometimes, following orders can help them rediscover their path."

"What about the bruises? He's been hurt."

Jean leaned against a side table and looked at me, arms crossed over his chest. "Jacob has anger which needs to be used in a way that endangers no one. He fights, the men place wagers, and he is no longer so angry."

"But—"

"He is loup-garou, *Jolie*, and enjoys the fight. I promised you I would not allow him to be truly harmed, but you must let me deal with him in my way."

I ran my hands through my own hair, fighting the overwhelming exhaustion that had been building since we arrived. I had to admit Jean's logic made sense. Jake had been a Marine. He was hardwired to follow orders and respect authority, and he'd mostly been floating alone since the loup-garou attack. And he did have a lot of anger to work off.

"You're right." Man, I hated to admit that. Jake would take orders from Jean before he would do anything Alex suggested. The Warin cousins loved each other, and hated each other, and had way too much baggage. "What I don't understand is, what's in this for you?"

"Allies are always of value." He walked to me and put his hands on my shoulders, then leaned down and kissed me on each cheek. "Welcome to my home, Drusilla. We will talk more. For now, I have someone who will help tend to your *toilette*, or certainly I would be pleased to be of service myself."

Ah, there was the Jean I knew, and I had to smile—until I felt the dried blood on my face crack and a dark reddish-brown flake fell on the shredded remains of my red dress. I felt a blush spread across my face at the picture I must make.

I'd kill for a shower, but somehow I didn't think plumbing had been invented in this version of Barataria. "You aren't even going to ask about the elf?"

Jean's jaw tightened. "As I said, we will talk afterward."

Oh, goody.

A soft knock sounded from the open doorway, and I turned to see a young woman standing shyly outside.

"*Bonjour*, Josefin." He motioned her closer, and she stepped in with a quick, wide-eyed glance at me before looking down. I tried to imagine what I must look like to a pretty, young mulatto girl of the early 1800s, standing here in my bare feet, half of a short red dress, a coating of dried blood, and hair that probably looked like a rat's family palace. I'd be afraid to look at me too.

Jean rattled off some instructions in French, then turned back to me. "Josefin will bring you water and clothing. I will have food brought for you once you are ready."

"Thank you." I began to relax, and breathed normally for the first time in hours, which was sad considering I was hiding out in a pirate lair in some time-warped version of reality. "Before I go, can you get word to Alex that I am here and safe? Please?"

That grin again—more of a smirk, actually. "*Certainement.* I will inform *le petit chien* that you are a guest in my home, and that it was I to whom you came for assistance."

Oh good Lord. Well, it was the best I was going to get, and at least Alex, "the little dog," wouldn't be planning my funeral. He'd just see it as one more ridiculous situation I'd landed myself in to reinforce his feelings that my life was too chaotic for him to handle. What else was new? Only that it made me profoundly sad.

With a lot of pointing, pantomime, and my pidgin French, Josefin and I managed to get through bath time without a disaster. She brought several buckets of heated water and poured them into a large tub in a small, windowless room located off a bedroom—an early nineteenth-century version of en suite. She sat in a chair near the door, just out of sight, and hummed to herself while I took stock of my injuries with the help of a mirror she'd brought me. It was ornate silver, heavy, and polished to a bright shine. I wondered from what Spanish ship Jean had plundered it.

Shampoo hadn't been invented yet, so I had to wash my hair with rich, oily soap that smelled slightly of coconut. Josefin had sprinkled some type of lavender-scented liquid in the water, so I ended up smelling like either a Caribbean courtesan or a tropical drink that would be served with little paper umbrellas.

I'd kill for some aloe, hawthorn, and ground hibiscus to make a healing potion. I had cuts and concrete scrapes on both arms and one side of my face, and my ribs were killing me. Sadly, I had enough experience with such injuries to know they were bruised and not broken since I could move without screaming. My feet were cut and sore.

On the bright side, at least I hadn't been chopped at with an ax. Maybe I could make a shopping list for someone to pick items up for me in Old Orleans. I wanted to be healed and ready for a fight before I went home. In the back of my mind, I was already hatching a plan that included the aid of a certain piratical member of the historical undead. Jean Lafitte could help us catch the Axeman, if I could talk him into it.

I also wanted Rand healed and back to his fully powered, glowing self before he had to meet Mace Banyan again. I wasn't sure what I was going to do about my elven non-husband, but I had a feeling his continued existence might be closely tied to my own.

If the necromancer controlling the Axeman had simply wanted me dead, he could keep sending the killer back again and again until my luck ran out. But I suspected the necromancer also wanted to play with me, drag this out, make me wonder where his killer would turn up next. Anyone who liked playing games that much would love the idea of killing me not at the hands of the impersonal Axeman but using Jean Lafitte.

The irony of it would be irresistible. I just had to work out the details, including convincing Jean to go along with it and figuring out a way to keep him from actually being controlled by the necromancer and killing me. If we pulled this off, God only knows what I'd owe him.

I wrapped myself in one of the towels Josefin left for me, and stood looking uncertainly at the gross bathwater, tinged pink and brown with blood and dirt. I wouldn't let that poor girl haul it out for me. I took the bucket, filled it, and walked to the door of the bathing room.

Josefin tittered when she saw me. *"Non!"* She took the bucket and poured the water back into the tub, then reached in and pulled out a plug I hadn't seen. I leaned over and saw some rough piping leading from the bottom of the tub through the floor. Fancy.

Josefin rattled on enthusiastically, and I smiled. The only words I understood were "Monsieur" and "Lafitte." And really, in Barataria, what more needed saying? The man could afford the best rudimentary plumbing available.

She motioned for me to follow her, so I hitched the towel

around me more tightly, trailed her into the bedroom—and stopped. I hadn't really looked around it before, assuming it was a guest room. Judging by the pirate lounging on the bed, looking right at home, my assumption had been misguided.

34

My mouth went dry, and I couldn't think of anything to say. If the garments piled next to him were any indication, Jean had managed to rustle up some clothing. "Uh, can you excuse me while I dress?"

We would not be discussing anything with me in his bedroom wearing a towel.

His blue-eyed gaze traveled leisurely—and blatantly—from my face to my feet and back. I knew some good French words for that. "*Cochon*. Go away. Vamoose. *Au revoir*."

I doubted it was the first time he'd been called a pig, and he seemed to take no offense. "You cannot blame a man for being a man, *Jolie*." He chuckled and rolled to his feet. "I will grant your privacy, however. Josefin will help you dress."

I wished Josefin would leave as well but after assessing the clothing on the bed, I realized I needed an instruction manual. I looked at the girl helplessly and she giggled, pulling out a cream-colored garment that consisted of two tubes connected at the top by a band. When I shrugged, she held it up to herself.

Holy crap. It was a cross between crotchless panties and

silk long johns. That was so not going to happen. I shook my head and dug my nice little red bikinis from the pile of clothing in the bathing room and put them back on. God would forgive me for a little judicious recycling.

Josefin collapsed into a chair, laughing, and I imagined the stories she'd take home with her about the filthy idiot woman who didn't know how to bathe or dress.

She held out what I decided was a corset. Crafted of ivory linen and silk, it looked more like a vest than anything too Victoria's Secret, so I shrugged into it, looking at the laces and pulling at strings. It was really lovely, with delicate embroidery in floral patterns hand-stitched into it.

Too bad Josefin's English was nonexistent. I'd love to know how many different sizes of lingerie Jean Lafitte had hanging around his bachelor pad, just waiting for the proper woman to need it.

I started lacing myself in, and the girl shrieked, now laughing so hard tears rolled down her cheeks.

"*Non, non.*" She turned around, miming a lacing motion behind her back.

Ack. I was wearing it backward. Sighing, I slid into it the other way and turned for her to lace me up. "Not so tight. Need to breathe. Bruised ribs." I flapped my arms in a bellowing motion.

The corset created way more cleavage than I was accustomed to showing, but who was going to see it? Certainly not Monsieur Lafitte. And it kind of held my ribs in place and helped with the pain.

I picked up a simple chemise and tossed it aside, along with a pair of what looked like silk stockings. No wonder women in the olden days kept their virtue intact so long—it was too much trouble to get dressed and undressed. Although the open-air bloomers would have made certain bodily functions and sexual acts convenient.

The only remaining garment was the dress, and I held it up. A beauty, probably stolen from a ship bound for the fashionable ladies of New Orleans. It had a velvet bodice of deep indigo blue that gathered under the bust in an empire waistline, with a champagne-colored skirt flowing beneath. Very 1815 haute couture.

With Josefin's help, I slipped it over my head and discovered all that cleavage was still exposed. Otherwise, it fit perfectly. It was even the right length, surprising since modern clothing always had to be hemmed for me.

Along with the mirror, I'd been given an ornate silver brush, and I ran it through my damp hair, which had started curling from the sea air. Josefin took the brush from me and directed me to a seat, where she tugged out curls and pulled hairpins from her skirt pocket, working until I barely recognized myself in the little mirror. I looked like a wealthy nineteenth-century lady. We'd see how long that lasted.

I was as presentable as I was going to get, and I could eat an undead horse. I also wanted to make sure Jean hadn't killed Rand. Eventually, I might hire him to dispose of the elf, but for now I felt at least partially responsible for him, like a nanny with an entitled, ill-tempered, six-foot-tall toddler.

"Monsieur Lafitte?" I motioned for Josefin to go ahead, and she led me from the room onto the verandah and down two doors, back into the main parlor. There seemed to be no hallways in the interior of the house, but I noticed both the front and back were open, allowing air to circulate.

Jean sat in an armchair, long legs splayed, smoking one of his little cigars. He rose to his feet when I came in. The door snicked behind me, and I turned to see Josefin had left us alone.

"You look lovely, *Jolie*. The gown shows off your . . ."

I held up a hand, my face growing warm. "Don't finish that sentence. I know what it shows off." The dress weaved provocatively around my legs as I walked through the room, making me wish I'd worn the chemise as well as a shawl to cover the cleavage. "Where is Rand?"

"Bah, do not concern yourself with the elf." Jean pointed to a side table that had been laid out with bread, cheese, and some type of dried meat. "You must eat."

I didn't even ask what the meat was, but took some of everything. I knew ladies should be proper and eat like birds—at least that's what Mammy told Scarlett in *Gone with the Wind*—but I thought the rule should be suspended when in the company of the undead. Or so I told myself. Plus, I hadn't eaten since lunch at Liuzza's yesterday, or today, or . . .

"What time is it? What *day* is it?"

Jean handed me a snifter of brandy, and I took a sip. "Time is irrelevant here, *Jolie*. But in your world, it is Sunday morning."

We'd been gone more than twelve hours. "Did someone reach Alex? Where is Jake?"

Jean shook his head. "You have too many men with whom to concern yourself, Drusilla. Had you availed yourself of my offer to live here, your life would have been much simpler, *oui*?"

Couldn't deny that, although I suspected life with Jean

Lafitte, even an immortal Jean Lafitte, wouldn't be without its challenges.

He'd returned to his armchair, and I sat on the nearest end of the sofa with a small plate in my fabric-covered lap. I asked the question that had been needling me since I'd seen him stretched across his bed. "Do you keep gowns and underwear for women in all sizes and colors for whenever the need arrives?"

He smiled. "I had hoped you might come to my home one day and wear these garments chosen especially for you."

Uh-huh. He was so full of crap. "And about Alex?"

I stuffed another bite of bread in my mouth and washed it down with brandy. It was good brandy; my head was already buzzing. There was probably a rule of etiquette about ladies guzzling brandy on a Sunday morning too, but we were in the Beyond and it was dark outside.

"*Oui*, Drusilla. Word was sent to Monsieur Warin that you are safe. What has happened to bring you here with this elf?"

Well, that dampened my appetite. The memory of my home in flames sat heavily on my heart, and the pain of loss outdid the bruised ribs in making it hurt to breathe.

I'd have to mourn later. I set the plate back on the table and gave him the short version of the Axeman's activities so far. "We know the necromancer is targeting me. Rand helped me escape into the transport at his house." I swallowed hard and blinked back white-hot tears. "The Axeman burned my house down. I doubt anything is left. I guess if it weren't for Rand, I'd have burned up with it." I remembered trying to run back inside and him hauling me physically away from it. I needed to be nicer to him.

Jean's eyes narrowed. "Monsieur Randolph claims to be your husband. Is this true?"

I choked on my brandy, coughing out a quick "no!" I wasn't sure how, but I had to get Rand under control and rid him of the notion that we were going to be more than business partners, sort of, apparently forever. Good Lord, Alex was right; I did attract chaos like flies to bad chicken.

"I bonded with him to give him leverage within the Synod, in exchange for getting rid of the loup-garou virus. Mace Banyan found out I'd been exposed to the virus, and planned to use it against me. It was my best option."

Jean stared into space a few moments. "It might have appeared to be your best option, but I fear this bonding will make you a more serious threat if the rumors about power struggles within the Synod are true. Some say the elves wish to challenge the wizards for control of the borders by taking over the Interspecies Council."

Holy crap. "You think Mace Banyan kidnapped me, thinking it would get the wizards to break the truce and start a war?" If so, the staff was nothing but an excuse. And Rand had complicated things more with this bonding business, of which I'm sure he was aware.

"I do not know, but it would not be a great surprise." Jean leaned forward and propped his elbows on his knees. His indigo shirt matched the bodice of my gown, and his fawn-colored pants were the same color as my skirt. It couldn't be coincidental. "Do you wish me to kill Quince Randolph? It would be my pleasure to do so, and rid you of this burden."

"No!" My heart stuttered, and I realized that no matter what a mess I'd made of things, it could always get worse.

"He's a member of the Elven Synod now. Killing him would be a disaster. I'll figure some way out of this. You haven't done anything to him already, have you?"

"Of course not, *Jolie*." Jean's smile left me pretty sure that wherever Rand was, he wasn't basking in comfort, being supplied with a bath and luxurious clothing and plates of food. On the other hand, Jean would realize helping a member of the Elven Synod would work to his favor. He was piling up IOUs like a banker during a recession.

As annoyed as I was with the elf, I thought he'd suffered enough physical pain. "I don't want him hurt, especially since he saved me from the Axeman." Well, unless I hurt him myself. "Promise me."

To seal the deal, I trotted out Jean's favorite three-word endearment: "I'll owe you."

He laughed, getting up to pour himself more brandy. "Very well." He held up the decanter and raised an eyebrow.

"No, thanks." I'd had just enough liquid courage to plow into my next request. "Speaking of owing you, I need your help."

With a total know-it-all smirk, he planted his smug (and quite attractive) butt next to me on the sofa. I hated owing Jean. He had no boundaries when it came to repayment.

His arm rested alongside mine as he leaned toward me. "Tell me your heart's desire, *Jolie*, and I shall be pleased to provide it." His voice was husky and silky at the same time. It made me uncomfortably aware of how close he was sitting, and annoyed with myself for noticing.

I stared deep into his eyes and said just the thing to cool his ardor. "Come back with me to New Orleans, to lure out the necromancer."

Worked like a charm. He got up and prowled behind the sofa, eventually throwing himself into his chair again and slinging a long leg over the side. "Why would I do this, Drusilla? If the *maître des mortes* controls me and you are the target, he could force me to kill you, or worse. Why would you wish this?"

What was worse than dead? "I can't go back without a plan to flush out—"

The beachside door flew open and Mace Banyan burst into the room, apparently shoved by Jake, who followed closely behind. "Keep your hands off me, you rabid hound!"

Talk about bad news blowing in. Mace straightened his clothing and glared at Jake. I liked seeing Mace wolf-handled.

"Monsieur Banyan, to what do we owe this . . . pleasure?" Jean rose from his chair like Sebastian when he'd spotted a squirrel outside the window. Playtime and dinner, all rolled into one package. I felt another pang of guilt, wondering if Sebastian had survived the fire.

"Mr. Lafitte, I have cause to believe two of my people are being held in Barataria against their will. I demand their release." Mace didn't glow, but the air around him literally shimmered with power, giving him a not-quite-solid, wavery look. Like the Princess Leia hologram in *Star Wars*.

"Help me, Obi-Wan. I have an elf that needs caning." I held my brandy snifter up in salute. It really was excellent brandy.

Mace noticed me for the first time and didn't seem pleased. "*You*. I should have known when we learned our transport had been used to go to Old Barataria that you'd be up to your . . . cleavage in it. Glad to see you're dressing for the only part you're fit to play."

I'd had about all the elven nonsense I could handle for this week, so I did what any self-respecting Green Congress wizard would do in my situation. I hurled the heavy cut-glass brandy decanter at his head.

Surprised, he didn't duck in time, and it glanced off his forehead with a satisfying crack before crashing to the floor and shattering into a brilliant carpet of glass.

"Sorry about your decanter, Jean. I'll buy you another."

"It is of no concern, *Jolie*."

Mace rounded on Jean, rubbing his forehead. "Release my people immediately—both of them—or suffer the consequences."

"What do you mean, both of them?" I propped my hands on my hips in my best impression of a pirate stance. "Who do you think is here?"

Mace's eyes narrowed. "I told Quince Randolph to stay away from you, but he is stubborn and ambitious." His anger sent an uncomfortable electrical charge into the air. "I thought Vervain would talk him out of using you to drive a wedge into the Synod by involving the wizards in our affairs. Since she's here with you, apparently you've corrupted her as well."

He took a step toward me, a move echoed by both Jean and Jake. "Consider this a declaration of war between the wizards and elves." His voice was low and menacing. "And you will not win."

35

War? What was the Elf King smoking? "Look, Mace, I don't know what you think has happened, but I haven't done anything to interfere with the Synod. You kidnapped me, remember? All Rand did was get me out before you killed me."

He took another step toward me, causing both Jean and Jake to visibly tense, but I closed the rest of the distance between us myself. I had no tolerance for bullies, and that's all Mace Banyan was—a bully who could make the air around him shimmer. Plus, I'd been drinking.

"No one is being held here against his will, you arrogant ass." Unless Jean had other prisoners, but I didn't want to go there. "Rand is here with me by choice, and after what you did to him, if anyone should be declaring war, it's him."

Mace sent an eyebrow northward. "Defending him, are you? Then where is he? Why are you dressed"—his eyes traveled to my chest and paused, his mouth quirking in a way that made me want to slap his lips off his face—"like a pirate trollop? And where is Vervain?"

My breath hitched, not at the pirate-trollop moniker, since

that was regrettably accurate, but because he didn't know about Vervain. How was that possible? I searched his face for some sign of duplicity, but saw only anger and that elven arrogance I'd come to detest. Normally, I'd have been absorbing emotions like crazy since I was in the Beyond and didn't have the staff, but I couldn't read elves.

Jean's anger fed into mine, however, as he stood to my left, feet apart and arms folded across his broad chest as if he were commanding a ship. Jake leaned against the wall behind Mace, his posture casual but his eyes sharp.

Well, wasn't this fun. "Jean, where is Rand? He needs to tell Mace what happened."

With a curt nod and a wave of his hand, Jean dispatched soldier Jake to fetch my big, blond, elven albatross. I sure as hell hoped Rand knew how to defuse this situation. I was starting to think life on Grand Terre as Jean Lafitte's pet wolf might have been preferable to this political circus, and that was without factoring in the Axeman.

We stood in a triangle of tense silence for a couple of minutes, until Rand finally stalked through the door ahead of Jake, his pretty face now only marred by a scowl. All that glowing and chanting must have helped him heal. He wore jeans and a shirt of soft golden-brown flannel I recognized as Jake's.

Rand got in Mace's face without a pause. "What the hell are you doing here, threatening war? Threatening my mate?"

God help me. To keep my mouth shut, I literally had to bite my lower lip so hard I tasted blood. If I had to play the mate role to back Mace away from warmongering, so be it. I forced myself forward to stand beside Rand and didn't flinch when he took my hand. Mace had to be neutralized until I could talk to Elder Zrakovi and find out what the hell was going on. Assuming he knew.

Mace looked at our joined hands and laughed. "Nice try, but I will not formally recognize her as your mate until I've talked with Vervain."

Rand looked at the floor and began chanting softly. When he looked back up at Mace, his skin had taken on a golden glow, and the hand I held grew uncomfortably hot. I was beginning to suspect the fire elves did more than rub two sticks together to kindle a flame.

Mace took a step backward, his eyes widening as the meaning of Rand's display hit him. "Vervain is dead." He didn't ask it, simply said it in wonder. "As her eldest, you are Synod." He bowed slightly, as if it pained him. "So be it."

That was it? It was that simple? And did "eldest" mean Rand had siblings? Did I have elven in-laws?

"You must accompany me to Elfheim. The Synod must meet and hold the ceremony." Mace turned mocking eyes to me. "Along with your mate, of course."

"As leader of the Synod, you'll recognize our union now, in front of these witnesses. We don't need your recognition for it to be valid, but I won't have you going back to Elfheim and pretending you know nothing of it." Rand had stopped glowing but his voice, which with me was either flirtatious or petulant, deepened with a weight of power. Who *was* this guy?

The two men silently engaged in some kind of long, mental pissing match.

Mace blinked first. "If you insist." He pulled a small folding knife from his pocket and flicked it open. In my peripheral vision, I saw Jean straighten.

Mace drew the blade across his left palm and dragged his right index finger through the blood that welled along the cut. That finger was not going anywhere near my mouth. As if sensing my thoughts, Rand clasped my hand more tightly.

Chanting the same language Rand had used earlier, Mace reached toward Rand, who lowered his head. Mace traced a figure in blood on Rand's forehead. It looked like a cross between a peace symbol and a stick figure. Continuing to chant softly, Mace swept his finger through the blood again and turned to me. His voice was calm and even, his finger unhesitant as he traced something on my forehead I could only assume was the same figure as Rand's. But when they met mine, his dark eyes held pure hatred.

He might have agreed to this, but he didn't like it, and his expression told me he'd never accept it.

Damn it, I felt like a clueless pawn in the middle of some elven power war whose outcome would be monumental. And I didn't even understand the rules.

"Wait for me outside and let me say good-bye to Dru," Rand told Mace. "I'll go back to Elfheim with you to meet with the Synod. She has business to attend to in New Orleans."

"You can say your good-byes in front of me. Surely your mate isn't shy."

I recognized a dare when I heard one, and so did Rand. He turned his back to Mace and pulled me in front of him, out of Mace's view. Fiddling with the button of his shirt, he reached inside and carefully slipped out the staff. Still cracked, unfortunately.

Pressing it into my hands between us, he pulled me to

him and kissed me. I kissed him back through gritted teeth—
not easy, but possible. Finally, he pulled his mouth up to my
ear. "The wood is cracked, but the core is repaired. Stay out
of Elfheim, no matter what."

I hid the staff in the folds of my billowy skirt as he turned
and stalked out the door, leaving Mace to direct his parting
shot at Jean. "This is twice you have opposed us, Mr. Lafitte,
first in Antoine's last month, and now again. We will not
forget."

36

After Mace Banyan's performance, convincing Jean to return to New Orleans had proven surprisingly easy. All it took was sharing Rand's theory that the elves—maybe even Mace himself—were behind the necromancer who was controlling the Axeman. Mace had made it onto the pirate's most-hated list, and Jean had both a long memory and unlimited time in which to wreak havoc.

Neither would fight fair, but I'd put my money on the pirate, if for no other reason than Mace could be killed and Jean couldn't. Plus, once Jean's true enemy in his mortal life, always his enemy. I can't imagine his immortal self had changed that much. Jean could wait, plan, and get revenge at his leisure.

While Jean tended to some mysterious, pressing business—I always thought the fewer details I knew about his dealings, the better—Jake walked me back to the transport. I had Jean's key card to the Eudora Welty Suite at the Hotel Monteleone in my pocket since I didn't know what kind of shape my house was in. Besides, we'd all agreed it would be better for me to stay off radar until we had our plan set.

"You coming back to New Orleans once the elves have settled down?" I'd promised myself I wouldn't pressure Jake. For one thing, it always backfired. For another, there was Alex to consider. I'd done my share of sending mixed signals between the Warin cousins, but I had made my choice and he was back in New Orleans.

Jake walked a bit farther before answering. "I like it here, DJ. I like working for Jean, at least for now." He gave me a sidelong glance, and I could sense his trepidation. He was afraid I'd argue with him.

I took his hand. "I understand. You do what you need to do. I'll tell Alex you're okay."

He smiled, and I caught my first glimpse of the dimples that had done me in the first time I met him, back in the first days after Katrina. In hindsight, those days—which had seemed so chaotic—had been much, much simpler. "I doubt he's worried about much besides wringin' my neck, sunshine."

I laughed. "You guys can pretend you don't care about each other all you want. I know better." Bottom line: No matter how angry Alex got at Jake, he'd want whatever was best for him, and vice versa. Jean had made me realize that, for now, Jake needed to stay here. He needed to be a good soldier. He needed to fight off his anger. He needed to stay out of his own head.

As for Alex and me, we had to smooth things out, whether it meant being together or just relearning how to back away and be friends again. The close call with the Axeman, and this forced separation, had made me realize I wanted to see where our relationship could go. I wanted it so desperately my chest ached. But I couldn't be someone

I wasn't, and only Alex could decide if the chaos of my life was something he could live with. Whatever conclusion he came to, we had to come out as friends on the other side. We had to.

Jake and I walked up the rise in silence and hugged before he turned and started back toward the beach. I stepped into the transport set into the marshy sand and watched him walk away. I didn't know when I'd see him again, which hurt. What happened to him wasn't fair, but if Hurricane Katrina had taught us anything, it was that sometimes fairness was only a lucky twist of a capricious wind.

Ignoring the stares from tourists, I trudged through the plush Monteleone lobby as fast as my bare feet could slap along the cold marble floors. Fortunately, it was busy midafternoon check-in time, so none of the hotel staff paid any attention to the limping woman in an early nineteenth-century gown flashing too much cleavage, clutching her ribs, and holding on to a two-foot-long cracked stick of wood as she rushed through their fine establishment.

I stepped onto the elevator with a young couple wearing blinding white tennis shoes—the sure sign of tourist-hood. New Orleans wasn't the cleanest city, and most of us quickly abandoned white footwear unless, like shrimp boots, they could be hosed down.

The couple tried to stare at me without staring, but finally I said, "Pirate reenactment. Lost my shoes." They laughed and said how much they loved New Orleans. Such spirit. Such zest for life. Such character.

They had no idea.

I'd been up for more than twenty-four hours with very

little to eat, so the closer I got to Jean's suite, the more exhaustion weighed on me. I needed a shower, something from room service (charged to the account of "John Lafayette"), and a nap, in that order.

First, though, I had to call Alex and see if he was too angry to sit down and talk strategy after Jean arrived. Whatever we did, Alex and Ken needed to be in on it.

He answered his cell on the first ring. "Where the hell is she, you son of a bitch? I might not be able to kill you permanently, but I can make you suffer."

It took a second to realize he'd seen the Monteleone on his caller ID and thought it was Jean. "It's me, Alex."

A heartbeat of silence. "Where are you? What room?"

I flipped over the key card I'd thrown on the coffee table, but it didn't tell me a number. "Eighth floor. Eudora Welty Suite. I—"

"Do. Not. Move."

"I—" I'd been about to say give me an hour for a shower and bring me something to wear, but he'd already hung up.

Damn, this wasn't going to be easy. I wanted to wrap my arms around Alex, to have him hold me and tell me everything was going to be okay. I didn't want to argue with him, or feel like I couldn't be what he wanted.

I figured there was time for at least a quick shower before he arrived—twenty minutes to drive to the Quarter and another ten to find parking. It should be longer than that before Jean arrived.

Groaning, I shucked bits of period clothing along the thick carpet as I shuffled toward the bathroom. I glanced around the bedroom suite, wondering if Jean had left anything of interest, like clothing. The color scheme of royal blue and cream carried over from the huge sitting area outside, with a brass chandelier overhead. Too bad I didn't have time to plunder fully, but I did open the armoire and find a thick white hotel robe on a heavy wooden hanger next to shelves piled with folded pirate clothes.

The hotel would charge for the robe, but I was racking up debts to Jean at an alarming clip. What was one more?

The warm water, soap, and shampoo stung my cut and bruised feet, but turned my sore muscles to rubber. I was healing at a nice, slow, wizard rate. The concrete scrapes along the side of my face had scabbed, but I had a big, dark bruise the shape of a bedpost across my rib cage where the Axeman had slung me.

When I was growing up, I never saw Gerry come home with bruises and cuts and broken bones. I'd like to think the world in which I was a sentinel had gotten a lot more brutal than his pre-Katrina days. I didn't much like the other option—that I wasn't very good at my job.

I'd just toweled off and shaken the loose water out of my hair when I heard Alex calling my name. The man must have sped through town and parked on the flipping sidewalk. And how did he get in the suite? It sounded like he was right outside the bathroom—

"Wait!" I scrambled for the hotel robe as he opened the door. "Let me—"

"God, DJ." I barely had a chance to see the dark circles under his eyes before he'd pulled me against him. One arm held me to his chest so tightly it hurt my ribs, while the other hand touched my hair, my face, my shoulders. "You scared the shit out of me. When I saw your house . . ."

I'd ask about the house eventually. Right now, I had everything I needed, and as much as I wanted to be cool and sexy and detached, all I could do was wrap my arms around his waist. Everything was such a damned mess. I don't know how long we stood that way, him rubbing my back and holding me close.

Finally, he loosened his grip and I stepped back, wiping my eyes with the too-long sleeve of the robe.

"Where have you been?" His voice was rough, and his control was shot. I could feel the emotions rolling off him, making me shiver. Fear, relief, anger, all in one big shapeshifter tangle.

"Didn't you get my message?" I grabbed his hand, holding it between mine. I needed to touch him.

"I got this stuck under the windshield wiper of my truck." He dug in his jeans pocket with his other hand and pulled out a folded sheet of paper. He shook it out and held it up. Expensive-looking, handmade paper with two words of looping, ornate handwriting I recognized as Jean's: "Drusilla lives."

Oh good Lord. I should have known not to trust Jean to do more than the bare minimum. "I'm sorry. I asked Jean to get word to you that I was in the Beyond, at Barataria. I had to escape through a transport and didn't want . . . I couldn't . . ." The tears started again, and I dashed them away impatiently. Of all the times to turn into a whiny girl, this wasn't it. "Is Sebastian . . ." I couldn't finish a sentence.

Alex hugged me again. "He's okay. I found him hiding in the bushes behind my house about twelve hours after the fire. I should've known you were with Lafitte, but I was afraid the elves had you, especially with Randolph missing too."

"He's—"

Alex stepped back and placed a finger across my lips. "It's gonna be complicated. It's gonna give me a headache. Probably acid reflux too. And I'll end up doing something illegal. So don't tell me. Not yet." He leaned down and kissed me, then traced his fingers across the cuts on my face, following his fingers with his lips.

This was a bad idea. We had too much unresolved. We had too much . . . *damn*. He slipped his hands inside the robe.

His voice was low and husky against my ear. "Were you wearing that lace-up thing I found on the floor out there?"

I struggled to breathe as he worked his way down my neck. "Corset. Yeah. Wearing."

He growled against that sensitive spot where neck meets shoulder and nudged the robe aside till it slipped off and puddled at my feet. "Take it home with you. I want to see you in it."

Uh-huh. I could do that. As soon as I finished unbuttoning his stupid shirt. How many buttons did one shirt need?

By some stroke of divine providence, I opened my eyes while Alex's back was to the door to the outer suite and I was camouflaged by his body. So my "holy crap" was muffled by my dive for the floor and the abandoned robe.

Jean lounged in the doorway, grinning. "Do not mind me, *Jolie*. I would enjoy the sight more without *le petit chien* in the way, but"—he shrugged—"*Je prends du plaisir où je peux en trouver*."

I think that translated roughly as taking pleasure where

one found it, and I hoped he wasn't suggesting a threesome because as intriguing as that sounded in theory, it was a horrible idea.

I'd like to say I was woman enough, but I really, really wasn't.

37

The Eudora Welty Suite was beginning to feel like home, which was pathetic since it was much nicer than anyplace I'd ever lived or probably ever would.

After a nap, another shower, and a couple of good meals, I'd bought emergency magical supplies using my own credit card. Alex had miraculously found my abandoned purse in my driveway beside the slightly baked rental car. With the supplies, I cooked up a couple of simple potions on a hot plate I'd bought and set up in the suite's abbreviated kitchen.

After going through my grounding ritual and making up a new mojo bag, I wrapped my sore ribs in athletic tape, strapped a lightweight Kevlar vest over a T-shirt, then pulled my enormous new white Hotel Monteleone sweatshirt over that. I looked like the Michelin Man.

The elven staff, sturdy and straight as it could be inside its coating of duct tape, fit into a sleeve I'd stitched to the thigh of my new jeans, using a portable sewing kit from the gift shop and the denim I'd trimmed off the bottom where they were too long. Made a great camouflaged holster. I tucked a silver knife into a boot and clipped a small grenade to my belt loop within easy reach; Alex had retrieved it from my mantel. He thought the Axeman had found the grenade I'd left on my worktable and triggered it after setting my house on fire. Thus, the explosion.

I'd pulled my hair into a ponytail, then braided it and wrapped it in a low knot at my neck, minimizing its effectiveness as a handle with which to haul me around. Lesson learned.

Everything I wore except the knife and grenade were the products of a quick shopping trip in the Quarter. They were also the only clothing I now owned besides a robe stolen from Jean Lafitte and some underwear from an overpriced Quarter boutique. Alex had broken the news that little from the upstairs of my house would be salvageable except for Gerry's black grimoires, which appeared to have been protected with some kind of spell. The downstairs of the house was iffy because of smoke and water damage from the firefighters.

In theory, I knew it was all gone, that a big chunk of my life had disappeared in smoke and flame. I hadn't seen it, though, so it didn't seem real. Not seeing it helped me tuck it away in the back of my mind, where it waited like a coiled rattlesnake, waiting to spring up and sink its poison into me. I knew it *would* strike, but not when.

My watch had been crushed when Rand tackled me on Magazine Street and dragged me away from the fire, so I paced the suite, watching the minutes crawl past on the digital bedside clock. Jean was late, and I wasn't sure whether to be worried or annoyed.

He'd gone to L'Amour Sauvage to see Etienne and let slip the details of my plans for the evening. I thought it was risky for him to go alone and had urged him to take Alex or Ken or Rene—or even pull Dom or one of his other men out of the Beyond. Jean was convinced his vampire buddy had no role in the Axeman business.

I thought his trust was misplaced. Sadistic Lily had been in Etienne's office on my first visit, which gave him a connection to the elves. And the snippet of the phone call I'd overheard the last time I saw him kept replaying in my head. Etienne Boulard was up to something, and now Jean was an hour behind schedule.

I jumped when my new cell phone rang, its preset ringtone sounding like something from a Martian disco. My nerves were shot.

"Where are you?" Alex spoke in a stage whisper. He and Ken were waiting at my house, where I should have been twenty minutes ago.

"Jean still isn't back. I'm afraid he's been compromised. Etienne might be our guy."

Alex chuffed into the phone. "You want to change the plan?"

I did a quick mental run-through of different scenarios. "I'll come without him and hope he got the message delivered. If the vampire's taken control of Jean and is sending him to kill me, I don't want to be trapped at the hotel with all these people nearby."

One thing about the *Jean-as-necromancer-bait* plan worried me. I didn't know if I could kill him, even knowing he was trying to kill me, even knowing he'd come back to life in the Beyond and heal as good as new. Last time we'd tried to hurt each other was early in our relationship, and even then I wasn't sure either of us was serious about it. I sure as hell couldn't blow him up with a grenade.

But we both knew the risks and had agreed that, if this worked, it was the best chance to catch the necromancer. If it didn't work, nothing lost.

Jean, Alex, Ken, and I had gone through every scenario we could think of to keep Jean from falling under the necromancer's true control. Mostly, it consisted of him interpreting the necromancer's commands very literally. *Kill DJ* could be interpreted as *Kill DJ someday*. Or *Stab the girl* could mean any girl, or a stab wound to the toe.

Rand had made a quick, tense trip to New Orleans before returning to Elfheim—he'd taught me an elven spell that might help me track the line of magic from my attacker back to the necromancer, regardless of whether it was the Axeman or Jean being controlled. He was convinced one of the elves was behind this whole mess, and had gone back to Elfheim to spread the word that I'd be at my house tonight, digging through what was left after the fire.

I'd called Adrian and told him the same thing, explaining why I needed a few days off from my elf lessons. He actually asked if I needed help, which surprised me.

And just to cover my bases, I'd called the necromancer Jonas Adamson and set up a phony meeting with him next week to talk about new potions regulations, slipping in the information about my evening plans.

If Etienne, Adrian, Jonas, or a Synod member was either our leak to the necromancer or the necromancer himself, we should be in business.

I pulled the sweatshirt down to cover the grenade and headed down the softly lit, thickly carpeted hallway of the Monteleone's eighth floor and back through the lobby.

My hand trembled as I hit the remote to unlock Ken's

nondescript tan sedan that had been left on the curb with his NOPD hangtag in view. God, I hoped this plan worked. Prayed the staff would power Rand's tracking magic and be one of the elven skills I could control. He'd written down the words and told me what should happen, but it was all guesswork.

I also prayed nobody else I cared about got hurt.

As we'd agreed beforehand, I parked on Nashville beside the house instead of in the enclosed parking area behind it, the better to make a getaway if needed. Even in the illumination from the streetlights, the house looked a mess, and for the first time I realized how hard this was going to be—not the necromancer tracking, but seeing my home in ruins.

I fingered the crime scene tape crisscrossed over the back door, then ducked under it and went inside. I let out a whoosh of breath, relief draining the adrenaline from my muscles at the sight of my kitchen, or what little I could see of it from the wash of light coming from the street and the fluorescent lanterns Alex and Ken had set up around the rooms. The power had been cut to the house the night of the fire.

Alex and Ken were here somewhere, watching, waiting.

The acrid odor of charred wood, smoke, and damp burned my lungs and made my eyes water. The old Formica kitchen table with red-covered chrome chairs I'd found at a garage sale sat undisturbed but for a coat of ash from the ceiling above it. It could probably be saved. Dried mud covered the wooden floor.

I swallowed hard and stopped at the doorway into the double parlors. There hadn't been much left in here anyway since I'd even destroyed my lawn chair, but the old millwork had been water-soaked. Some of it might be salvageable, but it was hard for me to look past the ruin to see the redeemable.

Most of the things in the room—bits of jewelry, a shoe, a seared pan I'd used in my library for stirring charms—shouldn't have been there. They belonged upstairs, where Alex had told me nothing was left and the floor was suspect. Everything I'd worked for lay mixed in with chunks of plaster or covered in inky sludge, all the more gruesome for the shadows cast by light from the lanterns sitting in two corners of the room.

I knew it was just stuff, but sometimes stuff is important. Sometimes, stuff holds us together. Stuff bookends our lives, and stuff defines them.

I don't remember dropping to my knees. I was just suddenly there, flashing back to my first look at the wreckage of Gerry's house after Hurricane Katrina had sent the Seventeenth Street Canal flowing through it. I couldn't help but go back, the first of the losses that had lined up like macabre dominoes over the last few years. The loss of my house became the final domino that threatened to bring back every unshed tear I'd choked down.

How much loss should one person have to endure? How much *could* one person endure? I'd asked that question before, but the hits kept coming, pressing so hard on my heart I couldn't breathe, weighing so heavily it seemed as if I should sink through the floorboards.

Arms reached around me and the last voice I expected whispered, "Hush, baby girl." Eugenie sank to her knees beside me, pulled me into her arms, and rocked me like a child.

If God was listening, maybe He'd sent her as a gift.

Someone else I thought I'd lost but who'd made her way back to me.

"I'm sorry." My voice was ragged with sobs, but I finally choked out that inadequate excuse for an apology. For not being able to tell her who and what I was. For the damage to our friendship. For hurting her and letting it go on so long without finding a way to make it right.

"Shhh. I'm sorry too. I let things that don't matter get in the way of protecting what does matter. Us. You're still my best friend, DJ."

"You too." I hugged her back. "I will tell you everything when tonight is done. Everything. I swear it."

And I meant it. I couldn't pay lip service to our friendship and then lie to her at every turn.

A clatter in the guest room, followed by a curse, reminded me why we were here. Alex came into the parlor as Eugenie and I clambered to our feet, both sniffling and puffy-eyed. Ken remained out of sight. Probably praying for God to spare him from women crying during a stakeout.

"I told her how Rand tricked you into helping him," Alex said. "But Eugenie, you need to go home. We're trying to set up the arsonist."

Good cover story. "We think he'll come back if I'm here. We're trying to trap him." I hugged her and whispered, "Thank you. I'm glad you were here with me when I saw this."

"Me too." She looked tired, and I realized with shame I'd been so angry and hurt myself I hadn't thought about how hard this mess with Rand had hit her. She'd fallen heart-first for a man who didn't exist, at least not in the way she thought.

"Come on, let me walk you home." Alex's gaze met mine

over Eugenie's head, and I nodded. We needed her safely gone.

Before they reached the door to the kitchen, a crash of splintering wood and breaking glass sounded ahead of them. Eugenie was already screaming by the time the Axeman came within my line of vision, swinging his weapon of choice in his meaty right hand. If possible, he looked even more gross than the last time I'd seen him. More burned skin. Fever-bright eyes.

Alex shoved Eugenie toward me. "Get her out of here!"

She'd gone from scared to hysterical, screaming nonsense syllables and pushing me away. "He's not even human, DJ. Look at him! Why doesn't somebody shoot him?"

The Axeman had stopped to look at her. "I'm not human, and as soon as I kill her, I will kill you." With every word, he took a step closer, and Eugenie's breath came in such short, rapid gasps I feared she'd hyperventilate.

I prayed for forgiveness and slapped her—hard. It worked, at least for the moment, and she looked at me with big eyes and a pink handprint on her cheek. "Is that him? The Axeman?"

"Yes, now go!" I herded her toward the front door. She whimpered, her eyes darting from me to the ax-wielding horror show now charging at Alex.

"Front door," I said, shoving her in that direction. "Go home. Lock your doors. We'll explain later. GO!"

I turned back as the Axeman propelled Alex hard against the fireplace, the mantel cutting him across his upper back and knocking the wind out of him. He slid to a seated position on the slate hearth, wheezing, leaving the Axeman free to lumber toward me with a feral growl and a raised ax.

Fumbling in my pocket, I finally got my fingers on the immobilization charm, thumbed the top off the vial, and flung the contents at him.

Time and movement seemed to slow as Eugenie charged in front of me at the same time the dustlike particles of the charm flew forward. They hit her in the face, and she keeled over with a thud. Where had she come from? She must have circled the room to try again to reach the back door.

The Axeman laughed, spittle running down a chin and lips that were still blackened from our last encounter, with skin hanging in shreds from raw muscle and meat. "You missed, wizard. My turn."

Great, not only was he a charred undead killer, he was a comedian.

He started toward me again, but former fullback Alex hit him with a kidney shot from behind. They hit the ground, grappling, punching. The Axeman had dropped his weapon, and I kicked the ax away from them. It hit the fireplace and sent up a cloud of dust.

Ken ran in from the guest room with his gun drawn, but he seemed unsure what to do.

"If you can wound the Axeman without hitting Alex, shoot him!" I shouted. "Don't kill him, though." I needed him alive, in an undead sort of way, to run the elven ritual.

I pulled the staff from its holster and from my pocket tugged out the paper with the ritual words Rand had told me. I'd written them phonetically and began chanting: "Gan fod-e meister"—Alex howled, and I faltered, looking up and screaming as the Axeman buried a huge knife in the front of his shoulder, exposing muscle and bone. Alex fell to his knees.

Feeling underneath the big sweatshirt, I found the grenade and unclipped it from my belt loop. I needn't have bothered; the explosion of Ken's gun was deafening.

The Axeman didn't fall, but he stopped and shouted a bunch of gibberish at Ken, something about demons and hell and heavenly realms. I bent over my cheat sheet, holding out the staff, trying to block out the noise, and hoping Ken could handle it. "Gan fod-e meister Mahout, " I whispered, the words coming out fast and jumbled. "Rowyn-e gal wary pwer o dan I daflu goleuni ar y ffordd ohut." *As the master of Mahout, I call upon the power of fire to illuminate the way of magic*, Rand said it meant, although I'd have to take his word for it.

I pointed the staff at the Axeman, currently trying to shake off an enormous golden dog whose teeth were buried in his thigh. Alex had shifted, and his alter ego Gandalf's shoulder was raw and bloody. Gandalf whimpered as the Axeman shoved him away with a powerful kick of a huge, booted foot into his midsection.

I focused all my native physical energy into the staff, then released it, praying the taped-together staff worked, the ritual chant did its thing, and the Axeman didn't burst into flames and go back into the Beyond. If that happened, this would all have been for nothing.

Instead of the red ropes of flame I'd come to expect from the staff, a violet glow spread from me to the Axeman. His gaze met mine, and I saw it all in my head—and he didn't want me there.

"I'll kill you, wizard!" I was barely aware of Ken trying

to slow him down with what looked like a banister off my half-burned staircase while the killer advanced on me. I closed my eyes, focusing on the line of magic, mentally tracing the violet band like a piece of yarn as it stretched out of my house and away, east on Magazine Street. I mentally sped along it, following it through twists and turns until it ended at a spot I recognized. Just a little farther . . .

"DJ, down!" Ken shouted, and I shot my eyes open just as the Axeman wrapped me in a bear hug and took me to the ground. I squirmed underneath him as he pinned my hands and bared blackened, sharp teeth.

I gagged on the stench, and screamed when a gunshot exploded near my right ear and the Axeman's shoulder burst like a ripe melon, raining meat and hot blood over me. He went limp on top of me but didn't begin fading, so he still lived.

"Goddamn son of a bitch." Ken pulled the Axeman off me and slapped a pair of silver handcuffs on him. He disappeared into the guest room and came back with a pair of shackles, which he used to fasten the Axeman's ankles together. Old Axel wouldn't be chasing me down again anytime soon. I hoped.

I rolled to my hands and knees, panting. "I think he's still alive. Good job."

"Was that fucking thing *ever* alive?" Ken was breathing hard after dragging Axel in front of the fireplace. The killer was regaining consciousness, and bellowed when he realized he'd been shackled.

I approached him cautiously, wiped blood off my elven cheat sheet, pointed the staff at him, and repeated the charm. This time, I was able to close my eyes and focus harder. I followed the purple trail of magic all the way to the door of L'Amour Sauvage and into the back office.

Etienne Boulard was not at his desk, but Adrian Hoffman was.

38

I didn't have proof that Etienne Boulard was the necromancer since I didn't actually see him, but the circumstantial
evidence was damning. And freaking Adrian Hoffman had
sold me out.

Alex had shifted back, pulled on his clothes, and curled
on his side, breathing hard. He stared at me a moment, then
choked out a laugh. "You look like Sissy Spacek in *Carrie*."

Good thing red was my color. And my only clothes were
ruined. What a cluster. Except I knew exactly where to go,
and I needed to get there fast.

"Yeah, well, you look like last week's hamburger. You
gonna be okay? I need to check on Eugenie."

"Yeah, I'll heal."

My friend still lay in the doorway, her eyes wide and
shocky. I knelt next to her, and her focus shifted to me.
It didn't seem to calm her any. I stroked her hair. "I'm so,
so sorry." Again. I couldn't seem to do anything right
by her.

I shifted around to look at Alex. He'd managed to sit up,
but his shoulder was going to take a while to heal. "Ken, can

you take Eugenie home? You'll have to carry her. The charm should wear off in about another hour."

He nodded. "She's gonna have questions. What should I tell her?"

I pulled a chunk of flesh out of my hair and turned my back so I could dry heave in semiprivacy. I might have to go vegan.

Eugenie had closed her eyes, her skin like porcelain in the lamplight. She looked frail. "Tell her the truth." I raised a blood-encrusted eyebrow at Alex, and he nodded. "Tell her everything."

Amazing what a person can do in fifteen minutes with the right incentive. And I had a lot of incentive. I charged to the head of the line at L'Amour Sauvage and didn't wait for the bouncer to wave me through. I wanted to see Etienne and Adrian, and to find out what happened to Jean Lafitte.

Alex was on my heels. He hadn't finished healing his own shoulder wound yet, but we needed everybody. Ken was babysitting Eugenie. As soon as he could calm her down and make sure she wasn't in shock, he'd be meeting us here. I'd even called Rene, but he was out hunting in the wilds of north Louisiana with his brothers Claude and Cheney and couldn't get back before midnight, though he'd been willing to try. I hoped everything would be over by then.

I'd taken a fast shower at Alex's and thrown on one of his Ole Miss sweatshirts. It came almost to my knees but it covered up the grenade. My jeans, with their modified staff holster, were bloodstained. I had to wear them anyway. Pantless necromancer-chasing? Not a good idea.

At the end of the bar, I stopped at the sight of Adrian

sitting alone in a booth, his vampire significant other notice-
ably absent. He had his head propped on his hands as if he
had the mother of all headaches, so he didn't react when I
slid in the booth facing him. I raised my voice to be heard
over the din. "Where's your feeder?"

He looked up at me slowly and blinked, his eyes bloodshot,
face haggard, expression confused. It was a startling difference from the last time I'd seen him here with Terri, arrogant
and making plans to resume our lessons in elven magic.
"Etienne sent her on an . . . errand."

His eyes darted around the bar, finally settling back on
me and Alex. "I thought your house burned down and you
disappeared. You were safe. Why the hell did you come
back?"

Gee, and he sounded so happy to see me. "You must not
have gotten my message. I managed to track the Axeman's
necromancer back to L'Amour Sauvage using some of my
useless elven magic. And guess who the trail led me to?"

Adrian sat up straighter and assumed his normal—i.e.,
condescending—demeanor. He still looked like a cat that had
been dragged through a washing-machine wringer, but it was
an arrogant cat. "It might have led you to this bar, but it
didn't lead you to me. Etienne is in the back office with your
friend Lafitte. The Regent was behind everything."

"I'm not sure what part you played yet, but you played
one." I left the booth and started toward the back hallway.

Behind me, I heard Alex ordering Adrian to stand up.
"You're going with us."

I hung a left at the hall and stopped outside Etienne's
office, resting my ear against the door to try and hear if
anything was going on inside. The noise from the bar was

too distracting, though, and the door was heavy. Wrapping my fingers around the doorknob, I took a deep breath, said a quick prayer, and turned it, making sure Alex was behind me.

I eased the door open, but I needn't have bothered. I even looked behind the door and in the adjoining bathroom, into which Etienne, having no need of such facilities, had installed a roomy recliner and video setup. I did not want to know what went on in there.

"I thought you said they were here." I turned to look at Adrian. "Or are you and your fangy girlfriend covering for her boss?"

"Don't be absurd." Adrian looked in the bathroom as if I might have missed a large French pirate and his vampire crony hiding inside, then prowled behind Etienne's desk. "There's a transport here—they obviously left."

I circled the desk and stared at the floor. Damn it, he was right. An interlocking circle and triangle had been chalked onto the hardwood. I knelt and touched a finger to the chalk and a tingle of magic shot up my arm. "It's fresh." I looked up at Adrian. "But a wizard had to power it. Where did you send them?"

A deafening pop and a choked sound brought me to my feet. Alex lay on the floor, curled in a fetal position. Adrian backed himself into a corner. And the man who stood over Alex with a gun was red-haired and smiling. Jonas Adamson, our friendly new age necromancer.

Damn it all to hell and back. "You? Why?" Why would a registered necromancer risk getting messed up in this? "What happened to Green Congress solidarity and all that crap?"

Jonas Adamson shrugged. "Money, why else? Power. But mostly money."

Adrian reached behind a chair and pulled out a length of rope. Good, he could slip up behind Jonas and choke him.

Instead, he knelt beside Alex and began tying his hands behind his back. Holy shit. They were both in on it? "Adrian, what the hell are you doing?" He worked for the Elders. His father was the freaking First Elder.

"I had no choice," Adrian said, kneeling and binding Alex's hands and feet. He dragged Alex into Etienne's private screening room and closed the door. Alex wasn't conscious yet, but the bullet had hit his thigh and he'd cracked his head on a chair when he fell. I didn't see enough blood to think it had nicked an artery. I thought he'd be okay. I, however, was in the room with two lunatic wizards.

I moved away from the transport, easing toward the office door, but Jonas's gun barrel tracked my movements without wavering. Adrian looked nervous, but the necromancer was cool and steady.

I focused on Adrian. "It's not too late to get yourself out of this. Whatever they're offering you, it can't be worth it."

He looked at the floor, and for once his voice didn't hold an ounce of arrogance. He was scared. "This wasn't about money. One of the elves, Lily, found out my father was First Elder. She threatened to expose my involvement with Terri. It would jeopardize his position and I'd never . . ." Adrian broadcast a swirling mix of fear and shame. "I was just supposed to let them know where you were, nothing more." His voice dropped to a whisper. "It got out of control."

No kidding.

So it had been Lily all along. Rand's theory that she

might be making a play to gain control of the Synod was probably right. It would put her in a position to break truce with the Elders and then fight for top position in the Interspecies Council. If a war broke out, she'd have gotten rid of the only wizard who could fight elven magic with elven magic. And with Jonas, she had her own wizard weapon in hand.

Adrian proved he couldn't keep his mouth shut by continuing to talk. "I need you to understand. At first, Lily just wanted the staff out of your hands, even though no one else could use it. Jonas and the Axeman were supposed to scare you into giving it up—you weren't supposed to be hurt. Once she saw your elven magic went deeper than just using the staff, she wanted you dead. Then you bonded with Randolph, and that sealed it."

Damn it. "And keeping your father from knowing about your vampire girlfriend was worth helping them kill me?"

He took a deep breath and squared his shoulders. "It's out of my hands now."

"You can still salvage this, Jonas." I turned to the necromancer, who'd been listening to Adrian with amusement. "I'll pay you *not* to kill me. Whatever Lily offered you, I'll pay double." Jean Lafitte had deep pockets and would be delighted if I owed him even more favors.

Jonas raised an eyebrow. "And make an enemy of the elves? Forget it. They're nuts. If Lily didn't kill me, your mate would. And if he didn't kill me, sooner or later Mace Banyan will find out about all of this. Hopefully, by then, Lily will be in charge and I'll be a rich wizard living in Elfheim."

Mace Banyan was innocent?

"You are both pathetic losers, you know that? Look, I'll make a deal——"

A sharp pain in my head cut off further words, and I had a brief glimpse of something new before darkness overwhelmed me: a close-up view of a woman's shiny black pumps.

I heard the voices long before I was able to slit my eyes open to the same hardwood floor. I was still in the office at L'Amour Sauvage.

Above and around me as I lay on my left side, an argument was in progress between Jonas, Adrian, and a woman. I recognized Lily's voice. She must have cracked me over the head with something when she slipped in behind me.

"Let Lafitte kill her." Jonas's voice grew louder and softer, in and out, up and down——he was pacing. "You said Randolph told you the staff is broken. Without it, she can't win."

Good for Rand. He'd given me an advantage, at least.

"Quince Randolph can't be trusted." Lily's voice came from right in front of my head. "He went too far in bonding with her. Kill her now, one of you. We can't risk her escaping from Lafitte and ruining everything."

A well-toned pair of ankles in black heels moved in front of my shuttered eyelids and I fought a wave of nausea. I gritted my teeth, sending sharp pains through my jaw and into my skull. What the hell had she hit me with? At least I could lay here and recuperate while they argued about who was going to kill me. Lily didn't seem to want to get her hands dirty, and my fellow wizards were stalling.

"I didn't agree to kill her, not that she doesn't deserve it,

arrogant little twit. I'll have nothing more to do with it."
Adrian's voice was muffled—he was farther away than the
others. "You said let you know of her whereabouts and you'd
keep your mouth shut about Terri. That was the deal.
Nothing more. I shouldn't have let it get this far. Now we've
shot the enforcer."

Lily's shoes clicked out of sight and I heard the video
room door opening and then closing again.

"The enforcer needs to die too. You have no choice unless
you want your father to find out about your little vampire
habit, Adrian. Think you'll ever make Elder if they know?"
Lily laughed, a musical, tinkling sound that set my heart
thudding. She'd sounded a lot like that at my elven
regression.

"Fine. Tell whoever you want." Adrian's boots came to
rest in front of my face. "Kill her yourself, or let your chum
Jonas do it. I won't help you anymore."

"You two are cowards." Lily's feet stopped an inch from
my nose. "Jonas, do you have control of Lafitte?"

"Not yet. He's been taken to the site and restrained but
I have to get closer to control him. I'm still sending orders
to the Axeman but he isn't responding. I think he's been
caught."

I had to think smart if I was going to live through this.
There were too many factions involved. My biggest advantage was the staff, pressing into my leg from inside its sheath.
Lily and her buddies thought it was broken. I had no idea
where my bag, premade charms, or cell phone were.

I had another weapon too. I closed my eyes and focused
my mind on Rand, visualizing his face, his voice. *In trouble.*
L'Amour Sauvage office. Need help. I didn't know if it would

work with me in New Orleans and Rand in Elfheim, but it couldn't hurt.

Adrian's loafered toe tapped on the hardwood near Lily's pumps. "Why don't you just fry her brains with your elven magic? It almost killed her before."

"It doesn't work on her since the bonding." Plus, Lily needed her hands to stay clean if she was going to overthrow Mace as head of the Synod and then take on the wizards for control of the Interspecies Council.

Lily's shoes disappeared from view. "You know, I rather like the idea of using Lafitte against her, and forcing him to do something he objects to." Her voice came from behind me now. "We can't kill him, but he'll suffer because of what we make him do. Jonas, you'll be living in Elfheim and he won't dare come after you there. You're the only one implicated except Terri. Etienne's kept his hands clean. Adrian, the pirate doesn't know you're involved and if you want to continue drawing breath, I'd suggest you keep your mouth shut."

Every freaking one of them was a part of this except, ironically, the two I'd been most angry with—Rand and Mace.

Something fell to the floor with a bang, and I prayed they hadn't seen me flinch. Thank God I had on Alex's huge sweatshirt or they'd see my heart pounding. How could I slip the staff out without them see—

"Ow!" What felt like the sharp toe of a high heel whacked my upper back. Damn, that hurt, and I couldn't stop the instinctive arch as the muscles around my spine drew in on themselves. I rolled to my back and Lily leaned over me, her pale hair and face made even more washed-out by her basic black dress.

I smiled at her. "You really should wear pastels. Black looks like shit on you." My words were tough, my shaky voice far from it.

She assumed the same smug smirk I'd seen on Mace Banyan and Rand. The elves must practice it. "You've rested enough, my meddling wizard. Time to go and see your friend the pirate."

I tried to sit up, but as soon as I raised my head, the room spun. Whatever she had hit me with had probably given me a concussion. From behind, Jonas jerked me to my feet, then had to hold on to my arm to keep me from toppling over again. I couldn't decide which hurt worse—my head or my back or my bruised ribs.

"Let's get this over with." Jonas shook me like Sebastian with his rubber rat, making the room tilt. I might have to throw up. "I have dinner plans."

God forbid my death should interrupt his dinner. I snaked my right hand toward my thigh—these people needed to meet Mahout in a bad way. Before I could get my hands on it, Jonas shoved me roughly toward Lily. She stepped out of the way so I hit the floor inside the transport. Jonas chanted behind me, and his words, plus the compression of air around me, told me we were going on a trip to Six Flags.

39

A cold front had pushed in from the north, and an icy rain was falling when we landed in the transport at Six Flags. After Katrina, the park's electricity had been cut to everything except the streetlights in the outer lots. Along with the rain, the sparse lighting added shadow-buildings and giant mutant roller-coaster ghosts to the general ambience.

I heard Jean before I saw him. I couldn't understand the words, but I recognized the sentiment. He was giving someone a verbal beat down in French. Shivering, Alex's sweatshirt growing heavier as it soaked up the rain, I finally saw him near the big laughing clown head, arguing with Terri while handcuffed to one of the dead light poles. He stopped speaking when he saw me, something like sorrow and resignation crossing his face.

Jonas shoved me toward them. I tripped over a concrete barrier and stumbled into Jean.

"*Jolie*, I was hoping you would elude them." He glanced over my shoulder at Terri. "I fear my trust in Etienne was misplaced. When I arrived, he was not there but his assistant trapped me." He rattled the handcuffs, but that light pole—and, thus, Jean—wasn't going anywhere.

I took stock of my companions as they huddled in the nearest storefront, wondering who to take out first as they argued about the best way to use Jean against me. I didn't see Etienne, but Terri could probably do that fast-moving vampire thing. Adrian had his Blue Congress skills. Lily's mental magic wouldn't work on me now, thanks to Rand, but God only knew what else she could do. And Jonas could control Jean, at least in theory.

If they were going to leave me out here in the rain and ignore me, they'd pay. Easing the staff from beneath my soggy sweatshirt, I aimed it at the roof of the wooden building they were huddled in and shot a nice stream of elven-bond-enhanced fire directly over Jonas's head.

They screamed and scattered as the roof sparked and sizzled, caving in on top of them in a hiss of smoke. Thanks to the rain, I didn't get the eruption I wanted, but I got a diversion.

I studied the handcuffs and wished I had a handy charm or potion. "I'm going to try to use the staff on these cuffs but it might burn you," I told Jean.

"Do it, *Jolie*."

While I used short bursts of energy against the cuffs, I talked. There were much bigger things than me at play here and my odds of surviving weren't great. Terri had already escaped the collapsed building, and the others wouldn't be far behind. Then they'd turn their attention back to me.

"They're afraid of you—afraid you'll go to the Elders." I kept my voice low and spoke quickly. "If I don't make it out of this, go to Zrakovi. Tell him that Lily, Adrian,

Jonas the necromancer, and the vampires are all involved. I think the vampires and Lily are conspiring to overthrow Mace Banyan for power in the Synod, and then present a united vampire-elf force against the Elders. I think Mace and Quince Randolph are not involved. Together, the elves and vampires outnumber the wizards, and they want to take control of the Interspecies Council. Remember. Zrakovi needs to know."

"You will not die here, Drusilla." Jean whispered so softly I strained to hear him. "Kill the necromancer first and I will be able to . . ." Jean's eyes glazed and he looked past me. He didn't blink, even with the rain pelting his face and dripping from his lashes.

I turned to see Jonas crouched outside the collapsed storefront, chanting and moving his fingers in intricate patterns, twisting a spell. "*Courir, Jolie!*" Jean said, his voice choked, straining, urgent. "My will fails me. Run!"

I took off, pulling out the staff as I ran at a ninety-degree angle from Jean. I aimed over my shoulder and let out a blast of my elven-bond-induced fire, aiming at Jonas. Broad red ropes flew straight at him, but Lily had been watching me. She shoved him aside, leaving the fire to blow a hole in the concrete wall behind him. The building didn't collapse, but at least I'd bought some more time while Jonas regrouped.

I ran onto the midway of storefronts but stopped when I got out of their view and peered back at them around a partially collapsed wall. Terri had released Jean, and he ran toward Jonas and Lily. The elf had a freaking pistol, standing guard while Jonas crafted his spell again. Jean stopped halfway to him, and his shoulders stiffened.

Crap, Jonas had regained control.

I held out the staff, ready to take another shot, but Jean was between me and Jonas. Instead, I looked behind me, trying to make out the dim shells of storefronts that lined the midway. I needed to hunker down and figure out a strategy.

I ran toward a hulk of a building—some type of souvenir stand, back when the world was normal and Six Flags was full of laughter and music. Halfway there, I went sprawling on the wet cement, and twisted around to see the bottom section of a concrete planter. In the rain and shadows, this was like running an obstacle course blind.

As if on cue, a rainbow of neon lights flickered, then shone in a steady glow along the walkway, even from shops missing doors, windows, or even front walls. At the far end of the fake French Quarter midway, the carousel began to twirl, its empty swings flying outward, tinny jazz music playing at a frenzied pace, orange and gold lights twinkling around the ornate top. Blinding and brilliant even through the sheets of cold rain.

Holy crap. The ghost of Six Flags Past had been resurrected. It was classic Blue Congress magic—creation and re-creation, and if I hadn't known he was doing it to help Jean find and kill me, I'd have given Adrian props for being able to maintain this kind of magical illusion on such a large scale.

I spotted Jean rounding the end of the first storefront. He slowed when he saw me, his movements mechanical and stiff. He was fighting Jonas from sheer force of personality.

Running again, I darted into a darkened corner and through an alleyway between buildings. Behind them, back in the shadows, I half fell, half jumped over trash and rotted storm debris. Finally, I found a dark corner in which to hide. This was the same building I'd used while running from the Axeman. The store's front wall was missing, and most of its rear. I'd have an escape route.

I steadied my breath and wiped the rain off my face, thankful the adrenaline had at least cleared my head of the dizziness. I couldn't just run from Jean. Eventually, he'd catch me. He'd been right; I needed to take out Jonas Adamson. Without the necromancer, the spell on Jean would be broken and, now that he wasn't tethered to a light pole, he'd be one hell of a backup.

I slipped through the hole in the back wall, using my hands to feel my way along the plain concrete rear of the faux Vieux Carre stores, retracing my route to the walkway entrance.

I'd like to blow Lily's pale elven ass straight to Elfheim, and if she landed on Mace Banyan, all the better. He might be innocent of trying to have me killed, but he wasn't innocent. Might as well throw in Betony as well. And Rand, just for good measure. Anything smacking of elf was on my bad list.

By the time I reached the back of the last store, I was ready to shoot something. My best shooting range with the staff had been six feet and closer, so I needed to get near the entrance to the storefront Jonas was using for his magical setup.

I scanned the area, looking for another place to run for cover, and decided on the remains of the giant clown head. It was in a relatively unlit area, about the width of a basketball court from where I crouched, and I could get to it without running through the open part of the midway.

Another quick look around the corner didn't reveal my pirate, so I sprinted for the clown . . . and skidded to a stop on muddy ground as Jean stepped from behind it. The muscles in his face stretched taut, his eyes dark swirls of anger. I knew the anger wasn't directed at me, but at the wizard issuing orders.

"Come to me, Drusilla," he said softly. "Let us end this."

I pointed the staff at him and willed a brief burst of my magical energy into it, jerking it left at the last second and hitting the giant clown—which even after the fire was so huge I couldn't miss it.

Its blue cap and right eye exploded in a burst of plaster shards and dust that mixed with the pouring rain, and knocked Jean off his feet. Just the distraction I needed to run toward the building where I'd last seen Adrian and Terri.

Slipping and skating across the muddy ground, I raced around the carousel, which still careened madly, throwing orange and gold sparks from its equipment room door. Adrian must be getting tired; the music had gone from tinny to warbly, and the bright array of red and gold lights around the carousel's top flickered on and off.

I heard a boom and thought it was thunder, until I found myself facedown in the mud, my right shoulder a mass of throbbing, fiery pain. I tried to push myself up, but my right arm collapsed under me. Part of my mind registered that I'd been shot, but my legs kept wanting to run.

A strong arm around my left arm jerked me to my feet. "I am sorry, *Jolie*. They ordered me to shoot the wizard, so I shot at the necromancer. The elf shot you. I'm being ordered to hold you."

Jean was shouting, but his voice sounded muffled and

distant. At first I thought the rain was muffling the sound around us, including Jean's voice, but when the carousel behind him tilted at a thirty-degree angle I realized how close I was to passing out. If I fainted, I died—simple as that. Jean wouldn't be able to intentionally misinterpret his instructions indefinitely.

Whimpering as torn skin and ligaments created shards of pain that sliced through my body, I slipped my right hand into my pocket and pulled out my only remaining charm, thumbing off the top and flinging it at Jean's arm.

"*Mon Dieu*." He released me and held his arms out into the driving rain. My acid charm wasn't made to work in these conditions, and most of it washed off. I only made it a few feet before he caught me again.

My legs almost gave way when he grabbed my right arm, the pain so sharp the Axeman might as well have chopped off my arm at the shoulder. So this was what it felt like to be shot. It sucked.

Jean slowly pulled his dagger from its resting spot under the wide black belt he wore when in fighting-pirate mode. I'd studied that dagger before: triangular blade, razor sharp, wicked. It would hurt like hell too.

I jerked away from him enough to raise the staff between us with my left hand, but I shook so badly it might as well have been a twig from a pine tree. He grasped my hand and held it steady, lowering the staff until its tip rested over his heart. "Do it, Drusilla. They have ordered me to stab you in the heart, and to do it now. I fight it, but I cannot change the order to something that will not kill you."

"I can't." My voice was nothing but a whisper, and I felt hot tears mingling with the cold rain on my face. "I can't do it." I knew that for the historical undead, the real death had already occurred, and that Jean would not truly die from anything I did. But it was still using my magic to willfully, seriously hurt someone I cared about. I'd never done that before, and now I knew it wasn't in me.

Holding the end of the staff steady against his chest with his left hand, he raised the dagger with his right, pressing it against my breastbone. "I cannot stop this, *Jolie*. You must save us both."

He pressed the point of the blade through the waterlogged fabric of the sweatshirt, barely breaking skin but doing just enough to bring me out of the gray haze that threatened to overwhelm me. "God help me," I whispered, and sent a burst of magic into the staff.

I smelled the burn of flesh and fabric, even in the rain, and Jean dropped the dagger as he crumpled to the ground. I knelt with him, stroking his cheek, easing him onto his back. His dark blue eyes cleared, and he smiled. Seconds later, he died another death, and I felt part of my soul die with him. Everyone who had a hand in this was going to pay. I didn't know how, but they would.

Jean's body had already begun to fade into the Beyond when the lights went out. The music from the carousel died with the tortured whine of a dying animal. Only then did the sound of shouting voices filter through the rain.

Clutching my right arm against my body to keep from jostling my shoulder, I struggled to my knees, and finally got to my feet. Taking a final look into the shadows where Jean had died, I began to run toward the voices. I had a bill to settle.

40

A glow emanated from inside the storefront where everyone had taken refuge after I collapsed their first hangout. I limped toward it like a crippled homing pigeon. Jonas would know Jean was gone, which made him impotent and shifted the bulk of the danger to Terri and Lily.

Adrian was too big a coward for me to consider him a threat. He'd done something boneheaded, gotten caught, and let things spiral out of control.

Grateful for the sound-muffling effects of the rain, I stopped outside the east wall of the building to catch my breath, and hazarded a quick look into the open storefront. I wasn't sure how much of my serious case of the shivers came from the cold, from fear, or from injury.

Add hallucinations to the shivers. There seemed to be a hell of a lot more people in that open storefront than there should have been. I held my left hand over my eyes like an awning to keep the rain out of them, squinting to try and figure out who'd joined the party and forgot to invite me.

Alex. Unless I was really hallucinating, he was here. His right leg was red from blood but he was upright, looked pretty well healed, and I'd never been happier to see him. The adrenaline drain of knowing he was nearby almost sent me to the ground again. He stood behind Terri, an arm clamped around her waist and a gun to her right temple, yelling at Adrian, who sat on the ground with his head in his hands. There was no sign of Jonas.

I couldn't understand what Alex was saying because Rand, Lily, Betony, and Mace were all standing a few feet away, shouting at each other. The whole freaking Elven Synod was at Six Flags.

The situation looked well in hand, so I stepped into the open storefront. It took a few seconds, but eventually all eyes turned to me and all talking stopped. Did I know how to make an entrance, or what? I still held the staff in my left hand in case the elves decided to resort to violence in front of Alex, but I thought Rand's presence would be enough to keep them in check.

"DJ. Thank God." Alex pulled the gun away from Terri's head and shoved her toward Adrian, then came to me. He started to hug me, but stopped when he saw my right shoulder. "You've been shot. Where's Lafitte?"

He'd stood in front of me and let me kill him, that's where.

"He's . . ." I stared at Alex's hand. "Is that a *nail gun?*" Why the hell was the king-of-all-weaponry, badass enforcer using a nail gun?

"Wooden nails." He shook it in Terri's direction. "Got her attention."

Terri was whispering to Adrian, but I couldn't summon the energy to deal with them yet. "How'd you know to come here?"

"Rand got your mental SOS and came to L'Amour Sauvage. He found me in that room off the office. He could trace you here through your bond."

Thank God. "What's up with our pointy-eared friends?" Elves didn't have pointy ears, but I figured it would annoy them. Judging by the seething looks from Lily and Mace, it had. Betony looked stunned, and Rand was headed my way. Awesome.

"What do you know of elven involvement in the attempts to kill you?" Rand glowed a little from within, as if the scene needed any more weirdness. His words were formal, but the eyes that raked me from head to mud-covered boots, pausing on my blood-soaked shoulder, were lit with blue flames.

Leaning on Alex, I filled him in on Lily's involvement, and Etienne's, and Terri's, and Adrian's. And lest I forget, the absent Jonas Adamson, who was probably trying to figure out a way to escape both the wizards and elves with his life.

I dropped my voice. "Here's what I could piece together. At first, they wanted the staff destroyed, just to ensure I wasn't able to use it to help the Elders if the truce was ever broken. Etienne was going to help Lily overthrow Mace for control of the Synod, then form some kind of super-alliance against the wizards to take over the Interspecies Council. When Lily saw how much magic I could do through the regression, and then we bonded, destroying the staff wasn't enough. They had to destroy me to neutralize you and carry out their plans to take down Mace."

"Then Lily has incurred the penalty of my choice, including death if I so wish it." Rand was shouting again, this time at Mace.

"Not here." Mace gave him granite-face, but he'd been

listening and was clearly shaken. "We deal with our own, and you'll have your wish. But it will be after a formal meeting of the Synod at our Place of Counsel. Tonight. She can't come." The latter reference to me. Like I wanted to go anywhere near Elfheim.

Grabbing Lily's hand and dragging her roughly behind him, Mace pounded past me, going out of his way to brush my injured shoulder. The room turned gray, and I ground my upper teeth deep enough into my lower lip hard enough to draw blood again. I would not faint in front of those freak-show elves even if I had to stay alert by chewing my own lips off.

"You going to be okay?" Rand's voice was soft. "I'll be back as soon as I can. We need to talk."

I leaned against Alex, reminding Rand where my allegiances lay. "You know where to find me." Besides that, every time Rand said *we need to talk,* something horrific happened.

Only after Rand left did I notice that Terri and Adrian had disappeared. We weren't far from the open transport. Oh no he didn't. "Take me to L'Amour Sauvage. Adrian's not getting away with this."

"You're not going anywhere but to . . ." Alex paused, the pounding of the rain outside filling up the space while he went through the same mental litany as me. I couldn't go to a human hospital. I needed to be treated by a wizard. My house was in ruins. I couldn't even sleep in my car under the Claiborne Avenue overpass because my rental car had been hauled away after the house burned. It would be too easy to find me at his house, just in case some of the elves decided to drop in for a chat.

"You can take me back to the Monteleone afterward and we can call a doctor on retainer for the Elders, but first, Sauvage. And before that, we need to talk to Zrakovi. He needs to deal with Adrian and issue a warrant for Jonas Adamson." I gave Alex a short, garbled version of everything I'd overheard. "He needs to know that Adrian's up to his neck in this and I'm not letting him sweep it under the First Elder's rug."

Alex clipped the nail gun onto his belt and pulled out his cell phone. While he talked—he was really much better than me at reports, even verbal ones—I finally let myself thump to the floor, propping against the wall. It hurt to breathe. On the positive side, my shoulder hurt so badly, my bruised ribs and possible concussion felt almost normal.

"DJ?" Alex touched my good shoulder, startling me awake. Had I fallen asleep or passed out?

"Help me up." My words slurred but I couldn't seem to straighten out my tongue.

Alex ignored my outstretched left hand, leaned over, and picked me up, careful not to jar my shoulder. "You aren't in any shape to go anywhere. I'm taking you to my house. Zrakovi's sending a doctor."

"Have the doctor go to L'Amour Sauvage. I need to see this through." This was personal; Adrian had sold out one of his own. "Please."

Alex made a growling noise, which I translated as a yes. I let him play caveman and carry me to his truck, settle me into the passenger seat, and fasten my seat belt. When he wanted to cover me with the Saints throw from his backseat, I called a halt. "Alex, I'm okay. Really." I did take the throw with my left hand and wipe the water off my face and hair, then handed it to him to do the same. We both looked like we'd been fished out of Lake Pontchartrain.

His eyes, normally the warm color of Hershey's finest chocolate, were dark pools of angst, and he was broadcasting a tangle of relief and fury and confusion. The man had the most complex emotional signature I'd ever felt. "I don't like it, but I understand why you need to see. But if you start bleeding again or you faint, we're out of there."

By the time he'd walked behind the truck, climbed in the driver's seat, and called Zrakovi with the change of plans, I was half asleep.

"Talk to me," Alex said. "Stay awake."

I rolled my head to look at his profile. "I think I have a concussion." Or excessive blood loss, or shock. Take your pick.

I couldn't see his expression as we pulled out of the dark parking lot and sped back toward the I-10, but his voice was soft. "Go through it. Tell me what happened when you got to L'Amour Sauvage."

Savage Love. What a perfect name. Love was savage, and it hurt.

I started talking. I probably told him the same things more than once. Alex asked questions and kept me awake, but he couldn't make me alert. When we pulled into an illegal loading zone near the vampire club, I blinked in confusion because I didn't remember driving through town.

He slapped his FBI hangtag on the rearview mirror, and zeroed in on my shoulder. "You're bleeding again. You sure you're up for this?"

"Yes," I lied. I wanted to curl up in a ball and sleep. I wanted to hide out in Old Barataria, swinging in Jean's hammock until this all went away. I wanted to go home with Alex and make love as if pleasing each other was all we had to worry about the rest of our lives. I wanted to do anything but deal with more crappy prete and wizard politics.

I opened the passenger door, took a deep breath, and tried to swing my legs out. Wasn't happening.

"Stubborn woman." Alex lifted me out of the truck and set me on my feet. I wavered a moment, and we both waited to see if I could right the ship before it sank onto the sidewalk. I stayed upright. Yay me.

He flashed his FBI badge as we walked past the lines waiting to enter the club. Pretty Boy opened his mouth, looked at us, and closed it again. He shoved a clipboard at me, a silver pen attached to it with a velvet ribbon.

"What is it? I've never had to sign anything before."

"It's a waiver of responsibility," Pretty Boy snapped. "You're bleeding. Christ, you might as well wear a flashing chartreuse *hors d'oeuvres* sign on your head."

Yikes. I hadn't thought about that.

Neither had Alex. He stared at my shoulder with renewed concern. "Uh, DJ. Maybe you better—"

"Get me to the office or I will faint."

I knew I needed medical care but if I could hang on just a little longer . . .

On our way toward the back hallway, I glanced at the table I'd come to think of as belonging to Adrian and Terri, but of course it was empty. I wondered if Terri had taken him to hide out in Vampyre—a part of the Beyond I didn't care to visit. As Jean Lafitte had noted one time, if I were ever to go there, the vampires, unrestricted by human and prete council law, would eat me.

I walked into Etienne Boulard's office without knocking. He sat behind his desk, fingers steepled in front of him, and didn't look surprised at the intrusion. I heard Alex close the door behind him, and when he stepped beside me, he held his modified nail gun. That, Etienne looked surprised to see.

"Do enforcers carry nail guns these days?" He had the gall to look amused, so Alex raised the nail gun and fired. A sharp, wooden nail shot across the room and embedded itself in the wall behind Etienne's head.

"Next time I'll aim lower and to the right." Alex spoke with the don't-screw-with-the-enforcer drawl he saved for special occasions.

Etienne's nostrils flared. "Terri is not here. I dared not leave her to your primitive justice system and ordered her to Vampyre under house arrest, although I assure you she will be punished for getting mixed up in this."

Yeah, well, he wasn't getting off that easily. "We know about your plot with Lily, and that you referred her to the necromancer Jonas Adamson." I hobbled to the chair facing him and fell into it. I felt Alex at my back. "And did you realize that Adrian, the wizard who'd been ratting on my whereabouts, was the son of the First Elder?"

For the first time, Etienne looked rattled. "What?"

So he hadn't known that part of it. Interesting.

He rose and began pacing. Alex shifted the nail gun back and forth, keeping it trained on the vampire. "I thought he only worked for the Elders in a minor role. *Merde*." Etienne looked past me, and I turned, trying to keep my shoulder stiff. The sofa on the back wall was partially blocked from view by the open door. But I could see enough of it to tell there was someone lying on it.

Alex stepped over and swung the door shut. The person lying on the sofa was Adrian. He wasn't moving.

Alex holstered his nail gun and knelt next to the sofa, placing fingers against the side of Adrian's neck. He shook his head at me. "He's dead." He shifted Adrian's head to the side. "And he's been fed on recently. No other injuries that I can see."

She drained him? I stared at Adrian's body several moments before the truth hit me like a falling Mardi Gras throw. "They're turning him. Oh my God, they're turning the son of the First Elder?"

I swiveled back to Etienne too fast, and had to clutch the arm of the chair to stop the room from spinning, which in turn sent a dagger of pain from my shoulder to . . . everywhere. "You're freaking *turning* him," I whispered.

"I didn't know about his father, and it was his idea," Etienne said. His voice was calm but his eyes weren't. "He wanted to become one of us to be with Terri."

My mind whirled with the possibilities afforded by a vampire who was also the son of the world's highest-ranking wizard.

"Turned who?" Elder Willem Zrakovi stood in the doorway, looking from Etienne, to me, to Alex, and finally behind him, to Adrian. He caught on a lot faster than I had. "Oh dear."

Not one for hyperbole, Zrakovi.

41

Thanksgiving dawned cold and clear. I sat with Eugenie in her kitchen, drinking coffee before she headed to Shreveport for family time. We'd had three days to come to terms with this new world she'd never known about, and three days to rekindle our friendship. We still had a ways to go, but we'd gotten a good start.

"So that guy I met before Alex's Halloween party really *was* Jean Lafitte? For real?" Eugenie practically quivered with excitement.

"For real. He should be back in town next week. I'll reintroduce you." After I had a long, serious discussion with her about Jean's unique system of bartering favors, which sometimes bordered on the morally ambiguous. She was still half excited, half perplexed by this grand new world Ken Hachette had introduced to her. He'd told her a lot more than Alex or I intended. I think he just wanted someone else with whom he could share the horror of it all.

I wore a borrowed button-front purple blouse and a denim skirt because I could get in and out of them with my mending shoulder. Eugenie had found me a matching sling to rest my arm in, packed a few other things she thought I could wear into a small bag, and was getting ready to deposit me at the Hotel Monteleone. I'd spend my homeless holiday watching the flat-screen TV in Jean's hotel suite and eating turkey and oyster dressing from room service. Sounded perfect.

Eugenie had a few hours before her flight to Shreveport, but needed to go on a mystery errand she'd asked me to help her with. She had invited me to spend Thanksgiving with her family, but sitting with someone else's relatives at Thanksgiving seemed even more pathetic than sitting alone. I'd called my grandmother, finally, to let her know my house had burned. After a few short minutes of conversation about how I should move to Alabama, get married to a nice, steady man, and give up magic, I realized I'd rather spend Thanksgiving alone than with my own family too.

Pathetic.

"You about ready to go?" Eugenie retrieved her small, tapestry-covered suitcase from the corner and shoved a heavy tote bag into my usable hand. I hefted it onto the table and looked inside. "What is this?"

"It's that good andouille and crawfish boudin we got in LaPlace yesterday, and the caramel doberge I picked up at Gambino's."

"They won't let you take this on the plane." Besides, I had plans for that doberge. Seven thin layers of cake, caramel frosting, and at least ten pounds on my hips overnight. And here I thought she'd dragged me all over the river parishes yesterday to keep me from wallowing in self-pity. "At least leave the cake. It'll get crushed. I'll take it to the hotel with me."

Eugenie eyed me with way too much wisdom and not an

ounce of pity. "You aren't going to sit in that dead pirate's hotel room and eat caramel cake by yourself all day, girl."

No, if she took the cake, I'd sit there and eat Cheetos and Reese's Peanut Butter Cups by myself all day. I'd already stocked up.

"Alex gone up to Picayune to spend Thanksgiving with his folks?"

I shrugged, then winced at the pain that shot through my shoulder. I needed to pick up some different body language to indicate my cluelessness. "Dunno. Probably." I wondered if Jake would make a holiday appearance before heading back to Jean Lafitte's fight club.

I hadn't talked to Alex all week. He'd been called off on another enforcer assignment that Ken had been kind of vague about. Something involving gremlins.

I wanted to phone him, but hadn't worked up the nerve—plus, phones did work both ways. I wanted us to try again, even if it meant decluttering my life of its natural chaos. But I worried that this last episode might have scared him away for good. I thought he might be avoiding me and using gremlins as an excuse.

I followed Eugenie to her car and climbed in with my bag of sausage and cake.

"Ken tells me there's a big meeting going on with your . . . people. Are wizards people? I've always thought of you as a person."

I sighed and shifted the bag away from my immobilized arm. "Yeah, we're people. Well, some of us more than others." Ken needed a muzzle.

No way Eugenie needed to know about the troubles in preteville. The Elven Synod, Vampire Regents' Council, and entire Congress of Elders were planning a big sit-down after Christmas to figure out what to do about Lily, Terri, Etienne, and the newest baby vampire, Adrian. The only reason for waiting so long: the Elders had their own housecleaning to do, which might or might not involve removing Geoffrey Hoffman as First Elder, depending on what he knew, when he knew it, and how far he was willing to go to protect Adrian. The final formation of the Interspecies Council was on hold.

I'd been ordered to testify before both the Elders and the bigger prete council, along with Rand, Jean Lafitte, the now-incarcerated Jonas Adamson, who'd been found hiding in a barroom in Old Orleans and been reported by none other than Louis Armstrong, and the Axeman, who'd be brought back by another registered necromancer.

Just shoot me now.

Eugenie hadn't mentioned Rand since the great unveiling, and neither had I.

He'd come back to town yesterday, which I only knew because he'd been knocking at my mental door, trying to communicate. I was growing adept at ignoring him mentally, and planned to ignore him physically when he tracked me down at the Monteleone. Because he would. He was persistent, if nothing else. I didn't know how I felt about my non-husband—it waffled between outright hatred, reluctant tolerance, and morbid fascination. Until I figured it out, I didn't want to talk to him.

Eugenie bounced the car through Mid-City on pothole-pocked streets that were mostly deserted. Everyone had something to do on Thanksgiving Day. "Where is it we're going exactly?" She was supposed to drop me back at the hotel before heading to the airport.

"Just something I want you to see." Eugenie looked smug, turning right on Carrollton and heading north.

"And you're going to have time to take me back to the Quarter and then get to the airport? I could drop you off and keep your car if you aren't afraid for me to drive left-handed." I couldn't believe I was in my late twenties and didn't have a car, a house, or a stick of furniture to my name. What I did have was a staff and a pile of black grimoires, protected by such a complex of spells I doubt they could ever be destroyed. Alex had boxed them and taken them to his house till I had a place for them.

I needed a serious self-pity party, with cake. I eyed the tote, wondering how I could get the cake carrier out from underneath the sausages without Eugenie noticing.

The fact we were headed into Lakeview didn't hit me until the car nosed onto Marconi Drive and sped north through City Park. "Where in the world are we going?"

She grinned and didn't answer, turning left on Harrison and driving toward the Seventeenth Street Canal, whose levee breach had been the major culprit in the post-Katrina flooding of New Orleans.

The only place of interest in this neighborhood—and when she turned right on Bellaire Drive I knew it's where we were headed—was my childhood home. I'd grown up with Gerry only a few blocks from the levee breach. After the flood, I'd had his ruined house gutted and the interior reframed, but nothing more. I couldn't bear to do it.

"Euge, I don't want to go to Gerry's house. I really, really don't." Especially on Thanksgiving. It still hurt too much. Eventually, maybe my good memories would outweigh the horrific sights I'd seen here after Katrina, but not yet. If I closed my eyes, I could still smell the mold, visualize the jumble of Gerry's belongings, feel the squish of inky sludge beneath my feet as I walked through.

Half the houses in Lakeview had been torn down after the Katrina flooding had left them unfixable, and empty lots took their places. Others had been rebuilt, higher and stronger. Quite a few, like Gerry's house, were gutted and ready to be filled in like outlined drawings in a coloring book. Empty shells.

Eugenie pulled in the driveway to the house on Bellaire— two stories with a balcony on the front of the second floor. All the original doors and windows had been blown out by floodwater, and the new panes still had stickers on them. The spray-painted X from the National Guard units searching house-to-house for bodies had long since disappeared thanks to new siding.

"Why are we here?" Was this some warped attempt to make me thankful that I had not one but two uninhabitable houses? Because it wasn't working. I had my heart set on self-pity with snacks. "This is a bad idea."

"You got your key?" She opened her car door, and had to walk around and open mine since my right arm was immobilized and my left was full of food. I struggled out, and she gave me a little shove toward the house. "I need to get something out of the trunk. Go on and let yourself in."

"What is wrong with you? Did you spike your coffee this morning?" I glared at her a moment while she rummaged in her trunk. "Oh, good grief. Fine."

Laying the tote bag with my cake carefully on the hood of the car, I forced myself toward the new front door that looked exactly like the one I'd come and gone from every day between ages six and twenty-one. I should've gotten its replacement in a different color or style.

As I turned my key in the stiff new dead bolt, I heard her trunk lid slam, then her car door. By the time I turned around, she'd cranked the car and was backing out of the drive.

"Hey!" I hobbled back into the small front yard and watched her taillights disappear up Bellaire Drive. The bag with the andouille and doberge cake sat on the sidewalk.

Well, crap. Looked like I'd be spending Thanksgiving alone in a house full of ghosts and no TV. On the bright side, I had the cake and Rand had never been here, so he might have a harder time finding me.

I grabbed the bag and returned to the front door. The entry foyer hadn't been tiled yet, and the staircase stretching upstairs was unfinished wood. I closed my eyes and took a deep breath, waiting for the assault of mold or mildew, but I only smelled the clean, tart scent of freshly cut wood, Sheetrock . . . and coffee. Definitely coffee.

Hanging a right off the foyer, I followed the scent down the short hallway into what had been Gerry's family room. I clutched the wall with my good hand to keep from falling over in shock. Where the sludge-filled carpet had been, a thick rug covered the plywood subflooring, its dark jewel tones setting off the heavy leather sofa and chairs around it. Candles burned on coffee and end tables. A fire burned low in the fireplace, which had a new mantel.

"Welcome home, DJ."

I whirled to find Alex behind me, holding two glasses of wine. "How . . . when . . . Eugenie?"

He smiled, and I realized it seemed like a lifetime since

I'd seen that sexy crease that formed beside his mouth. "She was in on it. I've been working here this week—working and thinking."

I set the bag on the counter in the kitchen that stretched just off the living room, noting the roughed-in countertops holding a microwave and mini-fridge and a bunch of bags from Rouse's that smelled like turkey and stuffing. I ran my fingers along the plywood serving as makeshift counters, and blinked away tears. Alex had seen into my heart and knew what I needed more than I did myself.

I thought I needed cake. He knew I needed a home.

"Hey, no crying on a construction site." Alex came in the kitchen and handed me the wineglass. "Did you see your new back doors?"

More tears threatened when I turned to see the French doors that opened onto the raised deck in back, where before there had been an old sliding glass contraption that wouldn't lock. I'd tried to get Gerry to replace it for years. "How did you know?"

"Jake told me you mentioned it once. He's been here helping me all week." I must have looked shocked, because Alex shrugged. "He's going to be okay, DJ. He'll come over by transport a few days a week to take enforcer runs, but he's going to stay in Barataria with Lafitte's people for a while. The enforcers have okayed it, and I think it's best."

I watched a squirrel race across the backyard, the big, reinforced levee wall rising behind it. If Alex thought he'd get an argument from me, he was wrong. "Jean knows how to help him. I'm glad he's staying there."

"Do you mean that?" Dark brown eyes bored into mine. "No regrets?"

I smiled and watched the squirrel make another trip. "Sure, I have regrets. I regret he ever got turned garou. I regret I made things worse instead of helping him." I turned to face Alex, because he needed to hear this once and for all. "I do not regret choosing you, even if you decide my life is too chaotic and screwed up."

Because God knows it was.

He took the glass from me and set it on the counter alongside his. I closed my eyes as his arms wrapped around me, pulling me close. I didn't even care that my shoulder felt like a blowtorch had been set against it.

He rested his chin on top of my head. "We'll figure it out."

Sounded good to me. "Any ideas on how we do that? Because I have a few ways we could start."

"Are you flirting with me?" He brushed a soft whisper of a kiss across my lips, and I winced as a mental *ping* zapped through my head from my non-husband.

"I am flirting," I said, flipping up every mental barricade I knew how to construct. We would not be having a metaphysical threesome. "Is it working?"

It was.